THE FIRES OF ATLANTIS

Books in the *Babylon* Series (Reading Order)

THE FIRES

OF

ATLANTIS

BOOK 4 IN THE BABYLON SERIES

SAM SISAVATH

The Fires of Atlantis
Copyright © 2014 by Sam Sisavath

All rights reserved.

Disclaimer: This is a work of fiction. Names, characters, businesses, places, events and incidents are either the products of the author's imagination or used in a fictitious manner. Any resemblance to actual persons, living or dead, or actual events is purely coincidental.

Published by Road to Babylon Media
www.roadtobabylon.com

Edited by Jennifer Jensen & Wendy Chan

Cover Art by Creative Paramita
Formatting by BB eBooks

ISBN-13: 978-0692287514
ISBN-10: 0692287515

To everyone who helped make the series what it is
– THANK YOU.

Separated, but not out of the fight.

Gaby has been captured by a familiar figure from her past. Some might take captivity lying down, but they aren't Gaby.

Will and Danny are close on Gaby's trail, but their rescue mission is detoured in a city under siege by a very dangerous new breed of ghouls. The reunited ex-Army Rangers will face their toughest fight yet if they want to get out alive.

Back on Song Island, Lara prepares for an impending attack. She receives unexpected assistance from a man named Keo, an ex-mercenary with his own agenda.

Meanwhile, the survivors' radio broadcast has elicited surprising responses from around the globe. It might be the start of a resistance against the ghoul domination...if Lara can keep everyone alive long enough.

Where The Purge begins, the Gates hold, and the Stones crumble, the Fires will burn...

PRELUDE

"TO ANY SURVIVORS out there, if you're hearing this, you are not alone. There are things you need to know about our enemy—these creatures of the night, these ghouls. They are not invincible, and they have weaknesses other than sunlight. One: you can kill them with silver. Stab them, shoot them, or cut them with any silver weapon, and they will die. Two: they will not cross bodies of water. An island, a boat—get to anything that can separate you from land. Three: some ultraviolet light has proven effective, but flashlights and lightbulbs with UV don't seem to have any effect. We don't know why, so use this information with caution. If you're hearing this message, you are not alone. Stay strong, stay smart, and adapt. We owe it to those we've lost to keep fighting, to never give up. Good luck."

BOOK ONE

S.E.R.E.

CHAPTER 1

KEO

THE SCAR TINGLED whenever it got cold. And it was cold at night, even in October in south Louisiana. If he thought about something else—like Gillian, or better yet, Gillian in a bikini walking along a stretch of beach waiting for him—it was easy to forget that someone had very recently tried to carve his face like a jack-o'-lantern. The scar was a reminder of three months of running and fighting.

Remember when you didn't give a damn about anyone but yourself?

You're really getting soft, pal.

The earbud in his right ear *clicked*, interrupting the silence he had been enjoying for the last hour while waiting for darkness to fall. A voice said, "You're putting your life in the hands of some girl you don't know from Adam. If that doesn't make you the dumbest man still alive, it's gotta be pretty close."

"You know what they say about lives," Keo whispered into the throat mic. "The only thing certain is death and taxes. And since good ol' Uncle Sam isn't around anymore to collect the latter, where does that leave us?"

"You and us up a creek, San Diego."

"So what else is new?"

"Leave the man alone with his death wish, Shorty," a second voice said.

"We should be on Song Island right now, Zach," Shorty said. "Wasn't that the point of coming down here in the first place? But instead, we're stealing people's silver and turning them into bullets.

What a big ol' waste of time."

"Song Island's not going anywhere," Zachary said. "It'll be there when we get there. Besides, if the lady on the radio's right, this could change everything. We might actually be able to kill these things. What did she call them?"

"Ghouls," Keo said.

"Sounds about right."

"We could have at least tried this closer to the water," Shorty said. "Safer."

"Since when did you start playing it safe?" Keo asked.

Shorty snorted. "We should have stayed on the boat. Wait for one of them to get close to the pier and test this theory out. Coming out here is stupid, Zach."

"We tried that last night," Keo said.

"This is too risky…" Shorty insisted.

"Life's a risk, especially now," Zachary said.

Keo couldn't help but smile to himself. Shorty called him crazy, but he wasn't the one who had voluntarily spent his nights in the ground wearing a ghillie suit while the bloodsuckers were running around—sometimes on top of them. He had been calling them *creatures*, *monsters*, and *bloodsuckers*, but the woman on the radio referred to them as *ghouls*. He guessed it was as good a name as any.

The woman on the radio also told him silver would kill these things.

I guess we'll find out tonight…

He focused on the creature in the center of his weapon's optic. It had been a good nine seconds since he acquired his target and laid the red dot directly over something that used to be a forehead. It was pruned, like someone's asshole. He shouldn't have been able to see the creature from this distance, but there was a full moon out tonight and he had a good perch.

"You guys could have stayed on the boat," Keo whispered. "You didn't actually have to come out here with me. I could have done this myself."

"Someone had to watch your ass," Zachary said in his right ear. "You're used to working alone, kid, but we're not."

"Your funeral."

"What a nice thing to say," Shorty said. "I should have stayed at the park. You know what's the best thing about sleeping on a boat?

Not being surrounded by a few thousand ghouls."

"A few thousand?" You're being overly generous there, Shorty. There's got to be a few tens of thousands of the bloodsuckers out tonight…

"Well?" Zachary said.

"Well, what?" Keo whispered back.

"The one you got in your crosshairs right now. I assume it's the same one I'm looking at. You going to shoot it or not?"

"Why so anxious? The two of you don't even believe it'll work."

"Can you blame us?" Shorty said. "Silver bullets? Come on. That's crazy."

"Right. Silver bullets is crazy," Keo said. "Because all of this is perfectly sane."

Zachary chuckled. "He's got you there, Shorty."

Shorty wasn't buying it. "I'm just saying. Why would silver bullets work when good ol'-fashioned lead don't?"

"The lady on the radio says it works," Keo said.

"You don't even know who she is."

"She sounded pretty sure of it. And she got the rest of it right. Sunlight, bodies of water… We know for a fact those work, too."

"All right, all right," Zachary said impatiently. "So get it over with and let's see once and for all. I'm freezing my ass off out here, and Shorty's all pruned up so much I might not be able to tell the difference between him and those ghouls pretty soon."

"Just don't accidentally shoot me in the ass," Shorty said.

"No promises."

"Relax," Keo said. "You're hiding inside the building while I'm up here on the rooftop. The only one who should be worried right now is me."

"Don't miss," Shorty said. "As I recall, you're not much of a long-distance shooter."

"This isn't much of a shot."

"You hope."

He tuned out the two men, along with the soft wind blowing through his hair and across the rooftop, scattering loose gravel around him.

Nice and slow. Breathe.

Keo tightened his forefinger against the trigger of the MP5SD. The long barrel of the submachine gun was steady against the brick edge in front of him. From his vantage point, he had a clear look at everything for a good block and a half. There were, at the moment, a handful of the creatures moving from building to building, but he didn't have any illusions that that was the full extent of their numbers.

Where you find one, you find a hundred...or a thousand...

The one he was staring at stood underneath a streetlight. He imagined a pool of white circling the thing's head, but of course there was no such thing. The city was pitch black at night, and had been for the last few days ever since he and Allie's two boys arrived.

Nice and slow.

The creature was forty meters farther down the street. It wasn't a terribly difficult shot. Your average Boot Camp graduate could have made it standing on his head with an M4 rifle. But he didn't have a carbine. The MP5SD was a close-quarter combat weapon and was not designed for long-distance shooting.

Still, it was only forty meters. Even an up-close-and-personal shooter like him could probably make this shot.

Probably.

Breathe. Nice and slow.

Just breathe...

He squeezed the trigger and the 9mm round was away, the soft *pfft!* sound of the gunshot echoing slightly in the darkness, most of it muffled by the highly effective stainless steel suppressor connected to the end of the gun barrel. The noise made by the bullet casing as it ejected, then flicked through the air, before *clinking* on the rooftop was almost louder than the shot itself.

He watched through the scope as the creature jerked its head back and slumped to the sidewalk in a pile.

Holy shit.

"Holy shit," Zachary repeated in his right ear.

"Sonofa*bitch*," Shorty said, sounding slightly breathless.

Keo pulled the submachine gun back just in case the moonlight decided to give away his position on the rooftop. Below him, the creatures were converging on the dead one, their black-skinned and gaunt forms more silhouetted shadows than actual figures. What were they thinking now? Shock? Fear? Confusion? Did they even still think at all?

"So, was it worth it coming out here tonight?" Keo whispered into the throat mic.

"Yeah, yeah," Zachary said. "Stop gloating and get back down here before they spot you."

Keo grinned, got up, and moved across the rooftop, keeping his profile as low as possible by bending at the waist. He snatched up his pack along the way, very aware of the *crunch-crunch* of his boots against the loose gravel floor. He slung the MP5SD as he reached the stairwell door and pulled it open, careful not to make a sound—or more than necessary, anyway, since it was impossible to be completely silent these days—and slipped inside.

He flicked on a small LED flashlight to navigate his way down the enclosed room, the only noise the soft *tap-tap* of his boots against concrete. He fought against the instinct to turn and flee when faced with darkened corners. Not too much, though; that instinct was what had kept him alive all these months, and it didn't pay to water it down.

He flicked off the flashlight and entered the fifth floor through another door.

Zachary and Shorty were exactly where Keo had last seen them—still crouched at the window on the far side, peering through night-vision binoculars at the streets below. Zachary's beaten and well-used Browning BAR rifle rested against the windowsill, while Shorty's Winchester rifle was on the floor within easy reach. Both men wore jeans and black shirts, far removed from their ghillie suits and Robertson Park.

Chilly air filtered in through some of the broken windows up and down the floor, including the one in front of Zachary and Shorty. The office building was nestled in the heart of downtown Lake Dulcet, and in the daylight, it looked hauntingly abandoned like all the rest around it. The place didn't look any better at night, but it was one of the few large structures that hadn't revealed any signs of ghoul occupancy. It also had everything he needed, including a tall enough perch with an easy view of the area and a place to shoot from that couldn't be traced back. Or at least, he hoped not.

"Silver bullets. Now I've seen everything," Zachary said, looking over his shoulder at Keo. He was in his forties, with a thick patch of beard and a face, like Keo's and Shorty's, that hadn't seen a decent soap or shower in weeks. "Maybe we should call you Tonto from now on."

"Because I'm half-Korean that means I can't be the Lone Ranger?" Keo said.

"I was thinking more because you're a smartass troublemaker."

Keo grinned. "I hate horses, anyway."

The young man sitting next to Zachary, Shorty, remained fixed outside the window with his binoculars. "Man, you really stirred them up. They're running around like chickens with their heads cut off. You better hope they didn't hear that gunshot."

"Did you hear it?" Keo asked.

"No."

"Then I'm guessing they couldn't hear it, either."

"You *hope*," Shorty said. "You know what I say about hoping these days?"

"What's that?"

"Nothing."

"I don't get it."

"Because there is no hope. Get it?"

Keo smirked. "You suck at this."

"Whatever," Shorty said. He lowered his binoculars and glanced at Zachary. "We locked the lobby doors, right?"

"Yup," Zachary nodded. "Why?"

"Nothing, just wanted to make sure," he said, and Keo thought the young man might have shivered slightly in the semidarkness, but that could have just been his imagination.

Keo crouched next to them at the window. He looked out at the shadows gliding up the street in their direction. After all these months, he still couldn't quite get used to watching them moving around at night. This was their world now. There was no mistaking that. They—he, Zachary, and Shorty, and all the other humans still running around out there—were the outliers. The exception to the rule.

Santa Marie Island. That's where you should be. With Gillian. On the beach.

Soon. Soon…

He could see the dead ghoul he had shot, farther down the sidewalk and left to lay where it had fallen. He had done that. Killed it. With a silver bullet. The reality of it was still a little hard to grasp.

But there it was. The evidence.

Daebak.

It had taken them days to collect enough of the valuable metal and find an Archers store in the city with the right bullet-making supplies. Despite Zachary's and Shorty's doubts (which he shared, if he was being honest), they all wanted to believe. The creatures had been unkillable except by sunlight for so long that just knowing you could take them out even at night was a game changer.

"You can kill them with silver," the recording had said. *"Stab them, shoot them, or cut them with any silver weapon, and they will die."*

Damn straight.

"Silver bullets," Keo said. "If she's right about that, what else do you think she knows?"

"The bodies of water and sunlight we already know," Zachary said. "I don't know where we'd get industrial strength ultraviolet lights, though."

"I knew a couple of guys that grew some plants using those," Shorty said. "I don't know if they were industrial strength, but they looked pretty big to me."

"I know one thing. We're making a lot of silver bullets tomorrow."

Shorty glanced at Keo. "Nice shot, by the way. I didn't think you could hit a trash dumpster with that German peashooter."

"You'd be surprised what a peashooter can do in the right hands," Keo said.

"I bet. You ever gonna tell us what you used to do before all of this?"

"This and that, and some of those." Keo leaned back against the wall and pulled a half-eaten granola bar from his pack and took a bite. "Next stop, Song Island?"

"After we make a shitload of silver bullets," Zachary said. "As much as we can carry."

"What about knives?"

"Silver knives?"

"Yeah."

Zachary nodded. "Good idea. Give me a day, and I can come up with a lot more silver-based weapons."

"Take your time," Keo said. "It's not like we're going anywhere tonight—" He stopped in mid-sentence.

Zachary glanced over. "What?"

Keo looked across the empty floor at the stairwell door. He was still chewing, but there was no taste anymore. "Are you sure the lobby's sealed?"

"Like I told Shorty, yeah. Why?"

"I thought I heard something."

"Like what?" Shorty asked.

"Moving."

"What kind of moving?" Zachary said.

"Moving."

"That narrows it down," Shorty said just before he picked up his rifle and laid it across his lap.

Zachary pulled away from the window and faced the stairwell door. He stopped moving—even stopped breathing entirely—and listened. After a moment, he shook his head, eyes searching out Keo's again. "I don't hear anything. You sure you heard something?"

"Pretty sure," Keo nodded.

"Shorty?"

Shorty shook his head. "Maybe all those months being chased through the woods by that Pollard guy's got him spooked."

"You didn't hear anything?"

"Nope."

Zachary looked back at Keo. "What do you think it was?"

"I told you. Movement."

"From the floor below us? You mentioned the lobby…"

"Somewhere below us." Keo dropped the unfinished granola bar and tightened his hands around the MP5SD. "Definitely below us."

"Maybe you're just imagining things," Shorty said. "Maybe killing that bloodsucker's got you overly excited."

"I don't get overly excited."

"First time for everything, San Diego," Shorty said.

Keo flashed him a slightly annoyed look. He didn't really like Shorty all that much, and he was sure the feeling was mutual. Keo preferred the older Zachary's company. Shorty was a couple of years younger, and his insistence on calling Keo *San Diego* was getting old real fast. The only reason the kid had come along with them in the first place was because he was tied to the hip with Zachary, who had his own reasons for wanting to reach Song Island.

"Are you guys loaded with silver?" Keo whispered.

"We just made the nine mil rounds for your peashooter, remember?" Shorty said.

Zachary's eyes remained focused on the door across from them.

If he heard or saw anything, he didn't say it. After a while, he looked down at Keo, sitting to his right—Shorty was to his left—and said, "Are you sure—"

He never finished because Zachary's words became slurred, then stopped becoming words entirely, and instead took on the form of a scream as his body jerked backward toward the window, as if he were being sucked out by a vacuum.

Keo lunged away from the wall and unslung the MP5SD as he watched, with a mixture of horror and disbelief, as two of the creatures clung to the windowsill outside the building and *pulled Zachary through the opening.*

One of them had a fistful of Zachary's scruffy long hair while the other had a viselike grip over the lower half of his jaw, quickly clamping down on Zachary's screams and turning them into muffled cries for help instead.

And all Keo could think was, *How did they get up here? Did they…crawl up the side of the building?*

He didn't know they could do that. He didn't know the ghouls could do a lot of things.

"Zachary, fuck!" Shorty screamed as he too stumbled away from the wall, spinning around and lifting his rifle.

Shorty fired, his first shot splattering the left eyeball of one of the ghouls outside, the round punching through the back of its head and disappearing into the cold October air, continuing on. The creature, too, kept on going—pulling Zachary's struggling body through the window along with its partner.

Then Zachary disappeared from view.

Keo stood, frozen, even as he heard Zachary screaming like a banshee from outside. The screaming went on for what must have been two or three seconds, though it sounded more like two to three minutes.

Jesus Christ, how long does it take a man to fall down five floors?

Both he and Shorty flinched involuntarily when they heard the *thump!* of flesh and bones striking the sidewalk outside.

"Shorty," Keo said. "We gotta go."

"Zachary," Shorty said.

If he had more to say, he never finished it. Instead, he might have gasped audibly when two of the creatures—different ones, this time (or were they?)—reached up from below the windowsill, grabbed the frames, and pulled themselves upward until their faces were visible in the opening. Grotesquely deformed features, like nothing that could possibly be mistaken for human, peered through the window at them.

"We gotta go!" Keo shouted.

Keo backpedaled from the glaring eyes, lifted the submachine, and fired. He hit one of them in the face and the creature let go of its grip, dropping back into the night. Keo was momentarily shocked by what had just happened. He had shot these things more times than he could count and they never reacted that way. He had even seen Shorty put a .308 round through one of them a few seconds ago, and it didn't even flinch.

But this one...this one *went down*.

Silver bullets. Silver bullets!

The second one had managed to hook its spindly legs into the window frame, like some kind of insect, and was in the process of pulling itself through the opening when Keo shot it in the chest. It let go and dropped backward, swallowed up by the darkness.

"Shorty!" Keo shouted. "Let's go!"

But Shorty didn't move, not even when deformed shapes began climbing through the windows to their left and right along the floor. It was too dark for him to see anything beyond moving shadows. Not that Keo had to guess what was happening around him, because as soon as he killed the first two bloodsuckers, two—three—*five* more were trying to crawl in through the exact same space that had just been vacated.

Gather some supplies. Make some silver bullets. Go find Gillian.

What could possibly go wrong?

He flicked the fire selector on the submachine gun to full-auto and opened fire.

"Shorty!" he shouted over the *clink-clink-clink* of bullet casings falling against the tiled floor around him.

Silver 9mm bullets ripped through flesh and kept going, and the creatures fell like dominos in front of him, others swan diving back out of the window.

Then *Boom! Boom!* as Shorty began shooting. It was a bolt-action rifle, and each shot required him to manually reload. Keo remembered all those days on the road trying to convince the kid to switch to something more practical. But Shorty wouldn't go for it. He was married to his Winchester.

Stupid kid, Keo thought, shouting again, "Shorty, come on!"

Because Shorty's .308, as devastating as it was to a human body, was like throwing pebbles at the ghouls. His bullets tore through them, and some even hit the ones behind them—and it still kept going even then—but it didn't stop them. Not for a moment. Not even for a millisecond. Keo wasn't sure if the creatures even felt the bullet impacts.

"Shorty!"

He was backpedaling and firing, spraying from left to right, watching the bounding forms stumbling and falling. They were converging from every side now, literally pouring in through the windows across the floor, the *tap-tap-tap!* of bare feet against the carpet like a dozen stampeding herds at once.

Too many. Always too goddamn many…

Even as they collapsed left and right and over each other, more were climbing through the windows every second. Every half-second. He found breathing difficult as the floor began filling up with their stench. There was a never-ending stream of them, and he guessed this must be what it was like trying to hold back a flood with your bare hands.

And Shorty was standing in front of him, shooting and smashing the buttstock of his rifle into the creatures as they surged toward him. He was backpedaling, but not fast enough. Too slow. *Way* too slow.

"Shorty, goddammit!"

He didn't know if the other man could hear him. Probably not. Shorty didn't seem capable of moving any faster, and soon—

They were on top of him. Driving him to the floor.

Shorty started screaming.

Then the sea of black tar began changing directions and converging on Shorty. He saw Shorty's hand sticking out of the squirming mass of shriveled skin and bony limbs.

Keo turned and ran, reloading at the same time, dropping the long, slender magazine. He didn't have to look to perform the task. It was second nature by now.

He made a beeline for the same stairwell door he had come through earlier.

The tsunami of bare feet slapping against the floor burst through his eardrums as the creatures gave chase. He guessed not every one of them was going for Shorty anymore. How many were back there on his heels? A dozen? Hundreds? *How many undead things could fit into one floor*, he wondered.

Too many. Always too damn many…

Keo didn't look back. It was pointless because he knew what was back there. And he didn't want to see Shorty's death. He couldn't even hear the kid's screams anymore. He couldn't hear his own breathing, for that matter—only the relentless pounding in his chest.

Around him, their stench overwhelmed the stale odor of the abandoned floor.

They were fast, but he was faster. A steady diet of beef jerky and protein had kept Keo lean, and the nearly three-month long jaunt through the woods, being hunted by psychos with assault rifles, had forced him into the best shape of his life. He was also blessed with a long stride, one of the benefits of being six-one.

He grabbed for the stairwell door with his left hand, his right still wrapped around the MP5SD with the forefinger against the trigger. He twisted the doorknob with one fluid motion, pulled the door open with another, and was greeted by total darkness—

—*except for the pair of yellow, crooked teeth coming at him.*

He squeezed off a burst, slicing the creature in half. It fell soundlessly, thick clumps of black liquid splashing the wall behind it.

Silver bullets. Silver fucking bullets!

Keo jumped over the shriveled-up dead thing.

Sounds—coming from below this time. That meant he couldn't go down. Which wasn't his first choice anyway, but it would have been nice to actually have a choice.

So what was left?

He glanced up the flight of stairs, just as—

—*THOOM-THOOM-THOOM* as they crashed into the stairwell door behind him with the intensity of rabid dogs that hadn't eaten in days, weeks, maybe months.

He went up.

They were coming. Fast-moving bastards. The manic *tap-tap-tap!* of bare feet slammed against the solid concrete of the stairwell, echoing along the length of the confined space. He didn't look back, didn't look down. The rush of wind caught up to him from behind as the fifth-floor stairwell door was flung open and they poured inside, the very distinctive splatter of feet against black blood spilled by the dead ghoul ringing in his ears.

He reached the rooftop door faster than he expected and burst outside, boots *crunching* against familiar loose gravel. He darted across the wide-open spaces, intimately aware that he was going to run out of space soon.

Very, very soon.

Darkness, moonlight, and a pair of smaller buildings around him, including one directly in front. A two-story building, with a bar on the first floor and living quarters on the second. He had scouted it earlier in the day with Zachary but hadn't gone inside because the windows and doors were locked. The most important thing, though, was that the windows were not covered, which meant there were no nests inside.

That was the good news.

The bad news? The building was three stories down, with just over four meters of empty space between rooftops. It was going to be a hell of a drop if he couldn't make the jump.

London Bridge is falling down, falling down…

Shut up!

They flooded out of the stairwell behind him and were battling against the loose gravel. He wondered if it looked nearly as comical as it sounded.

I should have brought a camera.

He unslung his pack, and with a meter left until he reached the end, flung it and watched it disappear into the night. He glimpsed the edge—was he running to it, or was it coming to him?—and lunged forward with his left leg, landed solidly, and catapulted himself up and over and forward through the cold, chilly Louisiana air.

So this is what it feels like to fly.

The rooftop of the building next door came into view as he plummeted back down through the darkness, way faster than he had anticipated. He tried to pick up where his pack had landed while he was still in the air so he wouldn't have to waste time looking for it later—

—If my legs aren't broken when I land—

—and saw it lying almost near the far edge. Jesus, how the hell had it gotten that far?

I must be stronger than I look.

He almost laughed out loud, but before he could put thought into action, the flat rooftop was there and he managed to land in a crouch, his momentum carrying him forward into a tuck and roll. He snapped back up on one bent knee, shocked and joyous that he was still alive, that neither one of his legs were broken even though pain shot through both and up his thighs, his entire body seeming to vibrate for a few seconds afterward.

Daebak!

He was on his feet instantly and rushing toward his pack. He snatched it up and slipped it through his arms as—*thoomp! thoomp!*—two of the creatures landed on the rooftop behind him.

He glanced back, saw them floundering like fish out of water, bony arms and legs snapping in every direction and at one point actually became entangled with one another. But that didn't last, and they quickly became two separate creatures again—

He shot them and watched them drop, even as more fell out of the inky black sky like raindrops, landing one after another...after another. Bones snapped and broke, then another, then another still—not that it stopped any of them.

They kept coming—falling over and over, then actually on top of one another when they ran out of space. And still they kept dropping out of the sky...

Keo backed up until cold air was brushing against his backside. He looked over his shoulder at empty space, having nearly backpedaled right off the edge. There was a catwalk below him.

He emptied the remaining 9mm rounds into the mass of creatures in front of him, watching as they stumbled and fell, still amazed that they were going down, that he was actually killing them for once.

Killing them again? Re-kill? Whatever.

When the submachine gun ran empty for the second time, he slung it and dropped off the edge without looking back. It wasn't a steep fall, only a few meters, though it felt like more. He landed on the catwalk with a loud *bang!*, the structure threatening to buckle under him, to pry itself free from the brick wall it was fastened to.

But it held. Miraculously, it held.

The window in front of him was closed and Keo was prepared to smash it open with his weapon, but when he grabbed the bottom and tried to open it, it actually slid up for him.

Hallelujah!

He pushed it all the way up and dived inside, turned, and slammed the glass back down just as one—two—*five* of the creatures landed on the catwalk outside. *Whomp-whomp-whomp!* There were so many coming down at once that they started falling on top of each other's heads and shoulders, then bounced off and tumbled over the railings.

The first creature to right itself slammed its fist into the window and cracked it, but it must not have been strong enough because the window held. At least, until another one of the ghouls joined the first one with its own flailing fist. Then a third and a fourth began ramming their entire bodies—one was using its skull—until the glass panes began cracking under the frenzied assault.

Keo took a couple of steps back, ejected the magazine, shoved it into his pack, and pulled out a fresh one from a pouch around his waist and slammed it home. He shot the first ghoul that made it through the jagged opening in one of the panes. It fell forward into the room, landing awkwardly on its skull.

The others continued scrambling inside, undeterred, fighting to be the first one in.

He strafed the window, emptying the magazine, and watched with morbid fascination as the mass of black, pruned flesh and skeletal bodies corralled within the four walls of the catwalk outside. The congestion didn't slow them at all, and even more were falling out of the sky like endless raindrops.

Silver bullets or not, he wasn't going to stop them. Not even close.

He fled, making a run for the door, grabbing it and pulling it open without a problem, and lunged into darkness. His eyes quickly adjusted, picking out the banisters at the other end of the hallway. Keo ran for it when his forehead hit something soft. He slid to a stop and looked up at a rope dangling from the ceiling.

Crash!

From below him on the first floor, the unmistakable noise of glass breaking.

Then another *crash!*, followed by another...

He grabbed the piece of rope and yanked it. The frame of the attic door appeared in the darkness as it opened up from the ceiling.

Keo grabbed the ladder and pulled even as something smashed into the door behind him.

Thoom-thoom-thoom!

He shut the noises out—from below him, from behind him—*everywhere.*

Scrambled up the stairs and ignored the last few steps and jumped upward onto the wooden scaffolding above. Clouds of dust that had been gathering for the last year erupted around him. Twisting, he grabbed the ladder and pulled it up, making sure to bring the dangling rope along with him. Before the door could slam shut and join the tumultuous symphony of chaos exploding below him, Keo grabbed it at the last second, slowing its speed, and cautiously—painfully slowly, almost as if in slow-motion—tapped it shut.

Darkness swamped him, taking away what little light he had with the attic door open. The *tap-tap-tap* of bare feet against the wooded hallway floor filtered up from the room below him, overwhelming everything, including his own ragged breathing. There were no peepholes, so Keo had to only go with what his ears could pick up.

Footsteps on the stairs, rushing down, then up, then down again.

They were searching for him, an endless wave of the creatures moving through the hallway below, in and out of doors and rooms.

Keo moved into a sitting position facing the door in the floor, the submachine gun resting between his legs. Something small and furry scrambled next to him in the darkness, brushing up against his right arm. It was all he could do not to open fire on it. Instead, he gritted his teeth and listened to the creature burrowing through attic insulation, more afraid of him than he was of it. Or maybe that was just wishful thinking on his part.

He glanced at his watch, the hands glowing in the suffocating darkness.

It was hours yet before morning.

He sat and waited and did his best not to breathe in the dust around him. The place probably had asbestos, too. Just his luck. He had survived the end of the world only to get mesothelioma. Now that would really suck.

His body had already begun to itch from the close proximity to insulation. He battled the urge to sneeze and had to cup his mouth and nostrils with one hand.

Below him, the endless *tap-tap-tap* of bare feet continued unabated, like an ocean's wave lapping against a beach, soft and soothing and promising safety and shelter from the darkness.

He wondered if Gillian and Jordan and the others had made it to Santa Marie Island after all. If they were waiting for him on the beach right now, wondering why he hadn't made it there yet like he had promised. Would Gillian understand when he finally arrived and explained what took him so long?

"See, there was this crazy guy with a small army hunting us…"

She might have even found someone else after giving up on him ever showing up. It would serve him right. Maybe Mark was the lucky guy…

"Keo. You promise me. You'll follow us to Santa Marie Island," Gillian had said to him when they had their last conversation.

"Yes," he had answered. *"I promise. Reserve a spot on the beach for me. I also wouldn't mind if you were wearing a bikini when I get there."*

How long ago was that? It seemed like another lifetime now.

This'll teach you to make promises you can't keep, pal…

CHAPTER 2

LARA

"THIS IS YOUR way of making me hate you, is that it? Because it's working. First you let me think you were dead, then I learn you're alive, and now you're telling me you're not coming home. Are you purposefully trying to piss me off, Will?"

He didn't answer right away, and for a moment she wondered if hearing his voice for the first time in nearly a week had been just an illusion, something her grief-stricken mind had conjured up in order to spare her the pain of believing she had lost him for good. Maybe it was all a bad dream. She'd had plenty of those since he left the island with Gaby on Jen's helicopter.

"Will? Are you still there?"

"I'm still here," he said finally.

He sounded so close, as if she could reach out and touch him. She had to remind herself that he was alive, something she hadn't been sure of until yesterday when Danny found him outside of Lafayette. That should have been all that mattered, but at the moment she couldn't stop her anger from boiling to the surface.

The guilt immediately washed over her, and she struggled to control it.

"So say something, Will…"

"Lara, you know there's nothing in this world I want more than to come back to you right now. I just can't. Not yet."

Of course not, Will. If you did what you wanted instead of what you needed to do, then you wouldn't be Will, would you? You wouldn't be the man I love.

She sighed. "Forget for a moment that I'm this close to getting in a boat and hunting your stupid, inconsiderate ass down for leaving me hanging. Forget that for one moment. Take emotion out of it and think about this logically, Will. You're hurt. You're bleeding. You've been shot. You need to come back to me. I need you to come back here so I can make sure you don't die."

"I will." He sounded tired, as if the weight of the world was on his shoulders. Which was to say he sounded exactly the way he always did. "But I can't. Not yet."

"Can you even trust this Kellerson? What if he's leading you into another trap?"

"He's not. I've made sure of that."

"How?"

He didn't answer, and Lara realized she didn't want to know.

Will does what he has to. What he needs to. Like he always does.

That's why he's Will.

"No, don't tell me," she said. "What about Roy?"

"He should be back at the island in a few hours with a passenger. Her name's Zoe. She's hurt, so you'll have to take care of her for me."

"Carly warned me you'd find someone else out there."

He laughed, and Lara couldn't help but smile.

"We were sort of thrown together," he said. "I think you'll like her."

"Is she okay?"

"She was shot, too."

Who hasn't been shot these days? Lara thought, but said, "How bad is it?"

"I wasn't sure if she would live, but she's a tough one. She was in one of those blood farms when all of this began."

"How did you two meet?"

"She was working in one of the camps the collaborators were running. The one Josh was in charge of."

Josh.

Lara still couldn't believe it. Eighteen-year-old Josh, who followed Gaby around like a lost puppy when she first met them all those months ago. But as difficult as it was for her to believe that Josh had changed so much, it had been even more of an ordeal for Gaby.

Will's hurt. Gaby's missing. And Josh has become the enemy.

How did it all go so wrong?

"When I was shot, she saved my life," Will was saying. "I owe her everything, Lara."

"Then I'll have to thank her when she gets here."

"She's a doctor, so once she's better, she'll be a big asset to the island."

"Oh, a doctor. A *real* doctor, you mean."

He laughed again. "It's not like that."

"No?" she teased.

It had been so long since she'd had the opportunity to have a little fun at his expense. The fact that he was still alive made her a bit giddy, and Lara was glad she was alone in the third floor of the Tower so no one could see. She could be herself with Will, but these days, other people expected more out of her. Too much, sometimes.

"She could never replace you," he said. "No one could. Not in a million years."

"Good answer," Lara said. "Though I'm sure if she wanted to replace me, it wouldn't be much of a challenge. She is, after all, a real doctor."

He went quiet again, and she wondered if she had gone too far.

"Will, it's just a joke."

"It's not that, Lara."

"What is it, then?"

"You can do this. It's in you to lead."

"That's not my job. That's yours."

"I'm just a grunt."

"Bullshit."

"It's true. I've always been just a grunt. Give me a gun and a target, and I can handle it. But you… You're smarter and stronger than I'll ever be."

Her chest tightened. The way he had said it—so earnestly and with so much conviction, as if he believed every word of it with every fiber of his being. At that moment, she wasn't sure if she should be proud or scared. It was probably a little of both.

"Danny told me how you handled the West and Brody problem," Will said. "You did good, babe."

"Thanks."

"Just like I knew you would."

"Then you had more faith in me than I did."

"Don't doubt yourself, Lara. You survived The Purge."

"I was lucky."

"It wasn't luck. It was persistence and that strength I mentioned before. You have it in you to lead, Lara."

"Will…"

"That's why I know the island will be fine without me for a few more days. Or however long it takes to find Gaby. When I've done that, I'll come home. There's nothing I want more. Nothing in this world than to hold you and kiss you again."

"You still love me?" she asked.

It sounded like something only a lovesick teenager would come up with even to her own ears. But she couldn't help herself, and she wasn't the least embarrassed by it. Not here. Not with Will.

And she had to know…

"More than anything," he said. "More than anything in this world. There's nothing I wouldn't do for you. Absolutely nothing."

His voice was steady, heartfelt, and she wanted to cry but didn't. Because that was something a teenage girl would do, too, and she hadn't been that in a long time.

She sat up straighter in the chair instead.

"Do you believe me?" he asked.

"Yes," she said softly.

"But I need to find Gaby first. I have to try."

"I know." She took her fingers off the transmit lever and took a breath, then gathered herself, grateful for the cool wind sweeping into the Tower through the four open windows around her.

"Lara," Will said.

"Yes…"

"I'll see you soon."

She smiled, pressing the transmit lever. "Go find Gaby, then come home. The island and I will still be here when you get back. I promise."

HOURS AFTER HER conversation with Will over the radio, Lara stood at the end of the pier and watched the pontoon through a pair of binoculars. Blaine and Bonnie were standing on the boat, with Roy and the woman sitting in chairs as they glided smoothly across Beaufont Lake. Blaine was behind the steering wheel, Bonnie leaning to one side, her long auburn hair blowing wildly in the breeze.

Lara smiled at the sight. Even on a fast-moving boat, her face splashed with too-bright sun and no makeup, Bonnie still looked like a supermodel that had just stepped off a runway. It was almost unfair for every other woman on the island.

"As milady requested, the infirmary's ready for its newest customer," Carly said, coming up behind her. "Though I have to say, it's a good thing Roy's bringing back medical supplies, because we're running dangerously low."

"I know," Lara said.

Their dwindling medical supplies. It was one of the reasons Will and Gaby had gone out there in the first place. There were other reasons, but there was no getting around the fact that they had suffered too many injuries lately.

Everyone's hurt. Everyone's shot up. Every day, surviving gets harder and harder.

I could use you back here with me right now, Will.

"You know, there's an easier solution to this problem we keep having," Carly said.

"I'm listening…"

"Stop getting shot or stabbed."

"Now that's an idea. I'll bring it up at the meeting later tonight."

"I get credit for it, right?"

"Absolutely." Then, Lara added, "Danny'll be all right, Carly."

"I know," Carly said. "I just realized this is the first time we've really been apart, that's all."

Carly watched the pontoon coming toward them and absently played with her red hair. Lara was always surprised how much older her friend looked despite being just twenty. Carly had been a teenager when they first met, but then you grew up fast or you didn't grow up at all these days.

Adapt or perish, right, Will?

Lara took Carly's hand and squeezed. "He'll be fine. The two of them out there? Those collaborators don't stand a chance."

Carly smiled back at her. Or tried to. "I know. So why does it take me so long to go to sleep, and I keep waking up in the middle of the night?"

"Because you love him."

"So that's it?"

"That's it."

She sighed. "Love's depriving me of my beauty sleep."

"Amen, sister."

They both laughed.

"Please don't say that ever again," Carly said.

"Shoot me if I ever do," Lara said.

"Deal."

Lara glanced down the pier at Jo, who was standing on the boat shack at the other end with a shotgun poking out from behind her back. The sight of the tall, skinny girl with the weapon was borderline absurd. Lara waved, and Bonnie's little sister waved back.

"Has she fired that thing before?" Carly asked, looking back at Jo.

"Not yet," Lara said. "I don't want her to, either. She might hurt herself."

"I'm more concerned about her hurting me with that thing."

"Let's all hope it doesn't come to Jo saving us with a shotgun." Lara unclipped her radio and said into it, "Maddie, what do you see?"

"The lake's clear from up here," Maddie said through the radio.

Maddie was back in the Tower, pulling overwatch with the M4 rifle equipped with the ACOG scope. Just like with the beach, someone was always in the Tower to keep an eye on the surrounding lake and the shore to the east and south of them. Another one of Will's protocols that everyone had taken to heart, because the alternative was unacceptable.

We're like a well-oiled machine. If by machine *you mean a bunch of amateurs with dangerous weapons they don't actually know how to use.*

"No traffic on the roads?" Lara asked.

"None that I can see," Maddie said. Then, "Lara, when you're done down there, I need to see you back up here."

"Something wrong?"

"Something good."

Carly and Lara exchanged a curious look.

"I was playing around with the radio and I heard something that you're going to want to hear," Maddie continued.

"What is it?" Lara asked.

"I think you should hear it for yourself. It's hard to explain. But your message, the one you sent out into the world? Someone just responded to it."

"Is that good?" Carly asked.

Lara shook her head. "I have no idea. Can you...?"

"Go. A boss lady's work is never done."

Lara sighed.

Boss.

The very idea that she was the "boss" of anything, much less an island full of desperate survivors, still sounded wrong in so many ways. Despite what Will had said this morning, Lara had doubts. But then, she always had doubts. It stuck with her when she went to sleep and when she woke up.

Doubts. There were always doubts.

Carly must have seen the look on her face. She smiled and patted her on the shoulder. "Get used to it. When Will comes back, we'll have to call you guys co-bosses. You'll be CBL."

"CBL?"

"Co-Boss Lady."

"How long did it take you to come up with that?"

"I spent all night thinking it up. I mean, I couldn't sleep anyway. Awesome, right?"

"Yeah, no," Lara said.

<hr />

"THIS IS THE United States government, trying to reach the person or persons responsible for the message that has been broadcasting across the radio frequencies. If you can hear us, please respond. I repeat: This is the United States government, trying to reach the person or persons responsible for the message that has been broadcasting across the radio frequencies..."

"The United States government?" Lara said.

"That's what they're claiming," Maddie said. "Though Uncle Sam sounds like a sixteen-year-old virgin if you ask me."

Lara was back on the third floor of the Tower, staring at the ham radios sitting on the table. She had used one of them to talk to Will earlier. There were three, with the most visually interesting one connected to a laptop by a tangled mess of wires duct-taped together. That radio was still broadcasting, sending out the recorded message, though they had muted the sound on their end.

The second radio sat undisturbed on its own part of the table. It was tuned in to a very specific frequency—their little private designated emergency channel, because no one else but Song Island's residents knew to monitor it.

The voice they were listening to now was coming from the third radio. The all-purpose one, free and clear of any special use.

"…trying to reach the person or persons responsible for the message that has been broadcasting across the radio frequencies…"

"Is it a recording?" Lara asked.

"Doesn't sound like it," Maddie said. "You can tell he's reading from a script, but he's definitely doing it live on air." Then, "Should we answer it?"

"I don't know."

What would Will do?

"The less people that know about the island, the better," Lara said. "It's fine to bring new people like Bonnie's and Benny's groups every once in a while, but when we start opening the place up to just anybody…."

"Lollapalooza," Maddie finished.

"I don't know what that is."

"It's an alternative rock concert. I went to it once when they came to Austin a few years back." She waved her hand. "Never mind. Neither here nor there. But is it possible? Do you think the United States government really is still functioning out there?"

Lara shook her head. It had been nearly a year since they knew of anything even remotely resembling an official government broadcast. To hear it now, out of the blue, was unreal. The fact that they were responding to *her* message was, frankly, unsettling.

"Is it just on the FEMA frequency?" Lara asked.

"As far as I know," Maddie nodded.

"How long have they been broadcasting?"

"No idea. I heard it about thirty minutes ago while playing around with the radio." She shrugged. "It gets boring up here by yourself."

"…this is the United States government," the voice repeated on the radio, "trying to reach the person or persons responsible for the message that has been broadcasting across the radio frequencies…"

Lara reached for the radio's microphone and lifted it to her lips but didn't press the transmit lever right away. She took a deep breath, and then, only then, answered. "This is the person responsible for the broadcast, responding to your message. Over."

She released the lever and waited, but the only response was silence from the other end. The "sixteen-year-old virgin" had stopped broadcasting.

Lara pressed the transmit lever again. "Hello. If you can hear me, please respond. Over."

She waited five seconds, then ten…

"Hello," a voice finally answered. It was different from the one she and Maddie had been listening to. Older, with an authoritative tone that came through even over the radio. "Who am I speaking to. Over."

"Identify yourself first," Lara said.

"Colonel Beecher," the man said. "Commanding officer of what currently remains of the United States of America."

She looked back at Maddie, who frowned. "That can't be a good sign. My dad used to say the military is good at a lot of things, but running a democracy isn't one of them."

Lara turned back to the radio. "I wasn't aware the military had taken charge of the country, Colonel."

"I assure you, I didn't come to this command voluntarily," Beecher said. "As far as I know, we're it. We haven't been able to make contact with any other civilian or military authority. So I'm left to assume there is no one else out there. Now that I've identified myself, would you mind responding in kind, Miss?"

"My name is Lara."

"Lara, it's good to hear your voice. We have a lot of questions."

"Such as?"

"Are you in charge over there?"

No. Far from it. I'm so out of my depth I feel like I'm constantly drowning, except people keep telling me I'm doing fine. Great, even.

God help us.

"Yes," she said into the microphone.

"Where are you currently located?" Beecher asked.

Nice try.

"That's not information I'm willing to divulge at the moment,

Colonel."

"Is there a reason?"

"I don't trust you."

Beecher chuckled. "Fair enough. It's a dangerous world out there. It's difficult to know who to trust."

"Agreed."

"So what *can* you tell me, Lara?"

"Ask, and we'll find out together."

"All right." Beecher paused for a moment. Then, "First of all, the silver. We've been trying to kill these things for nearly a year, then overnight your broadcast changed everything. How in God's name did you know about silver?"

"Trial and error and a lot of experience," she said. "My turn, Colonel."

"Fire away."

"Are you willing to say where you're located?"

"We're in Colorado. Five miles out of Denver."

"Are you in some kind of bunker?"

"Nice try," Beecher said.

She smiled. "Your turn."

"Now that you brought it up, are you under or aboveground?"

"Aboveground. You?"

"Both."

"Now who's being cute?"

Another chuckle. "I don't mean to be. Have you ever heard of Bayonet Mountain?"

"No."

"It's an old 1950s Cold War bomb shelter designed to withstand an atomic bomb. As it turns out, it works just as well against ghouls, as you call them. That's where we are now. My men and a sizable civilian population."

"What's your definition of *sizable*, Colonel?"

"At the moment, just over 4,000 military personnel and civilians," Beecher said. "How about you? How many do you have over there?"

She looked back at Maddie, who mouthed back, *"Four thousand?"*

Lara took a breath and said into the microphone, "We have, uh, just slightly less than that, Colonel."

"Can you say how many?" Beecher asked.

"Not at this time."

"Fair enough. So tell me, Lara. Any ideas about how to take back the planet from these bloodsucking bastards?"

That made Lara pause.

"Lara?" Beecher said. "Are you still there?"

"I'm still here, Colonel."

"Did I say something wrong?"

"No. I'm just not sure why you're asking me that question. You're the one with 4,000 people with you, including soldiers. I'm just a civilian."

"You're more than that. Your message saved our lives, Lara. Learning about silver has turned the tide for us." He paused again. Then, "You don't have a clue what you've done, do you?"

She didn't, because she had put out the message at Danny and Roy's insistence. Lara was still grieving what she thought at the time were Will's and Gaby's deaths. The radio message was supposed to give whoever was still out there hope, but in so many ways it was to give *herself* hope.

"No," she said finally. "I guess I don't."

"You gave us a fighting chance," Beecher said. "Your broadcast changed everything, and I'm willing to bet there are others monitoring this frequency right now, who have been waiting for someone to lead them…"

CHAPTER 3

GABY

THE SPORK WAS white and plastic and flimsy in her hand. It was one of those disposable utensils that came in cases of a thousand. It barely held together as she picked her way through the baked potato, so it was a good thing the toughest food on the brown cafeteria-style tray were strips of shriveled bacon, dirty brown rice, and two buttered biscuits.

As for its ability to penetrate the human skin, well, she didn't have very high hopes. They didn't even trust her enough to give her one of those plastic butter knives. As if she could actually stab anyone with it. Of course, that wouldn't have kept her from trying, though the point was moot since she didn't have one.

"You barely touched your food."

She rubbed her thumb along the teeth of the spork. The two middle claws were probably too weak to puncture anything as tough as human skin, but the two flanking teeth were twice the size and just as sharp. Better yet, they were reinforced by the oval-shaped spoon connected to them. So, pretty tough, as far as flimsy plastic utensils went.

"Gaby?"

Even if she couldn't get the plastic teeth through flesh, she might still be able to dish out some hurt. It wouldn't be a killing blow and she probably couldn't dig deep enough to sever a major artery, but there were possibilities—

"Gaby!"

She looked up at him. "What?"

"You hardly touched your food," Josh said. "You should. We're celebrating."

"What are we celebrating?"

"My birthday."

"Your birthday?"

"I turned nineteen last month. I was going to tell you when we met in the park, but... Well, you know."

She nodded. "Happy birthday."

"Thanks. Too bad we don't have any cake. Do you guys have cake on the island?"

"I don't know."

"Oh well, I guess it doesn't matter." He smiled. "We're not kids anymore. Do you realize that? We're both nineteen. Damn. When did that happen?"

She sat across from him, the frail portable table between them. The tabletop space was so limited that a quarter of their trays dangled off the ends. Josh had eaten most of his potato, wrapped in aluminum foil and baked over a grill, and was shoveling a sporkful of brown rice into his mouth. He seemed to have grown since the last time (*Days? Weeks? How long have I been here?*) she had seen him back at the camp in Sandwhite Wildlife State Park. In another couple of weeks, his hair would be long enough to tie in a ponytail. She wondered if he had left it long on purpose, or if he was too busy for a barber because of the demands of his new job.

What was the job interview like, Josh?

"I know it's not a lot," Josh said, almost apologetically. "But it's more than most of the people here get to eat. We have to ration the food until we can grow more in the fields. Most of them are still eating MREs and stale bagged chips. Cans of SPAM, if they're lucky. We found cases of those in a warehouse outside Shreveport. Mountains of them. I guess it's true what they say. When the world ends, only the cockroaches and SPAM will be left."

I'm supposed to be grateful for this. Potatoes baked over a grill. Strips of bacon. Dirty brown rice.

"Where did you get the bacon?" she asked.

"Wild hogs. They're all over the place. Somehow, they managed to survive all this time; I have no idea how. We already have farmers raising them, and in a few years they'll be plentiful and everyone will be eating bacon and biscuits in the mornings. Oh, and eggs, too. Plenty of chickens are still running around out there. When we're done, the farms will be the biggest part of the towns." Josh picked up his water bottle from the floor and twisted it open. "You never asked me how I found you at the pawnshop."

"How did you find me?"

"She told me. The blue-eyed ghoul. Kate."

"Will's Kate…"

"Uh huh. After the black-eyed ones located you, she told them to stay back, to wait until I got there. I guess they sort of jumped the gun a bit, but I arrived just in time, didn't I?" He smiled, probably expecting her to acknowledge it. "She knew you were important to me. Because you are, Gaby."

She rubbed her thumb against the teeth of the spork again before glancing over at the closed door to her left. There was a man on the other side named Mac. He took turns walking around the second floor hallway with another one of her guards, Lance. It was afternoon and sunlight was visible through the open window across the room, so Mac was out there because Lance had the night shift.

She turned back to Josh. He was wiping his hands on a handkerchief before stuffing the wool cloth back into his shirt pocket. Josh didn't wear a hazmat suit when he came to have lunch with her. She wondered if he still did. Mac and Lance didn't wear one, either. In fact, it had been a while since she had seen a hazmat suit on one of the collaborators.

"What do you want from me, Josh?"

He didn't answer right away. Maybe he didn't have an answer. Or, more likely, he just wanted her to wait. Josh did that these days. He had the power, and he knew it. The old Josh, who would do anything to please her, was long gone. The transformation showed in the way he walked, the way he sat, and in the way he looked at and talked to her. She used to adore his shyness, but there was none of that anymore.

This Josh…he knew who he was. *What* he was. And most of all, he understood and embraced the authority he wielded. Over the others, over the town, and most of all, over her.

Finally, he said, "I just want you to understand what I've been doing here, that's all."

"And what's that, Josh?"

He stood up and walked across the room to the window, looking out at the street below. Her eyes went to the chair and she wondered if she could take Josh out with it, then break off a leg and use it on Mac.

Maybe…

"How many times have you stood here and looked out this window?" he asked.

"What does it matter?"

"Just answer me, please, Gaby."

"Plenty of times."

"And what do you see?"

"I don't understand what you want me to say."

"It's just a conversation, Gaby." He sounded a bit exasperated. "When you look outside, what do you see?"

"People."

"That's right. People going on with their lives. Little kids not scared of walking in broad daylight. *This*, Gaby, this is what we've always wanted, don't you remember? To live freely. To not be afraid. Isn't this what we talked about all those times in every dark and stinky basement we've ever hid in since the world ended?"

She stared at him, trying to understand. This new Josh, who was so different from the boy she had known. Where did this Josh come from?

"I did this, Gaby," he continued. "I helped them put all of this together. Those people down there, they're going to live out the rest of their natural lives. And all they have to do is give a little blood every night and teach their children to do the same."

You're breeding a race of slaves, Josh.

"What's so bad about that?" He was watching her face intently. "Tell me, Gaby, what's so bad about what I've done here?"

You don't know. You're so deep in it, you're incapable of seeing it.

"What?" he said, narrowing his eyes at her.

Gaby realized she had been smiling at him.

"Share with the class," he said, the annoyance creeping back into his voice.

"I get it now," Gaby said.

"Get what?"

"That you're delusional."

He opened his mouth to argue, but stopped and sighed instead.

"Don't say that, Gaby." He sounded genuinely hurt. Or maybe it was just more playacting. "Please don't say that. I did all of this for you."

"Stop saying that."

"It's true."

"Stop saying that, Josh. I want nothing to do with this place." She could feel her patience slipping and did her best to rein it in. Emotion was the enemy here. *(Stay in control!)* "Get it through your head, Josh: I don't want any part of this."

He walked silently back over and gathered up the sporks, dumped them on her plate, over her uneaten potato and strips of bacon and dirty brown rice, and stacked the trays together. "I'm leaving tonight to help out with another town." His voice was still calm, even-keeled. Josh had mastered his emotions. Somewhat. "I don't know when I'll be back. Maybe a few days. Maybe a few weeks." He picked up the trays and walked to the door without another glance in her direction. "Mac!"

The door opened and Mac leaned in. He had an AK-47 slung over his shoulder and was wearing a camo uniform that made him look almost like a soldier, though she guessed Will and Danny would disagree. Lance had been wearing the same identical clothing the last few days, and so had other men with guns she had seen on the streets.

Is this another one of your doing, Josh? Turning collaborators into soldiers?

"Grab the chair," Josh said before stepping outside the room.

Mac came inside and walked over to the bed. He gave her a sharp look, almost daring her to do something, as he picked up the chair.

"How's the head?" she asked. "Stitches holding up?"

He smirked. "Keep it up. Your boyfriend won't be here forever." He had said that last part almost in a low whisper, as if afraid Josh would overhear.

He's afraid of Josh. This grown man is afraid of a nineteen-year-old teenager who was in high school last year.

Mac exited and slammed the door after him. She heard the familiar *click-chank* of the deadbolt sliding into place on the other side.

When she was alone again, Gaby stopped fighting and let her stomach growl and wished she had at least eaten the potato. Or the bacon. When was the last time she was going to get a chance to eat fried bacon again?

At least they had left her the water bottle. She picked it up from the floor and drank greedily. It was warm—but then, they all were these days. The liquid helped soothe her throat, which still hurt from the night at the pawnshop when one of Josh's people had struck her with the butt of his rifle. It was Josh who had wrapped her up in a ball, his hazmat suit saving the two of them from the horde of ghouls rushing into the room. He had saved her, but what about…

Nate.

He had been there too, though Josh refused to tell her what had happened to him. Josh wouldn't even tell her if Nate was alive or dead. Or worse—if he had been turned. It was Josh's way of punishing her, letting her know that, ultimately, he held all the cards.

Because he did. All fifty-two of them.

She walked to the window, hoping that staying active would keep her hunger temporarily at bay. They had left her plenty of clothes. Or whoever used to live in the room before her had. The jeans and T-shirt fit fine, and there were even socks, but no signs of shoes of any type. Not that she needed to wear shoes at all. The only place they would allow her to go was a single bathroom two doors down the hallway. She hadn't even made it far enough to the end of the second floor to see down to the first.

Gaby looked out at the sun-streaked streets below, just in time to catch Josh emerging from the building and climbing into a waiting green Jeep. As far as she could tell, they were keeping her in some kind of boarding house. Not exactly a hotel, but one of those bed-and-breakfasts. That explained the other rooms. She heard plenty of people coming and going over the last few days, even if she never actually got the chance to lay eyes on them. If this was some kind of prison, she was the only one locked up.

Her view of the outside world was revealing, even through the metal burglar bars fastened over the window. She didn't know if hers was the only one secured like a prison cell. The bars were so tightly pressed against the frame that it was impossible to stick her head out far enough to see around her.

The driver waiting for Josh wore the same type of uniform as Lance and Mac and looked at least twenty years older than the kid he was picking up. The two men exchanged a perfunctory nod, but nothing resembling a salute. As the Jeep moved away from the curb, she waited for Josh to look up, perhaps sensing her, but he never did. She watched them drive off until they disappeared up the street.

"I'm leaving tonight to help out with another town," Josh had said. *"I don't know when I'll be back. Maybe a few days. Maybe a few weeks."*

And maybe I won't be here when you get back, Josh.

She looked around at the room.

Of course, getting out of this place was easier said than done. Besides the round-the-clock guard outside her door, she had no weapons, and they had taken away anything that could even remotely be used as a weapon ever since she had nearly killed Mac with the nightstand the first day she woke up.

But Gaby didn't for a second think about giving up the idea of escape. She couldn't, even if she wanted to. Surrender wasn't a part of her DNA. It had never been, and the end of the world hadn't changed that.

Take all the time you need, Josh. I won't be here when you get back…

SHE DIDN'T GET another visitor for the rest of the afternoon. There were no clocks in the room, so she had to use the sun outside to tell time. That and the noise, because the people on the streets were most active in the mornings and afternoons, but as it got darker, the activity died down and the town became ghostly quiet.

They still remember. This place might have become a safe haven, but they still remember what's out there when the sun goes down.

After four days in L15, she had become used to the sight of people on horseback and kids in shorts running around the street. There wasn't any danger of getting run over because there were so few cars in town. And you knew when a car came, because it was usually one of those big Army transport trucks settling yet another group of people. She wondered how long those vehicles had been coming and going. Sooner or later, the space would run out, and then what?

Another town. L16, maybe. Or L20.

L30?

How long had they been building these places, she wondered, and how many more were out there right now? In Louisiana, and in the other states?

What about around the world?

The sight of pregnant women had also ceased to become a novelty. She watched them from her window with a mixture of sadness and pity. Did they know what they were getting into? Of course they did. Josh had told them. Or whoever ran this place when Josh wasn't here. She didn't think Josh was actually responsible for the day-to-day operations. He was like an overseer, coming and going as needed.

The sun was already fading over the rooftops across the street. She didn't need a watch or a clock to tell her that it was almost six. It would be dark in less than thirty minutes. Sometimes sooner, when you least expected it.

Night is not our friend. Not anymore.

She glanced back when the doorknob behind her jingled and Mac pushed the door open. He looked in cautiously, as if expecting her to be lying in wait for him. Gaby almost grinned at his reluctance.

"Dinner, your highness," Mac said, with just enough of a smirk to get across his disdain for her.

A young girl who Gaby had never seen before squeezed her way past Mac. Gaby's entire world in L15 up to this point had revolved around Josh coming in the afternoons and evenings, and Mac standing outside her door in the day and Lance at night. The girl brought a newness that stirred curiosity and suspicion in Gaby.

And who might you be, little girl?

She wore a white sundress and had short black hair cut to complement a round face. She looked all of thirteen, with big brown eyes that gave her a rare vibe of innocence, something that was in short supply these days.

She smiled at Gaby. "I brought you dinner."

"Thank you," Gaby said.

The girl was carrying a brown plastic tray with a red apple, a baked potato in aluminum foil, (*Potatoes again?* she thought, just as her stomach growled), and two pieces of bread with something that looked like ham placed with care between them.

"Where should I put it?" the girl asked her.

"Put it anywhere," Mac said impatiently behind her.

"But I don't want it to get dirty."

"Just put it anywhere, for God's sake."

"On the bed's fine," Gaby said.

She smiled at the girl and got a pleasant response. "Are you sure?" the girl asked. "Peter would kill me if he saw food on my bed."

"I won't tell him if you don't."

That elicited another bright smile. The girl walked over to the bed and put the tray down over the duvet. She stepped back and seemed to hesitate for a moment.

"Get on with it," Mac said behind her.

"I'll come back later—for the tray—when you're done," the girl said. There was something about the way she looked at Gaby—a strange, almost anxiousness in her voice—that made Gaby even more curious.

"Okay," Gaby nodded when the girl didn't say anything else.

"Come on," Mac said. "I don't have all day."

The girl hurried back to the door. Mac held it open for her then slammed it shut after them and immediately pushed the deadbolt into place on the other side.

Gaby stared at the door after them.

What was that about?

SHE SAT ON her bed, eating everything on the tray. She devoured the potato skins and apple core and crumbs from the two slices of bread. Homemade bread. She could tell. Her mom couldn't make bread to save her life, but her friend Anna's mom could. The ham was delicious and fresh. They weren't from a frozen package like on the island. She guessed the townspeople got it from the same pigs as the strips of bacon Josh was boasting about earlier.

She thought about the girl as she ate and watched nightfall blanket the world outside her window. She had gotten used to leaving it open. The sight of candles and flickering lanterns from the buildings around her brought a sense of normalcy she didn't realize she had missed until now.

But it was the girl in the white sundress that stayed at the forefront of her mind. The kid had wanted to say something, but the presence of Mac had discouraged it. What was going on behind those big eyes?

It was pitch-dark outside when she finished her meal and found herself back at the window, looking past the buildings and at the woods beyond. L15 was ringed by woods. Dark and natural, their trees teeming with things she couldn't see. Things other than the animals on the branches, the birds perched among the crowns. Things that were moving on the ground, restless…

Ghouls.

She shivered involuntarily. They were out there right now. Somewhere. She couldn't see them, but she could feel their presence beyond the town limits. The people around her could, too. That was why L15 shut down well before nightfall, why everyone—despite the arrangement, despite the promised safety—still operated under the assumption it wasn't safe to wander outside in the dark.

How many were out there right now, in the woods? Hundreds? Thousands? Easily thousands. The creatures always seemed to know where people congregated. And there were a hell of a lot of people here, right now, in these buildings around her. What was keeping them from coming in one of these days?

Or maybe the better question was, *who* was holding them back…

THE GIRL WITH the round face and the big eyes came back five minutes later, still wearing the sundress, while Gaby was at the window. Mac did his usual look-inside-first move before letting the girl in. Then he stayed behind at the open door, watching Gaby like a hawk. He was so consumed with her that he didn't pay any attention to the girl.

"Get it and let's go," Mac said.

The girl hurried inside and picked up the tray, glanced briefly at Gaby—sideways, so Mac couldn't see their brief exchange *(Okay, now what was that about?)*—before leaving again without a word.

"Sleep tight," Mac said. "Don't let the bed bugs bite, princess."

"Can I ask you something, Mac?" Gaby said.

That caught him by surprise. He hesitated, then said guardedly, "What?"

"Have you lived it down yet?"

"Lived what down?"

"Almost getting your head bashed in by a girl with an end table."

He grunted. "Yeah, you keep bringing that up, princess. Like I keep telling you, one of these days your boyfriend might not be in charge anymore. Those things out there? Those bloodsuckers? They've been known to change their minds."

Mac gave her a big grin, one that was intended to scare her.

It didn't work. "Josh thinks you're a pussy. He told me himself. Can't stand you. Says you don't bathe."

His face turned slightly pale even in the semidarkness of her room, and he was about to respond when he apparently decided against it and left without a word instead. Gaby sighed when she heard the deadbolt snapping into place. She didn't think very highly of Mac, but the man was damn good about always locking her inside.

The girl had left without a word while she was talking with Mac. Gaby cursed herself. Why hadn't she paid more attention to the kid instead of wasting her time with—

Then she saw it. A piece of folded paper, tucked underneath the duvet near where the tray had been.

She hurried across the room, suddenly terrified Mac might choose tonight, of all nights, to come back in for a last-minute check before turning the shift over to Lance. She picked up the paper and walked toward the door on tiptoes, making as little noise as possible, and leaned against the wall and listened.

Mac, moving around, the *creak* of his heavy combat boots against the floorboards.

Gaby unfolded the note. It was a small piece of what looked to be from a sheet of 8x11 piece of writing paper. There was writing on it in black pen, the letters drafted in fine, almost elegant cursive letters. Which meant the girl didn't write it. Gaby had known plenty of girls at thirteen—herself included—and none ever had this kind of penmanship.

She scanned the letters, her eyes widening with every line she read:

"If we help you escape, will you take us with you? Destroy this when done."

Gaby re-read the note again just to be sure her desperate mind hadn't accidentally (purposefully?) "rewritten" the note for its own purposes:

"If we help you escape, will you take us with you? Destroy this when done."

THE FIRES OF ATLANTIS 41

No. It was still the same.

"If we help you escape, will you take us with you?"

Gaby folded the note back up until it was barely the size of her thumb, then slipped it into her mouth and swallowed.

SHE WOKE UP sometime in the middle of the night to the sound of footsteps outside her door. They were too quiet, someone walking on tiptoes, to be Lance. So quiet, in fact, that she only heard it because she had been sitting on the bed waiting for it, or something like it, for the last few hours.

The second floor was partially lit by a portable LED lantern hanging from the ceiling somewhere in the middle of the hallway, between her door and the staircase on the other side. It was rechargeable, and she had seen Mac taking it down to recharge every morning when he showed up for his shift.

There was definitely a figure moving against the hallway light now, visible as elongated shadows through the slit under the door. The figure stopped, shifted *(crouched?)*, then the sound of paper sliding across the floor.

Gaby climbed out of bed and raced toward the door just as the figure stood up and turned to go. "Wait," Gaby said, whispering just loudly enough to be heard. She snatched up the paper—the same size as the other one—and pocketed it. "Don't go."

The shadow turned, then someone pressed against the door. A soft, familiar voice whispered, "You're awake."

Gaby smiled. It was the girl in the sundress. "What's your name?"

"Milly."

"Milly, who sent you—"

"I have to go," Milly said, cutting her off. "He's coming back."

"Wait—"

But Milly was gone, the barely audible *tap-tap* of bare feet against the hallway floor, before a door opened and closed softly seconds later. Gaby was certain Milly had disappeared into a room somewhere further down the hallway, which meant she lived in the building and was one of the many unseen neighbors that came and went every day.

A few seconds later, loud footsteps—like thunder compared to Milly's—climbed up the stairs and moved across the hallway.

Lance.

She got up and tiptoed back to her bed, lay down, and pulled the duvet over her chest and under her chin as the footsteps got closer. Lance moved with all the grace of a bear wearing combat boots.

Gaby closed her eyes when she heard the metal scraping—the familiar noise of the deadbolt sliding free. The door opened a crack and dimmed LED lights flooded into the room. She imagined, but didn't open her eyes to see, Lance's familiar hulking frame in the doorway, making sure she hadn't escaped while he was gone.

A few seconds later, the door closed and the *click-chank* of the deadbolt once again locked her in.

She sat up, took out the note, and unwrapped it.

It was the same black ink written in the same careful cursive handwriting:

"First light. Be ready. Destroy this note."

Gaby re-read the note again, making sure she didn't miss anything, before folding it back up and swallowing it.

She looked over at the window and the darkness outside.

"First light" was sunrise. The *"Be ready"* part was obvious.

What wasn't clear was what they were planning. She didn't believe Milly was acting on her own, and the careful handwriting proved it. So Milly was working with someone. Who? Maybe her father. Or a brother. Maybe just a friend. Gaby was no expert, but the handwriting looked like a man's. Then again, for all she knew, it really could just have been little Milly. Was that possible?

She lay back down and closed her eyes. If there was some kind of escape being planned for tomorrow, she had to be ready. And that meant getting as much sleep as possible now so she would be alert for tomorrow.

"First light…"

AN HOUR LATER, she was still awake.

An hour after that, she gave up trying to sleep altogether.

Gaby climbed out of bed and did push-ups on the floor. She had been keeping up her strength ever since she first opened her eyes in L15, knowing that eventually the time would come when she would need it, so the sudden burst of physical activity wasn't anything new to her body.

She did thirty push-ups, then threw in fifty sit-ups, hoping to tire herself out enough to get the sleep she needed. When that still didn't work, she shadowboxed in the dark, careful to stay away from the window where someone outside could see her.

She didn't stop until she was covered in sweat and her body was sore all over.

When she lay down on the bed for the second time, she had no trouble falling asleep.

"First light. Be ready…"

CHAPTER 4

WILL

"WE GO IN, hit the bars, deflower the virgins, and we're outta there with no one the wiser," Danny said. "Easy peasy."

"What about the guys with guns?" Will asked.

"Weekend warriors. We'll be nice and give them a couple of rounds' head start. But that's as far as I'm willing to bend over for these bozos." He glanced back at Kellerson. "What do you think? That strike you as fair?"

Kellerson stared blankly back at him. He couldn't have said a word even if he wanted to, not with a strip of duct tape over his mouth. His hands, resting limply in his lap, were bound at the wrists. The pinky and ring finger of his left hand were missing, and blood was seeping through the fresh gauze Will had put on the man this morning. Kellerson was quickly becoming more trouble than he was worth.

"Not much of a conversationalist, huh?" Danny said.

"He's shy," Will said. "Cut him some slack."

"'Cut him'?" Danny snorted.

Will smiled. "No pun intended."

"What pun? Oh, you meant those missing fingers of his?"

They were hidden in the woods, looking out from cover at what used to be a small town called Downer Plateau. There was a good kilometer of open clearing and small roads between them and the town, now referred to by the collaborators as simply L15. Behind them, hidden by trees for at least another three kilometers, was

Interstate 49, the primary road through this part of Louisiana.

L15—or what parts of it he could see—had been a good-sized place once upon a time. Big enough for thousands of people to call it home. It was connected to the interstate by a state highway, and from what he could see most of the buildings were concentrated around a central main street. The place gave off an old-fashioned vibe, which was exactly what the ghouls and their human collaborators were going for.

"We think it's because they want us to start over," someone had once told him. *"A fresh start. The cities are filled with reminders of the old world. Our achievements, our art, our evolution as human beings. Out here, surrounded by farmland, woods… It's like going back to our roots. No power, no electricity… It's easier to believe the last two centuries never happened."*

It wasn't a bad place, if you were looking to start all over without actually beginning from scratch. The people moving around the streets were there willingly. Children poked their heads out of apartment windows, and every now and then he heard the *clop-clop* of horseshoes on roads meant for cars. The last collaborator town he had been this close to had armed men on rooftops and walking the streets. But there was a noticeable lack of anything resembling "the enemy" at L15.

He looked back at Kellerson again, leaning lifelessly against a tree. The man's face was white, his eyes hollow, and Will kept expecting him to bolt any second, but losing two fingers must have taken all the fight out of him. That, and he just didn't look like he had the strength to stand up, much less think he might be able to outrun them.

"L15," Will said to Kellerson. "That means there are fourteen more towns just like this one?"

Kellerson nodded and mumbled something behind the duct tape.

"How far does the number go? Twenty? Higher?"

Another nod.

"Thirty?"

Kellerson seemed to think about it, then shrugged.

"You don't know for sure."

Nod.

"I guess you were right," Danny said. "Little buggers have been busy while we were twiddling our thumbs back on the beach and drinking piña coladas."

"Looks like it."

Will glanced at his watch. 4:14 P.M.

Two hours before sunset. Even with the ATVs Kellerson and his men had been using (when they weren't tooling around in their armored Humvees), it had taken him and Danny too long to travel from Lafayette, where they had parted company with Roy and Zoe earlier this morning. He couldn't afford to let Zoe go yesterday after she had been shot, not until he was sure she wouldn't die on Roy while they were en route. Zoe was a doctor, and those were more valuable than bullets these days.

"It's going to be dark soon," Will said.

"Of course it is," Danny said. "If it didn't, then this would just be another boring jaunt through the woods. And I forgot my jaunting pants at the island."

"Shoulda packed appropriately."

"Shoulda, coulda, but didn'ta."

Will gestured at Kellerson, who pushed himself off the tree with some effort, turned around, and began marching back through the woods. There was enough light splashing through the trees around them that Will didn't feel like he was walking through a nest of ghouls, something that you had to take into consideration these days, especially when you were close to an area filled with humans—or prey, to the creatures. They *crunched* dried leaves and *snapped* twigs under them, the noise swallowed up by birds perched along branches.

"You think he's back there?" Danny asked. "Our little buddy Josh?"

"If she's there, he's probably there, too."

"Kid's got it bad. I remember the last time a girl had me so head over heels. Of course, it never occurred to me to sell out the human race for her affections. Then again, Dad always did say I lacked ambition."

"If only he could see you now."

"Yeah. Take that, Pops."

They hadn't gone more than a few minutes before Will heard it—felt it, really. He grabbed Kellerson and pushed him down onto one knee, while at the same time he and Danny went into a crouch and looked to their right through a small grouping of trees.

They were less than forty meters from the highway that connected the town to the interstate, and Will had previously spotted a couple of vehicles—both trucks—coming and going. At the moment, he caught a flash of red paint, then dull green. A pickup truck up front, followed by an Army five-ton transport, its thick tires kicking up clouds of dust in its wake.

"Haven't seen those in a while," Danny said. "My ass hurts just looking at them."

Will reached over and peeled the duct tape half off Kellerson's mouth. The man sighed with relief and sucked in a deep, fresh breath.

"Those five-tons," Will said. "Are they always full when they show up at these places?"

"Yeah," Kellerson nodded. He sounded hoarse, even though he had just drank some water a few hours ago. "The kid believes in efficiency, and he's been organizing everyone into a military mindset. Thinks he's a major or something."

"The kid." Josh.

You actually entrusted one of your operations to an eighteen-year-old kid, Kate? Really?

"How many does a town like L15 hold?" Will asked.

"Maybe two or three thousand," Kellerson said.

"How many dickheads do they have watching that many people?" Danny asked.

Kellerson shrugged. "Anywhere from ten to twenty."

"Ten to twenty for a few thousand?" Danny wrinkled his nose. "You telling a fib, Kellerson? Want Willie boy here to start working on those toes next?"

"He doesn't get it, does he?" Kellerson said, looking at Will.

Will slapped the duct tape back over Kellerson's mouth.

"Get what?" Danny said. "You BFFs have a joke you wanna share with me? Come on, I'm starting to feel like the third wheel here."

"He means they don't need a lot of guards," Will said. "The people in these towns are here of their own free will. They don't *want* to leave. My guess is, ten is more than enough, and twenty is overkill."

"So what you're saying is, when we finally get around to going in there guns blazing, they won't be throwing their virginal daughters at us?"

"That's an affirmative."

Danny grunted. "Well, damn. I certainly signed up for the wrong road trip, didn't I?"

THEY WALKED FOR another hour until they reached the spot where they had stashed the camouflage ATVs earlier—a small group of buildings about half a kilometer from I-49. It was a homestead connected to the highway by a spur road that hadn't looked traveled even before The Purge. The house's main building was a bungalow flanked by an empty garage. A long red barn, the paint badly chipped by neglect and weather, squatted in the back with a rusted-over tractor out front. The place was as out-of-the-way as they could find on short notice.

The ATVs were hidden inside the barn among the unused bales of hay and horseless stables. Walking the rest of the way to L15 had been necessary. Sound traveled these days, and the roar of all-terrain vehicles would have been obvious to even a deaf man.

There hadn't been much of the bungalow to explore, and their biggest worry was the decayed sloping roof falling down on them. They found what they were looking for in the back of the house, hidden behind rotting twin doors that opened up into an underground cellar. There wasn't much inside except for old tractor parts and stacks of cinder blocks under dust-covered tarps. They cleared out just enough space in one corner and dropped their bedrolls and supply packs.

Kellerson sat down in one corner on the dirt floor. Will let him eat a stick of beef jerky and gave him a bottle of water to wash it down with. When he was done, Will covered his mouth back up before he could say a word. The fight had gone out of Kellerson about the same time Will threatened to take the collaborator's third finger.

They found a way to lock the doors by looping coiled steel cables around the handles and snapping a padlock in place. When that didn't look like it would hold against a prolonged assault, they stacked the cinderblocks in front of the entrance, then threw the heavy tarps over them to make sure not a single inch of space could be seen from the other side. The creatures had proven themselves too smart at detecting people to take any chances.

If their luck did happen to run out, at least they had plenty of the right ammo to fend off an attack. Danny and Roy had left Song Island well prepared, and Will had taken all of Roy's before they parted company this morning. Roy took the regular ammo because in the daytime, any ol' bullet would do. Will and Danny carried two heavy bags and two tactical backpacks with them, stuffed with a combination of what Danny and Roy had brought and what they had salvaged from Kellerson's dead crew. Dead men didn't need beef jerky, bottled water, and spare ammo. The portable ham radio he had been using to communicate with Song Island was among the supplies.

Will looked down at his watch's glow-in-the-dark hands: 5:34 P.M.

"You think she's still alive in there?" Danny asked. He was chewing loudly on a stick of jerky.

"Gaby?"

"No, Yoko Ono. Yeah, Gaby."

"She's Gaby."

"Yup. That's her name, all right."

"What I mean is, she'll be fine. She's a survivor. You should have seen her at the hospital."

"Yeah?"

Will nodded. "Yeah."

Soon, the only evidence that Danny was even leaning against the dirt wall next to him was the sound of chewing. Somewhere to his right, Kellerson was breathing deeply. How the man could make so much noise while only inhaling and exhaling through his nostrils was a mystery. Will had considered removing Kellerson's duct tape to make it easier on him, but it never took long for the man's crimes—those that Will knew for a fact, and likely more he didn't even know about—to come up again, and it took all of Will's strength not to execute him on the spot.

Night came, and they heard scurrying outside almost immediately. The soft patter of bare feet against hard ground vibrated through the dried dirt around them.

Will flicked the fire selector on his M4A1 rifle from semi-automatic to full-auto just in case.

"You nervous in the service, son?" Danny whispered somewhere in the darkness.

Will smiled.

"I'll huff and I'll puff, and I'll blow your flimsy cellar doors down," Danny whispered.

A soft *click* as Danny flicked at his carbine's fire selector.

Will sat back against the cool dirt wall and groped his pack for the all-too-light bottle of painkillers. He shook out two Tramadol and popped them into his mouth, then swallowed without chewing. He pulled up his shirt and ran his palm over the stitching along his right side and considered it a good sign he didn't feel any wetness. His left arm had numbed over since yesterday, and he hadn't felt anything more than the occasional slight tingles coming from his left hip in a while. Either the pills were working, or he had become used to them.

What he wouldn't give to have Lara look him over. The last thing he needed was an infection. Battlefield wound treatment was a crapshoot at best, but leaving them for days was just asking for it.

Of course, having Lara treat him meant going back home. Back to Song Island.

And he couldn't do that. Not yet. Not while Gaby was still out there…

AROUND MIDNIGHT HE drifted off, waking up two hours later to let Danny sleep.

Each time Will woke up, he could hear Kellerson moving erratically in the darkness, possibly from a nightmare. Or it could be the bugs and hairy legs of spiders crawling up and down his body. Will felt them too, but they were small enough that he didn't bother chasing them off. He did slap a few that wandered too close to his neck and face, squashing them against his palm, then wiping the leftover goop on the floor.

When he was awake, he listened to the occasional movements on the other side of the cellar doors, like rats scratching in the walls. He wasn't surprised they were out there, though it did make him more than a little uncomfortable they were this close. There was no one in the house, and surely they must have already searched it a hundred times since The Purge, so why were they back?

But the creatures' presence in the area didn't surprise him at all. There were people nearby in L15. Humans that had given up liberty for salvation. Blood for safety.

"They're not like you, Will," Zoe had said to him once. *"They're not soldiers. They're just trying to survive the end of the world the best they can."*

I would rather die first.

Danny woke up two hours later, and Will went back to sleep.

◄▬▌ ▐▬►

HE FELT THE heat building inside the cellar with the morning, and small slivers of sunlight flitted through the barricade in front of him when he opened his eyes. Not much light, just enough to illuminate parts of the room.

He sat up and soaked in the peace and quiet of a waking world. The birds had already begun chirping, and Will thought about Lara, about waking up next to her and wishing he were there now instead of sitting inside a room literally dug out of the ground.

After about an hour of tranquility, he stood up and woke Danny, who had been sleeping soundlessly next to him.

"I'm up, I'm up," Danny said. "What's for breakfast?"

"Beef jerky."

"That's what we had yesterday."

"Ain't life grand?"

"I could have stayed on the island and eaten pancakes. Speaking of which, you know what else Sarah found in the kitchen freezer?"

"What's that?"

"Jimmy Hoffa. Turns out he was in there this whole time."

"You don't say."

"I just did. Sheesh. You never listen." Danny looked over at Kellerson, sleeping awkwardly on his side across from them. "Should we wake up Sleeping Beauty?"

Will looked at Kellerson for a moment. He had been thinking about what to do with the collaborator for some time now and had even devoted one of his two-hour awake times last night just to mull over the question. The possibilities were endless. Some were bloody, others were cruel, and there were a few merciful options in there, too. Each time he had to weigh the lives Kellerson had taken against the man's fate…all the bodies Will knew about, and all the ones he didn't…

Finally, Will said, "We should put him out of his misery. He's already served his purpose."

"Kinda rude to just kill the guy after he's been so helpful," Danny said. "But hey, you know what they say about karma and bitches and all that good stuff."

Will was reaching for his Glock in its hip holster when a faint noise from outside the cellar drew his attention.

"You heard that?" Danny said.

"Yeah," Will said. He moved toward the doors and began removing the barrier they had put up there last night.

The noise they had both heard was a faint wet *pop* sound, something they wouldn't have detected eleven months ago when the world was still alive.

As he and Danny were throwing cinderblocks out of their path, they heard it again. This time it wasn't a single sound, but a continuous rattling *pop-pop-pop*. They knew exactly what it was and where it was coming from.

Behind them. L15.

Gunshots.

CHAPTER 5

GABY

SHE STOOD NEXT to the door, just out of the path of the sunlight pouring across the length of the room through the open window. Her back was pressed against the wall, and Gaby willed her breathing into slow beats to allow her senses to concentrate on what was outside the second floor at this very moment.

Mac was out there again, moving around loudly. He might as well be stomping cockroaches in boots. The man would be carrying his usual gear, including the AK-47, a belt with full ammo pouches, and a sidearm.

"First light. Be ready."

It was first light, but no one had come.

Not Milly the girl or her accomplice. She knew Milly wasn't working alone because of the first note she had received: *"If we help you escape, will you take us with you?"*

The "we" was the dead giveaway. *If* this was real. She didn't put it past Josh to play games with her, though that was a worst-case scenario. There was no reason for Josh to deceive her now. Not after he had won. She was locked inside a room and not allowed to leave for any reason except to use the bathroom. In every way that mattered, she was at his mercy, so it was doubtful he would stoop so low as to mess with her head.

No, this wasn't some elaborate trick. It had to be real.

Probably.

She wished she had a weapon, something that could break

bone—or at least puncture skin. She had her hands, but it wasn't nearly as easy to incapacitate someone with your fists as the movies made it out to be. She had learned that the hard way during sparring sessions with Will and Danny. Regardless of what kind of an advantage she had over a man, when it came to hand-to-hand fighting, she was still shorter, smaller, and weaker than her opponent. Girl power be damned, she would rather have a weapon.

Gaby glanced down at her watch: 7:36 A.M.

More than twenty minutes since the sun rose over the tree lines ("*first light*") and bathed the town in a welcoming orange glow. To look at it, you wouldn't know L15 was a town built on lies and desperation—

Voices, coming from the hallway outside.

About time.

Gaby slid closer to the door, leaving just a foot of space between her and the hinges, the doorknob on the other side. She was dressed in jeans and a T-shirt, with socks but no shoes. Josh hadn't responded to her requests for shoes. Just another way to control her, to keep her at his mercy. He was good at that these days.

"Already?" a male voice said. *Mac.*

"I gotta go do something after this," a soft female voice answered. *Milly.* There was a hint of anxiousness. Gaby hoped Mac didn't notice.

"Like what?" Mac said.

"What do you care?" Milly countered.

"Don't be a smartass."

"I'm just saying, if I don't give her her breakfast now, I won't be around for another couple of hours. Peter's got me busy today."

"Okay, whatever," Mac said. "Hurry up."

The familiar sound of the deadbolt sliding, then the doorknob turning. A second later the door opened, followed by something hard and plastic *clattering* against the floor. She recognized the sound. It was one of the food trays.

"What—" she heard Mac start to say a split-second before Milly backpedaled through the open door, fumbling with a handgun in her small hands.

Oh, hell, this is the plan?

Mac was moving quickly through the door after Milly, reaching one hand out toward her. "Give that back to me, kid. What are you doing? Are you crazy? Give that back to me!"

He was so concerned with Milly—no, about *his gun in her hands*—that he didn't do his usual due diligence. He didn't look around to make sure she wasn't lying in wait for him.

Now now now!

Gaby pushed herself off the wall and had gotten one step toward Mac—the sound of her bare feet pulling Mac's eye away from Milly and over to her—but neither one of them managed to do anything before a fourth body slammed into Mac from behind. Arms snaked around Mac's waist as the new figure's head buried itself into the small of the guard's back. The whole thing was so awkwardly executed that Gaby actually found herself staring in astonishment.

Mac let out a loud surprised grunt as he was thrown forward by the surprise attack. He slammed into the wooden footboard of the bed with his stomach and bent over awkwardly at the waist, the AK-47 slung over his shoulder swinging wildly around him. He attempted to right himself when the other man hit him in the back of the head with a brown maple wood rolling pin, swinging the kitchen object like some kind of hammer, and *thwack!*

Another burst of pained sounds sprung from Mac's mouth as he slumped forward again, his body draping over the bed's footboard. The attacker staggered back, gasping for breath, while Milly stood nearby holding the handgun, looking impossibly frightened.

Gaby took a step forward and the attacker whirled on her, rolling pin rising to strike. Gaby ignored him and made a beeline for Mac. She grabbed the AK-47 and pulled it free. A small pool of blood had clumped at the back of Mac's head, and he didn't fight her as she took his rifle away.

The man and Milly were looking at her, their labored breathing filling the room as if they had just run a marathon. The man was in his mid-thirties and tall. He wore slacks and a T-shirt, but what got her attention was the Garfield apron around his waist. He opened his mouth as if to say something but ended up just sucking in more air instead.

Gaby held out her hand to Milly and the girl anxiously gave up the handgun. It was an automatic, almost entirely stainless steel except for a strip of laminated wood along the grip. *Smith & Wesson SW1911TA* was engraved along the side. It looked a hell of a lot more expensive than the Glocks she had been trained on, and she wondered where Mac had gotten something that fancy.

"What now?" the man said, his eyes focused on her. She couldn't tell if he looked disappointed or confused. "Jesus, I thought you'd be older."

"Sorry to disappoint you," she said.

"I didn't mean—I just thought—"

"That I'd be older. I got it. Close the door," she said to Milly.

The girl stepped over the plastic tray and the spilled food and closed the door. Gaby grabbed Mac and hauled him off the foot-board, dropping him to the floor on his back. Dull, pained eyes stared up at her, but if she was afraid Mac would fight, she didn't have to be. It was entirely possible he wasn't even seeing her at the moment. He was alive, if barely, because she could still hear him breathing.

"What are you doing?" the man asked behind her.

She didn't bother to answer him. Instead, she unclasped Mac's gun belt and pulled it off, along with the holster and ammo pouches. She cinched it around her waist and instantly felt better with the weight. These last few days, walking around without weapons was like being naked in front of the world. The Smith & Wesson slid easily into the hip holster, and though it didn't have silver bullets in the magazine, it was better than no ammo.

"How many of you are there?" she asked, busying herself with Mac's boots. He was a few inches taller than her and she expected his boots to be a little larger as a result, but she was surprised when they fit her as well as they did.

"Just us," the man said. "What are you doing now?"

"Stop asking stupid questions," she snapped. "You know what I'm doing."

Gaby pulled off Mac's camouflage jacket and slipped it on. It was slightly big around the shoulders, but luckily Mac wasn't fat. She took off his watch and put it on her wrist.

"Maybe I should take the rifle," the man said.

"You know how to use one of these?" she asked.

"How hard could it be?"

"Right. I'll keep the rifle."

She got up and walked over to the door and opened it just a crack. She looked out at the empty second-floor hallway with Milly standing next to her, eyeing her curiously.

"Where is everyone?" she asked the girl.

"At work," Milly said.

"Work?"

"Everyone has assigned work details," the man said. "I work in the kitchen downstairs, and Milly is the server girl."

"Hostess," Milly said.

The man smiled. "Sorry. Hostess."

She glanced back at the two of them. There wasn't much of a resemblance, so she crossed out father and daughter. Not brother and sister, either.

"I'm Peter," the man said, holding out his hand.

She shook it. "Gaby."

"Milly told me. How are we getting out of here, Gaby?"

She stared at him for a moment. "You don't know?"

He shook his head. "We were hoping you might have a plan."

"Are you serious? You're the ones who are supposed to be rescuing me, not the other way around."

Milly and Peter exchanged a look.

"Never mind," Gaby said. "Tell me about the town. How many collaborators are here?"

"Collaborators?" Peter said.

"The guys in the uniforms with guns."

"Oh." He thought about it. "Seven. Four left yesterday, but four more came with the new group of arrivals."

"Is that too many?" Milly asked eagerly, still watching her face closely.

Gaby shook her head. "No. Seven is doable."

I hope…

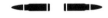

THEY WERE KEEPING her in a bed-and-breakfast just as she had guessed. That accounted for all the rooms on the second floor. According to Peter, except for her, everyone came and went as they pleased, though the building was reserved for singles.

Milly and Peter had their own rooms, and they disappeared inside them while Gaby stood watch at the top of the stairs. The first floor below her was empty, with everyone having already left for their "jobs." Peter was still around because he worked in the kitchen while Milly assisted him.

"It sort of worked out perfectly for us," Peter had said. "Besides Mac, there won't be anyone here to stop us from leaving."

"What about outside?" she had asked. "Where are all the other guards?"

"Walking around most of the time. You probably already know this, but this isn't exactly a prison. They're not going to stop anyone from leaving. Well, except you."

Gaby had seen the way Peter looked at her more than once. He had questions, but he had (smartly) decided to keep them to himself for now. He didn't really have the look of a chef, but then most of the people around L15 were probably doing things they didn't think they would be doing before The Purge. She certainly had no idea she would be sneaking around a bed-and-breakfast with an AK-47.

Milly and Peter came back a few minutes later, both carrying large backpacks. Too large.

"What's in there?" Gaby asked.

"Clothes," Milly said. "And other stuff."

"What kind of other stuff?"

"Deodorant, tooth paste, toothbrush…"

"Get rid of the clothes."

"Why?"

"Take only what you need."

"But I need my clothes," Milly said.

"Get rid of the clothes," Gaby said again.

Milly sighed and went back into her room.

Peter looked after the girl, then over at Gaby. "I, uh, just have socks and underwear. And some personal stuff."

She nodded. "That's fine."

"How old are you, anyway?" he asked. She guessed that was one of the questions that had been swirling around in his head since they met.

"Old enough," she said.

"I thought you'd be older."

"You said that already." Gaby glanced over as Milly came back out of her room with a noticeably lighter backpack. "Is there a back door?" she asked Peter.

He nodded and moved to take the lead, but she put a hand on

THE FIRES OF ATLANTIS 59

his arm.

"I'll go first," she said, stepping ahead of him. "Just tell me where to go."

"Down the stairs, turn right into the back hallway," Peter said.

She moved down the stairs, the rifle in front of her. She didn't particularly like the AK-47, but she knew how to use it. Although she was more familiar with the M4, there were other rifles on the island she had trained on over the months. Will always told her it was fine to have a favorite, but not at the risk of being ignorant of the rest.

As Peter promised, there was no one on the first floor. The emptiness made her nervous, with the main entrance looming in front of her. She glimpsed two figures standing across the street, both wearing camo uniforms similar to the ones Mac and Lance wore and the jacket she had on now. The uniforms made it easier to pick them out from the civilians. The last thing she wanted was to shoot someone who was just trying to survive the end of the world. The ones with guns, on the other hand…well, she could live with putting them down.

She turned right and led Milly and Peter into the back hallway. They followed (too) closely behind and made too much noise. There was a door at the end, sunlight filtering in through a security window. She reached it and looked out, past the sidewalk and at the buildings across the street. Large trees encircled the town in the near distance. Figures—men and women, and some children—moved along the sidewalks.

She looked back at Peter, then Milly. They were watching her anxiously.

"We're going to walk out of here like we belong," she said. "Act normally. Walk normally. *You belong here.* Don't draw attention to yourselves, but don't look away from anyone, either. Got it?"

They nodded back.

"If anyone calls your name, respond," Gaby continued. "You're doing what you're supposed to do—going about your business."

"Okay," Peter said.

"Got it," Milly nodded.

"I don't see any vehicles except the ones the guards drive," she said to Peter.

"There aren't that many still left in town," Peter said. "There are a couple of trucks and some ATVs parked near the administrative building."

"Can we get to them?"

"I don't see how. Besides you, those are the only places they actually guard."

She could see it in Peter's eyes again. It was the question that had been going through his mind: *"What's so special about you?"*

But he didn't voice it, and she was glad. Gaby didn't feel like explaining her relationship with Josh. It was complicated. *"See, there's this guy, and he's in love with me, but he has a really screwed up way of showing it."*

It sounded messed up even in her head.

"What about the horses?" Gaby asked. "I've seen them around."

"There's a stable on the south side, but there are people watching it. They're not armed, but I don't think they're just going to give the animals to us."

"They won't have a choice."

"Can you really just shoot them?"

She stared at him, wondering if the shock on his face was real. "Yes," she said matter-of-factly.

"I don't want to do that," Peter said, and shook his head. "Can't we find another way?"

"I'm open to suggestions."

"I want to leave this town, but not if I have to kill to do it."

"You bashed Mac's head in pretty good upstairs."

He flinched. "That was different. He's one of the guards, and it was necessary. These other people...they're not dangerous."

She could see the conflict on his face, and he reminded her very much of Nate.

Where are you, Nate? Are you dead? Are you out there somewhere? Are you one of those things now, lurking in the darkness?

"All right," she said. "Then we'll have to go on foot." She looked back down the hallway. "The highway is back there."

"The interstate," Peter nodded.

"Then what's on this side?"

"The farms, woods, and Hillman's Lake, where they get the water."

"And beyond that?"

"I don't know. I've never gone past the lake. I don't think anyone has except the guards."

Gaby took a breath. Milly smiled back at her, looking strangely confident in what they were about to do. Gaby couldn't fathom what was going through the kid's head at the moment. The last thing she was feeling was confidence. She wanted to escape, but she always thought she'd only have herself to take care of. Dragging a thirty-something guy and his, well, whatever it was Milly was to him, was never part of the plan.

Finally, she nodded. "All right. Remember: You belong here. Act normal."

"Normal," Peter said. "Right."

She turned back around, opened the door, and stepped outside into the bright sun, gripping the AK-47 tightly in front of her, forefinger sliding comfortably close to the trigger.

SEEING AND FEELING the warmth of the sun from her apartment window *(prison cell)* was one thing; actually being outside walking under it was another. She had forgotten how freeing and comforting the daylight was. Even with all the potential dangers around her, Gaby couldn't help but take a moment to soak in the clean air.

The first sound that reached her after stepping out onto the sidewalk was loud hammering from across the street. A dozen men were carefully lowering a large rectangular sign—a gaudy monstrosity featuring a woman lying on her side, barely clothed—to waiting hands below them. There was a second, plainer sign leaning against the building with writing that read: "Housing #14."

Other buildings around her were being similarly repurposed, their old signs either already redone or in the process of being replaced. They seemed to be working from right to left, probably depending on what they needed. With the constant arrival of new five-ton transport trucks on a regular basis, she imagined they had dozens, maybe even hundreds, of new people in need of homes every day.

Salvation comes at a price. Your blood. Your soul. Your future.
I'd rather die first.

"Let's go," she said quietly.

They started up the sidewalk, making a beeline for the end of the street. The road curved left out of town, but the tree line in front of her beckoned, promising safety within the woods beyond. Gaby set a calm, almost leisurely pace, smiling and nodding and exchanging looks with everyone they passed. No one wore uniforms, which helped to set her mind somewhat at ease, and she allowed herself to lessen the pressure against the AK-47's trigger.

She expected to see men on horseback, but there were none. Instead, the streets and sidewalks were filled with civilians. Men, women, and children. And pregnant women. It wasn't hard to pick them out of the crowd. There were a *lot* of them.

"How many pregnant women are in town?" she asked Peter.

"A lot," he said. "Over a hundred. There are more women here than men. I asked around, and it's the same in all the other towns."

She could see for herself that he was right. For every man or boy she saw, there were at least two females. Some pregnant, others not. And there was something else she noticed: They were all young and healthy.

Perfect birth-giving age. To squeeze out babies for the monsters.

Gaby's mood darkened.

I'd rather die first…

"Peter!" a female voice shouted.

Gaby looked over as a woman in her twenties walked briskly across the street toward them. She was slim and attractive, with long black hair that fell all the way to her waist. She wore a white one-piece dress and beamed at the sight of Peter. Gaby searched for the telltale signs of a baby bump, but there wasn't one.

"Hey, Anna," Peter said, smiling back at the woman.

"Where you off to?" Anna asked.

"Um, to the lake."

"What's going on at the lake?"

Peter glanced at Gaby, and she could see him struggling for an answer. Lying, apparently, didn't come easily to Peter.

"They wanted me to look at some plants they found," he said. "To see if they're edible."

The woman stopped in front of them, and bright green eyes settled on Gaby. "Hi."

"Hey," Gaby said.

"I haven't seen you around before. Did you just arrive?"

"You know everyone in town?" Gaby asked, injecting just enough annoyance into her voice to let the woman know it wasn't her job to question her. She was, after all, the one wearing a uniform (or at least, Mac's boots and jacket) and holding a rifle.

The woman was properly chastised. "I guess not."

"Right," Gaby said, and looked away.

Anna smiled at Milly instead. "Hey there, kid."

"Hey, Anna," Milly said. The girl smiled, playing along. She was definitely a more convincing liar than Peter. "How's Bobby?"

"He's okay. Working at the barn with the horses now."

"That's cool."

Anna looked back at Peter before her eyes shifted over to Gaby again. "So, I'll let you guys get back to work."

"Okay," Peter said. "See you around."

"Yeah, sure." She gave Gaby a pursed smile before walking off.

Gaby looked after her.

She knows.

She must have been unconsciously raising the AK-47 when she felt Peter's hand on the rifle's barrel. "No," he said softly, shaking his head. "Please. She's a good person."

They're all good people until they shoot you in the back, she thought, but said instead, "Whatever. Let's go."

She started up the sidewalk again. Peter and Milly followed in silence for a moment, their quickening footsteps sounding almost in tune to the hammering across the street.

Gaby risked a quick glance over her shoulder.

Anna, farther back down the street, was watching after them, and her eyes met Gaby's again.

"Pick up the pace," Gaby said.

She began moving faster, dodging people in their path. If they were indifferent to her before, they became slightly alarmed as she moved aggressively around and sometimes through them. Gaby measured the difference between them and the woods.

Fifty yards, give or take.

Her pace quickened and she was almost moving at a trot now. "Hurry."

"What's happening?" Peter said.

"Just hurry!"

Peter and Milly already looked out of breath and they weren't any closer to the tree lines. The girl probably hadn't built up much of a stamina delivering food, and Gaby could already see the strain on her round face. Peter didn't look any better. She guessed cooking for people in the bed-and-breakfast hadn't done him any favors, either.

Forty yards…

…thirty-five…

"Hey!" a male voice shouted behind them.

Gaby looked over her shoulder a second time.

Anna was standing next to a uniformed guard, the woman pointing after them. The man was too far back for her to make out any details, but she could easily discern the M4 hanging at his side.

"Stop where you are!" the man shouted.

The hell with that.

She took off, shouting, "Run!"

She knew Peter and Milly were close behind because she could hear them gasping, their sneakers slapping against the pavement. People stumbled out of their way, others hurrying into open doors. Men working on a building across the street stopped what they were doing and stared curiously.

A gunshot *pinged!* against a metal sign hanging four feet above her head. Gaby ducked reflexively, even though she didn't really need to.

She picked up even more speed.

Twenty yards…

She glanced back and saw Peter holding onto Milly's hand, the two of them somehow keeping pace despite the sweat and veins popping out along their temples and foreheads.

God, they're out of shape.

Gaby didn't stop. Didn't waste precious seconds shooting back at the guard. The first gunshot would already be bringing other collaborators. One or two, she might have been able to prevail against in a stand-up fight, but if even half of those seven showed up, she was a goner.

No, not seven. Six. Because Mac was probably still bleeding on the second floor of the bed-and-breakfast right now.

Death by roller pin. Now that's a hell of a way to go.

Ten yards…

…five…

She finally reached the end of the sidewalk and darted into the woods just as the man fired again, the *pop-pop-pop* of a three-round burst chopping into the branches above her head. She heard Milly scream and glanced back at the girl's terrified face. Peter had picked her up and was cradling her like precious cargo as he struggled to catch up.

"Keep running!" she shouted.

He might have nodded, she couldn't be sure. But he didn't stop, and that was all that mattered. Milly was clinging to his neck, her face shoved against his chest. She might have also been whimpering, but Gaby couldn't be certain with her own heartbeat slamming against her chest.

As she ran, Gaby wondered how long it would take Josh to hear about her escape and come after her. How many men would he commit to getting her back under his thumb? That would probably depend on how badly he wanted her. At the moment, she didn't particularly care. She had weapons again and freedom, and she'd be damned if she was going to give up both of those things now.

Come and get me, Josh.

Come and get me if you can...

CHAPTER 6

KEO

SUNSET DELUCA DRIVE, with its commercial buildings and vast parking lots to one side and the crystal clear waters of Lake Dulcet on the other, made for a great morning walk. The only sounds came from the soles of his boots against the pavement, a welcome distraction after last night's near miss. The wind blew through the palm trees and birds glided through the air with all the time in the world. He could almost believe there was nothing wrong with the universe, that at any moment the area would be filled with tourists snapping photos.

Keo walked under streetlights and alongside dead cars, most of them still with keys in their ignitions. But minus gas or working batteries, they were useless. There was surprisingly little traffic, with only the occasional sedan or abandoned truck to break the monotony of gray concrete and random spurts of weeds. He had traveled this stretch of the city dozens of times, and the silence never failed to make him just a little bit uncomfortable.

It was noon by the time he finally made it back to the marina.

He stepped out of the street and onto the cobblestone walkway, dodging the same three white trucks that had been parked there since the day he had arrived with Zachary and Shorty. He took note of each truck's windows and their current positions and was satisfied they hadn't been moved or tampered with since yesterday morning.

The marina had three long docks and sixteen slips, with the middle section capable of hosting eight vessels while the outer two were able to hold four each. There was only one boat in the entire place at the moment. A sailboat with blue along the sides, about thirteen meters long. It was spacious enough to house five or six comfortably, with an American flag fluttering proudly at the stern. Inside the cabin, they had found photos of a family of six. A nice-looking group of people with blue-blood genes in expensive polo sweaters and Ralph Lauren slacks.

The fact that there was only one lone sailboat in the entire marina was a bit of a mystery. Inside, they had found emergency rations, nonperishable food, and cases of bottled water, which led Keo to believe the cruisers had arrived only recently. Maybe they docked, went into the city, but never made it back onboard. In a way, it was similar to how Mark and Jordan had been surviving since the end, which would mean the previous owners knew about water being a sanctuary from the monsters.

So where were they now? Maybe out there, somewhere.

Or dead, like Zachary and Shorty.

That wasn't entirely true. There were worse things than death these days...

The problem with the sailboat was the size. Thirteen meters was big, and the vessel wasn't designed for single-handed sailing. Even with Zachary and Shorty, two men who were even more novices at this than he was, it would have been a chore to manage the boat along the veins of the river heading south—

Engines.

Keo was about to climb over the boat's fender when the noise cut through the silence of the city. It was impossible to miss. Sound already traveled long distances these days, but mechanical noise was like shouting through a bullhorn.

Car engines.

He finished the climb and dropped down, flattening himself against the sun-bleached white deck. He unslung the pack and slid it in front of him, then laid the MP5SD on top of the nylon fabric. He pulled the zipper and took out the small binoculars and peered through it, past the railing in front of him.

He tracked two vehicles moving fast down Sunset Deluca Drive.

Trucks.

A sleek black GMC Sierra and a white Honda Ridgeline. They were staying close together, clearly moving in tandem. He waited for both vehicles to flash by and keep going, but instead they began to slow down—

Crap.

—before stopping completely in front of the parking lot and behind the three white trucks.

And my luck keeps getting better and better.

Two men, wearing clothes Keo didn't think he'd ever see again, climbed out of the GMC in camo uniforms and combat boots, with sidearms and ammo pouches attached to web belts. They looked like soldiers, but Keo knew better. There were no American soldiers anymore. You would need an American government to still be around for that. Besides, these guys didn't actually look like servicemen. Keo had been around guys in uniform almost his entire life, and these jokers looked more like civilians dressing up for Halloween. Even the shade of their camo was wrong.

One of the men reached into the large GMC and pulled out a tan-colored FN SCAR assault rifle. The second, bigger one had an M4. He was wearing some kind of an assault vest with a radio in a pouch, which the man pressed now. A loud squawk, then muffled voices, but they were too far away for Keo to eavesdrop.

He was caught in no man's land. Escaping into the cabin behind him was a non-starter. He had only two real options at this point—fight or flee. He couldn't flee. There was nowhere to go unless he wanted to go for a swim.

Which left fight.

Because there was no way these men were going to leave now. Even if they didn't know the boat existed before showing up, they would have to be blind not to spot the white-painted forty-meter mast sticking up into the air like a beacon. If these bozos came any closer and looked for more than a few seconds, it would be impossible to miss the only boat in the entire marina.

So he wasn't terribly surprised when the fat man began walking up the middle dock toward him.

If it weren't for shitty luck...

He watched Fatty turn sideways to move between two of the trucks in the parking lot, barely making the tight squeeze. His eyes, predictably, saw the docked sailboat right away as soon as he was through.

Keo slipped the binoculars back into the pack and picked up the submachine gun. He pressed as much of his body against the deck as he could in order to lower his profile even further. The railing would hide him somewhat, but if the man came any closer...

He flicked the fire selector on the MP5SD from fully automatic to semi-auto. The sound suppressor would do a lot to hide the gunshot, but the other guy standing outside the Ridgeline would notice pretty quickly when Fatso fell down.

Humpty Dumpty sat on a wall...

He couldn't see up the dock anymore, so he had to rely on his ears. Heavy footsteps approached him at a slow pace. Keo didn't think the man could hurry if he wanted to because of the girth he was carrying.

How do you stay fat at the end of the world? Now, that's a nice trick.

"—see the boat, but I don't see anyone," the man was saying.

"Well, someone's gotta have sailed that thing here," a voice said through a radio. "The kid said it wasn't here a month ago when he last came by."

"Maybe he got it wrong."

"Kid swears by it."

"Okay, okay, I'll check it out."

"Careful you don't slip and fall into the water," the other man said, chuckling. "I'm not jumping in there after your fat ass."

"Har har," the fat man said. "You're a funny guy."

Keo had been counting the man's loud footsteps, and when he got the right number, he rose up on the deck of the boat with the MP5SD in his hands.

The man was halfway up the dock when he froze at the sight of Keo.

A painful second, then two, ticked by.

The man groped for the radio and tried to lift it to his lips when Keo shot him once in the chest. He watched the man stagger for a moment, a shocked expression spreading across his generous face. Keo shot him again between the eyes, and the big man dropped to the wooden boards, his bulk making a loud *thump!*

Keo quickly threw himself over the boat's fender and onto the dock. He raced back toward the parking lot with the MP5SD in front of him.

The man with the SCAR was running up the parking lot when he spotted Keo and slid to a stop.

Keo squeezed the trigger twice, putting both rounds into the man's chest. The "soldier" stumbled but didn't go down. Instead, the man actually put a hand back against one of the white trucks to steady himself.

Bulletproof vest? Cheater!

Keo put the third bullet in the man's face, the silver 9mm round obliterating the nose in a shower of blood and bone. This time, the man dropped.

He reached the end of the marina and pushed on, passing the second dead man, whose radio squawked, a voice shouting through, "Milton? What's going on out there? Milton?"

He slipped around one of the trucks instead of going between them. He flicked the fire selector to fully automatic as soon as he reached the parking lot and came up on the Ridgeline just as both front doors opened and two more uniformed men clambered outside. The passenger was trying desperately to unsling an M4 carbine, while the driver had managed to get a silver Colt 1911 automatic out of its holster and was aiming it over the hood of the truck.

Keo shot the passenger first because he was the closer target, stitching the moving man with a quick burst and catching him in the chest with three rounds. His fourth, fifth, and sixth bullets shattered the Ridgeline's window and Keo glimpsed faces inside the truck, in the back, and heard screams.

Female screams.

The driver fired over the hood of the truck. Too fast and his hands were shaking, throwing his aim off. Barely. Keo still heard the *zip!* as the bullet nearly took his head off anyway.

He went into a crouch and lost sight of the driver on the other side of the truck momentarily. Not that that seemed to stop the man from shooting. He fired off two more shots, then a fourth one, the *clink-clink* of his bullet casings landing on the ground.

Keo stayed low and crab-walked sideways when the driver appeared from around the hood. Keo shot his legs out from under him, and the driver screamed as he slammed into the parking lot.

He got up and rushed over, kicking the fancy Colt under the Ridgeline. He ignored the driver's screams and circled the truck before leaning into the open driver-side door and looking into the backseat.

Two faces, both draped with long hair, peered back out at him.

One of the women, a brunette, held out her hands—showing scarred palms—as if to let him know she wasn't armed. The other one had dirty-blonde hair and seemed to be trying to disappear into the floor of the truck.

"Outside," Keo said.

He stepped back and waited for the women to come out. They did, reluctantly, shaking with every step. They clung to one another, staring at Keo, then at the driver rolling around on the ground next to them. The driver's eyes, like the women's, were glued to the bloody stumps that used to be his legs.

Keo made a quick tour of both vehicles, searching for hidden passengers that didn't exist. He gave the area a once-over and listened for sounds other than the driver screaming behind him. His own gunfire had been suppressed, but the driver's Colt might as well have been artillery fire against the stillness of the city.

He walked back to the women. Both wore cargo pants and cotton undershirts underneath long-sleeve work shirts covered in sweat. They looked dirty, but then again, he was probably not much of a prize himself at the moment, especially after running for his life and spending all night inside a smelly attic.

"We should go," the brunette said.

"Go where?" Keo said.

"Anywhere, as long as it's not here."

"Why?"

"There are others out there. Nearby."

"How near—"

He hadn't gotten the question out when he heard them.

Car engines.

And they were coming in his direction...*fast.*

◄━━▮ ▮━━►

"ARE THEY AFTER you or me?" Keo asked.

"These new guys? I don't know. The ones from earlier were taking us back," the brunette, Carrie, said. "But it's not like we're important or anything; we just had the bad luck of being at the wrong place at the wrong time. What about you? They went to that marina looking for someone. Are you important or something?"

"No. I'm just some guy trying to get to Texas."

"What's in Texas?"

Gillian.

"Be quiet for a moment," he said.

They were inside an abandoned lakeside bar called Bago's, about half a kilometer from the sailboat that Keo needed. From here, using a pair of binoculars, he had a direct line of sight to the marina across Lake Dulcet. Carrion birds were gathering in the air above the parking lot waiting to feast, except they couldn't because there were men below them. Living men, moving around in familiar camo uniforms.

One of the men that had arrived five minutes ago started shooting into the air, scattering the birds. At least for a little while. Soon, the creatures had circled back around to where the bodies were. It didn't look as if they were going anywhere anytime soon.

There were two new vehicles in the marina parking lot, and they had dumped six more men with assault rifles. Keo watched them from the safety of Bago's for nearly twenty minutes as they searched through the bodies, the vehicles, and then the lone sailboat at the end of the dock. When they were satisfied he wasn't there, two of them opened fire on the boat with their carbines, the *pop-pop-pop* filling the air for ten full seconds. When they were finally empty, they reloaded…and poured more rounds into the vessel.

Shit. There goes my ride to Texas.

They didn't stay behind to watch the boat sink. Instead, they headed back to the parking lot, where one of them drew his sidearm and shot out all four tires on the already bullet-riddled Ridgeline while his friends picked up the bodies and loaded them into the trucks. Two of them climbed into the GMC and the three vehicles drove off.

Except they didn't all go in the same direction. Instead, they headed off in separate paths, spreading out into the city. That was a search formation if he ever saw one. The closest truck came within 200 meters of Bago's before turning and disappearing eastward. The only bright spot was that not a single one of them headed south, which was the direction he needed to go.

Yeah. Bright side. Get it where you can, pal.

"They're gone," Keo said, lowering his binoculars and putting it away.

"Thank God," Carrie said behind him.

She and the blonde teenager, Lorelei, sat at a booth eating canned food from the supplies they had salvaged from the two trucks before running off. There were boxes of ammo and more weapons in the back of the vehicles, but Keo kept things efficient—as much supply as they could carry and still run. Everything else was superfluous, including two women he didn't know until very recently.

He had thought about leaving them behind but couldn't bring himself to do it. Maybe it was losing Zachary and Shorty last night, or maybe it was the thought of what Gillian would say if she found out he had abandoned two desperate girls just to get to her.

Gillian.

Was she even still alive out there? Did she even make it to Santa Marie Island months ago?

He didn't know, but that only meant he had to go there and find out. Whatever happened, he had to find out for sure…

Of course, doing that would have been much easier with the supplies he had left behind on the sailboat. The silver rounds they had made, the bullet-making materials, and those stacks of silverware they had collected but never got around to melting down. Losing the boat hurt in more ways than one.

In the boat's place, he had two women he didn't know from Adam and a world of trouble. Those uniformed men definitely hadn't come looking for him. They had gone there looking for a boat, but not *him* specifically. Besides, the only person who knew he existed at all and wanted him dead was, himself, dead.

Burn in hell, Pollard. You and your son.

"I don't understand why we didn't just sail away on your boat," Carrie said. "I almost had a stroke running here, and we barely made it before those guys showed up."

"Not enough time," Keo said.

"How long would it have taken to get a boat ready to sail?"

"More than what we had."

"Oh."

He sat down on a stool and finished off the can of peaches he had left open on the bar counter. He ate while trying to ignore Carrie as she watched him intently. She was an attractive girl, mid-twenties, with high cheekbones and a long, slender figure. The other girl, Lorelei, looked all of sixteen and hid behind her long hair. She barely talked, and for a while Keo thought she might have been a mute, but no, she just had very little to say, at least to him. She did whisper into Carrie's ear every now and then. They acted like sisters, but there was no obvious resemblance.

"Those guys back there," Keo said, "the ones that went looking for my boat. You said they were taking you somewhere?"

"They were taking us back to the town."

"What town?"

"L11."

"Never heard of it."

"It's what they call it," she said and shrugged.

"L11," Keo repeated. "Sounds like something the military would come up with."

"You were in the military?"

"God, no." Then, "Those guys back there. They weren't soldiers, either."

"No. They just started dressing in those uniforms recently. Before then, they ran around in hazmat suits and gas masks."

Hazmat suits and gas masks? Now that rings a bell…

"You say there are more of them around?" Keo said. "Besides the ones we've seen already?"

"A lot more." She looked anxiously toward the window. "How long are we going to stay here?"

"Until I'm sure no one else is going to pop up. Then we'll leave." He glanced at his watch. "Still six more hours until nightfall. Relax."

"Relax. Right."

"Do your best."

Carrie went back to scooping syrup-drenched pieces of fruit into her mouth with one of the cheap plastic sporks they had found in the back of the Ridgeline. Lorelei, meanwhile, ate ravenously from a can of SPAM.

"Tell me about this town," Keo said to Carrie.

"What about it?"

"Why did you run away?"

"You really don't know? About the towns?"

"'Towns'? So there is more than one?"

"That's why it's called L11," she said, watching him carefully, maybe trying to gauge if he was messing with her. When she was certain he wasn't, she continued. "There are dozens of them in Louisiana alone. That's what I heard, anyway. The one we escaped from was called L11."

"L11," Keo repeated again. "So there are ten more before it. And more after it?"

"Yes, I think so. I don't know for sure, but I've heard the stories."

"And there are people in these towns? How is that possible? What happens at night? How do they keep the bloodsuckers out?"

"You don't know?" she said again. "Where have you been all this time?"

"In the woods. I guess I'm a little behind the times."

"Have you ever been to the camps?"

"These are different from the towns?"

She nodded and told him, and Keo listened intently.

Carrie explained the camps filled with survivors. The towns like L11, where the creatures stayed out. And humans donating blood every day. "The agreement," as Carrie put it. Then there were the pregnant women. He found that the hardest to swallow, but when he stared at the women and saw the very real fear on Lorelei's face underneath her hair, he believed it. Every single word of it.

"Goddamn," he said when she was finished. "So they're working for those things? The enemy?"

"Yes," Carrie said. "They watch over us in the daytime."

"But that's not all they do."

"No. They do a lot of other…things."

Keo nodded. Suddenly the presence of those men in hazmat suits and gas masks trying to kill him in Robertson Park made sense. Or as much "sense" as selling out your own species to bloodsucking creatures made any sense, anyway.

"You're taking this well," Carrie said, watching him closely.

He shrugged. "I've seen some crazy things in my life."

"Crazier than this?"

"Not this, but I've seen people do some crazy things to survive."

He spent a few minutes rolling all the information he had just absorbed over in his head in silence. A year ago he wouldn't have believed a single thing Carrie had just said, but what was possible and impossible had been upended for good in the last eleven months. These days it seemed anything was not only possible, but likely.

After a while, he glanced back at her. "You said they wanted to impregnate you."

"Yeah. That's why we ran."

"Were the guys too ugly?"

Carrie rolled her eyes. "It's not the sex. It's what happens after-ward. With the babies." She looked almost imploringly at him. "You understand, right? Why we couldn't stay? Why we ran?"

He nodded and thought about Gillian. "I understand."

She nodded back gratefully then returned to eating her canned fruits with the flimsy utensil.

"One of the men I shot mentioned a kid over the radio," Keo said. "Was that why they were there?"

"I heard them talking on the radio," Carrie nodded. "One of the kids spotted your boat at the marina. That's why they were checking it out."

"'Kids'?"

"They have eyes everywhere. Kids. Eleven, twelve-year-olds. They're all over the cities on bicycles. Some on skateboards."

"Skateboards?"

"Whatever they're used to and can get them from place to place the easiest, I guess."

"What do these kids do, exactly?"

"They're spies. Lookouts. Their job is to go around the city looking for survivors. The guys in uniform come later. That's how they found us. One of those stupid kids spotted us and the trucks swooped in."

"Kids on skateboards, towns, camps, and pregnant women car-rying babies to feed the ghouls," Keo said, shaking his head. "Next thing you know, you're going to tell me Santa Claus and the Tooth Fairy are real, too."

"'Ghouls'?" Carrie said.

"That's what she calls them."

"Who?"

"The woman on the radio."

Carrie stared at him like he had a third eye. Then Lorelei joined in.

Keo sighed. "My turn, I guess."

He told them about the woman on the radio. The repeating message. Bodies of water. Sunlight. Ultraviolet. And silver.

"Is she right?" Carrie said. "About everything? I know about sunlight, but the others…"

Keo nodded. "She's right about pretty much everything. The only thing I can't be sure of is the ultraviolet light. Hard to test that one out without the right equipment, and I have no idea where to get those."

"But silver…"

"It works. I was testing it out last night." *And got Shorty and Zachary killed doing it,* he thought, but left that part out. Instead, he said, "The boats at the marina. Do you know what happened to them? That sailboat was the first and only vessel I saw since I arrived in the city."

Carrie shook her head. "I don't know. I spent most of my time in the camp before they relocated us to L11. It's weird, though. Those marinas are usually filled with boats."

"You used to live around here?"

"The east side," she nodded. "That's where we were headed when they grabbed us."

"What's over there?"

"My old house."

"That's it?"

She looked embarrassed. "I couldn't really think of anywhere else to go. I don't even know what I expected to find there. Everyone I know is gone. I just didn't…know where else to go."

Lorelei reached over and clutched Carrie's arm tightly. The two girls exchanged a brief private smile, an attempt to give each other strength that he wasn't entirely sure was successful.

Keo watched them closely for a moment. The teenager, hiding behind her hair as if it were an invisible force field, doing her best not to draw attention. The older Carrie, who would have been pretty if not for the dirt and grime. They looked beaten and tired and in so many ways were the exact opposite of Gillian.

Or, at least, the last time he saw Gillian.

Was she even still alive out there?

He had to know. And that meant finding a boat. Maybe somewhere down south.

He had to go down there anyway…

"Have you ever heard of Song Island?" he asked Carrie.

"Yes," Carrie said, looking back at him. "It's on Beaufont Lake. I used to go fishing with my dad down there when I was a kid. Those were some of the best times of my life. Why?"

"I was told there might be people there. The plan was always to find out one way or another if they're still there before I headed off to Santa Marie Island."

"An island," Carrie said. "It would make sense, wouldn't it? Because the creatures—the ghouls—wouldn't be able to cross the lake. Do you think that's why all the boats are missing? Maybe the soldiers are going around destroying them so no one can use them to get to these islands?"

"That's one theory."

"You said going to Song Island was the original plan. Is it still the plan?" Carrie asked anxiously.

He nodded, thinking about Zachary, who had come with him specifically to find out what had happened to his friends who had gone to Song Island, following the siren call of a radio message promising shelter and security many, many months ago.

"I owe it to a friend to make a pit stop there first," Keo said.

CHAPTER 7

GABY

HORSES. THEY SENT the guys on horses after her.

Like a posse in a Western. Now I've seen everything.

But instead of six-shooters and Winchesters, this posse was carrying assault rifles and semi-automatic pistols. They were wearing identical uniforms, combat boots, and two of them had caps to keep the sun out of their eyes. There were four and they were spread out in pairs of two, which told her they weren't complete dummies.

She kept that in mind as they moved slowly through the woods, sometimes ducking to get under low-hanging branches. The only positive she could find was that they didn't appear to be expert trackers and seemed to be searching randomly, perhaps hoping to just stumble across her. So there was that. It had been hard enough keeping Peter and Milly on course, but it had been downright impossible to get them to stop stepping on every twig in their path.

This is what it's like to run around with civilians. How did Will and Danny ever do it?

She gripped the AK-47 tighter. Mac had done her a favor and kept two magazines in his pouches, with two more for the M1911. Unfortunately all the bullets were regular ammo, which meant she had to get out of the woods by nightfall. If she was caught in here without silver to defend herself with...

Gaby looked down at Mac's watch: 9:13 A.M.

Plenty of time.

That was the other good news. Night wasn't her friend anymore, but she had plenty of time to find shelter. Of course, that might be harder to do than she had expected, given the lack of civilization inside the woods—

"What now?" Peter whispered behind her. He was so close she could feel his breath against the back of her neck.

"I don't know," she whispered back. "Maybe we can wait them out."

Milly moved nervously behind them. They had been crouched in the same spot for the last thirty minutes, waiting to see how the guards would proceed. She had expected a stronger chase and was surprise they had only sent four. Then again, she had to remember they didn't have that many in town to begin with.

You don't need a lot of guards when no one wants to leave.

Well, almost no one.

She looked back at Peter and Milly. She had a lot of questions for them: Why leave and why now? The questions had been nagging at her ever since they entered the woods. No one else in town had seemed interested in abandoning the safety of L15. The woman Anna, who had sold them out the first chance she got, was proof of that.

"What?" Peter said when he caught her staring.

Gaby didn't say anything. She turned away and took in their environment for the tenth time in as many minutes. They were surrounded by trees and bushes, with the sound of Hillman Lake behind them. Forty yards from the shore, give or take. Close enough to make the heat just slightly bearable.

The closest two men on horseback were moving away from them before turning right. Gaby listened to the fading *clop-clop-clop* of the horseshoes against soft earth. Every now and then there was the squawk of radios as the men communicated back and forth in muffled voices.

Gaby glanced back at Peter again. "How big is the lake? Can we go around it?"

He shook his head. "It's big. Half a kilometer. It would take too long to circle it."

"How deep?"

"You mean you want to cross it?"

"Where else are we going to go? If we can't go around it and we can't head back toward town, there's only one direction left—across the lake."

"It's pretty deep," Peter said. "There are shallow ends—"

Crack! A bullet slammed into a tree trunk two feet from Peter's head, cutting him off. He flinched with his entire body, instinctively dodging flying bark as the gunshot echoed loudly around them.

"Go!" Gaby shouted.

Milly and Peter launched to their feet and raced off behind her. She stood up slightly, gripping the AK-47, and searched out the source of the gunfire the best she could, though it was like looking for a needle—

There! A man sitting on a horse sixty yards away.

He was taking aim at Milly's and Peter's fleeing forms when her movement drew his attention. She was still swinging the AK-47 around when he snapped off a shot with his M4, but his horse was moving under him and his bullet sailed harmlessly over her, chopping a branch free above her head.

Gaby took careful aim and fired—and *missed!*

Dammit! she thought, and was about to fire again when the horse, responding to her near-hit, reared up on its hind legs and tossed the rider as if he were nothing more than a nuisance. Long, luxurious brown mane flashed in the air as the animal turned around and galloped off, leaving its rider on the ground.

The man had lost his rifle as he went down, and he was scrambling to find it when Gaby shot him in the back, right over the ass. Or did she actually hit him in one of his cheeks? The man screamed, whether in surprise or pain, she wasn't sure. He gave up on locating his weapon and began crawling to safety, his bleeding backside in the air, facing her.

Now that's a sight.

She lifted her rifle to shoot when the man somehow half-crawled, half-lunged behind a big tree.

Gaby took a step forward to finish the wounded man off when another horse pushed its way through a thick bush in front of her, with another uniformed figure swaying in the saddle. They were still far away—almost eighty yards—and hadn't seen her yet. Gaby decided not to risk a shot at this distance and instead turned and fled in the same direction that Peter and Milly had gone.

Or, at least, the same general vicinity. Her only hope was that Peter was smart enough to grab the girl before she could get too far ahead of him and lead her somewhere safe.

The first thing she had noticed when she fled into the woods earlier was that it was a massive place. It reminded her of Sandwhite Wildlife State Park, but minus the trails, which made it wilder and more unpredictable. If she thought every inch of Sandwhite looked exactly the same, she couldn't imagine getting lost in here. Thankfully, there was Hillman Lake to her right, so if nothing else, she always knew which direction would lead her away from the town and the pursuit.

She had been running for two straight minutes at a full sprint before she finally heard the noise she had been waiting for. The *clop-clop-clop* of horseshoes, bearing down on her fast.

She looked over her shoulder. Nothing. But not being able to see the incoming rider wasn't the same as him not being there. She could almost feel him gaining on her, and she could definitely still hear him getting closer.

Clop-clop-clop!

Clop-clop-clop!

Gaby pulled up to a stop and slid behind a tree. She hugged the gnarled trunk and waited, using the momentary respite to suck in air and did her best to control her breathing, but it was like trying to hold back a freight train.

She was still gasping for breath, trying to temper the adrenaline coursing through her like wildfire, when a man on a horse galloped past her. Like the others, this one was wearing a camo uniform and he was holding onto the reins for dear life with one hand while clutching an M4 rifle at his side. He didn't look entirely comfortable in the half-second or so that it took him to ride past her.

Gaby didn't let him get too far ahead. She pushed away from the tree, took aim, and shot the man in the back. He must have pulled on the reins reflexively because the horse let out a furious whine as it slid to a stop, horseshoes digging trenches into the ground.

As the animal settled and the man on top of it hung on, Gaby took two quick steps forward and took aim again, but before she could squeeze off another shot, the man collapsed from the saddle. He crumpled onto the ground on his belly, legs twisted awkwardly under him, and lay still.

The horse didn't stick around. It turned and ran back—*right at her!*

Gaby stepped into the animal's path and threw her hands into the air, waving them wildly to gets its attention. She got it, all right, not that the large brown charging thing with magnificent flowing mane had any intentions of stopping for her.

"Whoa!" Gaby shouted. "Whoa, horse!"

She didn't have time to process how stupid she must have looked (or sounded) before the horse came within a foot of running her over like she was an annoying gnat. She lunged out of its path, going sideways at the last second, losing the AK-47 at the same time she crashed into some underbrush headfirst.

By the time she picked herself back up, the horse was running freely through the woods until there was nothing left of it but the gradually fading *clop-clop-clop* echoing back and forth among the trees.

She sighed and struggled to her feet. "Stupid horse."

Right. The horse is the stupid animal and not you, who just tried to flag it down like it was a taxi. Keep telling yourself that, girl.

She snatched up the assault rifle and jogged over to the dead rider. Gaby robbed him of the M4 and pocketed his spare ammos and a small first-aid kit. She pulled out his holstered sidearm—a 9mm Glock—and stuffed it into her waistband.

Voices, coming from behind her. "Greg! Where the hell are you?"

She didn't hear galloping, so the man had to be on foot. Gaby didn't stick around to find out for sure. She slung the newly acquired carbine and hurried off, feeling much better with her pouches stuffed with spare magazines and an extra handgun in her waist. The extra weight made her move slower, but she didn't want to risk throwing anything away.

"A soldier who complains about having to carry too much firepower is a dead one," Will liked to say.

◄▬▬▬ ▬▬▬►

WILL AND DANNY had taught her a lot of things on the island, but tracking people wasn't one of them. She had no idea where Milly and Peter had gone, and although there were clues—a broken branch here, a snapped twig there—each time she thought she had picked up their trail, it suddenly changed again.

She entertained but quickly dismissed the idea that Peter was purposefully mixing up his footprints in order to throw her off. He didn't strike her as someone who had a lot of experience in the woods. She didn't either, but compared to him she might as well be one of those frontier woodsmen she had learned about in school. Peter was one of the town's cooks, for God's sake. A guy like that probably didn't spend a whole lot of time learning tracking—or in this case, hiding his tracks—from pursuers.

Of course, she could be wrong. What did she really know about them, anyway? What did she know about the girl? Besides the fact they were both clearly desperate to leave L15. They were the only two, from the looks of it. Was that suspicious? Maybe. Right now, though, she owed them for saving her life. Maybe she would have gotten out anyway on her own, but they had made it easier.

Even so, after about fifteen minutes of fruitless searching, the idea of heading off by herself was becoming more and more feasible.

What did she really owe them, anyway? Yes, they had helped her escape, but if they had run off on their own, they were beyond her help. The smart thing would be to keep going, cross Hillman Lake, and somehow reorient herself and head back south, back toward Beaufont Lake…

…*and Song Island.*

How long had it been? It felt like years since she had seen the white beaches and eaten the fresh fish and stood watch in the Tower's third floor—

Snap!

She spun around, lifting the AK-47 to fire—

"It's just me!" Peter shouted.

She sighed and lowered the rifle. He had come close to dying. Too close.

"Where's Milly?" she asked, keeping her voice low.

"Follow me," he said, lowering his voice to match her pitch. He started off and Gaby followed.

"Where's Milly?" she asked again.

"We found a place to stay not far from here."

"Is it safe?"

"I think so."

"You think so?"

"It looked pretty safe."

They walked in silence for a while, and Peter seemed to know where he was going.

"You're pretty good with that rifle," he said finally.

She remembered missing the horseman with her first shot. "I'm not that good with the AK. I was trained on an M4."

"Which one is that?"

"The black one."

"Oh."

"Where did you put Milly, Peter?"

"It's a cave, but it's pretty well hidden. I left her to come look for you."

Gaby grabbed his arm and spun him around. "You left her inside a *cave?*"

He didn't answer right away, and she could tell he didn't understand the accusatory tone in her voice. "Why? Isn't a cave safe?"

"Caves are *dark*, Peter."

The realization spread across his face. "Oh God," he said, and jerked his hand away before running off at full speed.

She fell in behind him, keeping one eye in front of her and the other scanning the woods. Her ears were up, listening for the familiar *clop-clop-clop* of horse hooves on soft earth. She didn't believe for a minute the remaining two guards on horseback hadn't converged toward all the gunfire. The fact that they weren't here yet worried her. Then again, maybe like Peter, they were more terrible at this whole woods thing than she initially attributed to them.

"Are we close?" she asked Peter.

"Almost there," he said, already sucking in air with every step.

She didn't know why he was breathing so hard. She was the one carrying two rifles, two handguns, and nearly half a dozen magazines. Even with all that weight, she was still matching him stride for stride. A part of her wanted to ask him what he did before all of this, but the other part—the survivor in her—didn't want to know. If he and Milly died today or tomorrow, it was better if she didn't know too much about them. It was a cold thought, but Gaby had gotten progressively good at detaching herself from her emotions these days.

Except with Nate.

What happened to you, Nate? Are you dead...or worse?

Peter finally slowed down as they came up on the mouth of a

cave, partially hidden among the trees and bushes. It was impossible not to notice the suffocating darkness staring back out at her.

"Milly," Peter whispered. He had stopped near the entrance. When there was no answer, he whispered louder, "Milly."

Gaby moved past him with the AK-47 in front of her, wishing badly for the magazine to be full of silver bullets. She flicked the fire selector to full-auto. Regular bullets didn't do a damn thing against the ghouls, but maybe enough of them at once…

"She's not answering," Peter said.

No shit, Peter.

Gaby took a deep breath and stepped into the pitch-black. Peter moved behind her, his footsteps tentative, his breathing too loud despite the fact he had stopped running more than a minute ago.

She stepped cautiously, allowing her eyes to adjust to the nothingness. The sunlight only penetrated the cave for a few precious yards, and it wasn't nearly enough to see with. She only managed four, then five steps before she was swallowed up by the pitch-black nothingness.

What are you doing? You don't know these people. You don't owe them this. You don't owe them dying.

Go back. Go back now!

She kept moving forward instead.

"Milly," Peter whispered behind her. "Where are you?" Then, much louder than he should, "Milly!"

Even as Milly's name echoed off the walls, the creature lunged out of the darkness at her, reaching with one hand, black eyes glistening *(That shouldn't be possible)* and a mouth full of devastating brown and yellow teeth lit up in a staccato effect as she pulled the trigger and the AK-47 leaped in her hands.

The creature jerked as bullets riddled its chest at almost point-blank range, and she heard a *ping!* as a round bounced off bone. That, more than anything, stunned and sent the ghoul tumbling to the damp cave floor. Not that it stayed down there for very long. It was back on its feet and moving toward her again a heartbeat later.

"Go!" she shouted. "Get out of here, Peter!"

Peter might have turned and ran, or maybe he just backpedaled. She didn't look back to make sure because she was too busy firing again. Split-second lightning flashed with every round she discharged, allowing her to see—

Them.

Because there was a nest. They had *stepped right into a nest.*

She fired from side to side, backing up, always moving, never standing still. The assault rifle got lighter in her hands as the magazine emptied. She held on and kept shooting and moving until she finally felt the warmth of the sun *(mercifully)* against the back of her neck.

Click!

She didn't stop moving, didn't think about the empty magazine, and instead swung with the empty rifle. She caught a creature in the cheek—its face broke in front of her, cheekbone *crunching*—and the blow tossed the ghoul into two others in the process of lunging at her.

Gaby swung again—this time to the right—and the barrel pierced the chest of a ghoul and impaled it all the way up to the hand guard. The creature staggered back, stunned by the blow, but somehow still managed to rip the assault rifle out of her hands as it fell away to the side.

She stumbled her way out of the cave and lost her balance, landing on her ass.

The sun! She was outside!

One of the creatures followed her out, mouth opening, jagged teeth snapping in an attempt to clamp down on her exposed arm—

The creature squealed as sunlight descended on it. The ghoul's flesh turned ashen and it vaporized before her eyes, and a second later bleached white bones that looked deformed for some reason tumbled out of the air and landed on the ground in a pile. The acidic smell enveloped the surroundings, and Gaby forced herself to start breathing through her mouth to keep from choking.

Hands grabbed her from behind and pulled her back, back, then finally up.

She unslung the M4 and pointed it at the silhouetted forms squirming inside the darkened mouth of the cave, just beyond the reach of sunlight. They had stopped their pursuit, the sun holding them at bay. She could sense their desperation, their rabid desire to get at her. It drove them crazy and they squirmed restlessly, and for a moment, just a moment, she thought one or two—or possibly all of them—might try to get her anyway.

But they didn't.

"Dead, not stupid," Will always said.

How many were in there right now, looking back at her and Peter? A dozen? A hundred? Was Milly one of them? The girl with the round face. Thirteen. Or twelve. She didn't know for sure. She should have asked, but Gaby hadn't wanted to know, didn't want to get too involved, to become committed to people who could die on her at any moment.

Because everyone died these days. Everyone...

Like Nate.

"Peter?" a soft female voice said behind them.

They spun around and saw Milly, wide-eyed and standing there, looking back at them.

Peter ran to her and scooped her up in a bear hug. She wasn't prepared for it and barely had time to register what Peter was doing before she was in his arms. Confusion gave way to happiness, and Gaby watched them embrace each other for a long five seconds.

Peter finally put her down. "You left the cave..."

"I heard noises," Milly said. "It was too spooky, so I left to wait for you out here. Then I heard all the shooting. What happened? What's in there?" She looked past them and toward the mouth of the cave and saw the bones, twisted and white against the daylight. "Oh."

"Come on, we have to go," Gaby said. "Everyone heard those gunshots."

She hurried off, and Peter and Milly followed.

"Where to now?" Peter asked.

"I don't know," Gaby said. "You have any ideas? You live here."

"But we've never actually been this far out of town."

"Never mind, then. We'll figure it out as we go."

She glanced down at her watch: 9:41 A.M.

Still plenty of time...

CHAPTER 8

LARA

"KINKASAN ISLAND," TAKESHI said. His English was good and came through crystal clear over the radio. "There are a few thousand of us here. Most are from Ishinomaki, but I've met some from Sendai and as far as Osaki."

"How did you know to get to an island?" Lara asked.

"We didn't," Takeshi said. "Not consciously. I think most of us just thought we needed to get as far away from the cities as possible. The ferries were running for hours…until they just stopped. That was the last I've seen of anyone from the mainland."

Lara looked over at Bonnie leaning next to the window with the binoculars. The former model had been listening to her conversation with Takeshi for the last few minutes, both of them riveted by his story. All these months of trying to survive on the road and to finally get confirmation that there were others out there like them who had managed to continue on, despite the odds, was exhilarating.

Takeshi, like the last few strangers who had contacted them over the radio, had responded only because of her broadcast. In so many ways, something she hadn't even wanted to do but did anyway at Danny and Roy's urging was becoming the most important thing she had ever done since The Purge. She couldn't help but feel a little pride in that.

"How did you know about FEMA, Takeshi?" she said into the microphone.

"American history," Takeshi said. "I've always been fascinated with your country. I told my girlfriend that once I graduated university, we would get married and move to Silicon Valley and start a new life. I'd work at one of your tech companies and she would teach Japanese in school."

"Is your girlfriend...?"

"Mako's here. We fled together. It was actually her idea to come to the island, where her family still lives."

Another pair of lovers lives on!

She smiled at the silly thought and was glad Bonnie couldn't see.

"Have you made contact with anyone else before you heard our recording?" she asked.

"Yes, there were a couple of Frenchmen, a few Englishmen, and I think some Chinese," Takeshi said. "It's been a while since I heard back from the Chinese, though. I didn't know about the islands, how the creatures—ghouls, as you call them—couldn't cross water. Which leads me to this thought, Lara; there are other islands nearby. Aji and Tashiro, to name just two. I should bring this up with the elders, tell them what I've learned. There must be survivors there, too. If not from the mainland, then those who never left."

"I hope so, Takeshi. It's worth finding out. Just...be careful."

"Yes. Always. We're always careful these days."

More survivors in and around Japan. How many were out there? More than she had imagined, as it turned out. The last year had seemed so dark and hopeless, and there were so many days (and weeks and months) that she thought they might have been the only living souls still moving, looking for safety from the darkness.

"How are you for food and water?" she asked.

"Kinkasan has everything we need," Takeshi said. "Food, water, even wildlife. We can survive here for centuries. We were lucky. Very lucky. A lot of people weren't."

She thought about all those months on the road, the loss of Harold Campbell's facility in Starch, Texas, and fighting for the island. Luck had a lot to do with it, but sweating blood and tears did, too.

"What else have you heard, Lara?" Takeshi asked. "I've been listening to your conversations with the American government."

He means Beecher. The Colonel from Bayonet Mountain.

"Not much," she said. "Everything I know was in the message and what I told Beecher."

It wasn't the whole truth, but as with Beecher, she didn't think Takeshi or anyone else listening to them at the moment needed to know everything. While talking to Beecher, she had to constantly remind herself that anyone could tune in.

Anyone, even the enemy...

Dead, not stupid, right, Will?

"I told the others about these blood farms and the camps you discovered," Takeshi said. "Why would anyone surrender their future like that? I don't understand it."

He must be young, she thought.

Before she could reply, a voice she hadn't heard before joined them. "Sorry to cut in without an invitation, folks, but glad to hear Japan's still in play." The voice belonged to an older man with an accent she couldn't place. "My name's Miller. Radioing in from San Francisco. I wanted to let everyone know we're still fighting the good fight over at the Bay, too."

"Good to hear your voice, Miller," Lara said. "Where in San Francisco are you?" Then she quickly added, "If you can reveal your location."

"It's no secret," Miller said. "They already know we're here, anyway. You won't be surprised to hear this, given your bodies of water theory—well, not theory anymore, I guess—but we've been getting by on Alcatraz."

"The prison?"

"It's more of a tourist attraction these days. A lot of us managed to grab a ferry when everything went to shit. Pardon my language. You're right; the bloodsucking bastards don't seem capable of crossing the water. Their human lackeys, on the other hand, don't have that aversion. They've dinged us up over the months."

"Collaborators. That's what we call them."

"As good a name as any. We've managed to fend off every assault so far, mostly because it's hard to approach the island without being seen and some of the survivors brought weapons with them."

"How many are on the island with you?"

"A few hundred. Mostly civilians. A pair of ex-law enforcement, like myself." He paused, then, "So, what's next, Lara?"

"What do you mean?"

"You started this. What do we do now? How do we take the planet back from these bloodsucking bastards?"

She pressed the microphone to answer, but when she opened her mouth, nothing came out. Instead, she let go of the lever and stared at the radio in silence.

"Lara?" Bonnie said behind her. "Something wrong?"

She shook her head. "No."

It was a lie. There was something very wrong here.

She didn't have any answers for Miller, and the fact that he and all the other strangers listening to them at the moment thought that she did didn't just perplex her, it *terrified* her.

"AM I GOING to live, Doc?" Zoe asked.

"I don't know; you tell me. I'm just a third-year medical student and you're the doctor, Doctor."

Zoe smiled back at her. The woman had very deep green eyes. "I've never been shot before. It's…a revelation. Have you ever been shot?"

"Once."

"Did it hurt?"

"Like a sonofabitch."

"Good. I thought it was just me."

Lara helped Zoe sit up on the small bed, then stacked two fluffy pillows between her and the wall. She looked better than yesterday when she first arrived with a hole in her side. Color had returned to her cheeks and her lips didn't look as deathly pale anymore.

Zoe let out a slightly pained sigh and looked around the room. It was an office that Lara had converted into an infirmary and stocked with beds taken out of a couple of unused rooms in the hotel. The shelves and cabinets were recently restocked with medical supplies that Roy had brought back with him along with Zoe.

"You came here just to check up on me?" Zoe asked.

I needed to get away from the radio, from all the questions, from people who wanted answers that I didn't have.

She didn't say any of that, of course. Instead, Lara said, "It's part of the job description. I don't have to tell you this, but don't do anything to aggravate the wound until it heals completely."

"What about a hot shower? Will promised me a hot shower."

Then, quickly, "I don't mean with him. I mean, you know, by myself."

Lara smiled, feeling strangely pleased with the other woman's awkwardness. "I know. And there'll be plenty of those later. As soon as you can get up and walk around."

"You know what they say, Lara. The worst patient is a doctor." Zoe looked down at the hospital gown she was wearing. It was really just bed sheets that Liza, Stan's wife, had sewn for them. "Is this...?"

"Bed sheets."

"Looks better than the hospital gowns I'm used to."

"When you're better, you can pick out some clothes. There are more than enough to go around, and I'm sure there will be plenty in your size."

Lara didn't tell her where the clothes came from. She, Carly, and the other survivors had brought clothes to the island with them, but a lot of it was already piled high in the basement under the Tower. The shirts and shoes and pants, along with equipment and weapons and ammo, belonged to people who had come to Song Island seeking salvation but had found a nightmare instead. Lara didn't like reusing those clothes, but Will was right about keeping them so they could focus their supply runs on the essentials like silver, food, and ammo.

Especially the silver. You could never have enough of that these days.

"Where did you go to medical school?" Lara asked.

"LSU," Zoe said. "You?"

"University of Houston."

"What are you guys doing in Louisiana?"

"We heard a voice on a radio. It's a long story." She picked up a bottle of water and handed it to Zoe. "Bottom line, we're here now."

Zoe's eyes widened when she touched the bottle. "Oh my God, it's cold."

Lara smiled. No matter how many times she heard that response, it never failed to amuse her. "You'll get used to it."

"Oh my God," Zoe said again. She fumbled with the cap and took a sip, then sighed with pleasure before drinking some more.

"We have plenty more where that came from."

"What is this, tap water?"

"The hotel has a huge water purification and filtration system.

As long as we have power, we have drinkable water."

"I can get used to this." She took another gulp and spilled some on herself but didn't seem to notice. "I can definitely get used to this." Then she looked around the room again. "Where's Will?"

"He's still out there."

"He is?" She looked stunned. "I thought he was the one who brought me to the island. That wasn't…?"

"That was Roy."

"Roy?" She shook her head. "I don't know who that is, but I think I might have called him Will a couple of times on the way over here."

Lara chuckled. "He mentioned that."

"You said Will's still out there? That's surprising. Every chance he got, he talked about coming back here. To you."

Lara felt a flush of embarrassment. Or was that pride? "He's looking for Gaby."

"The teenager?"

"Yes. She's still missing. Will's not coming back until he finds her."

Zoe nodded and took another sip of water. "He treated her like his little sister. I can see him going back out there for her."

There was a brief moment of awkward silence, and Lara thought Zoe might be purposefully trying to avoid looking at her for some reason.

What happened out there with her and Will?

She said instead, "You saved Will's life. Thank you, Zoe."

Zoe finally looked over and might have actually blushed a bit. "We're even. I wouldn't be here without him."

"Still, he told me what you did for him out there. Thank you for bringing him back to me. I don't know what I'd do without him."

"He loves you," Zoe said, and gave her a smile that seemed a bit too forced. "I've seen a guy in love before, but that man of yours…" She shook her head and laughed softly. "I hope he comes back okay."

"He will," Lara said with absolute certainty. "As soon as he finds Gaby, he'll come home."

"I don't doubt it," Zoe said, and looked away again.

The radio clipped to Lara's hip squawked just in time to spare the two of them from another round of awkward silence.

They heard Maddie's voice. "Lara. I got Will on the emergency frequency."

"Speak of the devil," Lara said.

"Say hi to him for me," Zoe said.

She nodded and got up to leave. "I don't have to tell you, right?"

"Hey, I have a comfortable bed and cold drinks," Zoe said after her. "I'm not going anywhere. Ever."

◀▅▅▏ ▏▅▅▶

"GOOD NEWS AND bad news," Will said through the radio. "What do you want first?"

"Will, how many times have I ever chosen the bad news first?" Lara asked.

He chuckled. "We found where they're keeping Gaby."

"That's great." Then, with reluctance, "So what's the bad news?"

"She escaped before we could bust her out."

"And that's bad?"

"Well, we're tracking her through the woods at the moment. The problem is, the woods over here are big. Massive. Twice as thick as Danny's head and three times as messy."

"Hey," she heard Danny say in the background.

Lara smiled.

She was on the second floor of the Tower with one of the radios. It was slightly smaller and more portable than the two above her on the third floor right now. She sat on the windowsill and looked toward the south side of the island, at the girls on the beach with Roy standing watch on the boat shack.

"Can you find her?" she said into the radio.

"That's the plan," Will said. "It's just going to be a little bit more difficult than we expected, that's all."

"Will, you took Danny with you because you thought you might have to fight your way into a town full of collaborators. Now all you have to do is find Gaby in the woods, and this, somehow, is more difficult?"

"I see your point."

"Anything else I should know?"

"They're wearing uniforms now."

"Who?"

"The collaborators."

"What kind of uniforms?"

"Army camo. Close to real thing, but not quite. With their names and from what I can tell, their state designation."

"State designation?"

"Louisiana for this lot. A boot-shaped patch. Real craftsmanship, too. They probably have a whole room of sweatshop kids putting them together. Oh, and a white star."

"What does that represent?"

"I don't have a clue, babe. Maybe it means they're all destined for stardom."

She smiled. "That doesn't sound likely."

"No." He paused for a bit, then, "How's Zoe?"

"She says hi."

"Up and about already?"

"Up, but not about just yet. You did a good job stabilizing her after she was shot, Will. Waiting a day before moving her was also smart."

"It's been known to happen."

"Long story short, she'll be fine with time and a lot of rest. You're right; it'll be nice to have a proper doctor on the island for a change."

"Is that real enthusiasm or self-pity?" he asked. She could almost imagine him smiling on the other end of the radio.

"Don't be an ass," she said.

He laughed. "She'll be good for us, Lara."

"We can definitely use someone with her skills. Which I guess is good and bad. Having it, and needing it."

"Hope for the best, prepare for the worst." Then, without skipping a beat, "Tell me about this Beecher guy."

"He says he's an Army Colonel, so I guess he outranks you."

"Only if the United States government is still in operation."

"He says it is."

"Anyone can say anything these days. Danny thinks he's the President of the United States."

"Hey, I was fairly elected," Danny said in the background.

"See?" Will said. Then, "Where did this Beecher guy radio from?"

"Someplace called Bayonet Mountain," Lara said. "Have you ever heard it?"

"Yes," Will said, but she noticed that he didn't elaborate.

"You've been there before..."

"Once or twice. Did he say how many were there with him?"

"He says over 4,000 people, including civilians. Is that possible? Is that place big enough for that many people?"

"The Bayonet Mountain I knew could easily fit twice as many. Three times, if necessary."

"So you really have been there. What for?"

"It's a long story, and right now I need to go hunt down Gaby. When I get back, I'll talk to Beecher. Try to suss him out."

"You think he's lying about something?"

"I don't know, but we have a civilian authority for a reason."

"This is coming from a soldier..."

"Exactly," Will said.

They didn't say anything for a moment.

Finally, she said, "Will."

"Yes."

"I love you."

"I love you, too," he said.

"Barf," Danny said in the background. "Get a fucking room, you two."

She ignored Danny and said, "Hurry up and find Gaby and come back home. I like hearing your voice and I'm not quite as pissed off as I was the last time we talked, but I need more than this. You understand? I need to see you in person."

"I'll be home soon. Leave a light on for me."

"How about a big lighthouse?" she smiled.

"That'll work, too," Will said.

CHAPTER 9

WILL

THE ATVS WOULD have taken them back to L15 faster, but the roar
of engines would have exposed their approach. That meant they
were forced to trek back through the woods on foot. They jogged as
much as they could with their full gear but spent most of the time
walking at a brisk pace before reaching the same clearing from
yesterday just beyond the edge of town. They took out binoculars
and peered through them.

The place looked calm, and he wouldn't have known a gunfight
had taken place less than an hour ago if he hadn't heard it for
himself.

"Everything looks pretty hunky dory in there," Danny said next
to him. "What gives?"

"Two possibilities," Will said. "Either the fight's over, or it's just
getting started."

"Which one of those is better for us?"

"That depends on who was doing the shooting and who was
being shot at, and if Gaby is involved. And if she is, that means she
made a run for it."

"That's a pretty big leap, chief."

"What else could it be?"

"Maybe the boys in uniforms were just letting off steam with
some target practice."

"Could be. But it was pretty short for target practice."

The lack of activity around the town was disturbing. A place filled with that many people shouldn't be that calm. There was no one running around, no one shouting or pointing, and no men with assault rifles searching buildings. It made him wonder if he had been wrong about Gaby being involved somehow. But if it wasn't her, then what was the gunfire all about?

It had to be her. The Gaby he knew would try like hell to escape, even if it cost her everything.

The girl's a born fighter.

"It's gotta be Gaby," Will said after a while.

"If she did make a run for it," Danny said, "wouldn't we have run across her? The first thing she'd do would be to head for the interstate."

"Maybe. They could have been keeping her on the other side of town. Kellerson didn't know her exact location."

"I'm glad we finally ditched that guy. Terrible conversationalist."

They hadn't really ditched Kellerson. He was still waiting for them in the cellar behind the house. Not that he had much of a choice. Will had left him on the same patch of dirt floor he had been sleeping on last night, still duct taped. The look on Kellerson's face had been a mixture of concern and elation when he saw them leaving without him. It wouldn't be long now before he realized they might not come back. Whenever Will started to feel sorry for the collaborator, all he had to do was think about Mercy Hospital, and it went away.

Clop-clop-clop.

Will looked up. "You hear that?"

"Are you kidding me?" Danny said. "What is that, a posse?"

Two men on horseback rode down the town street, the *clop-clop-clop* of metal horseshoes against cobblestone echoing in the quiet morning. The riders wore camo uniforms with assault rifles bouncing against their backs. Neither man looked entirely comfortable on top of the animals.

"Horses," Danny said, as if he couldn't quite believe it. "What is this, the Dark Ages? What's next, guys with bows and arrows? Pooping in the woods?"

Two more riders appeared from down the street, meeting the first two halfway for some kind of powwow. After a moment, they turned and headed off toward the other side of town, picking up speed as they went.

"That's definitely a posse," Will said, lowering his binoculars. "And they're headed to the other side. What's back there?"

Danny took out a folded map from one of his pouches and spread it on the ground. "Woods. Lots of woods. So many, they should call the place Woodsville. And there's a lake."

"The lake would explain why they chose this place. It gives them a water supply."

Danny folded the map back up and put it away. "What's the plan, Kemosabe?"

"Wait and see?"

"I'm not good at waiting and seeing. I'm more of an action man. That's what they used to call me back in college. Action Danny."

"Skirt around the woods, see what's happening on the other side, then?"

"Sounds like a better plan. Action Danny approves."

"Glad to hear it," Will said.

He got up and began moving alongside the clearing while still sticking to the woods. Danny kept pace behind him.

"You didn't tell me we'd be running this much," Danny said.

"Hey, I'm the one with bullet holes in me."

"Stop yer bitchin'. Those bullet holes are already a few days old. Plus, I was thinking..."

"Uh oh."

"Shaddup. Anyway, I was thinking, we shoulda brought Keller-son along. I've always wanted my own personal pack mule. You think he could have carried me, too?"

"Not without two fingers. Hard to get a grip."

"Yeah, well, whose fault is that?"

"He hesitated when I asked him a question."

"He said, 'Huh,' just before you cut off his pinky finger."

"What are you, Amnesty International?"

"I didn't tell you? They even sent me a membership card. That shit was laminated and everything."

It took them another twenty minutes of steady jogging before they reached the highway. It wasn't much to look at—two lanes with fading yellow dividers. There were steel guardrails along the sides that they had to climb over before darting across the open to the other side.

Back in the comfort of the woods again, they continued around trees and bushes before risking a run across open ground with L15 fading to their right. After another thirty minutes, they finally reached the other side of the woods.

Will didn't breathe easier until he had trees around him again.

They hadn't come to a complete stop when they heard gunfire from somewhere further ahead. The unmistakable clatter of assault rifles, and this time it wasn't a one-sided fight. There was clearly a back-and-forth gun battle going on.

They went down on one knee and listened.

"AK-47?" Will said when the shooting finally stopped.

"And at least one other rifle," Danny said.

"How many shooters?"

"Two, possibly three."

"Sounds about right. If it is our girl, it's four against one. I don't like those odds."

"She's a lot tougher than you think, Danny. You should have seen her at Mercy Hospital."

"Yeah?"

Will nodded.

"Damn," Danny said. "We should definitely open up that school we've been talking about. Danny and Will's School of Badassness. My name goes first, of course. Purely based on awesomeness, you understand."

"That goes without saying," Will said.

They got up and moved forward, toward the source of the gunfire.

⊲▬▮ ▮▬▶

MORE GUNSHOTS, THIS time coming from a different section of the woods, which told him they were going in the wrong direction and had been for some time. Either that, or the action was on the move.

There was something odd about this new round of gunfire—there was just a volley, the very clear indication of a single rifle firing on full-auto.

"AK-47?" Danny said.

Will nodded. "Yup. Plus, we're going the wrong way."

"That's the last time I let you drive."

They changed course, heading even deeper into the woods.

THERE WAS BLOOD on the ground. Fresh. Small splatters that led them to a brown horse grazing on grass next to a big oak tree, shading itself from the morning glare. The animal lifted its head when they approached, nostrils flaring in warning. When they didn't do anything, it went back to blissfully feeding.

The blood belonged to a man in a camo uniform sitting against a tree. His eyes stared off at nothing in particular, face frozen with an oddly perplexed expression. A still-wet pool of blood seemed to originate from his bottom.

"Ass shot," Danny said.

"Yup," Will nodded.

"Gregson" was written on a nametag over the man's right breast pocket, with a large but simple white star-shaped patch on the right shoulder. There was another patch, this one in the shape of a boot on his left side. After scrutinizing the "boot" for a moment, Will realized it was actually the state of Louisiana.

"Look at this," Will said.

Danny, who was busy watching the horse dine out, glanced over. "Whatcha find?"

"They're organizing. Names on uniforms. Regional declarations."

"Well, damn, it's about time they got their shit together." Then, "Hey, you know how to ride a horse?"

"Can't say I've ever ridden one."

"Don't you think that's weird?"

"What do you mean?"

"We're from Houston."

"So?"

"And we've never ridden a horse before."

"And I've never owned a Stetson or cowboy boots or a belt buckle the size of my head. What's your point?"

Danny shrugged. "Seems kind of wrong, that's all."

Will stood up and pointed at the ground. "There was another horse heading south. Let's see where it leads."

"Famous last words," Danny smirked.

THE FIRES OF ATLANTIS   103

THE TRAIL DIDN'T lead him to Gaby as he had hoped. Instead, it took them to two of the men on horseback they had seen earlier. One of the riders had climbed off his mount and was peering cautiously into the mouth of a dark cave. He saw something in there that he didn't like, and it kept him from getting too close to the opening.

A dead ghoul.

Will glimpsed nametags on their uniforms, along with the same white star and the Louisiana boot. He didn't bother trying to make out their names, though he and Danny were close enough that they could hear the two men talking just fine.

"Are we going in there to make sure?" the one still mounted asked.

"Fuck no," the one on the ground said. "I'm not going in there." He kicked at a deformed skull as if it were a soccer ball and watched it roll all the way into the cave, where Will saw something *(somethings)* squirming within the darkness.

"You see that?" the mounted one said.

"Yeah," the second one said before walking back and climbing into his saddle. "Freaks me out every time."

"What are we going to tell the kid?"

"The kid"? Will thought.

The second man reined his horse around. "We tell him the truth—that his girlfriend had the misfortune of trying to hide inside a cave full of the bloodsuckers and didn't come out."

"Girlfriend"? "The kid"?

They're talking about Josh and Gaby...

"Just like that?" the first one said.

"But more tactfully, of course," the other one said, chuckling.

"Of course."

Will and Danny watched them go.

When they couldn't hear the horses anymore, they stood up and made their way over to the cave.

"One guess what's in there," Danny said. He kicked dirt at the bones. They were almost pure white under the sun and looked malformed. He sniffed the air. "Lots of them, too."

"Why don't you go in to make sure," Will said.

"Maybe later. So now what?"

"Those guys are either smarter than they look and she's dead, or they're just as dumb as they look and she's not."

"That's so convoluted I bet you think it actually made sense, huh?"

Danny peered into the dark cave opening while Will looked around for tracks.

The ground was soft and malleable, which was both a good thing and a problem, because there had been a lot of activity around the area very recently. There were more than one set of tracks, both on foot and on horseback. He noted then quickly dismissed the horseshoes, along with the newest pair of boots belonging to one of the dismounted *(wannabe)* soldiers. With those out of the way, he was able to focus on three separate pairs of shoes. Two sneakers and one pair of boots.

"What's your Injun skills tell you?" Danny said, coming up behind him.

"Three people went inside—either separately or together, but they all went inside—the cave, and the same three came back out later and headed south."

"That's a good sign. Everyone who went in came back out."

"That's a very good sign." Will stood up and followed the tracks until they vanished through some underbrush. "Those two seemed convinced one of those tracks belonged to Gaby."

"The 'girlfriend' in question?"

"Yup. If they go back to town and tell Josh she's dead, that means she's free and clear of him."

Danny chuckled. "Now who's Captain Optimism?"

Will grinned. "Let's go find our girl."

"Let's," Danny said.

They headed off, Will feeling more hopeful than he had in days.

Gaby was out there. If he had to guess, the two with her were friendlies. That was the good news. The thought of Gaby having to face all of this alone bothered him more than he wanted to admit. It was his fault she was out here in the first place. Also his fault that she had gotten caught, because he had sent her on ahead of him.

Hang on, Gaby. Hang on a little longer…

◄▬▮ ▮▬►

AFTER ABOUT TWENTY minutes of steadily tracking Gaby and her two companions, it became clear they were using the lake— Hillman's Lake, according to the map—as a guide while traveling further south.

"We're going to have to stop so I can call in to Song Island," Will said. He glanced at his watch. "I promised Lara at least two contacts a day."

Danny made an exaggerated whipping sound.

Will grinned. "Until then, what's up ahead?"

Danny fished out the same map. "If they keep along the lake, they'll run across a place called Dunbar about thirty-five klicks south. If they turn left between here and Dunbar, they'll be heading toward a place called Harvest."

"I know Harvest."

"Fun times?"

"Oodles."

"Tell me about it never. In the meantime, what the hell's in Dunbar?"

"No idea. She either has a map or one of the people she's traveling with knows the area. Anything smaller that's worth stopping for between us and there?"

"We're in the sticks, buddy. They probably have towns out here that have been around since the days of Tutankhamun."

"Who?"

"Tutankhamun."

"I don't know who that is."

"Egyptian pharaoh. He's the dude all you uneducated types call King Tut."

"You been sneaking off to read again?"

Danny smirked. "It's amazing what you can shove into your learning hole when you're bored."

"Carly know you've been shoving things into inappropriate places?"

"Oh, the things you don't know about that little demon red-head—"

The whine of an engine cut Danny off and sent both of them

into a crouch among the tall grass. They scooted over behind a large tree and put it between them and the lake just as the noise turned into the roar of an outboard motor.

It was an aluminum twenty-footer, gray sides reflecting back the sun as it skidded smoothly across the lake's surface. There were two men onboard, one sitting on a swivel chair on the bow cradling an M4 while the other stood behind the steering wheel near the center. Both were wearing the same uniforms as the ones they'd seen so far.

They watched the boat disappear up the lake, the man up front glancing around and talking into a radio.

"Lake patrol?" Danny said.

"Looks like it," Will said.

"First uniforms with nametags and now this? Looks like our boy Josh has really whipped these naughty buggers into shape."

"Looks like it."

"Is that all you can say?"

"Sounds like it."

"Better."

After the boat faded into the distance, they got up and continued alongside the lake, but this time sticking closer to the thicker parts of the woods to keep from being spotted. The good news was that they could hear the motors coming from a distance, which gave them plenty of time to hide. After all, no one had ever accused the collaborators of being subtle.

"You know what this means, right?" Danny said after a while. "About the kid."

Will nodded. "Yeah."

"We see the kid, we gotta pop him. He's getting too dangerous to let run around out here. Him and his newfangled ideas are begging for a reckoning."

"A 'reckoning,'" Will said, grinning at him. "What are you, John Wayne?"

"I'm just saying. The kid's become a royal pain in the butt cheeks."

"Even if we popped Josh, it still wouldn't stop what's happening out there with the camps and towns. Kate probably has a hundred more like him running the show for her in the daytime. Take one of them out and she'll just replace him with another eager beaver."

"Yeah, well, I'd still like to put the kid over my knees and give him a good spanking," Danny said. "Bad boy, Josh. You've been a *very* bad boy."

Will recalled that day when he thought Josh had died. The eighteen-year-old had done something stupid and stood up during a boat chase and had gotten shot as a result. He had ended up falling into Beaufont Lake. How was Will to know the teenager would float back up later and turn into...this?

I should have put a bullet in him while he was drowning in the lake.

Still not too late for that, Josh.

Still not too late for that...

CHAPTER 10

GABY

"HE HAD A Mohawk," Gaby said.

"A Mohawk?" Peter thought about it for a moment before shaking his head. "I don't remember seeing anyone like that. And I would definitely have remembered a guy with a Mohawk. Milly?"

"What's a Mohawk?" Milly said.

"You don't know what a Mohawk is?" Peter asked, slightly amused.

"No."

"It's a hairstyle. Like in those cowboys and Indians movies."

"I don't like cowboys and Indians movies."

"Okay, um." He paused, then, "It's mostly a shaved head, except for the middle that stands up." Peter demonstrated by flattening his own hair and leaving just the middle section standing up. "Like this." He looked over at Gaby. "Right?"

She nodded. "Something like that. But shorter. You didn't see anyone with hair like that in town, Milly?"

The girl shook her head. "Nope. Was he your friend?"

"He's my friend, yes."

Was. Nate's dead. You know it. Stop pretending he's not. Josh would never have let him live even if he had survived that night. Maybe the old Josh would, but that Josh is long gone.

I'm sorry, Nate. You shouldn't have been there with me that night...

She walked on in silence and could feel Peter's and Milly's eyes on her back. She ignored them and continued to set the pace

THE FIRES OF ATLANTIS 109

through the woods, moving close enough to the shoreline to their right to get some of the cool breeze, but far enough that they couldn't be seen. Peter told her there were boat patrols along Hillman's Lake.

They had been walking for the last two hours, keeping to the shade provided by the trees. Every now and then she looked around her, expecting an attack by someone in a camo uniform. Josh's people. Or maybe Josh himself.

He'll never let me go. In his deranged mind, he's doing all of this for me.

"Where are we going?" Milly asked after a while.

"There's a place called Dunbar up ahead," Peter said. "A small city with a state highway running through it. We should be able to find shelter and food there, then figure out where to go next."

Song Island. Where else but Song Island?

"Are there a lot of people in Dunbar?" Milly asked.

"Well, there was supposed to be about 10,000 people," Peter said. "I'm not sure now."

"Is it close to the interstate?" Gaby asked, looking back at him.

He shook his head. "It's about thirty miles from Interstate 10."

"You've been there."

"I used to live there before I went to New Orleans for work."

"They took you from New Orleans?"

"Uh huh."

"What were you doing there? What was 'work'?"

He smiled. "What, you don't think I was a cook in my previous life?"

"Call it a hunch."

"Human Resources," Peter said. "Boring job, but it made use of my degrees. Of course, I wish I had spent more time in the woods hunting or something. What about you? What did you do before all of this?"

"I was in high school."

"Oh," he said.

She smiled. "I'm nineteen, Peter."

"I thought you were older."

"You keep saying that. Why?"

"Why?"

"Why did you think I was older? Don't I look nineteen?"

The question was rhetorical, because Gaby knew she didn't look nineteen. The Purge aged you and she hadn't looked—much less felt—nineteen in a year.

"I don't, I'm not…" he stammered. "I wasn't sure, that's all."

"Sure of what?"

"Milly didn't tell me you were so young."

"I didn't?" Milly said, surprised. "I thought I did."

"You didn't," Peter said.

"Oh."

"What did she tell you about me?" Gaby asked.

"Not much," Peter said. "Neither one of us saw you when they first brought you into town. Yesterday was the first time Milly had actually seen you up close."

"So who did you think I was?"

"I just thought, because…you know."

"Because of what?" She watched him struggling with an answer. She took pity on him and said, "Because they had me locked up, you thought I was dangerous and you assumed dangerous meant older."

He nodded, grateful for the rescue. "Yes."

"Sorry to disappoint you."

"You didn't. That's not what I meant at all. I just couldn't figure out why they had you locked up in there, that's all."

"It has to do with him," Milly said.

"'Him'?" Peter said.

"The kid. The leader."

"Oh," Peter said. Then, "Is she right? What's his name? James?"

"Josh," Gaby said.

"What did he want with you?"

She didn't answer. Instead, she kept walking.

Peter took the hint and didn't ask again.

I'm not yours, Josh. Get that through your thick head.

I was never yours, and now I'll never be.

◄▬▌ ▐▬►

THEY CROUCHED BEHIND tall grass and watched the boat pass. There were two men in uniform riding on top, both heavily armed. The one up front looked bored, occasionally turning his head left and right.

"How often do they go up and down the lake?" she whispered to Peter.

"Once or twice a day, I think," Peter whispered back. "In the morning and in the afternoon. Everyone tries to get back to town before nightfall."

She glanced at her watch. "How far is Dunbar?"

"Probably four more hours of walking."

"'Probably'?"

"I've never actually walked there. If we pick it up, maybe three hours?"

"So let's try to pick it up."

She stood up and started off, but this time made sure to angle left for a bit until they had put more space between them and the lake. Milly and Peter followed as best they could, the girl already looking as if she was struggling with her pack. That didn't surprise Gaby. The thirteen-year-old was painfully thin, even though she and Peter had been living in L15, according to them, for over two months now.

They've had it too easy. Got soft. Meanwhile, I was in the woods with Will and Danny eating bugs and sleeping on dirt.

She sneaked a look back at them. They were moving too slowly, hampering her pace. Every now and then, she had to fight the urge to run off and leave them behind.

They saved your life. You owe them a little bit of patience.

For now...

<hr>

HILLMAN'S LAKE HAD ended about an hour back, and they were now walking alongside a two-lane state highway somewhere at the outskirts of the Dunbar city limit. They had passed a dozen or so farm houses along the way, with old structures that appeared barren from the road. Most of the city was still ahead, but at the moment there were just the walls of trees to the left and right of them.

Milly's pace had flagged even further and the girl was straining, both hands hooked around the straps of her backpack. The heat, simmering against the hot concrete road, didn't do them any favors, and they were all soaked from head to toe in their own sweat. It was

October in Louisiana. When the hell was it going to get cold? She couldn't wait, though she was starting to wonder if she would actually live long enough to see the seasons change. What she wouldn't give to be able to wear a jacket these days...

Peter was doing better than Milly, but that was probably because he wasn't always a cook in a nondescript town in the middle of nowhere. For a former Human Resources manager (whatever that was), he kept up with her well enough that Gaby stopped worrying about him. As he walked beside her, she couldn't help but think about Nate and that day in Sandwhite Wildlife State Park as they fled the men in Level B hazmat suits.

Are you still alive out there, Nate? Or are you one of them now?

"Was he a friend of yours?" Peter asked, his voice intruding on her thoughts.

"Who?" she said, though she already knew the answer.

"Nate. The man you were looking for. He was a friend of yours?"

"He is."

Was. He's dead. Why can't you accept it?

"Why?" she asked.

"I was just wondering," Peter said. "I'm sorry. I wish I could have told you more about what happened to him."

"It's okay. I don't even know if—" *he survived* "—they brought him back to the same town as me. They might have split us up."

Now you're lying to a stranger about Nate? Someone's delusions have gone into overdrive.

"When was the last time you saw him?" Peter asked.

"I don't know," she said. "I don't even know exactly know how long I've been in your town. The days are a little fuzzy."

"Maybe he's out there somewhere. You never know." He shrugged. "Look at me and Milly. Who would think we'd still be around? So many people have died, and we somehow managed to keep going."

"There's an island," Gaby said. "Down south. Have you ever heard of Beaufont Lake?"

"I've heard of it, but I didn't know there was an island on it."

"There is. I have friends there. After we spend the night in Dunbar and gather some supplies, that's where I'm going. You and Milly are welcome to tag along."

"Okay," Peter said quickly.

"That's it? You're not going to ask me any more about it?"

He grinned. "Gaby, you seemed to know a hell of a lot more about what's going on out here than I do. And you're damn well more prepared than I am to survive it. If you say this island is preferable to staying out here, then yeah, I'll take you at your word."

She shrugged. "Your funeral."

"Whose funeral?" Milly said behind them.

"Nothing," Peter said, smiling back at her. "It's just a figure of speech." He looked over at Gaby. "Right?"

"Right," Gaby nodded, but thought, *Maybe...*

"See?" Peter said.

Milly didn't look convinced.

"You never told me why the two of you decided to run," Gaby said, hoping to steer the conversation away from less depressing subjects.

"I was wondering when you were going to ask," Peter said. "What took you so long?"

"There were more pressing matters until now. Like staying alive."

He didn't answer right away. Finally, he said, "Things weren't what we thought they were. Back in town."

"What did you think it was?"

"Don't get me wrong. We went there with our eyes wide open. We accepted the contract with those ghouls, as you call them. But then people started disappearing."

"Disappearing?"

"Men, mostly. Guys who were more—I guess you would say— opinionated than most."

"I don't know what that means."

"They asked questions. Too many questions, as it turned out."

"Troublemakers?"

"Yeah, I guess you could call them that."

"Just the guys?"

"Just the guys," Peter nodded. "One day they're there, the next they're gone. Whenever anyone asked, the guards just said they were moved to another town. It wasn't like anyone could verify it. We were allowed to leave whenever we wanted—or so they said—but you know what's out there, so no one ever did. Plus, they never told us where these 'other towns' were."

"So you decided to run because some loudmouths were going missing?"

"No, it wasn't until someone I knew disappeared. A guy named Jake. He was a cop from New Orleans. Milly and I met him in one of those camps. Good guy, tough."

"How big was the camp?"

"What?"

"The camp you were in."

"Oh. Pretty big."

"How many people were there?" Gaby asked, remembering the size of the one at Sandwhite Wildlife State Park. All those people in one place, like rats looking for salvation from a sinking ship. Thinking about it always made her angry and sad at the same time.

"A few thousand, probably," Peter said.

She nodded. "So what happened to Jake?"

"He disappeared one night. Milly saw it happen."

Gaby glanced back at the girl, who confirmed it with a solemn nod. "What did you see?" Gaby asked her.

"The soldiers took him," Milly said.

"She has trouble sleeping," Peter said. "It's all those nights we spent running after everything happened. It still gives her nightmares sometimes."

Milly looked away, apparently no longer interested in the topic. Or trying her best to avoid it. In so many ways, she wasn't even close to being as tough as Lara's Elise, or Carly's little sister Vera. Thirteen or not, Milly didn't have either of those girls' survival instincts.

"What happened to Jake?" Gaby asked Peter.

"I don't know, exactly. I asked around—as discreetly as possible—but no one could tell me where they took him. The closest thing to an answer I got was from Howard. He's one of the guards. A good guy, as far as guards go."

Gaby wondered if "good guy" guard Howard was one of the men she had shot in the woods while Peter and Milly were fleeing. She said instead, "What did he say?"

"That I should stop asking about Jake." Peter walked quietly for a moment before continuing. "The day after that conversation, Howard started avoiding me. I figured it out pretty fast that I was going to be next."

"So you decided to escape."

"It seemed like the thing to do."

Gaby sneaked a glance back at Milly, then said quietly to Peter, "Why did you drag her with you?"

He shook his head, clearly offended by the suggestion. "I didn't. But she wouldn't stay behind. We've been together since all of this began, and I guess I'm the closest thing to family she's got left. I tried to talk her out of it. Hours and hours of conversation."

"He goes, I go," Milly said loudly behind them, with all the confidence a teenage girl who didn't know any better could muster. "Case closed."

Peter gave Gaby an exasperated *"See?"* look.

Gaby almost smiled but managed to stop herself in time.

People die around you, remember? These two can die at any moment. Don't get too attached.

Don't *get too attached…*

◄━▮▮ ▮▮━►

THE CITY OF Dunbar, according to Peter, had a population of 10,000. That was twice as many as Ridley, Texas, where she had spent the first eighteen years of her life. She expected the city to look more impressive given its size, but it reminded her too much of her hometown—spread out and unspectacular and…country.

After passing the empty acres of unattended farmland, they moved through the suburban areas filled with old and new houses. The bulk of the city was in front of them, gathered around State Highway 190. The highway was flat to the ground and would have looked like any other road if not for the signs. One pointed south toward I-10.

And beyond that, Song Island…

They stuck to the roads, maneuvering around the occasional abandoned vehicle. Homes, businesses, and gas stations flanked them. The afternoon sun continued to beat down mercilessly, further soaking her in her own sweat. All of it just made her miss Song Island more.

For a city that 10,000 people used to live in, Dunbar was abandoned and empty and dead. They waited thirty minutes near the outskirts and listened for noise or anything resembling life but didn't hear a single thing. The stillness continued as they made their way inside. Instead of making her feel better, the quiet only gnawed at Gaby, and she couldn't shake the feeling that they were being watched from the very first moment they stepped foot into the city limits.

"Ten thousand people?" she said.

"Doesn't feel like it, does it?" Peter said.

"No, it doesn't." She walked in silence for a moment. Then, "Look for a place to stay the night."

"Already?" Peter said, glancing down at his watch.

"We took too long to get here. And it's harder to find a safe place than you think."

Peter nodded. "What kind of place are we looking for?"

Gaby thought about the pawnshop. About Nate... "Something with a basement. Just to be safe."

"I'm hungry," Milly said.

"Can we look through the gas stations for food first?" Peter asked.

She stopped in the street as her own stomach growled. On cue, Peter's and Milly's joined in. The three of them exchanged smiles, and this time she wasn't able to stop herself in time.

"Yeah," she said. "We should probably find something to eat."

Gaby took out the Glock and handed it to Peter. He took it hesitantly, as if he was afraid it would go off if he gripped it too tightly. She gave him two spare magazines and he put it in his pocket.

"Be careful," she said. "If you run across one of them, don't fight or shoot, just run."

"Just run?"

"Shooting them will just piss them off. You saw what happened in the cave."

He nodded and turned the gun over in his hand.

"Have you ever fired a gun before, Peter?"

He gave her an embarrassed look. "Is it that obvious?"

"Just point and shoot."

"Where's the safety? I thought guns have safeties?"

"Glocks don't." She held up her forefinger and twitched it in front of him, the way Will had done to her all those months ago back on the island during the first phase of her weapons training. "That's

THE FIRES OF ATLANTIS 117

your safety."

"My finger?" Peter said, slightly confused.

"You don't pull the trigger, and the gun won't go off. Simple as that."

"Oh," he said.

"Here," Gaby said, and took the Glock back and handed him Mac's 1911 instead. "This one has a safety." She showed him the switch, then took back the magazines she had given him and passed over two new ones. "Be careful."

Peter felt a little better, and it showed on his face.

"Milly, stay with me," Gaby said.

The girl nodded quickly. "Don't gotta tell me twice."

"Nice," Peter said.

THEY SETTLED ON an Exxon gas station at the corner of Tripps and Meer and walked around a white pickup truck in the parking lot before passing two more vehicles frozen at the gas pumps. The convenience store was long and advertised "Beer Cigarettes Liquor." They were just hoping for some nonperishable food.

Gaby went inside first, Peter behind her, while Milly stayed outside on the curb, looking worriedly back at the empty street. There was an auto body shop called George's on the other side, flanked by two big red buildings, including a Mexican restaurant called Rosita's.

Peter fidgeted behind her, and she prayed to God he didn't accidentally shoot her in the back.

"Don't shoot until you're sure," she said quietly.

"Okay."

"I mean it."

"Okay," he said again.

For some reason she didn't believe him, but she kept that to herself. "Let's stick together, okay? You watch my back and I'll take the front. Try not to stray too far."

"Yes, ma'am."

She rolled her eyes. Was she being bossy? Probably. Then again, she was the one who had been out here for the last year. According to him, Peter went to sleep in one of those blood farms on the very first night of what Will and the others called The Purge and didn't wake up again in one of the camps until two months later. He wasn't exactly equipped to survive out here, especially dragging around a thirteen-year-old girl who had about the same experience as he did. Maybe that was a bit harsh, but she had no time to pussyfoot around when her life was at stake.

Gaby headed down the first aisle they came to, scanning and listening for sounds other than their own footsteps and Peter's slightly loud breathing. There was enough sunlight that she wasn't too worried about ghouls hiding behind the shelves. But there were other things just as dangerous as ghouls in the daytime.

The city's too empty. So why does it not feel *empty?*

They went through the aisle and found nothing of interest except some melted chocolate on the floor, little more than puddles of black and brown spots now. The M4 she had taken off one of the dead guards felt more at home in her hands than the AK-47, and it moved in front of her as they finished up with the second aisle. Despite the comfort level, the fact that the rifle wasn't loaded with the right ammo played havoc with her confidence.

"What's that smell?" Peter asked.

"Rotten food," she said.

"Oh."

"The freezer's at the back. They should have some water, too."

"Good, because I'm thirsty as hell. I know I should have prepared something last night, but it never entered my mind. I guess I'm not very good at this."

"I guess not," she said. "Stay alert."

"Can I ask you something?"

She sighed. He was talking too much. She didn't know why he was talking so damn much. Didn't he know they were in a precarious situation here? That there could be bad things waiting for them in the next aisle? Or in the next room? Or outside?

Why does this city not feel *empty?*

When she didn't answer, he said, "What's it like to kill someone?"

"You killed Mac," she said, hoping that would nip the conversation in the bud.

It didn't work.

"I think he's still alive," Peter said.

"He's probably brain-dead if he is."

That made him go quiet, and in the few seconds that followed, she felt a pang of guilt.

Jesus. What's wrong with me?

"It's okay," she said. "You did what you had to."

"I know," he said quietly.

She wasn't the least bit convinced he was okay with what he had done to poor Mac, but Gaby didn't know how else to comfort him. This wasn't the time, either. They were still moving inside a building they had never been in, in a city that may or may not hold dangers they didn't even know existed yet.

Later. I'll talk to him about it later.

They were turning toward the third aisle when a scream pierced the air, coming *from outside.*

"Milly!" Peter shouted.

He was already running before Gaby could turn fully around. She hurried after him, just in time to see him shoving the glass doors open and lunging outside.

Christ, she had no idea he could move that fast!

Gaby burst outside onto the sidewalk after Peter, the M4 swinging up and sweeping the large parking lot for threats.

There's something wrong with this city. Dammit, I should have listened to my gut instinct!

Everything was where it should be—the white truck and the two vehicles at the gas pumps. There was nothing out here that could pose a danger to them, so why were alarm bells exploding inside her head?

But everything was where it should be—*except for Milly.* The girl was gone.

"Where is she?" Gaby asked.

Peter was whirling around, the Smith & Wesson gripped too tightly in his right fist.

"Peter," Gaby said. "Where's Milly?"

"I don't know," he said. "I don't know!"

The girl's backpack was leaning against the curb. Gaby bent to pick it up when a loud cry streaked across the air, coming from down the street. Peter took off running in that direction with the same deceptive speed she didn't know he was even capable of.

Where the hell had he been hiding *that?*

She ran after him. Or tried to, anyway.

Another scream, this one just as pained and shrill, rocketing up the street and prompting Peter to run even faster. He seemed to know where he was going, where Milly's screams were coming from, and soon he had abandoned the highway and was turning into a side street with long, smooth strides.

Gaby followed as best she could. Gray and red and white buildings flashed by on both sides of her. Store and restaurant signs. Windows, some painted, others barren, reflecting back a streaking figure—her. Thank God she had tied her hair in a ponytail.

She swerved around vehicles in the streets, keeping sight of Peter in front of her. He had somehow added to the distance between them.

God, he's fast. Where is all that speed coming from?

She blamed her lagging pace on the rifle she was carrying along with the Glock in the hip holster. There were also the pouches around her waist, still stuffed with spare magazines even though she had dumped the ones for the AK-47.

Milly's voice, shouting, *"Peter!"*, coming from their left, and very close by.

Without hesitation, Peter turned into the mouth of an alley. Gaby was on his heels, and she was surprised to see that Peter had slowed down in front of her. As she began to catch up to him, she could hear his breathing hammering out of him in quick, pained bursts, flooding the narrow space along with their pounding footsteps.

There was a dead-end in front of them, along with a metal door that was opening and a figure darting through it *with Milly thrown over its shoulder.*

"Peter!" Milly shouted, looking back at them with hands outstretched and eyes wide with terror.

Gaby had never seen someone look so frightened in her life. Well, that wasn't true. Her mind flashed back to the kids from Mercy Hospital being taken away in the back of the Humvees. She had failed to save those kids. She didn't even know where they were at the moment or what had become of them.

Not again.

She didn't know where she got the burst of speed, but suddenly she was running past Peter. Then she was halfway up the alley when the steel door slammed shut in front of her. She didn't stop for one second. As she neared it, she reached out with one hand and grabbed the knob and twisted it and jerked the door back and slipped inside in one continuous, blurring motion.

Darkness.

It was pitch-black inside.

She stopped, the only sounds coming from inside her chest and through her mouth as she struggled to breathe. She swiveled the carbine left, then right, then behind her. Not that it did any good.

She couldn't see a goddamn thing.

Her eyes tried desperately to adjust to the blackness, but she could only see a few inches in front of her. It looked like some kind of hallway. She listened for footsteps, prepared to hear the soft patter of bare feet against tiled floor.

Ghouls! her mind screamed. *There are ghouls in here!*

Her finger tightened against the trigger.

She didn't know how long she stood there, swallowed up by darkness, but it must have only been a few seconds, because the alleyway door opened behind her and sunlight flooded inside. Peter hurried through, his breath flooding out in long gasps. In the brief few seconds that the door was opened, she confirmed that she was inside a hallway with old walls, peeling paint, and a vinyl-covered floor.

"Milly!" Peter shouted.

His voice echoed just before he let the door slam shut behind him and they were, once again, swallowed up by the same black void as a few seconds ago.

"Oh my God," Peter said, his voice breathless.

"What is it?" she said, keeping her eyes forward at…nothing. There was a big fat nothing in front of her.

"The door," Peter said, the panic rising with each syllable. "There's no doorknob on this side of the door, Gaby. I can't open it!"

Gaby glanced behind her, searching out the door, trying to find the doorknob in the sea of nothingness. She couldn't locate it, and the only reason she even knew Peter was standing next to her was the smell of his sweat and his out-of-control panting as he ran his hands over the metal door.

It's a trap. They led us right into a goddamn trap.

She heard a *click* before a stream of light flashed across her face, illuminating the peeling and old faded multicolored patterns over one side of the wall. Peter, with a flashlight, swiveled the light back to her. She winced, and he quickly took the bright light away.

"Sorry," he said.

"You brought a flashlight?"

"Yes. Why?"

"You've had it this entire time?"

"I—"

"The cave, Peter," she hissed. "Why didn't you use it when we were back in the cave?"

"I…forgot I had it."

"Jesus," she said, and looked away. "Never mind. Show me where we are."

He turned the flashlight down one side of the hallway, then swiveled around and did the same to the other side. There was a nightstand with a vase and dead flowers draped over the lid behind them. And beyond that, just a solid wall. The other side, on the other hand, showed an intersection about twenty yards further down, pointing left and right.

"Can you hear her?" Peter whispered.

She shook her head but then realized he probably couldn't see. "No. Can you?"

"No…"

"There's only one way to go. Can you find any windows?"

He moved the flashlight along the walls. First one side, then the other. They only saw old, discolored, peeling wallpaper. "Nothing," he said.

Of course not. Because it's a trap. They lured us in here.

You idiot!

"Keep beside me with the flashlight," she said. "If I turn, you turn. Got it?"

"Got it."

"Do you have your gun out?"

"Oh." She heard him pull the 1911 out of his waistband and cock back the hammer, the soft *click* sounding overly dangerous in the blackness. "Okay."

God, she hoped he didn't accidentally shoot her. The chances of that happening had been pretty high back in the gas station with the lights to see with. Now, with only the flashlight, she had a very bad feeling.

"Peter," she said.

"Yes?"

"See what you're shooting at before you shoot, okay?"

"Okay," he said uncertainly.

She sighed, then said, "Let's go," and started forward into the darkness.

CHAPTER 11

KEO

LAKE DULCET WAS a city of 23,000 or so people, about half the size of neighboring Lake Charles. It had a decent downtown and the surrounding areas were a concrete jungle like every other city. Despite the sun, it would have been a pleasant walk if Lorelei, who hadn't said a word when they first met earlier in the day, didn't suddenly transform into a chatterbox.

The teenager talked about everything. The ghost city around them, the fact that they were walking instead of driving, or how she needed a haircut. Keo tuned her out the best he could, but it wasn't nearly enough.

"Can't we get a car?" Lorelei asked. "There are so many cars around. Can't we use one of them? I'm tired of walking. How long have we been walking? It feels like days. Weeks. Months. Right, Carrie?"

"Uh huh," Carrie said absently.

Lorelei reminded him of Shorty. Annoying. Carrie was more like Zachary. Quiet, unless she needed to say something. Lorelei liked to talk, even if no one was responding to her.

"Look, there's a truck," she said behind him now. "It's nice. I like the color. Can we use that truck? Keo? Are you listening to me?"

"No," Keo said.

"Carrie?" Lorelei said. "What about the truck? Can we use that truck? My feet are so tired. I think my legs are about to fall off."

"We've only been walking for three hours," Carrie said.

"It feels longer. It feels like months."

"Well, it hasn't been months. Now be quiet for a bit, okay?"

Lorelei sighed and lapsed into silence. Keo was able to once again enjoy the stillness of the city and their unhurried footsteps. They kept to the shades provided by the buildings while Keo kept both ears open for the first sound of pursuing vehicles.

There were three trucks, likely more than two men in each one. Well-armed men playing soldiers. The uniform didn't bother him, but the weapons did. He had the submachine gun, but he was now saddled with two civilians, which put him at a disadvantage. All it would take was one of those cars to stumble across them by accident and he was screwed.

He thought about Zachary and why he was following up on a dead man's promise.

You really are the dumbest man alive, you know that?

Carrie had walked up beside him. "She's got a point."

She had light brown eyes, and despite the bruising around her mouth and cut lips, she was more attractive than he had given her credit for this morning. Like most women he had met since the world went to shit, Carrie had very few extraneous pounds on her, which helped exaggerate what he guessed was a generous B-cup under that white T-shirt.

He looked away before she could catch him sneaking a peek. "What's that?"

"Why didn't we circle back to the marina after the soldiers left and take one of those trucks? They looked in pretty good shape."

"They weren't. I checked when I first got there. No gas, and the batteries are dead."

"Oh."

"Besides, listen."

She did. "What am I listening for?"

"It's quiet."

"And?"

"Sound travels these days. Even if we could find a working vehicle, you don't think your friends would hear a car rumbling down these streets? There are three of them out there looking for us. All it takes is one. Right now, they don't have a clue where we're going. That's our advantage."

"Do we know where we're going?"

"South."

"I was hoping for a more concrete answer."

"South, until we fall into the Gulf of Mexico."

"Funny," she said, then glanced up, shielding her eyes against the sun. "You think we'll make it out of the city before nightfall?"

Keo didn't have to look at his watch before he answered, "No."

"What time is it?"

"Two in the afternoon."

"You didn't even look at your watch."

"I don't have to."

"It doesn't get dark around this part until after six. So we have four hours or so?"

"Sounds about right."

They walked in silence for a moment. Behind them, Lorelei was loudly unwrapping something. A few seconds later, he got a whiff of one of the Teriyaki-flavored Jack Link's jerky he had given them before taking off. One of the few foods he was carrying around in his pack from last night.

"She's eating again?" he asked.

"She eats like a horse," Carrie smiled. "Were you in the Army?"

"What makes you think I was in the Army?"

"You're really good with that rifle."

"It's a submachine gun."

"What's the difference?"

"One's a submachine gun, and the other's a rifle."

She smirked. "So were you in the Army or not?"

"Not."

"So how are you so good with that…submachine gun?"

"Experience," Keo said.

"Were you living in the marina?"

"I was lying low on the sailboat that they sunk. Me and a couple of guys. After we tested out the silver bullets, we were heading south down the lake. First Song Island to check up on it, then the Texas coast for me."

"What happened to your friends?"

The same thing that happened to the rest of the world. Their numbers came up.

"Bad luck," he said instead.

"That's it?"

"Yup, that's about it."

She didn't say anything after that, but he caught her sneaking a look at him every now and then. Not really at him, but at the scar along the left side of his face, very visible under the bright sunlight. Pollard's good-bye gift.

"What?" he said.

"How'd you get that?" she asked.

"I cut myself shaving."

"Must have been one hell of a shave."

"You have no idea."

THEY MADE IT to the outskirts of Lake Dulcet around five. Not quite within the city limits anymore, but not quite in the boondocks just yet, either. Lorelei was still grumpy about having to walk, though Keo was impressed with her and Carrie's stamina. With the sun already starting to dip in the horizon, he began looking for a place to hide.

They walked under the open sky along a street flanked by ancient looking power poles. Trucks were sprinkled in the parking lots of businesses and industries around them. He glanced backward, remembering the suburbs they had passed an hour ago, and thought about going back. Last night's run across the rooftops had convinced him he needed a place with a basement. Or, failing that, a place that could be easily defended. He couldn't hope to survive in attics the rest of his life.

"What?" Carrie said, walking beside him.

"The suburbs," Keo said. "I'm thinking we might have to backtrack to one of the houses we passed earlier. One with a basement."

Lorelei had stopped in the middle of the street. She put her hands on her hips and looked around. With her hair in a ponytail, she was actually a very pretty girl, if a bit too thin. The boots she was wearing that they had liberated from a shoe store a few kilometers back looked two sizes too big, but that was only because her legs were toothpicks.

"What about that?" Lorelei said, pointing.

Keo looked over at a large building inside some hurricane fencing.

"The warehouse?" Carrie said.

"No, the RV," Lorelei said.

It was a white recreational vehicle housed inside a garage with an open wall attached to one end of a warehouse. The RV sat in the shade, which only reminded Keo that he was sweating badly under the heat.

Carrie glanced over at him. "What do you think?"

Keo walked over and scanned the area. The grass inside the fence was burnt, mostly dead, with the occasional spots of weed. There were two, maybe three dozen groupings of gray cinderblocks, as if their owners had planned to build something in the wide-open spaces but never got around to it. Two swinging gates were closed tight with rusted-over chains and a large padlock. There was a gas station next door, its windows broken some time ago.

"What do you think?" Carrie asked again.

"Let's check it out," Keo said.

The fencing was cheap and stood only six-feet high. It was easy for Keo to scale; he waited on the other side as Carrie and Lorelei did the same.

"Couldn't you just shoot the lock?" Lorelei said as she struggled up the fence one inch at a time.

"Too noisy," Keo said.

"This is so hard…"

"It'll be easier if you climbed without talking."

"Whatever," she said, and threw her legs over the top and dropped down into his arms.

He set her down. "See?"

She made a face and looked around them.

Next, he caught Carrie as she came down. She was surprisingly light and he probably held onto her longer than necessary. He also noticed that her arms had conveniently gone around his neck as he lowered her to the ground.

"Thanks," she said, and actually blushed a bit.

"Sure."

He thought about Gillian, waiting for him on the beaches of Santa Marie Island…probably. For all he knew, she had never made it to the island. For all he knew, she and Jordan and the boat were somewhere at the bottom of a river…

Keo unslung the MP5SD as they moved across the wide-open spaces. Like the last five hours, the only sound he heard was a minor wind and their footsteps. The warmth against his face was growing unbearable, and he wiped at a fresh bead of sweat.

There were zero vehicles (other than the RV) inside the lot, which told him that the place was being used for storage. The lack of a sign or company logo was a bit confusing, though. Then again, if they weren't doing business out of here, the people who ran it wouldn't necessarily need to advertise. Even with all those excuses, the emptiness, combined with the encounter with the soldiers this morning, made him jumpy.

And I thought the woods were dangerous…

"You think the fence can keep them out?" Carrie asked, glancing backward.

"Not in this lifetime," Keo said. "But maybe it'll deter them anyway. If they've been through here before—and chances are they have—they won't bother coming in again unless we give them a reason to."

She gave him a doubtful look.

"What?" he said.

"You talk about them like they're smart. Like they can think."

"Carrie, look around you. What do you see?"

She did. Then, "I don't understand."

"They did this. One night. That was all it took. Now tell me—can stupid, mindless creatures that can't think do something like this?"

"I guess not."

"These things—these ghouls—might not be the smartest kids in class anymore, but they can still think and reason. Never, ever underestimate them."

She nodded solemnly.

"Come on," he said, "let's see what's in the bus."

"It's an RV," she smiled.

"Same difference."

The RV used to be white, but it was now a faded gray color with long brown and black patterns, like the Nike swoosh, from front to back. It was about thirty feet long and eleven feet high, give or take a few inches, and parked along the length of the garage, taking up the entire space with a few feet to spare up front. Despite the deflated tires and dust-covered windows, it seemed to be in relatively good condition.

"It looks cool," Lorelei said. "I've always wanted to travel around the country in an RV. My parents used to—" she stopped and didn't say anything else.

Carrie walked over and put an arm around the girl, and the two of them exchanged another one of their brief, private smiles.

"Stay here," Keo said. "I'll check the warehouse first."

He left them at the RV and walked around the warehouse. He ran his free palm along the building's side, feeling the heat that the metal walls had been absorbing all day. There were closed windows at the top, but too far to reach from ground level. Both front doors were locked, and pulling at them didn't get him anything. More layers of dust along the doors themselves and there were no telltale signs that they had swung open recently.

He located a smaller side door and two large ones at the back, but all three were similarly locked. It wouldn't have taken much to pry them open, but if the creatures—or one of their human lackeys—stumbled across the damage, they might know someone had taken up residence. If that happened, he'd have to defend a large property by himself. He could probably count on Carrie to lend a hand, but Lorelei, not so much.

I should just dump them. Both of them. Gillian would understand. Probably…

He headed back to the girls.

"Anything?" Carrie asked when he reached them.

"Doors are locked."

"Can we break into them?"

"We could, but we shouldn't. It's a big warehouse with too many access points. I doubt it'll have a basement or anything more secure than an office or a bathroom. If they catch us in there, we're sitting ducks."

"So where, then?"

"Let's check the RV first."

He wiped at the thick layer of dust over the security window on top of the RV's door. He peered through it, but despite the bright *(falling)* sun, he couldn't see more than a few feet inside. He glimpsed the driver's seat, the big steering wheel, and what looked like an empty can of Diet Coke on the floor.

"Stay out here," he said to the girls.

They looked back at him, as if to say, *"What, you thought we were going to go in there with you?"*

He smiled to himself then tried the door. It *clicked* open without a fight. He pulled it all the way open and slipped inside, sweeping the immediate area with the MP5SD. He took out an LED flashlight from one of his pouches and ran the beam over the seats in the middle. He was greeted by the very good sign of dust along the headrests and the smooth surface of a table to his right, half-encircled by a booth with plastic seats.

He moved up the aisle, boots squeaking softly against the vinyl flooring. There was a small kitchen complete with sink and range to his left. A dining table was fastened to the floor across from it, and more booth seating. Two doors at the very back. One opened up into a small bathroom and the other into a surprisingly spacious bedroom with a twin-size bed that had a wooden frame in one corner and an oak dresser on the other. There was a single window at the back, but it was blocked by the warehouse wall on the other side.

He rasped his knuckle on the solid fiberglass door and liked the sound he heard. It had a 12x21-inch tinted window at the top and a deadbolt lock on the inside. The odds of it withstanding a prolonged assault were good, especially with the dresser and bed as reinforcements.

Keo headed back to the front door.

Lorelei was leaning through the opening, giving him an anxious look. "Is it safe?"

"Safe enough," he said.

Carrie followed Lorelei up the steps. "Okay?" she asked.

He nodded. "It'll do. We only need it for one night, anyway."

"So," Lorelei said, "can we eat now? I'm starving."

Carrie smiled wryly at Keo. "I told you. Like a horse."

"Hey!" Lorelei said.

AS DUSK FELL, visibility inside the RV began to drop. Carrie sat in the booth across from Keo while they listened to Lorelei snoring inside the bedroom in the back. The teenager had gone to sleep almost instantly. Keo wondered if she was tired from all the walking or the talking. Maybe both.

Carrie had her legs pulled up against her chest, sneakers resting on the seat. "What now?" she asked after they had been sitting there in silence for a while.

Keo reached into his pack and pulled out a Glock, then handed it to her butt-first. "Just in case."

She took the gun and laid it on the table between them. Keo took out two spare magazines and placed them next to the weapon.

"How many of these things are you carrying around with you?" she asked, sounding amused.

"Plenty. Now, pay attention. It doesn't matter where you shoot them. As long as you hit them with a silver bullet, they go down. Understand?"

She nodded and picked up the magazines, putting them into her pocket. "So, you're like Chinese or something? I know you're Asian. But not the whole way."

He smiled. "'Not the whole way'?"

"You know what I mean."

"My mom was Korean."

"Ah. What kind of name is Keo, anyway?"

"Chuck was taken."

She stared at him, unsure how to process that response.

"You can take the bedroom with Lorelei," Keo said. "I'll sleep out here and keep an eye out."

"You sure?" she asked, the tiredness coming through.

"Yes."

"Thank you, Keo. For everything."

She picked up the Glock, stood up, and headed to the bedroom in the back.

Alone again, Keo pulled the tab on a can of Dole pineapple and sporked himself a nice big chunk dripping with syrup. He finished the entire can in a few minutes, watching as night fell outside the window like a canvas draping over the streets, the Spartan grounds within the hurricane fencing, and finally, the RV itself.

He picked up his MP5SD and put it on the table next to him, then leaned back against the wall. There was another window behind him, but it was blocked by the garage wall so there was no chance of anything coming through it. That only left three possible points of entry—the window directly across from him, the door to his left, and the front windshield. The windshield was mostly concealed by one of the other three walls, which really left just the window and door.

He closed his eyes briefly and thought about Gillian to help pass the time…

KEO WASN'T ASLEEP, but he had settled into a peaceful state somewhere been dozing off and wide alert. It was an old trick he had learned a long time ago, something that had become very useful when he found himself stuck up a tree recently.

When he heard the noise, he knew immediately what it was before he even opened his eyes, slid off the plastic seat, and glided across the RV to the other side and pushed up against the window.

Headlights speared the street, cutting across the fading light outside. From the sounds of it, a truck. Despite his limited perspective, he could tell it was moving erratically, headlights swaying left and right as it got closer.

One of the trucks with the soldiers? How did they find us?

Keo watched it near, wondering what was going to reach him first—the truck or the falling night. If he were a betting man…

Click.

Carrie squeezed out of the partially open bedroom door and looked across the darkened vehicle at him. He lifted a finger to his lips, hoping she could see, and when she quietly closed the door and walked on her tiptoes toward him, he guessed she had.

She flattened her body against the wall next to him. "I heard a car…"

He nodded.

"Did they find us?" she asked. "The soldiers?"

He shook his head. "I don't know."

The pickup finally came into view. It might have been red, but it was hard to tell against the falling night. The vehicle had begun to slow down a bit, but it was still swerving from lane to lane, clearly out of control.

"It's in trouble," Carrie whispered.

As if on cue, the truck flipped and a figure—thin, gaunt, and unmistakably *ghoul*—flew off the bed where it had been holding on and was slingshot across the night sky as if shot out of a cannon. It landed somewhere further up the road, well beyond Keo's line of sight.

The truck rolled on its side like a ball of steel and metal and aluminum, chunks of its frame firing off in every direction like missiles. Its bright front and rear lights shattered against the asphalt, showering the road with fireworks.

"Oh God," Carrie gasped.

Finally, the truck came to a stop, settling on its roof with a loud groaning noise as smoke flooded out of its crumpled hood. They heard the metallic *clinking* of car parts big and small rolling around the road and dropping from the overturned vehicle.

"We should go out and help them," Carrie said.

Keo didn't say anything.

"Keo..."

"It could be a trap. I can't tell if the truck is one of the three we saw earlier..."

A figure crawled out of the truck. It was a man. Or, at least, it had the size and large shoulders of a man, though Keo couldn't make out details in the darkness. The man *(?)* crouched and reached into the truck and was pulling something out (another person, maybe?) when he suddenly let go and staggered back, and two loud gunshots exploded across the empty city.

The man fired again and again and again.

Until he finally stopped, turned, and ran—*right at the fence in front of them.*

He leaped desperately and reached out for the top of the fence, just barely managing to get a handhold, and began to pull himself up. He was wearing slacks and a T-shirt. Definitely not one of those camo uniforms.

"He's not one of them," Carrie whispered next to him. "We should go help."

"It's too late," Keo said. He kept his voice calm, measured, and unyielding. "He's on his own."

"We can't do this. We have to help—" She gasped again when she saw them. "Oh my God. Oh my God..."

There was a tide of them, so many that at first he thought the night was actually moving, that it had somehow come alive. But no, it wasn't the darkness that had changed into a living thing, it was the living things *inside* it.

Ghouls. Hundreds, maybe more. Thousands?

He didn't know where they had come from, only that they weren't there one moment and then there was nothing *but* them. They swarmed toward the man, swallowing him up as if he were a fish trying to outswim the ocean itself. But he couldn't, and Keo heard the scream, the sound of gunshots that wasn't quite as loud as before because this time they were muffled by suffocating flesh.

Something grabbed onto Keo's arm. He looked down at Carrie's hand, her fingers digging into his skin. She stared out the window, face frozen in horror, the sight too frightening to comprehend yet too fascinating to look away from.

"Carrie," he whispered when he felt a trickle of blood along his arm.

She didn't hear him. Her eyes were transfixed by the amorphous blob moving outside the window, just beyond the flimsy hurricane fencing that would fall in a split-second if the creatures ever knew they were in there—

"Carrie," he said again, a little louder this time.

That did it. She looked over at him, then down at his arm, and quickly unfurled her fingers and pulled her hand back. "I'm sorry," she whispered.

"It's okay."

He slid down to the floor and took a handkerchief out from one of his pouches and wrapped it around his arm.

Carrie sat next to him, clutching her knees to her chest. She stared forward and rocked absently back and forth. "What were they doing out there, Keo? What in God's name were they doing out there?"

"I don't know."

"Everyone knows not to be outside at night. Everyone knows. Even Lorelei knows. *Everyone...*" Her voice trailed off.

Keo put his arm around her and pulled her against him. She came willingly, anxiously, and leaned her head against his shoulder. He could feel her trembling, and it wasn't because of the slightly chilly night air inside the RV.

"Go to sleep," he whispered. "It'll be better tomorrow."

"Will it?"

"Yes. I promise."

Carrie's body slackened against him and Keo tightened his grip on her with one hand, the other holding the MP5SD in his lap. He kept his eyes and ears open and knew he wasn't going to be getting sleep anytime soon. Which was okay. He was used to not getting a decent amount of sleep these days. Hell, these last few weeks and months…

He thought about Gillian, walking on a white sandy beach, barefooted. He wondered if she had given up on him by now or if she still looked off at the Gulf of Mexico every day, waiting for him to arrive, for him to finally make good on his promise.

"You promise me," she had said. *"You'll follow us to Santa Marie Island."*

"Yes," he had answered. *"I promise."*

"I'll wait for you. Just hurry."

That had been months ago. Did she still remember the exchange between them as vividly as he did? Was she even still waiting for him? There was only one way to find out.

First, though, he had to make good on a dead man's promise, and that meant going to Song Island…

CHAPTER 12

GABY

WHAT ARE YOU doing, you idiot?
Turn around. Right now. Run back to the door.
Do it.

And then what? There was no way out. No way to open the door. (She would need a doorknob for that.) No windows to climb out of, either. Not even a vent to crawl into.

They were inside the building, just like whoever had led them in here had planned it.

You're screwed. You're so screwed.

She must have sighed out loud because she heard clothes rustling as Peter, somewhere in the darkness with her, turned in her direction. Or she thought he did, anyway.

"You okay?" he whispered.

She shook her head before realizing he probably couldn't see, not with the flashlight beam in front of them instead of on her face. "I'm fine," she whispered back. "Keep the flashlight in front of us."

"Okay…"

They had been walking down a long, empty hallway toward another intersection for the last ten minutes, though it didn't seem as if they had gone very far from the alleyway door. That probably had something to do with the inability to see beyond the end of Peter's flashlight. She must have gripped and re-gripped the M4 at least a dozen times.

At least there was a window in front of them this time, even though it was covered up so thoroughly with thick slabs of wood that not a single sliver of sunlight managed to slip through. Peter's circle of light illuminated the occasional paintings of birds and ducks and flowers on the wall, along with end tables that held delicate-looking vases with nothing inside them.

It continued to be deathly quiet inside the building, not helped by the normal silence beyond the walls. It seemed as if she and Peter were the only two people still alive in the world at that moment, moving in the dark.

Moving in the dark...

She had trouble figuring out what kind of building they were in, much less its size. Maybe some kind of boarding house, judging by the hallways? Or an apartment building, maybe. Was there more than one floor? She hadn't come across any stairs yet, and there were no sounds above her. She had been so busy chasing Peter through the streets and then the alley that she hadn't taken even a second to take a look at the buildings around them. Her situational awareness, Will would say, had been utter shit.

How long had they been moving through the darkness? Twenty minutes? More? Less? Hard to tell. Hard to *breathe*.

But it wasn't hard to sweat. She was doing a lot of that. The thickness in the air was made worse by the boarded-up window. She assumed the rest of the windows in the place were similarly covered, which would explain the complete lack of ventilation. Peter was sweating almost as much next to her; she could tell because whenever they accidentally brushed up against each other—which was about once every other step—his sweat rubbed off on her exposed arm and vice versa.

They waited to hear from Milly or her captor the entire time. Noises, movements, as long as it was something *(anything)* that told them that she was still alive in here, somewhere. There was nothing except their dual labored breathing.

Crash!

Gaby spun around. Peter mirrored her action, his flashlight spinning a full 180 degrees until it exposed a small figure standing behind them.

A boy. Barely a teenager. His eyes bulged against the light, though he didn't look scared—just guilty, as if he had been caught doing something he wasn't supposed to. He wore dirty slacks and a

THE FIRES OF ATLANTIS 139

sweat-stained T-shirt, bright blue eyes looking back at Gaby through stringy brown hair that fell over his face. He couldn't have been more than twelve, and he stood next to one of the end tables, the vase on top of it having fallen down and broken on the floor.

The boy turned and ran.

"Wait, kid, stop!" Gaby shouted before chasing after him.

Peter was slow to react, but eventually his flashlight moved and the beam bounced up and down the dirty floor, erratically picking up the fleeing form. Gaby was close enough that she could see the kid—or at least, the outline of his shape—as he scrambled down the hallway.

Damn, he was fast. Which was becoming a theme today. First Peter had outrun her in the streets, and now this boy. Was she really that slow, or was the ammo really dragging her down? Maybe she should—

The boy glanced over his shoulder back at her while never breaking his stride.

"Wait!" she shouted. "We're not going to hurt you!"

If he heard her, he didn't care, because he soon turned right and kept going.

She grabbed for the corner and slingshot around the turn so she didn't have to slow down. The M4 bounced against her chest, all the magazines and equipment in Mac's web belt weighing her down like a ton of bricks. She was used to carrying the load, but not running full speed with them.

She glimpsed the boy's back up ahead. Jesus, he was fast. By the time she saw him again, he was already halfway to the side door, the same one they had come through earlier. Did he know it didn't have a doorknob?

"Wait!" she shouted. "Stop, goddammit!"

The boy didn't respond to her commands, but he was moving with purpose, as if he knew exactly where he was going. Which was where? More importantly, how had he gotten behind them in the first place? There was nothing back there…right?

Peter was still slow to catch up, and he was just now making the turn behind her when she was already ten feet up the hallway. She couldn't see where the alleyway door was, which wasn't a surprise since she couldn't see much of anything anyway. Finally, Peter's flashlight appeared, throwing a pool of light on the tiled flooring, peeling wallpaper—and up there, the boy again, racing like a little demon through the darkness.

The kid took another right turn.

Gaby primed herself to do the slingshot maneuver again, reaching out with one hand to grab the wall as she approached the corner—

Her vision—or what little of it there was—exploded as something smashed into her from the side just as she was starting to make the turn. She was flung across the narrow passageway and smashed into the wall on the other side and crumpled down to the cold, dirty tiled floor in a heap. She wasn't sure if most of the pain was coming from the blow that sent her flying, the impact, or from the M4 unwittingly digging into her stomach and chest as she slammed down on top of it.

She hurt. All over.

Was her back broken? That would explain why she could barely move her arms and legs. Maybe her spine had been snapped. Was that possible? She wasn't sure, but she couldn't breathe without feeling stabs of brutal pain, and it took every effort to turn her face away from the floor and to her side just so she could suck in a lungful of air.

Get up. Get up!

"Gaby!" Peter shouted, his voice not quite clear because he was still around the corner.

She managed to move her head, looked up, and saw the shape of a large figure standing over her. Was this what had hit her? A *man?* It hadn't felt like a man. It had felt more like a speeding train...or a dozen.

The man turned his head down the hallway as a bright beam of light splashed across his broad chest. She wanted to tell Peter to lift the flashlight up a bit so she could see the man's face, but she couldn't form anything that even sounded like words. Was she even still breathing? Of course she was. Wasn't she?

"Get away from her!" Peter shouted somewhere from the other side of the universe. "I'm warning you!"

Peter, just shoot him, you idiot.

The man's large legs backpedaled as Peter came closer, his footsteps getting louder.

Shoot him, Peter, shoot him!

She wanted to shout it out, but whenever she opened her mouth, the only thing that came out were short, labored gasps. God, her chest burned...

"Gaby—" Peter said, when there was the loud sound of something wooden hitting flesh and the bright beam of Peter's flashlight fell away from the big man hovering over her.

She heard the *clatter* of metal falling against the floor and rolling around before settling against a wall and illuminating the big man's shoes—well-worn Nike sneakers—standing next to her head.

Those same shoes squeaked as they moved past her and a thick male voice said, "Damn, you saw that, Harrison? *Bam!* She never had a chance."

"You idiot, get her weapons," another voice snapped.

"Oh, right," the first one said.

Gaby felt herself being turned over onto her back and rough, meaty hands pawing at the M4 and pulling it away. The same pair of hands groped her web belt and drew the Glock.

She was starting to get some semblance of feeling back in her arms and legs. She could move her fingers, which was a good sign. So she wasn't paralyzed after all. Right? God, she hoped so. She could only think of a few worse things these days, and being paralyzed was one of them.

"Did you kill her?" the second voice asked.

"Nah, I don't think so," the first one said.

"You don't think so?"

"She looks alive to me."

She was on her back, but Gaby couldn't see much of anything. These people seemed to be able to move around in the darkness just fine, though. She wasn't sure how that was possible. At least, not until a figure crouched next to her and leaned over. She looked up at a pair of round and green lights staring down at her.

Night-vision goggles.

"She's still alive," the man behind the goggles said. "She might wish she wasn't pretty soon, though."

More movement around her. There were at least four pairs of feet in the hallway now. Where did they all come from? And more importantly, how the hell did that kid get behind them in the first place?

So many questions. Pointless, stupid questions, because none of it mattered. Not to her. Not now.

It was a trap. A big, stupid, elaborate trap.

Milly. The kid in the hallway. The door that can't be opened.

And you fell for it like the big, stupid girl that you are.

Will would be so disappointed in you right now. So, so disappointed...

She struggled to keep her eyes open. The pain had become unbearable, and it was easier to lay still and absorb it, let it sweep over her entire body and think about how stupid she had been, how clueless, as she stumbled into their elaborate little trap.

Stupid. So stupid.

She found it easier to ignore all the voices around her. Ignore all the footsteps moving back and forth. Ignore the rough hands grabbing her and pulling her up from the floor as if she were a rag doll without any feelings.

There was the boy—the same one that had lured her down this path—as he played with her M4 rifle as if it were a toy. He looked up as they dragged her away, and she couldn't tell if that was innocence on his face or just a kid beaming with pride at a job well done.

◄▬▬▌ ▐▬▬►

SHE WOKE UP lying on her side. Her bones ached and she wasn't sure if she could still move her legs, but when she tried extending them, they seemed fine. She couldn't pry them apart, though, because they were pressed together at the ankles by a rope. Her head throbbed and opening her eyes to blinding LED lights didn't help.

She was inside some kind of basement. She could tell that much even while looking at it from the floor at an angle. The floor was cold and uncomfortable but that didn't stop her from feeling the sweat along her face, neck, and arms anyway. Someone had removed the camo jacket she took off Mac, and her web belt was gone.

And she was unarmed again.

Dammit.

A small figure was crouched in front of her. A girl, maybe fifteen, though it was hard to tell her age with the long, dirty-blonde hair covering half of her face, reminding Gaby of the boy from the hallway.

They use the kids. The bastards use the kids.

That immediately got her thinking of Milly. Where was she now? Was she fine? Safe? In danger? Given her own situation, Gaby thought it was probably too much to think that the girl was fine…somewhere out there.

The girl in front of her now was wearing cargo pants and sneakers and had a rifle lying across her lap. She recognized the weapon from the movies. Westerns with cowboys and Indians. Winchester? Was that what those were called? You cranked the lever to load a new round after you fired. Give her a carbine with a thirty-round magazine any day.

The kid had bright blue eyes that reminded Gaby of Lara. She was short, barely five feet, and there was a seriousness about the way she eyeballed Gaby that convinced her the girl meant business. Or, at least, she was putting on a hell of a game face.

She couldn't tell how large the room was because there was only one portable LED lamp in the entire place. It dangled from a hook along the ceiling, casting an ethereal halo around her, the girl, and…blood.

Why is there blood?

There was coughing next to her. Gaby pulled herself up from the floor and sat on her butt. It was difficult with the thick rope binding her hands, pulled so tight that it dug into her wrists. She looked to her right.

Peter was leaning back against the wall, his own hands bound behind his back. His face was red and purple and some other color Gaby didn't have a name for. His cheeks were puffy, his right eye swollen, and he peered back at her through fresh bruises that covered every inch of his face. His lips were cut and fresh blood clung to his sweat-stained shirt, and Peter didn't look as if he was breathing at all. There was surprisingly very little blood on the floor, which told her whatever had happened to Peter hadn't been inside here. He had been taken outside, then brought back…after.

"Peter, God, what happened?"

He shook his head, as if he wanted to talk but couldn't. His mouth quivered, and although she had only known him for a few hours *(has it only been half a day?)*, she felt something shattering at the pitiful sight of him. He looked in so much pain and his entire body seemed sapped of energy.

This wasn't the man who had rescued her this morning.

This man was...broken.

"Who did this to you?" she asked.

All he could manage was to shake his head. Barely.

She turned to the girl, still crouched in front of them, staring with those blue eyes. "Who did this to my friend?"

The girl stared blankly back at her.

"Can you talk?"

Nothing.

"My name's Gaby. What's yours?"

She saw something—a flicker—and was hopeful...for a brief second. Then it was gone in a flash.

Instead of replying, the girl stood up and took a step back, then another. She didn't look frightened, but there was a clear need to disengage herself.

She knows what's been happening. She knows what's going to happen. She's probably seen it before.

The trap. The boy in the hallway.

They've done this before...

The girl vanished into the part of the basement that was enshrouded in darkness, which happened to be most of it. There was a rustling of clothes as the girl settled back down. Then there was just silence.

"Gaby..." Peter whispered.

She looked over at him. Just saying her name seemed to have taken everything he had. "Peter, don't say anything. Just rest."

"Dangerous..."

"I know, Peter, I know."

He nodded—or tried to—and closed his eyes. He rested his head against the brick wall and seemed to drift off.

She looked around her again, taking in the room with a new eye, but didn't see anything remotely useful the second time around. Concrete floor, walls, and ceiling. Some kind of bomb shelter, maybe. Or just a really sturdy basement. She could imagine people in here surviving through The Purge and the months after. The door would probably be somewhere on the other side. And the only thing between her and it was a teenage girl with a rifle...

Her ears perked up at the sound of loud, grinding metal moving against concrete. Something opening. A door.

Then, footsteps approaching. Boots. Heavy combat boots.

A figure emerged out of the wall of shadows like some ghostly vision. But it wasn't a supernatural creature. It was just a man. He was large, in his early thirties, with short red hair and stubble that made him look older. He wore cargo pants and a sweat-stained T-shirt and had a Glock in a hip holster.

The man stopped in front of her and seemed to evaluate Peter for a moment. "I'm sorry about that," he said finally. "The boys got a little carried away." He looked at her. "My name's Harrison."

His voice sounded familiar.

The man in the night-vision goggles.

She remembered the bigger man, the one who had tackled her in the hallway, calling someone "Harrison."

"What did you do to Peter?" she asked.

"We had to be sure," Harrison said.

"Be sure of what?"

"What you were doing here."

"We're just passing through."

He nodded. "Yeah, that's what he said, too. I believe him. But we had to be sure you weren't dangerous, that's all."

"So you beat him half to death?" The anger rose inside her, surprising even herself. "While he's tied up? That takes a real man."

She expected indignation from Harrison, but instead he just shrugged indifferently. "You're not the first ones to come through here. And, like I said, there couldn't be any doubts. We had to be absolutely one hundred percent sure."

"So do you still have any doubts?"

"Not anymore."

"Then why are we still tied up?"

"We're sure there's just the three of you and you're passing through, but that's it." He went into a crouch and stared at her with dull brown eyes. "It's a dangerous world out there. The types of people who survive these days aren't to be trusted. You'd do the same in our shoes."

"Is that how you justify it?"

"I don't need to justify it. My people depend on me. Three strangers who I've never seen in my life aren't going to change what's worked for us for the last year." He stood up. "I'm sorry about your friend."

Bullshit.

"You can believe it or not," Harrison said, as if reading her thoughts—or maybe he just saw the look on her face. "It doesn't matter to me. Tomorrow we'll debate about what to do with you two—whether to cut you loose and send you on your way…or not. That's more than most people will do for you these days, so count your lucky stars. For now, sit tight."

"And the girl? Milly? What about her?"

"She's being taken care of."

"That's not what I asked you."

"She's staying," he said matter-of-factly.

"Did she tell you she wanted to stay?"

"No. But she's young, and she'll get over it." He looked behind him at the shadows—at the girl, who neither one of them could see at the moment but Gaby knew was still back there, watching and listening intently. "They all do, eventually. Kids are useful."

The boy in the hallway…

"What about him?" Gaby said, nodding at Peter. His eyes were still closed and it didn't look as if he had moved or made a noise—or even breathed—at all during her conversation with Harrison. "He needs medical attention."

"Like I said, it's a tough world out there," Harrison said, with all the sympathy of a lion feeding on fresh prey. "You gotta be strong to make it these days. It's up to him if he's walking out of here with you…or if you're going by yourself."

"You heartless *fuck*."

He snorted. "You should thank me. I could have found plenty of uses for you, too, but we're not that far gone yet." He leaned toward her and let his eyes bore into her soul. "But I can always change my mind later."

She didn't say anything. She also didn't look away. If he was trying to scare her, it wasn't going to work. At least, she hoped it wasn't working…

He stood back up. "Sit tight," he said with something that looked like a crooked grin before turning and leaving without another word.

She listened to the sounds of his heavy footsteps fading, doing her very best to control her rage. She wanted to leap up and lunge after him, bound wrists and ankles be damned, but that would have been stupid. He wasn't just bigger than her, she was also bound and hurt, and it wouldn't have taken much for him to beat her back down.

And she couldn't afford that right now. Beaten and bruised was okay, but she had seen what Harrison was capable of—saw it on Peter's face and God only knew what was happening under his clothes. If she wanted to save Peter, to save herself and Milly, too, she couldn't let that happen to her.

No, she had to bide her time, and that meant sitting still and listening to the same grinding metal moving on the other side of the room. Then the door slamming shut.

Finally, she allowed herself to breathe, to let all the anger flow away.

Stay alive. Nothing matters if you can't stay alive right now.

Gaby looked over at Peter again and felt a sickening knot in her gut. He looked even more awful than a few seconds ago, the discoloration around his face seemingly changing color at least a dozen times. The flesh around his right eye was now the size of a giant fist.

He's going to die. Tonight. Tomorrow morning. But he's going to die.

I'm sorry, Peter.

She sat back against the wall and closed her eyes and tried to think.

Options. What were her options?

Limited. But Will always told her there were options, some that were obvious, but most that were hidden. She just had to find them.

So what were her options right now?

She had to think.

Think!

Then it came to her.

The girl.

Gaby tried to find the small figure in the darkness, focusing in on where she last heard the girl moving around, the soft rustling of clothes.

"Hey," Gaby said.

There was no answer.

"Have you ever heard of Beaufont Lake?"

Still nothing.

"There's an island on it. Song Island. It's safe. There's even a hotel—"

The girl stepped out of the blackness with her head cocked slightly to one side. She had moved so quickly that Gaby was momentarily taken by surprise. There was a fleck of interest in the girl's eyes. "You said an island?"

"Yes," Gaby said. *Be careful. Don't spook her.* "Song Island. Have you ever heard of it?"

"No." She glanced behind her, as if trying to decide how to proceed. Maybe she was afraid of Harrison finding out she was even talking to the prisoner.

Easy does it. You have her attention now. Don't lose it…

"It's safe there," Gaby said. "There's a hotel. Electricity. Hot showers. Frozen food. And ice. When was the last time you had ice?"

The girl didn't answer.

"I can take you there," Gaby said.

The girl looked over at Peter, then back at her. "It's near here?"

"It's not far. A day's drive. Maybe a couple of days on foot."

The girl looked back into the shadows behind her a second time. With her hair out of her face, she was a lot younger than Gaby had first thought. Thirteen, maybe, like Milly.

"I know you don't want to be here," Gaby said. "I know you're just staying because you don't have a choice."

The blue eyes seemed to confirm everything Gaby had just said. Or was she reading the kid all wrong?

God, please don't let me screw this up.

"You can come with us," Gaby said. "With Peter and me. And Milly, too. Did you see Milly? She's about your age."

"They took her," the girl said.

"We can get her back and leave here, and you can come with us."

"To the island?"

"Yes, to the island."

Gaby did her best to control her rising excitement. She could almost imagine the girl's brain working, absorbing the information. But she had to tread lightly. The girl was taking a risk. She knew that much. Harrison had left her here because there was no way Gaby or Peter could escape in their condition. Certainly Peter had no more fight left in him, and it was hard for her to do anything when she couldn't even walk.

Even so, it bothered her that he had just left a little girl behind to watch them. Were the adults all busy somewhere with something else? Maybe there were guards on the other side of that door Harrison had gone through twice now. Maybe—

Concentrate on the girl! She's your opening! Seize it!

"What's your name?" Gaby asked.

"Claire," the girl said.

"I can take you with me, Claire. You'll be safe on the island."

"Because the bloodsuckers can't go there," Claire said.

"Yes," Gaby said. "How did you know—"

Claire whirled around and disappeared into the shadows.

"Wait, Claire," Gaby said, but the girl was gone. She wanted to shout but was afraid of making too much noise in case there were guards outside the basement door.

She sighed and leaned back against the wall, crestfallen. All her hopes of escaping with Peter and Milly died inside her and all she could do was look at Peter, asleep—or somewhere between asleep and dead—next to her.

I'm sorry, Peter. I'm not good at saving people. Nate could have told you that.

And Matt.

And Josh…

There was the quick patter of footsteps just before Claire reappeared out of the darkness. The rifle was slung over her back, looking absurdly big against her slight frame. There was something else, too: Claire was clutching a small black microcassette voice recorder.

Gaby opened her mouth to ask what was happening when Claire shushed her by holding up her hand. The girl crouched in front of her and pressed the play button on the recorder and held it out as a familiar voice came through the tiny speaker:

"To any survivors out there, if you're hearing this, you are not alone. There are things you need to know about our enemy—these creatures of the night, these ghouls. They are not invincible, and they have weaknesses other than sunlight—"

Lara! It was Lara's voice!

"—One: you can kill them with silver. Stab them, shoot them, or cut them with any silver weapon, and they will die. Two: they will not cross bodies of water. An island, a boat—get to anything that can separate you from land. Three: some ultraviolet light has proven effective, but flashlights and lightbulbs with UV don't

*seem to have any effect. We don't know why, so use this information with caution.
If you're hearing this message, you are not alone. Stay strong, stay smart, and
adapt. We owe it to those we've lost to keep fighting, to never give up. Good
luck."*

The message ended, and Claire clicked off the recorder. "You
said an island. Not far from here?"

Gaby nodded anxiously. "Yes. It's called Song Island."

"And she's right? The creatures can't go there?"

"Yes. She's right. They can't."

"She's not lying? You promise?"

"She's not lying. I promise." Then, "Where did you record that
from, Claire?"

"Donna has a small radio that she listens to every now and then.
It's our father's; he used to listen to talk radio on it. Donna thinks
the government might still be out there, but I told her it wasn't. A
few nights ago, we heard this. It keeps changing channels, so I
decided to record it just in case we couldn't find it again."

"Did you try to radio them back?"

"Can't. You can only pick up stuff with the radio."

"Do the others know about it? Harrison?"

"Donna tried telling him, but he doesn't believe it." She
frowned. "I think he doesn't care. He likes it here. The way things
are." She looked at Peter. "We don't, though."

"Who is Donna?"

"My sister." She glanced back at Gaby and narrowed her eyes a
bit. "How do I know the woman on the radio isn't lying? How do I
know *you're* not lying? Everyone lies. Especially adults. Harrison lies
all the time. He uses the kids to watch the roads and trick people.
Like he did with you."

"I swear I'm not lying, Claire."

Claire watched her intensely, blue eyes squinting as if she could
read Gaby if she stared long and squinted hard enough.

She's too young to look so old.

"And you'll take me with you?" Claire asked finally. "To the island? Swear it?"

"I swear it," Gaby said.

"And Donna?"

"Donna, too, if she wants to come."

Claire nodded, seemingly satisfied. She pocketed the voice recorder.

"Do you keep that with you all the time?" Gaby asked.

"Uh huh," Claire nodded.

"Why?"

"I don't know. I guess it gives me hope." She stood up and flicked another quick glance back at the shadows behind her. "What now? How do we get out of here?"

"Are there people on the other side of the door? Guards?"

"No. They left before you woke up."

Why? What's happening out there? Where are all the adults?

All those questions raced through her mind, but she forced them away. No guards. That was all that mattered. There were no guards outside the door!

"I need my guns, Claire," Gaby said. "Do you know where they took them?"

The girl shook her head. "No, but there are others."

"Others?"

"Guns. There are lots of guns on the other side of the door. How many do you want?"

"How many you got?" Gaby said, grinning back at her.

CHAPTER 13

WILL

"HOW MANY?" DANNY asked.

"A dozen, give or take," Will said.

"How many is 'give or take'?"

"A dozen or so?"

"Remind me to never let you do my taxes, Mister CP-Or So."

They were crouched just beyond the tree lines, watching the trucks roll by and up the road—Route 13, according to a sign they had passed earlier—and toward the city of Dunbar.

Lucky number 13.

The trucks were of various sizes and colors, some beat up, others brand new. They included a shiny silver F-150 that was hauling an orange and white U-Haul truck in the middle of the pack. Will glimpsed a couple of white stars and the state of Louisiana on the sweat-drenched uniforms of a couple of the men sitting in the back of the Ford as it flashed by him.

Josh's boys.

What are they doing here?

"Fourteen," Will said when the last truck had passed.

"You think they're tracking Gaby?" Danny asked behind him.

"I don't think so. Way too many cars for just one girl."

"Maybe our boy Josh is in one of them. Kid's in love. You remember what that was like? With the hormones going nuts? I wouldn't put it past him to commit this kind of force to recapturing her. Sounds like something a teenager would do."

"You're assuming he thinks she's still alive."

"Why wouldn't he?"

"The cave, remember?"

"Oh, right. I forgot about the cave."

"It was this morning, Danny."

"It's hot out here. My brain turns to soup in the heat. Give me a break."

Will grunted, then glanced down at his watch: 3:14 P.M.

Three hours until nightfall. Gonna be close...

"Did you see anything I might have missed?" Will asked.

"Like what?"

"Like something that'll tell us where they were coming from, or going?"

Danny thought about it, then shook his head. "Can't say, but then again, I don't know the area. You?"

"Nope."

"So, I have a question."

"Did you raise your hand?"

Danny raised his hand. "So, I have a question."

"What is it?" Will smiled.

"How do you think the ghouls know to avoid those betraying buggers now that they're no longer wearing the hazmat suits and gas masks?"

"Probably the same way they knew not to attack the guys in hazmat suits and gas masks in the first place."

"The whole hive mind thing. Someone gives the command and it goes out to the infantry. Someone high up. Like your buddy Mabry."

"Or one of his acolytes."

"Like, for instance, your ex-ghoulfriend Kate?" Danny grinned at him.

Will sighed. "Don't rub it in."

He sat back down on the hard ground and looked up Route 13. Dunbar wasn't a particularly big place, but like most country cities, it was spread out and separated into districts, with the suburbs circling the main business area. The whole place sounded dead at the moment, and Will could still hear the engines of the soldier's caravan moving away from them, fading with every passing second.

"Gaby probably went in there," Will said.

"Likely," Danny nodded. "If she's still alive…"

"Those soldiers seemed to think so back at the cave. So let's go find out, one way or another."

"Not like I got anything else to do."

Will got up and moved through the woods, keeping parallel to the road on his right. Danny followed, but only after making sure no one had sneaked up behind them while they were waiting for the cars to pass.

Gaby and her two companions had clearly been heading for Dunbar since leaving L15 behind. He had picked up multiple tracks moving alongside Lake Hillman and in this direction. *If* one of those prints had belonged to Gaby, that is. He still wasn't sure, but the odds were in their favor. This was Gaby, after all. If he knew one thing about her, it was that the teenager was a survivor.

"How're your wounds?" Danny asked after a while.

"My guts are still where they should be. Thanks for asking; I didn't know you cared."

"I don't, but Lara made me promise."

"You scared of Lara?"

"Hell yeah, she's five-five of balls of fury. I told you she's running the island now, right?"

"You mentioned that once or twice."

"Yeah, you really know how to pick them, buddy."

"What does that mean?"

"First Kate, and now Lara. I guess you have a type."

"Is that right?"

"Ball busters," Danny chuckled.

Will grinned. Danny probably had a point there.

THEY PASSED A train track, then a slew of old houses with peeling paint and rooftops that didn't look strong enough to withstand a harsh wind blowing in the wrong direction. There were too many open spaces, forcing them to dart from building to building as they followed the motor oil trails of the collaborator caravan up Route 13 toward the center of Dunbar.

After about an hour of skirting around the open, keeping to the same stretch of road but never on it, they finally sidled up to an orange building called Gaine's Meat Market near the very center of what Will surmised was the busy business section of town. A streetlight swayed back and forth in front of them, while half a block along Highway 190's four-lane stretch the trucks and ATV had made camp in the mostly barren parking lot of a strip mall. Heavily-armed men milled about the vehicles, doing…what?

Will and Danny leaned out from the corner of Gaine's with binoculars and watched the soldiers for a moment. The U-Haul sat almost in the center of the parked vehicles, but no one had pulled open the back doors, which further piqued Will's curiosity. It couldn't have been people inside, because trailers didn't have air conditioners and it would be suffocating under the heat.

"You think it's a coincidence they're here at the same time as us?" Danny asked.

"I'm not a fan of coincidences," Will said.

Danny sniffed him. "Not a fan of hygiene, either, from the smell of it. When was the last time you showered?"

"It's been a while."

"I can smell that."

"Stop sniffing me and take a look at the U-Haul."

"I am," Danny said, peering through his binoculars. "What about it?"

"They haven't opened it yet."

"You think there's something worthwhile in there?"

"Gotta be. Why haul it around?"

"Maybe it's dirty laundry. Or a washer and dryer to wash those sparkly uniforms. Look at them; they almost look like soldiers. How precious."

"Where would they plug the washer and dryer in?"

"Details, details."

"Look at the way they parked it. In the center."

Danny chuckled. "Isn't this what got you in trouble in the first place? This need to know everything about everything?"

"I'm just curious."

"Yeah, well, you know what they say. Curiosity killed the curious idiot."

"I'm not sure that's quite the saying."

"Details, details."

The men *(wannabe soldiers)* began spreading out along the streets, moving in pairs of two. He counted ten, then twenty—ten pairs in all. They were searching the buildings around them while a dozen or so remained behind with the caravan. It was a mixed bag of men— old and young, fat and skinny, and some sported ponytails or unruly long hair that stuck out underneath ball caps.

Try getting away with that in Basic Training, boys.

Weekend warriors or not, the fact that each man was carrying military-grade firepower made them just as dangerous as any enlisted man he had been around. They were wearing sidearms and he glimpsed the barrels of M4s, a couple of AK-47s, and one was hauling around a Belgian FN FAL battle rifle. Will wondered where he had gotten that. The weapon that people called "The Right Arm of the Free World" was a rare sight these days.

"Heads up," Danny said.

One of the pairs had come out of a Shell gas station in front of them and was moving up the street in their direction.

They pulled back from the corner.

"What's the call?" Danny said.

"Find out what they're doing here and if Gaby's still around."

"How are we going to do that?"

"Quietly."

"Oh, that's cute. When did you get so cute all of a sudden?"

"Must be the extra bullet holes," Will said.

"So that explains the whistling noise I've been hearing," Danny said.

WHAT'S IN THE U-Haul?

There was a gas tanker directly below them, and Will wondered how much fuel was left inside it and if it would be worth it to somehow drive it down to Song Island as an emergency reserve.

Hope for the best, prepare for the worst.

A tanker full of fuel would definitely help in a worst-case scenario. Of course, getting it there was the problem. That was, if they could get it working in the first place, which wasn't a given these days with cars sitting around collecting dust and rust for the last eleven months.

He fixed his attention back on the camouflaged pair walking on the street below them, carbines cradled in their arms.

Will and Danny had circled back around and headed up to the second floor of Gaine's Meat Market, using a catwalk in the back, but only after they had witnessed the soldiers searching it and, finding nothing, moved on. The last thing they wanted was for Josh's boys to show up unexpectedly and get them involved in a gunfight. That would bring everyone down on them, as well as stopping their search for Gaby in its tracks. They couldn't afford that. Not now. Will didn't know for sure, but he felt as if she was close. Now all he had to do was find her before someone else did...

He glanced at his watch: 4:15 P.M.

Two hours and change before nightfall. So was this it, then? Had the soldiers only stopped at Dunbar to spend the night? Did that mean they didn't have protection after nightfall the way they used to when they wore those hazmat suits? Or was he right and the ghouls just knew to ignore them?

Dead, not stupid.

"They coming back?" Danny asked behind him.

Will shook his head. "Don't think so."

"Good. Oh, by the way, I call dibs on the chair." Danny had settled down on a big, comfortable-looking black felt couch in the corner of the room and was stuffing his mouth with beef jerky from a bag of Oberto.

"How many of those do you have?" Will asked.

"Wouldn't you like to know." He threw his boots up on an ottoman and leaned back. "Turn on the AC, will ya?"

"I'll get right on it."

There was enough light coming through the curtains over the closed window in front of Will to see with, but it did nothing to help with the heat or the lack of circulation. Opening the window for some wind was a no-go after the soldiers had searched the room earlier. There was a chance one of them might remember that the window was closed if they should walk back in this direction. It was a small risk, but there was too much at stake to do something that stupid just because he couldn't stand a little *(or a lot of)* sweat.

Will glanced to his left, down the state highway and back toward the strip mall. He couldn't see much of anything from this angle. The soldiers left behind hadn't moved from their spots as far as he could tell, and the ones that had fanned out in pairs had begun to drift back one at a time as the hour dragged on.

What's in the U-Haul?

"You're still thinking about it, aren't you?" Danny said behind him.

"What's that?"

"The U-Haul."

"Nope."

"Let it go. We're here to find Gaby and get the hell outta Dodge. Keep your eyes on the prize, Kemosabe."

"You're not curious?"

"Of course I'm curious. But I'd also like to get home to Carly. This little adventure is fun and all, but I'm frankly tired of walking around with sweaty balls."

"Good to know, good to know."

"I'm just sayin'. A man needs more in life than a wet scrotum."

Will caught a flicker of movement out of the corner of his eye. It came out of nowhere and forced him to take a step back from the window before sliding against the wall.

A second later Danny was standing across from him with his rifle. "Company?"

"Not the kind I was expecting."

Danny followed Will's gaze to the rooftop of Tom's Billiard, a one-story building across the street from them. A lone figure in jeans and a black T-shirt was hurrying across the gravel floor toward the edge, where he went into a crouch and peered up the street with a pair of binoculars. He was looking at the same strip mall parking lot.

The one with the U-Haul…

What the hell is in there?

"Now how'd he get up there?" Danny said.

"Probably a ladder in the back."

"Not one of Josh's boys, from the looks of his outfit."

"Maybe a local."

The man unclipped a radio and raised it to his lips and spoke into it.

"I guess he's not alone," Danny said. "What are the chances that Gaby's with him, that she's drinking lattes somewhere around here?"

"Captain Optimism," Will smirked.

Danny chuckled. "Hey, we're due for a little luck."

"Gaby said that, too. Then she disappeared."

"You and your half-empty glasses. Can't you think positively for once?"

The man stood up and jogged back the direction he had come—the other side of the rooftop—where he leaned over the edge.

"What's he doing now?" Danny said.

"Taking a leak?"

"Should we be watching that?"

"What, you're not confident enough with your manhood?"

"Hey, the kid could be packing a cannon."

"Is that what Carly calls it?"

"She calls it lots of things. Paul Bunyan, her favorite glow stick, the nightstick to end all nightsticks..."

The man was pulling up a second figure from the side of the building. This one was bigger, with a round gut, and also wearing civilian clothes. He was carrying a faded green duffel bag over his shoulder.

"Oh, look, he's got a BFF," Danny said.

"Look at what he's carrying."

"About fifty extra pounds. So the poor guy has an eating disorder. Give him a break."

"No, over his back."

"Oh, yeah." Danny looked for a moment, then, "Looks like they're up to no good, these two."

"Yep."

"Should we stop them?"

"Nah. The enemy of my enemy is my friend. Besides, I really wanna know what's in that U-Haul."

"What if it's people?"

"People?"

"Like captives."

That hadn't occurred to him. "Good point."

"Really?"

"Hey, even the sun's gotta shine up a dog's asshole at least once."

"And I got a pretty bright asshole, too."

"Good to know, good to know."

The two men moved back over to the edge overlooking the

street. The fat one put down the duffel bag and unzipped it. He reached in and took out something long and metal. Will knew what it was before the sun glinted off the green camouflage barrel of the M40 rifle. Not the original M40, but a later model. Likely an M40A3 from the looks of it.

The fat man handed the Marine sniper rifle over to his friend, who took it and extended the tripod underneath the barrel before lying down on the rooftop on his stomach. He settled in behind the long scope and positioned his shoulder against the stock.

The kid's done this before.

"It's all fun and games until someone breaks out the peashooters," Danny said. "Then it's eyes and balls getting popped. Never good."

"They got friends, too."

Will nodded down the street, where two more men had appeared and were leaning out from the side of Tom's Billiard. One had an AR-15 with an ACOG scope and he was zeroing in, while the second one stood behind him peering down the street with binoculars while talking into a radio.

"Oh boy," Danny said. "Looks like we done run right into a good ol'-fashioned gunfight at the OK Corral. Question is, we wanna get involved in this?"

"Let's steer clear and see who comes out on top. The Clantons, or Doc Holliday and the Earps."

"Which one is the Clantons and which ones are the Earps, though?"

"Hell if I know. Does it matter?"

"Hey, you're the one who made the half-assed analogy. You tell me." Danny peered up and down the street for a moment. "You think there are more of them hanging around?"

"Gotta be. Whoever's coordinating this seems to know what they're doing. Probably a couple more snipers on a few more rooftops. If they're locals and this is their city, they'll know all the good spots, including all the ins and outs of the surrounding buildings."

"Ambush."

"Looks like it, yeah."

"Can't say I'm feeling sorry for the Earps."

Will grinned. "Josh's boys are the Earps?"

"They have the uniforms and the lot down there kinda look like outlaws, what with their sweat-stained shirts and AR-15s and whatnot."

"Let's go with that, then."

The sniper on the rooftop fired, the gunshot impossibly loud in the still city. The shot was still echoing when the man with the AR-15 below them began sending rounds up the street, the *clink-clink-clink* of his bullet casings flickering into the air and dropping one after another like loud metallic raindrops on the sidewalk.

"I wish we had popcorn," Danny said, dipping into another bag of Oberto and pulling out a big stick of jerky. "But I guess this'll have to do."

"Seriously, how many of those things do you have?"

"Wouldn't you like to know."

The gunfire continued unabated, the steady *pow!*, pause, *pow!* of the sniper rifle banging out a tune with the rapid *pop-pop-pop!* of the AR-15 as its melodic companion. They were clearly shooting at something, and Will wished he could see what, but his angle was all wrong.

He thought about moving, going to find another window in the building, when someone up the street unleashed with another rifle and the brick wall the two men were hiding behind flew apart. One of the men ducked behind cover, while the second one calmly pulled himself back and reloaded.

Then all hell broke loose, and the all-too-familiar rattle of dozens of assault rifles firing at the same time on full-auto filled the air. It was like rolling thunder, sweeping up and down the streets of Dunbar, Louisiana.

And all the while, Will's thoughts kept going back to the parking lot. To Josh's soldiers. And that one vehicle they seemed to be surrounding like precious cargo.

What's in the U-Haul?

CHAPTER 14

GABY

CLAIRE RETURNED TO the basement about ten minutes after disappearing up the stairs. She came back with a tall blonde girl, the two of them racing down the steps as if they were afraid of being caught. Which, Gaby guessed, wasn't too far from the truth.

The new girl looked all of seventeen and fresh-faced. Gaby couldn't remember when she last looked that innocent. The girls were definitely sisters—blonde, slender, and one of these days (probably soon) Claire was going to sprout and become just as tall as her sister. In the time it had taken them to come back, Gaby could tell Claire had already filled Donna in.

"When are we leaving?" Donna asked as soon as she climbed down the stairs.

"Now," Gaby said.

While waiting for the sisters, Gaby had time to take stock of their surroundings. She and Peter were being kept in the basement of a Veterans of Foreign Wars building somewhere in the center of Dunbar. Someone had converted the room into a bomb shelter, with two sections—the interior where she and Peter were being kept and an exterior portion with the stairs. There was plenty of light out here thanks to LED lamps hanging from hooks. Nearly thirty percent of the space was filled with weapons and ammo, with the rest reserved for nonperishable canned goods, cases of bottled water, plastic red cans of gasoline, an entire corner of propane tanks, and stacks of MREs in crates.

Gaby had grabbed one of the M4 rifles off the rack as soon as she saw them. The carbine had a nice pistol grip under the barrel and a decent, if not great, red dot scope mounted on top. She'd worked with worse all day, so this was definitely an upgrade. She had also snatched up a web belt and began stuffing the pouches with magazines. She was still choosing and adding supplies, shoving them into tactical packs and feeling better with every additional pound, when the girls returned.

"Grab Peter," she told them.

Claire and Donna helped Peter up from the floor and he hung between them, looking even paler and weaker than when Gaby had first managed to shoulder him into the outer room. His right eye was almost completely shut now, the skin around it giving off an abnormal appearance. Donna looked uncomfortable being this close to Peter, but she didn't say anything.

Gaby picked up a heavy-duty nylon bag from the floor and stuffed food and water into it before handing it to Donna. "Can you carry this?"

Donna nodded, taking the bag with her free hand. "It's either me or Claire, right? I mean look at her. She can barely carry herself."

"Hey, I can carry myself just fine," Claire said. "I'm still growing."

Gaby turned back to the gun racks and picked up an additional Glock, this one smaller than the one she already had in her hip holster, and held it out, butt-first, to Donna.

The girl looked at the gun, then at her. "I don't know how to use that."

"You want a rifle instead?"

"I don't know how to use one of those, either."

Gaby glanced over at Claire and the rifle slung over her back.

"Claire's been using that since we were kids," Donna said, picking up on Gaby's unasked question. "Our dad taught her."

"And he didn't teach you?"

"I didn't want to learn. I wasn't a tomboy like her."

"You were just lazy," Claire said.

"Keep telling yourself that, daddy's girl," Donna said.

Gaby stared at them for a moment. If she had any doubts they were actually sisters before, that would have gone away after listening to them. Only siblings bickered like that. She was pretty sure they weren't even aware of it because it came so naturally at this point.

"I'll take it," Claire said, nodding at the gun in Gaby's hand. "You can teach me how to use it."

"Later," Gaby said.

She shoved the spare Glock into her tactical pack, then flicked the safety off the M4. She walked over to the stair landing and glanced up at the closed door at the top. She stood perfectly still and listened but couldn't hear voices or sounds of any kind from the other side. Definitely no telltale signs that Claire and Donna's arrival had triggered some kind of an alert from upstairs.

"How many men did Harrison leave behind?" she asked.

"None," Donna said. "Just the women and children. Harrison took all the men to the north side of town."

"What's happening there?"

"Some soldiers showed up."

"Soldiers?"

"They looked like soldiers, anyway, but I don't know what soldiers would be doing around here. I didn't even know they were still around."

Because they're not. They're Josh's people.

She remembered the town guards in their nice and clean uniforms. She knew they weren't actually soldiers, just collaborators playing dress up. Not that it mattered now. What was important was that Harrison had marshaled all his forces to deal with it.

What was that saying? *"The enemy of my enemy is my friend"?*

"Are the women up there armed?" Gaby asked.

"Some of them," Donna said, before adding with some concern, "You're not going to shoot them, are you?"

"Only if I have to."

"They're good people. You don't need to hurt them."

"I won't if I don't have to." Donna didn't look convinced, but Gaby didn't care at the moment. "What's Harrison going to do? With the soldiers?"

"He's going to attack them."

"Why?"

"Because that's what he does."

"He's done it before," Gaby said. It wasn't a question.

"He says this is our city, that we have to fight to keep it."

Like with Peter, Harrison?

Gaby looked back and stared at the three people standing behind her. Really, *really* stared at them.

They looked back at her intently, anxiously.

Except for Peter, who hadn't looked any better since she handed him off to the girls. Despite their size, Donna and Claire were holding Peter up surprisingly well, but she could see Claire grimacing with the heavy weight. Peter was limp between them, as if he would fall and never get up again if they let go even just a little bit.

At first she had thought Harrison's people had only beaten Peter around the face during the interrogation (because Harrison *"needed to know for sure"*), but she knew better now. When she had helped him up from the floor, he had flinched with every contact regardless of where she touched him. And walking from one side of the basement to the other had been an ordeal she wasn't sure he would even survive.

At the moment, Peter was looking back at her with his one good eye. His right was never going to open again. He seemed to know what she was thinking, and he nodded. Or, at least, he motioned with his head in something that resembled a nod. It was mostly just a slight tremble.

"It's not just the broken ribs," he said. His voice was very low, coming out almost a whisper, because that was all he could manage, and even that seemed to take a great deal out of him. "I'm bleeding internally, too. This is the end of the road for me, kid."

"Peter..."

"My right eye's gone. I can barely see out of the left. I can't walk without feeling like every bone in my body's going to break apart at any second. I don't think I'll even make it up those stairs."

"What are you saying, Peter?"

"I want you to go. Take the girls, find Milly, and go."

He struggled against the sisters then somehow managed to untangle himself from them. They looked on worriedly as he stumbled over to the nearest wall and sat down. He let out a loud sigh, actually managing to smile back at the girls.

"Go," Peter said. "I'll be all right."

"You're going to die down here, Peter," Gaby said. She was surprised by her own matter-of-fact tone.

Damn. When had she gotten so cold?

He shrugged back, almost indifferently. "I'm thirty-six. You're just kids. This is your world now. *Go.*"

"Peter…"

"I'm not having this conversation, Gaby. Go, now, before it's too late."

"Too late for what?" Gaby was about to say when the first gunshot reached them as a slight echo—a wet, barely noticeable *pop* noise.

She knew it hadn't come from the hall above them. It originated from across the city, and it was quickly followed by a burst from an assault rifle. Then there was another shot and suddenly the city of Dunbar exploded with gunfire, the noise so intense that Gaby and the sisters found themselves standing perfectly still and listening to it, transfixed, for almost an entire minute.

Gaby finally snapped out of it. "How many soldiers are out there?" she asked Donna.

"I didn't see all of them," Donna said, "but it couldn't have been that many if Harrison thinks he can take them."

"How many men does he have?"

"Twenty-five."

Gaby glanced up at the basement door, this time with more urgency. "Is Milly out there, Claire?"

"Yes," Claire said.

"Are you sure?"

"I saw her."

"Okay."

Gaby looked back at Peter. He was holding his hand under his chin and there was blood in his palm. More red liquid coated his bloated, pale lips, and some trickled down his chin.

"Peter," she said softly.

He wiped the blood off on the floor and met her eyes. She saw resoluteness in them. A courage she didn't know he even possessed. "Get Milly, Gaby, and get her to the island. Please do that for me."

She took a step toward him. "Peter…"

He held up his hand to stop her. "I'm going to stay down here for a while. Rest." Then, he cracked a grin. Or tried to, anyway. "Enjoy the show for a while. Sounds like they're really having a blast, huh?"

She gave him a half-smile back. It was the only response she could come up with.

How did you say good-bye to a man whom you barely knew, but

THE FIRES OF ATLANTIS   167

who had saved your life? And now she was going to leave him down here to die, because she knew there was no way Peter was going to get out of the basement.

Not alive, anyway.

A loud, suddenly intense burst of *pop-pop-pop* from outside drew their attention again. The gunfire seemed to be coming at a faster clip now as more people were adding to the chaos. Twenty-five of Harrison's people were out there, according to Donna, and how many of Josh's soldiers?

All those people, all those guns, gathered in one place...

But she noticed something very clear about it, though: it was all coming from the *north* side, just like Donna had said. That left the rest of the city as a viable escape route, with the south in particular being, at this very moment, wide open.

"Go," Peter said. "Go now, Gaby. Save Milly, please."

Gaby nodded. She looked at him one last time, then turned and headed back to the stairs. "Let's go, girls."

Donna and Claire followed.

Gaby took the steps one at a time, her eyes fixed on the door, the M4 at the ready, the fingers of her left hand tightening around the pistol grip. She wondered if Peter was looking after them, if he would scream for her to stop at the last moment, just before she reached the exit. She didn't know if she wanted him to or if she was afraid he would.

Could she keep walking if he began calling her name? Could she just abandon him down here to die?

The hellacious back and forth continued outside, indifferent to what was happening with them in the basement at the moment. Those combatants out there didn't know and didn't care that a good man was dying, and that they *(me)* were going to leave him down here because he had become useless.

And in this new world, useless was the same as dead...

<hr />

THE BASEMENT DOOR opened up into a back hallway that joined with the main area of the VFW hall. There was another door to their left leading to some kind of office. The sound of gunfire, no longer constricted by the basement's concrete walls, was much louder and harder to ignore up here.

Gaby closed the door behind them and looked over at Donna. The girl wore shorts and a plaid long-sleeve work shirt, the sleeves rolled up to her elbows. She had on a belt with a knife in a sheath but no other weapons. Donna seemed to be carrying the bulky supply bag just fine—at least, for now. Gaby would have to keep an eye on her. She didn't want to lose anything in that bag, depending on how long it was going to take them to get to Song Island. If they couldn't locate a working vehicle along the way, it was going to be a hell of a walk.

Claire still had her lever-action rifle, which she gripped tightly in both hands. Gaby couldn't tell if the girl had ever used the weapon before (or at least, on a real live person), but she certainly held it as if she had and was willing and ready to put that experience to work if need be. Gaby wasn't quite sure if entrusting her life to a thirteen-year-old-girl and her seventeen-year-old sister was madness or desperation.

Oh, who are you kidding. It's definitely a lot of both.

The three of them stood very quiet for a moment and listened to the gunfire raging back and forth from the other side of the city. She couldn't tell who was winning. Hell, she couldn't even tell how many sides there were at the moment. There could just be two—Harrison's and Josh's—or a dozen, for all she knew. She was sure of one thing, though: it was definitely coming from behind them—not too far away, but not close, either.

"We need to head south," Gaby said. She glanced down at her watch: 5:09 P.M. "We're going to be cutting it pretty close, but we can't stay here tonight or we might never leave. So let's get Milly and get out of here."

She headed up the hallway toward the opening. Donna and Claire followed silently behind her.

"It's just the women and kids?" Gaby asked.

"Last time I was up here, yes," Donna said behind her.

As it turned out, the last time Donna checked wasn't recent enough, because when Gaby stepped out of the hallway and into the large main area of the VFW hall, the first thing she saw was a tall man sitting on a chair next to the twin front doors all the way across the room. He was cradling an AK-47 and looked bored, his head craned to one side as he listened to the gun battle outside with an almost wistful expression on his face.

Oh crap, Gaby thought when the man launched up from the chair at the sight of her.

But he had moved too fast, and instead of getting a grip on his assault rifle and putting it to use, he instead fumbled with it for a split-second. It was just long enough for Gaby to lift the M4 and shoot him once in the belly. The man stumbled back into his chair, tipping it over. He looked more stunned than hurt.

She shot him a second time, and he crumpled to the floor, the rifle clattering away.

There were kids in the hall, and they began screaming. The instant increase in decibel was so startling for everyone, including Gaby, that for a moment even the sound of gunfire from outside the building was drowned out by the cries.

Move move move!

Horrified faces turned toward her as Gaby rushed out of the hallway, the M4 in front of her, sweeping the room, looking for a target, anything that even resembled danger. Her left hand tightened around the grip as her right eye settled behind the sight.

The large hall was built to accommodate hundreds of people at one time, though at the moment there were only a couple dozen inside. Half of them were kids, the other half adult women. They all looked unarmed—or at least, no one reached for a weapon—when they saw her.

That is, except for the woman sitting at the bar with a shotgun resting on the countertop next to her. The woman was reaching for the weapon when Gaby swiveled the carbine around and stared at her. The woman froze and for a brief second, Gaby was sure the woman's hand would keep going.

But it didn't. Thank God it didn't.

Instead, the woman took her hand away from the shotgun as if it had become hazardous to her health.

"Sit down," Gaby said.

The woman did as ordered.

"Gaby!" a voice shouted.

Milly scrambled up from the floor across the room where she had been sitting with some kids and rushed toward her. A woman made a grab for her, but Milly managed to slip through her hands.

The thirteen-year-old practically barreled into Gaby and grabbed at her waist, almost knocking her over. It was a good thing Milly was barely eighty pounds soaking wet, or she might have sent both of them tumbling to the floor.

She put a hand around the girl's neck and hugged her back briefly. "You okay?"

"I'm okay," Milly said. "Where's Peter?"

"Peter's gone."

"'Gone'?" She squinted up at Gaby. "Gone where?"

"He's gone," Gaby said again, hoping the girl would understand. Milly did. Or she understood enough to frown.

"This is Claire and Donna," Gaby said. "We're leaving this city, okay?"

Milly nodded back mutely.

The kids had stopped screaming, but some were still sniffling. The women held them, fear and anger flashing across their faces as Gaby and the three girls moved toward the doors. They, like the windows around them, were reinforced with slabs of wood, with burglar bars on the outside.

"Keep moving to the door," Gaby said. She picked up the shotgun from the bar counter as they passed it by. The woman glared at her but didn't say anything. "Move from that stool and I shoot you, understand?"

The woman didn't respond, but she "understood," all right.

"Claire, the rifle," Gaby said.

Claire rushed forward and picked up the AK-47 from the dead man. She already looked ridiculous lugging the Winchester around, but now with the assault rifle too, the sight of her was almost comical.

Gaby turned around and backpedaled after the girls. She scanned the faces looking back at her. Some of the children were still crying, and others had their faces buried in the women's chests.

"Tell Harrison not to come after us," Gaby said loudly.

No one responded.

Donna had already led Claire and Milly outside. Gaby walked backward, careful not to step over the dead man (or into blood spreading out like tentacles from under his still body) and slipped through the opening. She was instantly reassured by the warmth of the bright sun *(It's still light out, thank God)* splayed against her back.

Donna pushed the doors closed as soon as Gaby stepped out-side. "What now?"

"We head south. After that, we'll figure it out. You lead the way."

She tossed the shotgun down on the sidewalk and took the AK-47 from Claire. They jogged across the street after Donna, who was already moving swiftly ahead with the heavy supply bag slung over one shoulder. She was definitely stronger than she looked.

Gaby glanced back at the VFW building, expecting the doors to open and the adult women to rush outside, guns blazing. Maybe they had hidden the guns somewhere and were scrambling for them now. Or maybe they had run to the basement and gotten the rifles down there. She wondered how they would react when they saw Peter bleeding to death down there. Did they know that was part of Harrison's MO? Claire knew, and so did Donna. She had a hard time believing a group of adult women didn't know, too.

I'm sorry, Peter. I'll take care of Milly for you. I promise.

The VFW hall's doors remained closed behind her, so she spun around before stealing a quick look down at her watch: 5:15 P.M.

Too close. We're cutting it way too close...

THEY LEFT THE streets as soon as possible in case they were being pursued. Fortunately, both Donna and Claire seemed to know where they were going. The two sisters led them through alleyways, then empty buildings, stores, and even diners. Whenever Gaby thought they had run into a dead end or cul-de-sac, the girls found a side or back door or knew a way around a fence or wall.

Gaby didn't know the path, but she knew where they were head-ed: south.

That was all that mattered. South took them back to Song Is-land.

South took her home.

South.

They spent almost thirty minutes steadily making progress to-ward the city limits, and the entire time Gaby could hear gunfire continuing unabated behind them. The battle seemed to just keep going and going, growing in intensity with every passing minute. She kept expecting it to die down as the fight wore on, but it never did.

Gaby kept her eyes on the sky. There were no clouds, and the sun was still bright. She guessed they had an hour, tops, before nightfall. Probably less than that. More like fifty minutes. A part of her wanted to start looking for a place to hide, but they couldn't afford that. Not yet. *Not yet.*

"The soldiers," Gaby said to Donna as the teenager guided them through a series of empty buildings near the edge of the city. "Have you ever seen them before?"

"Not these ones," Donna said. "But I've seen others come through in the past. Not soldiers, but guys with guns. Some of them wore those weird CDC suits."

She means collaborators in hazmat suits.

"They would search for supplies and keep going," Donna continued. "We have early warning systems all over the city, so when someone shows up, we know right away. Usually we can hear the vehicles coming for miles. Harrison decides how we react—either hide from them, or if he thinks they're easy prey, then lure them into a trap."

Donna glanced over at her almost apologetically when she said that last part.

Like with Milly, and the boy in the darkened hallway...

She wondered whatever happened to the boy. She hadn't seen him back at the VFW hall. Then again, she had been moving so fast, looking for adults with guns, that it wasn't as if she had actually paid attention to the kids.

"What makes these soldiers different?" she asked.

"Harrison says they're here for something and we have to stop them. But he always says that when he wants us to do something dangerous. It's always 'we this,' 'we that.' He's good at rallying the troops."

"But not you."

Donna shook her head. "Harrison's a bullshit artist. He's out for himself, and he's just using the rest of us to do it. Claire and me, and a lot of the others back there, just go along with it because it's safer in there than out here."

Gaby nodded and didn't ask anymore. She didn't blame the sisters for siding with Harrison. Donna was right. It was easier to survive in there, even under Harrison's thumb, than out here alone with just the two of them.

I would probably do the same.

They stopped to rest inside a Sonic Drive-In and Gaby looked out the front windows at train tracks. There were a couple of houses scattered on the other side of the streets and more businesses to the left and right of them. She listened, but the only sounds were the distant echoes of gunshots behind her.

Donna pointed at a two-lane highway with wide shoulders that ran across the tracks. "That's Route 13. It's got other names, but we just called it Lucky 13."

"Lucky 13?" Gaby said.

"You know, teenagers. Anyways, it leads straight through the countryside. Lots of fields, farms, that kind of stuff. On the other end is Interstate 10."

"How far?"

"About thirty miles. It'd be easier and faster if we had a car."

"You know where to get one that still works?"

"Harrison has garages around the city where he stashes working vehicles and gasoline."

"Back in the city?"

"Yeah."

"Any of them close to us now?"

Donna thought about it, then shook her head. "No, sorry. I should have told you about them earlier."

"It's my fault for not asking you sooner," Gaby said. Then, "What's between here and I-10?"

"Not a whole lot, unless you count farms. Guys from town used the highway for drag racing because it's essentially thirty miles of nothing. Sometimes the farmers complain, but most of the time they don't care. The Dunbar cops don't bother going out that far, either."

Gaby looked over at Milly, crouched silently next to her. The girl was glancing over her shoulder. At first Gaby thought she was listening to the fading gunfire but quickly realized Milly was turned in the direction where she assumed Peter was at the moment. Gaby didn't want to tell her that after all the back alleys and side streets and zigzag turns they had taken, Milly was looking in the wrong direction.

Instead, she put a hand on the girl's shoulder. Milly pursed her lips into an attempted smile. "Peter wanted me to get you to the island," Gaby said. "And that's what I'm going to do, okay?"

Milly nodded back in silence before looking away again.

"Okay," Gaby said. "Let's go. Once we're out of the city limits, we need to start looking for a place to stay the night, so keep your eyes open."

The others nodded.

Gaby lifted her M4 and slipped out of through the Sonic's glass doors. The three teenagers followed closely behind her with no one saying a word.

Behind them, the shooting continued in sporadic bursts, but now there were noticeably long lulls between sustained volleys. The gunfight was almost over. Gaby wondered who was winning before deciding that she didn't care. They could all go to hell as long as she was on her way south…

THE DARKENING SKY was like a physical heaviness trying to bury her along the shoulder of the road. She pushed on with the girls because there was no other choice. They couldn't turn back now. It was much too late for that. They had to keep going forward.

South.

Toward home.

Claire walked with the Winchester in her hands, looking every bit like a soldier. Her sister Donna remained up front, leading the way, even though there wasn't really much in the way of navigation. There was only forward. Milly kept pace alongside Gaby but was flagging with every passing minute. Pretty soon, the girl was going to ask to sit down to rest. Gaby kept waiting to hear those words and was surprised she never did.

Maybe she's tougher than I give her credit for.

The shooting behind them had mostly faded with time and distance. There were still occasional echoes, but it took a lot of effort to actually pick them out of the silence now. Instead of focusing on what was back there, she had been concentrating on what was around them. Or, to be more specific, what *wasn't* around them.

Gaby searched for a building, a house, or a store. Hell, even a

THE FIRES OF ATLANTIS   175

shack. Someplace where they could get out from under the open skies.

Too close. We're cutting it too close…

Donna wasn't wrong when she said there wasn't much between Dunbar and I-10. Route 13 was barren and low to the ground. The highway was surrounded by vast, flat, and empty scenery, and they were still too close to town to spot any farmland, not to mention the houses (shelter) that would be sitting on them. There were also no vehicles in sight. She hadn't spotted a car since they left the city behind twenty minutes ago.

"Donna," Gaby said. "We need to find shelter."

Donna nodded and glanced around them, turning a full 360 degrees. Gaby could practically see the gears turning inside the girl's head.

"Donna," Gaby said. "We need a place."

"I'm thinking," Donna said.

"Think faster," Claire said, sneaking a look at the darkening clouds above them.

"Shut up already," Donna said. Then, after a while, she turned to Gaby. "Okay, I know a place. It's not far from here, but you might not like it." And at Claire, "You're definitely going to hate it."

"I can take it if you can," Claire said.

"We'll see."

"Does it have a basement?" Gaby asked.

"It sort of has a basement," Donna said.

"Sort of?"

Donna shrugged. "We don't have a whole lot of choices, do we? It'll be dark in half an hour."

"Okay," Gaby nodded reluctantly. "Take us there."

Donna led them over to the ditch, then down into it and back up again onto the other side. They followed her across flat, undeveloped land for five, then ten minutes. With every step they left the highway behind, but there was no way to leave the graying sky above them. It chased them wherever they went, undeterred and inevitable.

DONNA WASN'T KIDDING when she said they might not like the place she had in mind.

It was a cemetery.

Milly's face grew paler as they neared the wrought-iron fences that surrounded the place. They walked alongside it for a minute or so before entering through the open front gates with a big sign that read, "Dunbar City Cemetery."

Donna seemed to know exactly where she was going.

"How far?" Gaby asked.

"Not too far now," Donna said. She glanced over at Claire. "So?"

"So what?" Claire said, putting as much defiance into her voice as possible. Gaby thought she wasn't entirely successful.

"You scared yet?"

"No."

"We'll see."

Donna led them off the main pathway and across the grass, all four of them moving with obvious urgency. No one had to say it. Not Gaby, and not Donna. Even Claire and Milly knew that time was running out for them. If it wasn't the skies above them, it was the tombstones jutting out from the weed-infested ground, along with the long-dead flowers and personal keepsakes scattered nearby.

How appropriate would it be if everything ended here tonight? It would be poetic if it weren't so damn depressing.

Gaby pushed the thought away and concentrated on the steps ahead of her instead, doing her best to ignore all the reminders of the dead and the grieving from their loved ones around them.

"How much farther?" she asked Donna.

"There." Donna pointed at a white structure flanked by two large trees that looked like ancient sentries that had been there long before man and would remain there long after.

Oh God. She wasn't kidding.

It was a crypt, and it was made of either concrete or white marble. She had a hard time distinguishing the material under the fading light. It wasn't particularly big, maybe the size of a small backyard shack. The front entrance was shaped into an arch and a rusted-over metal gate covered the front doors. "Evans" was engraved at the top in Roman alphabet.

"You've got to be kidding me," Gaby said.

"Hey, it's the only thing I could think of," Donna said. She turned to her sister. "So? You still not scared?"

"No," Claire said, though this time she didn't have a prayer of making it sound the least bit convincing.

"How are we going to get inside that thing?" Gaby asked.

"There's a key," Donna said.

"You have a key to a crypt in a cemetery?"

"No, but I know where they keep it. Well, these guys I know." Donna hurried over to one of the trees and crouched in front of it. She groped the ground around its base, pushing aside blades of overgrown grass. "It should be buried around here somewhere…"

Buried. She just said 'buried' in a cemetery.

Gaby waited for Donna to give her a hint that she had used 'buried' on purpose, a pun to break the ice. But she didn't.

She looked over at Milly, whose face had grown deathly pale during the walk from the front gates to the crypt. Even the usually taciturn Claire looked just a little bit disturbed as they watched Donna rooting about the grass.

"Eureka!" Donna said. She stood up and brushed dirty hands on her shorts. "I thought someone might have taken it for a moment."

She gave Gaby a half-terrified, half-elated grin before walking to the crypt and sticking a large old key into the lock and twisting it. The gate unlatched with a loud *craaaank*, like giant metal cogs grinding against each other. The painfully brown metal bars squeaked loudly as Donna pulled at them.

Gaby gave her a hand. It was heavy, like pushing boulders.

"You guys, um, played here?" Gaby asked.

"Not really, well, played," Donna said, grunting with the effort while trying to hide a bit of embarrassment at the same time.

She means they made out here. And…other stuff.

With the gate open, all Donna had to do was push the thick doors of the crypt inward. These, surprisingly, moved without much effort. They looked inside, using what little light was left to make sure the place was empty. Not that Gaby expected it not to be. Who would be hiding in there, with the doors locked? The place gave off the smell of an enclosed space that had been sealed for almost a year—maybe even longer.

It was surprisingly roomy inside, with a large rectangle-shaped concrete block in the center. There were none of the cobwebs or scampering bugs she always envisioned invading crypts like these. It looked amazingly well-kept, the people who owned it clearly having shown great care with whoever lay inside the coffin at the moment.

She looked back at Milly and Claire. They stared back at her, perhaps hoping she had changed her mind. "Let's go, girls."

The two girls stepped inside first, Milly groping the walls for support. They went all the way into the back, keeping as much distance from the coffin as possible. Gaby and Donna pulled the heavy metal gate closed after them. Donna stuck her hand out between the bars and locked it back up. She had clearly done all of this before. They stepped into the crypt and pushed the doors closed from the other side.

Gaby was prepared for it, but as darkness enveloped her inch by inch, she felt dread rushing down her body anyway.

We're inside a crypt. We're going to hide from the night inside a pitch-black crypt.

God help us.

Somewhere in the darkness, Milly might have sniffled. Then Gaby heard a *click* just before the beam of an LED light splashed across the walls, then illuminated the coffin and Donna, who was standing nearby. Claire was holding a small flashlight in the back.

"Where did you get that?" Donna asked.

"It's the same one I always carry with me," Claire said.

"Since when?"

"Since forever."

"Let me have it."

"It's mine. Get your own."

Donna sighed at Gaby, as if to say, *"See what I have to deal with?"*

Gaby smiled back. This very human moment was a welcome absurdity when they were trapped—voluntarily, too—inside a crypt with a dead body. How old was the body, anyway? And was it a man or a woman? Maybe they should find—

I'm going to throw up.

She unslung her pack and weapons, needing to move, to be doing something so she wouldn't entertain more idiotic thoughts like opening up a coffin to find out who was inside it. Claire helpfully shined her flashlight over so Gaby could see what she was doing.

She pulled out the bags of MREs and handed the girls one each. "Be careful with them. They can be pretty messy. Claire, help everyone with the flashlight. Why don't we all sit together so Claire doesn't have to move around too much?"

They moved to the very back and sat down on the floor. Claire's flashlight appeared as Gaby opened her MRE.

At least the room didn't smell too bad. There was a musty aroma, but none of the death stench she was expecting. Did all crypts smell this...nice?

"You, uh, played in here?" Gaby asked Donna.

"It's really not that bad," Donna said, again with just a shade of embarrassment. "It doesn't smell at all. You'd think a room with a dead body would smell, right?"

"It's probably the coffin. It keeps the body from the elements, so it doesn't...you know."

"I guess."

"No one ever found you guys out?"

"Nah. We always cleaned up after ourselves and we only came here at night. There's not a lot of people here at nights."

Gee, I wonder why.

"Where'd you get the key?" she asked. She didn't really need to know, but she felt it necessary to stave off the silence for as long as possible.

"It's a copy," Donna said. "This guy we know used to work here one summer. He made a duplicate and after he went off to college, it sort of became a thing within our group. Anyone who wants to use it can. Pretty cool, right?"

If you like making out in crypts while surrounded by the decaying bodies of other people's dead loved ones, then yeah, it's pretty cool.

She said instead, "I guess so."

"I mean, there's not a lot to do in Dunbar," Donna said.

There's less to do now.

"You guys lived in the city?" she asked.

"We had a farm about two miles on the other side of town. Dad, me, and Claire. Our mom passed away a few years ago."

"I'm sorry."

"Yeah, well, she was the lucky one, as it turned out. I guess we've always kind of been stuck around Dunbar our whole lives." Donna paused for a moment to eat, the sound of chewing and the (grateful) aroma of food filling the crypt. "I was really looking forward to getting out of town, too," Donna said after a while. "I guess better late than never."

They didn't say much after that, and there was just the sound of everyone eating.

After a few minutes of silence and darkness, Gaby heard Milly crying softly next to her. She put an arm around the girl and was glad Claire hadn't shined the flashlight at them to see what was happening. She knew enough to give them their privacy.

Gaby squeezed Milly's shoulder tightly and thought of Peter.

Probably dead now, back in the VFW basement. If not from his injuries, then when Harrison went back and found him. Or if not Harrison, then whomever he was fighting with and had killed him and his men.

There was another soft *click* from somewhere in the darkness, then Lara's familiar voice, slightly muffled by the recording, reverberated against the hard walls around them:

"To any survivors out there, if you're hearing this, you are not alone. There are things you need to know about our enemy—these creatures of the night, these ghouls…"

Gaby smiled and thought of Song Island.

South leads home.

Go south, young girl…

CHAPTER 15

WILL

"LOOKS LIKE THIS party's going to go all night," Danny said. "Are you sure our invitation didn't get lost in the mail?"

"Anything's possible," Will said.

"This is why you should always tip your friendly neighborhood mailman during Christmas. That, or invite him in for tea."

"I always knew you were a teabagger."

"I'll try anything once. Or thrice."

The gunfight had raged on for the better part of two hours, with Will and Danny content to watch (and listen) from the safety of Gaine's Meat Market. The sniper on the rooftop of Tom's Billiard across the street had left, replaced by two men with AR-15s who fired up the street at the soldiers, the *clink-clink-clink* of their empty brass casings pelting the street below them like never-ending raindrops. The two down on the sidewalk were also gone, and a woman with a ponytail firing calmly with an M4 had taken over.

Every now and then Will saw figures in civilian clothes running up and down the streets that were visible from his limited angle behind the window. They were almost always moving in pairs, all of them well armed, and he often saw them talking into radios. Which told him these weren't complete amateurs. Either they had been well trained or they had been out here surviving long enough to know how to fight as a unit.

Or, well, a unit-ish.

He was never going to mistake them for a Ranger battalion, that was for sure. Like Josh's soldiers, these were civilians playing at being weekend warriors. That didn't make them completely incompetent, but he had seen real soldiers, and these weren't them.

About an hour ago, they heard footsteps moving on the rooftop above them. The man (or woman) stayed up there for almost thirty minutes, pouring fire up the street. Eventually, he (or she) left, too, maybe for a better position elsewhere. The locals were moving around like busy bees, never staying in one place for too long.

The phrase *"The enemy of my enemy is my friend"* flitted across his mind throughout the two hours, but he had learned not to put too much stock in strangers with assault rifles. They could turn on you at a moment's notice, especially given the number of fighters he saw just outside his window alone. From the intensity and spread-out nature of the chaos, there were more of them across the city. The fact that they were fighting the ghoul collaborators from multiple angles was further proof these were dangerous people not to be underestimated.

And maybe the enemy of my enemy is also my enemy...

"You getting flashbacks, too?" Danny said after a while.

Will smiled across the window at him. "Just a little bit."

They were intimately familiar with the whole scenario playing out before them. The fact that the faux soldiers were clearly outnumbered and outmatched, fighting in a city they didn't know, facing what, from all appearances, were people who called this place home. People who knew all the angles and how to get to all the rooftops.

It's Afghanistan all over again. Minus the camels.

"It's almost just as hot, too," Danny said, pulling at his shirt collar for effect. "The only thing missing? That wonderful goat smell. Of course, you're making up for it."

"Glad to be of service."

"I'd settle for you taking a shower once per century."

"Yeah, well, can't do anything about that now."

Danny snorted. "Guess not. Who you think's winning, anyway?"

"If I was a betting man, I'd put money on the locals."

"That seems kind of wrong."

"You think?"

"I mean, I'm no fan of Josh's boys, but still... Uniforms and everything. I'm partial to a man in uniform, but don't tell Carly."

"Mum's the word."

The fight continued, gunshots like firecrackers, the insistent *pop-pop-pop* without end. But this gunfight had been going on for some time, which meant the soldiers were dug in, the strip mall parking lot they were calling a base likely providing plenty of protection. Was that on purpose? Had someone chosen that spot for its defensive capabilities? Probably not. He hadn't found the collaborators to be especially good at tactics. Then again, Kellerson had been pretty smart, and Will was quickly learning not to underestimate Josh.

Not that the fight was going to last for very long either way. Well defended or not, the soldiers were at a great disadvantage. They were pinned in, and sooner or later Dunbar's fighters would get just close enough to finish it. He could already see the locals surging up the street, taking over new buildings as they pushed forward. Already, the fight had almost completely abandoned their window, and they were now listening instead of watching what was happening.

Will glanced down at his watch: 5:52 P.M.

"They're cutting it close," he said. "It'll be dark soon."

"Speaking of which, we got a place to go when it's night-time time?"

Will looked around the room. He had been thinking about that, too, especially since it was becoming obvious they weren't going anywhere anytime soon. "This room looks decent. Barricade the door and window. Push comes to shove, there's the bathroom."

"Hide in a bathroom with you all night?" Danny wrinkled his noise. "Talk about torture." Then, "The kids still going at it out there? I can't see them anymore."

"Sounds like it."

"I guess they really, *really* want to kill Josh's boys."

"Or maybe they're just really curious about what's in that U-Haul, too."

Danny smirked. "You and the U-Haul. Remind me never to ask you to help me move."

Will peeked up at the darkening skies above them. Patches of shadows were spreading and the sun was dipping in the horizon like a giant orange ball. "Thirty minutes before nightfall. Give or take."

"Checked in with your girlfriend on the radio yet?"

"Aw, hell, I almost forgot. Thanks for reminding me—"

The *crack!* of a rifle cut him off.

It had been a few minutes since he last heard or saw anyone firing nearby, with the fight having progressed up the street, so the shot made Will instinctively jerk his head away from the window just as a neat hole appeared in the glass pane in front of him. The bullet kept going and embedded itself into the ceiling across the room. The point of impact had been so clean that the glass somehow managed not to break apart.

Will was twisting backward and almost fell. He turned his rifle into a crutch at the last second and just barely managed to stay on his feet.

Danny was already spinning away from the wall on the other side of the window and was firing down, shattering the glass panes as he squeezed off two, then three shots at whoever was down there.

Danny stopped shooting and pulled back. "You hit?"

Will reached up and wiped at a trickle of blood on his forehead. A small cut, barely a graze. "I'm good, I'm good."

"You don't look so good." Danny grinned, adding, "Oh, wait, never mind. That's just how you normally look."

"Tell me you got him, pretty boy."

"I dunno. He was pretty fast."

A loud series of gunfire from outside was proof that Danny had missed. The remains of the window exploded, showering them with pieces of glass. Danny yelped and dived to the floor before crawling away on his hands and knees. Will backed away as fast as he could, the *zip-zip-zip* of bullets slashing through the air around him.

Through the sound of shooting, Will picked up the unmistakable noise of pounding footsteps rushing toward them from the other side of the door. He spun around, dipped to the floor on one knee, and lifted his M4A1.

He waited one second, two—

The doorknob started to turn.

He fired, stitching the door with the carbine on full-auto. Left to right, then right to left, putting bullets in the walls around the door as well as the door itself just in case there were more than one and they were waiting in a stacking formation. That's what he and Danny would do if it were them out there.

He heard the telltale sounds of falling bodies and the clatter of weapons against wooden floor.

"Go go go!" Will shouted.

"Gee, and here I was going to take a nap!" Danny shouted back.

Danny scrambled up to his feet and raced to the big comfortable felt chair and snatched up his pack and slipped it on. He took aim at the door as Will jogged over and did likewise with his own pack. It was stuffed with emergency rations and ammo, but the rest of their supplies were in two other, thicker bags still on the floor.

The shooting behind them from outside the window had stopped.

"Radio?" Will said.

"I got it," Danny said. "Plus, some more Oberto."

"Seriously, how many of those did you bring?"

"That's for me to know and eat, and for you to look on enviously. The rest?"

"Ditch them."

Danny stood up and moved toward the door. He threw it open and Will slipped out into the darkened hallway first, stepping over two crumpled forms in jeans and T-shirts. Local fighters. He was careful to step around their pooling blood, too.

The stairs were down the hall in front of him, and he glided toward them now, listening for more footsteps besides his own and Danny's. They weren't really just going to send two into the building after them, were they? If so, whoever was in charge was either very confident or was strapped for manpower. After two hours of slugging it out with Josh's soldiers, maybe the locals had suffered their own share of casualties. He could only hope.

Either way, visibility was minimal without any source of light inside the narrow hallway, but he was lucky his eyes had adjusted to the state of semidarkness inside the room while he was watching the show outside for the last few hours. Somewhat, anyway.

He heard it: The muffled sounds of someone speaking through a radio floating up from the first floor.

The building was split into two sections—the store below and living quarters on the second, accessible only by stairs in the back of the property. To get to it, you had to move through a kitchen with linoleum tiles.

He heard the squeaks of tennis shoes racing across those same tiles now.

Will made it to the top of the stairs and looked down just as two figures appeared below him with rifles aiming up in his direction. They fired as soon as he poked his head out into the open, and the newel directly in front of him shattered, slivers of wood flashing around his head like missiles.

He pulled his head back, then stuck the M4A1 out into the open space and squeezed off a burst. He didn't expect to hit anyone, but scattering them was just as good. He was rewarded with more squeaking noises as the two below scrambled for cover.

Danny was crouched behind him, keeping a safe distance. "How many?"

"Two."

"Not so bad."

"They have position on us and they can afford to wait us out."

"That's bad."

"Any other way outta here?"

"There's a catwalk behind us that might work."

"Go for it," Will said, leaning around the staircase again. He glimpsed a head mirroring his action at the bottom of the stairs and opened fire, shredding a part of the handrail but missing the patch of sweaty dark hair completely.

He pulled back and listened to more muffled voices communicating back and forth below him. He couldn't quite make out what they were saying, but it sounded as if someone was giving an order and someone didn't want to follow it.

Weekend warriors.

Danny had moved toward the other end of the hallway and Will backpedaled after him now, reloading his rifle as he went. He kept both eyes on the stairs in front of him the entire time, ears open for the familiar squeaking of shoes. He stopped briefly when he stepped into a pool of blood, cursing as he changed directions to circle around the dead bodies.

"We good?" he asked, just loud enough for Danny to hear.

"Getting good," Danny said. A window opened and there was a brief silence for about five seconds, then, "You waiting for an invitation?"

Will turned around and ducked under the open window and stepped out onto the metal catwalk. Danny was already racing down the stairs below him, toward the familiar back alley of Gaine's Meat Market. Will knew it was getting darker from the second-floor window, but actually being outside and underneath the blackening skies told him he had underestimated the approaching nightfall.

Shit. This is gonna be tight…

He had been hoping they could hole up inside Gaine's until morning. It wouldn't have been an ideal situation, but given the gunfight outside and the need to find Gaby, who was probably still in the city somewhere (he hoped, anyway), leaving Dunbar now wasn't in the plan.

All that was out the window now after being discovered.

And now the sun was almost gone. What else could go wrong?

Cutting it close. Way too close.

A flicker of motion caught his attention just before a shadow appeared over one of the handrails down the hallway. Will flicked the M4A1's fire selector to semi-auto and waited patiently.

One second…

…two…

…three…

A head appeared up the stairs, peeking out curiously.

Will shot the man square in the forehead and watched the body disappear back down the stairs, the *thump-thump* of a full-bodied adult male sliding his way down each step until he finally landed at the very bottom.

"You coming?" Danny called from below.

Will slung his rifle and raced down as Danny pulled security in the alleyway. From back here, the only path was forward into the street. Will hopped the last few meters and landed behind Danny.

"Took you long enough," Danny said.

"Great view, I was just enjoying myself."

"Yeah, well, save that for your own time, buddy." He glanced at his watch and his face darkened. "Gotta be scootin', scooter. We're gonna be SOL in a few minutes unless Mister Sun decides to stay put."

"That ain't gonna happen."

"Way to be optimistic."

"Fuck optimism," Will said, slipping his rifle free, and together they moved toward the mouth of the alley.

The *snap* and *pop* of gunfire from up the street continued, though they were now coming at a much slower pace. Will imagined whoever was in charge of the locals were caught at two fronts—he and Danny down the street, and Josh's soldiers further up. The fact that they had only sent, as far as he could tell, three men was proof of that.

Then again, you know what happens when you assume...

Danny peeked his head out and scanned the street while Will looked back up at the catwalk behind them. There was still one more man up there, though it was probably a fifty-fifty chance he would continue onto the second floor alone. The smart move would be to backtrack and wait for reinforcements. He wondered how smart (or suicidal) the man was.

"Anything?" Will said.

"Looks clear," Danny said.

"You sure?"

"Pretty sure. Well, mostly sure."

"Good enough."

Quick movement as a head poked out of the window above him. Will fired, but the man pulled his head back inside just in time, and Will's bullet harmlessly chopped loose some pieces of brick.

Suicidal, then.

"That's our cue," Danny said, slipping out onto the sidewalk.

Will followed and they turned right, moving away from the fighting.

"We need to find shelter," Will said.

"Thanks for that suggestion. And here I was gonna run around like a moron for the next thirty minutes. What would I ever do without you?"

"I'm glad you finally realize that."

"It's Lara's fault. She's been filling my head with how great you are and shit. Frankly, I think she's delusional."

Danny turned left and darted across the empty street, then skirt-ed around a large six-wheel gas tanker with "Shell" written across its side parked in the middle of the road. Will was following him when—

Ping! A bullet ricocheted off the side of the tanker and disap-peared into the wall of a coffee shop.

"Incoming!" Will shouted, ducking and sliding behind the large vehicle for cover.

"Ya think?" Danny said.

Bullets slammed into the other side of the tanker, the *ping ping ping!* ringing out one after another after another. More rounds missed the vehicle entirely (how that was possible given its size, Will couldn't fathom) and slammed into the sidewalk and street around them instead.

Danny dropped, hugging the road, then peered underneath the small space that separated the gas tanker and asphalt.

"How many?" Will asked.

"Three," Danny said, rising back up.

"How far?"

"Sixty meters, give or take. Now would be a good time to flex some of that mush you call brain muscle."

Will was about to do just that when he realized that his shadow was gone and the suffocating heat had lessened noticeably. He didn't have to spend a precious second or two looking at his watch, either. An inky black coating had fallen over the streets and the last trace of sunlight had dissipated almost entirely.

Ah, shit...

"We gotta get out of the streets," Will said. "Danny—"

"Bar," Danny said, nodding at a building called Ennis further up the sidewalk. "They always have basements in bars, right? To store the beer and kegs and peanuts and all that good stuff?"

"You better hope so. Go!"

Danny went first and Will followed, ignoring the persistent *ping ping ping!* from behind him.

Ennis looked intact, and the door opened without a fight. The tables and counters had been put to use recently, and Will guessed the beer tap was either empty or had gone bad. Old bags of peanuts were scattered about the place, and someone had been using the custom-made coasters as Frisbees.

Danny flicked on his flashlight. He had slung his rifle and drawn his Glock, moving cautiously toward a back hallway. Will kept pace behind him, keeping his eyes on the front door. He could barely see the street anymore with the gloom that had fallen outside.

"The best laid plans of mice and men..."

The locals had stopped shooting, probably realizing Will and Danny were no longer at the gas tanker. Either that, or they had taken a look at the sky and realized for themselves what was about to happen. You didn't survive for this long without knowing when to run and when to stick around, especially in the evenings. More than he and Danny, it was entirely possible the locals had simply lost track of time. Anything and everything was possible during the heat of battle, and the locals had been fighting Josh's soldiers for a few hours straight now.

There was a metal door at the end of the hallway, the smooth surface glinting against Danny's flashlight. "Nice," Danny said. "Looks like a tough little hombre."

"Does it open?"

"Of course it opens. Why wouldn't it—" He grabbed the lever and twisted it, but the door didn't budge. "Aw, shit."

"No?"

"Locked."

"That's not good."

"I'd say it's fucking awful myself, but 'not good's' good too, I guess."

It had gotten even more miserably dark in front of Will, and in the same instant he noticed that, he also heard a sudden burst of gunfire and something else. Something loud and sharp, like a knife slicing through the heart of the city.

Screaming.

"You hear that?" Will said.

"I got ears, so yeah," Danny said, his voice dropping slightly.

Will scanned the hallway and saw two rooms. One was marked "Office," the other "Bathroom." He moved toward them and tapped on the office door. Solid wood, which was good. He knocked on the bathroom door and got back a dull, satisfying thud.

Metal. Much better.

"Bathroom," he said, and pushed the door open just as he caught movement coming from the front of the bar out of the corner of his right eye.

Will spun and squeezed off a burst as the first ghoul lunged at him. He shredded it, but even as it collapsed, he was already opening fire at the dozen *(two dozen?)* that followed it inside the building, little more than moving black silhouettes coming in through the windows and doors, scrambling over chairs and tables because that was apparently faster than running around them.

"Shenanigans!" Danny shouted just before he opened fire next to Will, the loud blasts of his Glock just a bit too close for comfort.

Their silver rounds tore into the creatures, ripping through yielding flesh and shattering the windows and pecking at the walls in the background. The last of the ghoul wave fell in front of them, caking the floor with flesh and bone and black, oozing blood.

Will quickly ejected the magazine and slapped in a new one. Danny was reloading the Glock behind him. They moved on instinct, without thinking.

Then he saw it: *a pair of bright blue eyes* staring at him from outside the bar.

It stood tall, like a human, outside in the falling night. He thought he would have gotten used to the sight of them by now—or, at least, not be as surprised to see them anymore. That wasn't the case, though, because they were such an anomaly. In a world overrun by undead things, these blue-eyed bastards remained freakishly supernatural in his mind.

There was something different about this one. The second he saw it, Will knew that it wasn't Kate or even Mabry, the only two blue-eyed ghouls he had ever seen. No, this was another one entirely, which prompted him to think with more than just a little bit of dread. *Jesus Christ, how many of these fuckers are running around out there?*

It stood proud and tall while the other ghouls flooded across the streets and up the sidewalk and crouched and kneeled around it like children worshipping at its holy feet. There had to be hundreds of them outside now, but since the initial attack, the rest hadn't come into the bar yet. They were forming a wall, their gathered mass blotting his view of the streets entirely until the only thing he could see was pruned black flesh moving under the growing darkness.

Will moved fast—faster than he had ever moved before, faster than he thought even he was capable of moving. He snapped the rifle up and squeezed off a single shot without the benefit of aiming—

—*and hit the blue-eyed ghoul right in the shoulder.*

It flinched at the impact, turned slightly, but *it didn't go down.*

It didn't go down.

Instead, it just grinned back at him.

Then the wall of black-eyed ghouls came unglued as the individual creatures broke into a run. They vomited through the windows and doors and moved like one single black entity, indistinguishable from the hundred others around them. They were not the least bit slowed down by the shards of glass clinging to the window frames that ripped into their flesh, or the bodies of the dozen or so dead already caking the floor in front of them, or even the furniture in their path.

"Aw, man, this isn't fair," Danny said behind him.

"Go go go!" Will shouted.

Danny pushed his way through the bathroom door as Will backed up and fired, putting ten rounds into the surging blob before he heard gunfire coming from behind him. Danny, firing, but not at the horde in front of Will—he was shooting *into* the bathroom.

Will knew what that meant even before Danny shouted, "No go! Bathroom's a no go! They're coming through the windows!"

He continued backing up, firing into the sea of ghouls. There were so many that their number suddenly became a problem as they tried, like rabid animals, to all jam themselves into the narrow passageway at the exact same time. The first creature that somehow managed to get through slipped on the congealed blood of the previous dead and flopped to the floor. But then it quickly righted itself and was moving up the hallway again, bringing more behind it.

Danny was backing up and firing beside him as the bathroom door, now in front of them, flew open and skeletal figures poured out of it. These new ones were quickly swallowed up by the unrelenting tide already pushing through the limited space. That, more than anything, was what held the creatures back, taking away their one superior asset: their sheer numbers.

Temporarily, anyway.

Danny was opening up with the M4A1 now, pouring silver rounds into the quivering mass alongside Will. The only source of light was the staccato effect of their nonstop weapons fire.

"Office!" Will shouted.

Danny spun around, but Will heard shooting behind him—again not directed up the hallway—before Danny shouted, "No go! More windows!"

Goddamn windows!

Will stepped into a pool of blood and stumbled over twisted bones that snapped apart under his boots. He ignored it, reloaded, and kept shooting.

They kept backing up, firing and moving, the creatures coming out of the office door in front of them now, too. They were so thin, their skin so weak, that the bullets punched their way through and hit one, two, sometimes three more of the undead things behind them.

But as effective as the silver ammo was, they still weren't effective *enough*. At least, not against the sheer volume of cracked teeth and black eyes literally filling up the hallway, growing bigger and higher in a pile of writhing flesh and tangled limbs. The creatures stumbled and fell and stepped over each other. Blood splattered the walls and floor and even the ceiling.

And still they came, climbing over their dead.

Relentless. Murderous. Rabid.

Will emptied his magazine, shouting, "Changing!"

Danny stepped up and unloaded into the freight train of flesh and bone and brown and yellow-stained teeth. There were so many bodies now that the creatures had begun to pile on top of one another, threatening to reach all the way up to the ceiling.

"Changing!" Danny shouted.

Will resumed shooting as Danny moved behind him and reloaded. He hadn't had time to look back to see just how close they were to the basement. A part of him didn't want to know, because as soon as they reached it, it would signal the end, because the locked door would seal their fate.

This'll teach me to run to the basement every time.

"Live by the basement, die by the basement."

He almost laughed out loud. Almost.

Instead, he just concentrated his full attention on killing as many of the pressing monsters as he could. They were close. *Too close.* He oscillated his fire from side to side, shooting at almost point-blank range. There was a surreal quality to the sight of them toppling back one after another as they climbed up on the growing mountain of bodies. But as soon as one disappeared over the pile, another— five—*ten* more took its place.

Then, finally, Will felt it.

The harsh and brutal cold of the basement's metal door pressing against his back, the chill seeping through his clothes and into his bones.

End of the line.

"Hey!" Danny shouted.

"Yeah?" he shouted back.

"You still wanna find out what's in that U-Haul?"

Will laughed this time as he stepped back and grabbed a fresh magazine out of his pouch and slammed it into the carbine. "Hell yeah!"

Danny was laughing, too, before the sound of his M4A1 firing on full-auto swallowed up every noise in the back of the hallway, with the locked basement door at their backs and the growing cemetery of dead *(again)* creatures in front of them.

They kept coming and climbing, pushing the layers of their own dead forward.

Now I've seen everything.

Will waited for Danny to finish shooting when he heard a soft *click-clack* behind him. It was such a small sound that it was almost completely drowned out by Danny's weapons fire, and Will wouldn't have heard it at all if he weren't standing directly against the metal basement door.

He spun around, lifted the rifle, and saw darkness gaping back at him.

The basement door was open and he could just make out the top of a flight of metal stairs leading down. But there was nothing down there—just a sea of empty blackness.

Behind him, Danny shouted, "Changing!"

"Door's open!" he shouted.

"The fuck?"

"Let's go!"

"You first!"

Will hurried inside and turned, waiting for Danny to dart in before he slammed the door shut. He turned the metal lever and heard the lock sliding into place a split-second before the ghouls crashed into it from the other side.

The impact staggered Will for a moment, but the door held.

They smashed into it again and again, the *thoom-thoom-thoom!* ear-splitting at such close proximity. The metal door and the surrounding brick wall shook and trembled with every impact, but they, too, held.

Thoom-thoom-thoom!

Thoom-thoom-thoom!

Will turned around. Danny was already facing the stairs behind them with his rifle aimed down into the darkness.

Thoom-thoom-thoom!

Will stepped up beside him. "Anything?"

"I saw movement," Danny said. He wasn't quite whispering, but it was close.

Will could hear his own heartbeat racing in his chest, and Danny's next to him, despite the nonstop banging coming from behind them.

Thoom-thoom-thoom!

"How many?" Will whispered.

"More than one."

"Human?"

"I couldn't tell ya."

Thoom-thoom-thoom!

There was a *click* and a bright LED flashlight beam sliced through the darkness and down the stairs, illuminating a dirty concrete floor. Danny moved his flashlight left then right, up and down, until the round beam washed over the barrel of a rifle pointing up at them.

Thoom-thoom-thoom!

The figure standing behind the weapon was a woman in civilian clothes, and she wasn't alone. Two other forms flanked her, both men, both armed. One of them, a familiar-looking lanky teenager, had an M40A3 rifle pointed up at Will's chest. The second man was peering behind the iron sights of an M4, and Will couldn't help but notice that the man's forefinger was trembling slightly against the trigger.

Thoom-thoom-thoom!

"This brings back memories," Danny said.

"Good ones?" Will said.

"Not so much."

Thoom-thoom-thoom!

Will saw additional movement out of the corners of his eyes, figures *(not ghouls)* emerging from the darkness to their left and right. Two more on his side and a third on Danny's. Assault rifles. Slacks and T-shirts.

Dunbar's locals.

"This is how it's gonna go down," the woman said. "The two of you put down your weapons and step back, and we won't shoot you down like dogs."

Thoom-thoom-thoom!

BOOK TWO

BLUE MOON RISING

CHAPTER 16

KEO

"ARE WE THERE yet?" Lorelei asked for the fifth time in the last three hours.

"Not yet," Keo said.

"How long have we been walking?"

"Not long enough."

"It feels like it's been days since we stopped. Can we stop and rest again?"

"We've already stopped three times."

"Yeah, but the last time was so long ago."

"It was thirty minutes ago."

"That's pretty long."

"We're almost there."

"That's what you said two hours ago. Carrie, can we stop and rest a bit?"

"One more hour, okay?" Carrie said.

Lorelei groaned but said, "Okay."

It took them most of the morning and parts of the afternoon, but after hours of walking and listening to Lorelei complaining, they finally reached the bridge he had seen on the map. The brown water below was part of a river, one of many that connected to Beaufont Lake, which would take him to Song Island. After that was the Gulf of Mexico and, if he was lucky, Santa Marie Island and Gillian.

Because you've been really lucky so far. Yeah, right.

Two lanes and fifty meters long, the bridge looked old and

cracked. There were no helpful marinas (or boats inside them), but someone had put a trailer park next to the shoreline on their right, while the left had been converted for warehouses. A couple of wooden planks partially submerged in water was the closest thing to a dock he could find.

Keo glanced down at his watch: 1:16 P.M.

They had made better time than he thought, which was a miracle given that Lorelei was hungry every other hour. They had also spent time raiding a few convenience stores along the way, replenishing what little supplies they were carrying. Other than that, he was frankly surprised they had gotten this far in just half a day.

According to the map, there were lakeside homesteads five kilometers on the other side of the bridge. And where there were homes by a lake, there were boats attached to docks. That was the theory, anyway, one formed before he found out the ghouls' human flunkies had been sinking boats up and down the lake. It all made sense. No wonder they sent two trucks and four men to scout the marina yesterday. A boat suddenly showing up, when they had been systematically sinking every one they crossed paths with, was a major anomaly in their world.

Still, all he needed was to find one boat, preferably a sailboat where he didn't have to scout for fuel to run an outboard motor. What were the chances of that happening? Who the hell knew, but it beat walking the rest of the way to Texas...

As they crossed the bridge, the heat seemed to double down on them. Lorelei was drinking from another bottle of water, her third since this morning, but Keo didn't bring it up. Lorelei eating or drinking meant the teenager was not complaining about something (her favorite topic being why they couldn't find a working vehicle when there were so many just sitting around), or asking him to rest for a bit.

"What about those homes?" Carrie said, looking at the rows of trailers parked to their right. "Should we look for supplies in those?"

"No," Keo said.

"You don't think there might be anything worth salvaging? There's an awful lot of them."

"Nothing we couldn't do without. Besides, we have enough on hand to get to Song Island. You still want to go there, don't you?"

"Of course." She gave him that earnest look again. "And thank you, Keo. For taking us there. I know you didn't have to. You could have left us behind at the marina too, but you didn't. I mean it. Thank you for bringing us along. Lorelei thanks you too, when she's not stuffing herself."

Lorelei smiled and nodded, but for once didn't say anything. She actually blushed a bit before taking another drink of water.

"We're not there yet," Keo said.

"But we soon will be," Carrie said. "Even if there's no one there now, the fish in the lake aren't going anywhere. We could stay there, Keo. If the creatures can't cross the water, we could stay there indefinitely."

"You think you can survive on an island by yourself? Just you and Lorelei?"

"You can learn to do a lot of things when you don't have a choice." She paused, then said, "Besides, it's better than out here. And you could always stay with us…"

"I can't."

"I know. Texas."

Galveston, he thought, but nodded instead. "Yeah."

"What's her name? Gillian?"

He nodded.

"She must be some woman."

"She is."

"I bet."

"Hey, how much further, guys?" Lorelei said behind them.

Keo pulled out a plastic bottle of peanut butter. He had been saving it since yesterday's raid at a Kwik-e-Stop convenience store. Keo held it out to Lorelei. "Here, have some of this."

"Oh wow, peanut butter," Lorelei said, taking the bottle. "I haven't had this in ages. Thanks, Keo!"

"Here's a spoon." He handed her a titanium spork from one of his cargo pant pockets. "Wash it when you're done. Thoroughly."

"I will!" Lorelei drifted back a bit as she enthusiastically twisted open the peanut butter lid and dug in, sighing with pleasure at the smell.

"Is that peanut butter still good?" Carrie asked him with some concern.

"Should be good for up to a year."

"You've been saving that up, haven't you?"

He smiled to himself. "I don't know what you're talking about."

HE HEARD THE roar of outboard motors from a kilometer away, prompting him to dart out of the small two-lane road and into the sparse grouping of trees on the other side of the ditch to his left. There was nothing on the right except undeveloped land, dried marsh, and a never-ending sentry of ancient power poles.

Route 410 was a long stretch of asphalt that ran through the countryside until it finally ended at the shoreline of Beaufont Lake, which was currently hidden in front of them though he thought he could smell the lake water already, and the air seemed a lot cooler than before.

They continued forward alongside the road, using the trees for as much cover as they would provide, which wasn't very much at all. Every minute brought them closer to the loud motor, which was as anomalous a sound as you could get these days.

Keo saw doubt in Carrie's face whenever he looked back. She was scared, and he guessed she had every reason to be after what she had been through. The idea was to stay clear of people—especially ones that were making so much noise—not walk right to them, which was exactly what they were doing now. Even Lorelei had gone completely silent, only occasionally picking at her nearly empty bottle of peanut butter.

After about twenty minutes of slowly walking toward the sound, they came across a group of old homes. That forced them to traverse one overgrown lawn after another, as well as skirting wooden fences with peeling paint. Most of the houses had boats in their backyards and some in the front, though the vessels didn't look as if they could still stay afloat on the water, much less sail. Keo took mental notes of the houses they passed. There was a two-story yellow monstrosity that looked like a good last-minute option in case they needed a place to hide—or fight—from.

He glanced at his watch: 3:21 P.M.

He smelled the familiar scent of fresh lake water before glimpsing the sparkling surface of Beaufont Lake moments later, visible even in the distance thanks to the clear day. Where housing was sparse and individualized this far back from the shoreline, the ones that crowded the more expensive lakeside properties were large and inviting, with private wooden docks with boats tied to them.

Boats.

Say, brother, can you spare one of those?

The outboard motors they had heard before had begun to fade and were now moving south down the lake. There were men standing around on one of the docks, and Keo glimpsed figures moving inside a two-story red house at the end of the street. Two Jeeps were parked in the driveway, and a man with an M4 stood on a boat launch watching birds flying in a V-shape pattern high above him.

Keo counted six men in all, wearing camo uniforms similar to the ones he had killed back at the Lake Dulcet marina. And these six were just the ones he could see from his position, about a hundred meters from the shoreline.

Carrie and Lorelei leaned out from the corner of the house, and Carrie's face turned noticeably paler at the sight of the uniforms. "Soldiers. They're from the towns."

"Do they all wear uniforms?" Keo asked.

"The ones I've seen recently, including those that tracked us down."

Keo took out a pair of binoculars from his pack and focused on a man moving up the street toward the red house. Like the others, this one also had a patch of Louisiana on his left shoulder and a star on the right side.

"What are they doing here?" Carrie asked. "Is there a town nearby?"

"I don't know," Keo said. "But from what you told me, there's not a lot around here that could sustain a population of any size for any length of time. You'd need plentiful food, supplies, and most importantly, water."

"There's plenty of water in the lake."

"Not safe drinking water. You'd have to constantly boil it to kill all the microscopic organisms unless you want the entire population getting sick. That takes too much time to do by hand, which is what they'd have to do since, from what you tell me, they don't have electricity in these places."

"No. It's sort of like going back to the old west. Everything's done by hand, though they do use propane and gas to cook sometimes and I've seen battery-powered lamps in some of the buildings."

"But no big machinery to treat the water. Those need electricity."

"The town I was in definitely didn't have electricity."

"A spring well would be ideal. But I don't see anything like that around here." He shook his head. "No, this looks a lot like a staging area to me."

"Staging for what?"

"Good question." He thought about it for a moment, then took out the map and scanned it. "According to the map, Song Island is about fifteen miles south from here…"

"So you think there *is* something on Song Island after all?"

"I don't know. It would be nice to know what these assholes are doing here, though."

Keo put the map away and pulled back around the corner, Carrie following suit. Lorelei had retreated halfway to the end and was now searching for something along the weeds at her feet. Keo was amazed how quickly she could switch from the girl he thought at first was a mute to the chatterbox who couldn't shut up, and now back again.

"What now?" Carrie asked in a low voice.

Keo didn't answer right away. Things had gotten complicated. Again. First losing Zachary and Shorty, then finding himself straddled with two civilians. Now, running afoul of heavily-armed men in uniforms. Whatever happened to the guy whose biggest worry was living up to the motto of "See the world. Kill some people. Make some money"?

Damn. I really have gone soft.

"Keo?" Carrie said. She was watching him closely. "What do we do now? Are we still going to Song Island?"

"We need a boat for that," he said. "I'm not sure we're going to find another one down the shoreline. If they really have been sinking boats up and down the state, they'd keep just what they need. The ones out there might be it."

"They're not just going to give us one—" She stopped herself. "Oh." Then, "You're crazy. There are too many of them."

"It wouldn't hurt to ask."

She stared at him in silence for a moment. "Are you being serious right now?"

A sharp *zip!* made him look back toward the corner.

Carrie opened her mouth to say something, but he quieted her with a finger to his lips. Behind her, Lorelei physically snapped her mouth closed, and her entire body started trembling noticeably.

Keo gripped the MP5SD and moved back over, then slowly leaned around the corner of the house. He wasn't sure what he was expecting, but it wasn't one of the "soldiers" standing with his back to them just three meters away, pissing into a dying garden. How the hell had the man crept up on them, unnoticed until now?

Sunlight bounced off the man's smooth and completely bald head, and he was humming some pop song Keo vaguely remembered as being popular before radio stations stopped broadcasting entirely. He was swaying a five-ten body from left to right and spreading a generous stream of urine over the shriveled flowers at his feet.

Keo leaned back and reconnected with Carrie's anxious eyes. He shook his head and slipped the submachine gun behind his back, then reached down and pulled the Ka-Bar knife out of the leather sheath strapped to his left hip.

Carrie tensed while Lorelei groped for her hand and held on.

The *crunch-crunch* of heavy boots on brittle grass sounded from around the corner. The noise was coming toward them, a realization that struck Keo a second before the man actually walked by while still zipping up his pants.

Either Lorelei or Carrie must have let out a gasp, because as soon as the man appeared next to them, he spun around, right hand abandoning his zipper and reaching for his holstered sidearm.

Keo lunged, and he didn't have all that far to go before he could shove the very sharp point of the Ka-Bar upward. The knife pierced the man's chin, slicing through a generous layer of fat, and kept going until it penetrated the bottom of the soldier's mouth and sliced through his tongue. The seven-inch blade didn't stop its momentum until the knife guard banged against skin.

Keo slipped behind the falling man, grabbing the pudgy figure around the waist. He caught the body as it went completely slack and lowered it to the ground before leaning the man against the wall of the house.

The girls had stepped back, Lorelei with her hands over her mouth to fight back a scream. Carrie looked stunned, but fine. At least, until Keo pulled the Ka-Bar out of the man's head—"Lewis" was written on his nametag—and there was a surprisingly loud *slurp* as blood poured freely out of the skewered chin.

Carrie made a gurgling noise before throwing up into the grass.

THERE WERE HOUSES along the shoreline, and from what he could tell, the soldiers were only staying at the two-story red building. So he made the decision to move sideways with Carrie and Lorelei instead of retreating back up Route 410 and found a house about 300 meters from their last spot (and the dead body currently occupying it).

It was a small white house, quaint compared to its neighbors, with a dirt driveway and an old red pickup parked up front. They hurried across the backyard and entered through a sliding glass kitchen door. Keo went in first with his MP5SD, Carrie and Lorelei following close behind.

He was surprised the women hadn't put up more of a fight when he suggested this course of action. He was almost sure they would battle him tooth and nail, the idea of sticking around in a place filled with soldiers almost as deplorable as being captured by them again, but they hadn't. Keo wasn't sure if that was because they trusted him (go figure) or if they were too shocked by what he had done to the soldier to think straight.

Either way, he was glad for the lack of drama. Working behind enemy lines was nothing new for him, but he preferred a quiet area of operation when possible. He had been doing this, in one form or another, since he was twenty-one. The organization paid good money for people who were willing to throw their lives away for a hefty paycheck. It wasn't as if he was good at anything else.

"See the world. Kill some people. Make some money."

Like its exterior, the inside of the house wasn't much to look at. The kitchen was tiny, as were the living room and a single bedroom on the other side. A wooden rickety dock extended from the side of the house into the lake, so walking on dirt was entirely unnecessary. There was nothing attached to the end of the dock, though he did find two fiberglass paddles leaning against the wall next to the side glass door.

Carrie and Lorelei were searching the cupboards in the kitchen for supplies when he returned. "Anything?" he asked them.

"Nothing worth taking," Carrie said. She stopped what she was doing and looked out the glass window. "What are we doing here, Keo? Shouldn't we be running?"

"Run where?"

"Away from here."

"There are only two directions to go—here or back up the road. Once they discover the body, and they will sooner or later, they'll launch a full-scale search. When that happens, they'll spot us from a mile away. There's nowhere to hide out there, Carrie. No place they can't find us before nightfall."

"And here…?"

"The less shitty of two really shitty alternatives."

He glanced at his watch: 4:16 P.M. Keo unclipped the radio he had taken from the dead man. It hadn't squawked yet, which meant the body was still undiscovered. He was surprised it was taking so long. Apparently the soldiers weren't nearly as organized as he had thought.

"Why did you take the radio?" Carrie asked.

"They're going to start communicating when they find the body," Keo said.

"So this way we can listen in on them. Find out what they're going to do."

"Yeah."

"Smart."

He smiled. "I've had recent experience dealing with assholes trying to kill me."

Keo went into the living room and sat down with his back against the wall, both eyes focused on the glass side door. Lorelei sat silently across from him, knees pulled up against her chest. She had reverted back to the frightened girl from yesterday morning at the marina. He thought he would be grateful for the quiet, but after a while he found himself missing the sound of her voice.

The radio finally squawked about five minutes later, and a man's voice said, "Lewis is dead." Keo picked up a lazy Southern drawl. "You should see him. Goddamn."

"What the fuck happened?" another man asked.

"Hell if I know," the first one said. "He's got a big hole under his chin where someone shoved a knife up into his face."

"Fuck."

"What I said."

"Everyone, sound off," the second man said.

Keo listened to three other voices calling out on the radio as ordered.

One of them was a woman, who said, "You said Lewis is dead? How the hell did that happen? I just saw him taking a piss about twenty minutes ago."

"Yeah, well, someone clocked him while he was taking the whiz probably," the Southerner said. "His fly's still open. Luckily, he shoved his little Lewis in before they took him out. Thank God for small miracles."

"Ouch, what a way to go," someone else said, and there was laughter.

I guess Lewis wasn't the most popular guy in the group.

"Shut the fuck up," the second man snapped.

Must be the leader of this little sideshow.

"Everyone get back to the OP until we can figure out what happened," the leader said.

"Travis," the woman said.

"What?" This was the Southerner.

"Lewis's radio. Does he still have it?"

There was a brief moment of silence before Travis finally responded. "No, it's gone. Shit."

"What?" the leader said. "What's going on now?"

"Lewis's radio is gone," Travis said. "Whoever killed him has it."

"That means they might be listening in on us right now," the woman said.

Looks like there's at least one with a working brain cell in the bunch. So why isn't she in charge?

"Fuck," the leader said, annoyed. "Everyone, get back here. *Now.* Until then, no one uses the radio."

The radio went dead after that. Keo waited to hear more, but they had completely shut down on him. He assumed they were going to switch radio frequencies as soon as they met in person, which, again, meant they weren't nearly as stupid as he had originally thought.

Carrie came out of the kitchen where she had been watching the back window and, probably, listening through the open door. "They found the body."

"Uh huh," Keo nodded.

"What now?"

"They're probably going to start looking for us once they meet up and come up with a plan."

"Then we should go before they get here."

He looked out the window at the empty dock. "We're not going to walk the rest of the way to Song Island from here, Carrie. And I'm not getting to Santa Marie Island without a boat." He gave her his best reassuring smile. "Besides, there's only five of them left."

"Only five?"

"Five's better than six. I've seen worse odds."

"Really? Where?"

"Have you ever been to Kabul in the spring?"

Carrie started to answer when he held up his hand and tilted his head to listen.

"What is it?" she said instead.

"Outboard motors." He looked back out the window. "They're coming back. The boat that left earlier."

"How does that help us? Doesn't it just mean the bad guys will have more people looking for us now?"

Keo smiled.

"What are you smiling at?" Carrie asked, annoyed.

"The guys at the house are meeting in person to change their radio frequency so I can't listen in on them anymore, remember? The ones on the boat don't know that."

"How can you be sure?"

He held up the radio. "I've been listening. There's no way the guys on the boat know about what's happening here. Besides, this thing has a max range of two miles."

"I still don't know where you're going with this."

"We need a boat. There just happens to be one coming toward us right now. The question is, do you trust me?"

She stared at him and didn't answer.

"Carrie. Do you *trust* me?"

She finally sighed and nodded. "Do I have a choice?"

"Daebak."

"What?"

"It means let's get us a boat."

IT WAS AN all-white twenty-footer with three guys inside. One stood behind the steering wheel in the center while the other two sat on a long plastic seat behind him, both cradling M4 rifles. They looked like men who had been on a long but uneventful trip and were glad to be back. The outboard motor was a Yamaha, about 200 horsepower from the sound of it, pushing the boat through the calm Beaufont Lake surface without any trouble.

It took the three men exactly fifteen seconds to spot Carrie standing at the end of the dock, waving her hands frantically over her head at them. It took them another ten seconds to slow down before he saw one of them on a radio, no doubt trying to reach someone at the house. He knew that was the intention because the radio he had picked up from Lewis squawked softly (he had turned down the volume) and he heard a male voice asking about "the woman."

Of course no one answered, because the men at the two-story red house had already switched frequencies, though he figured they could probably hear the boat coming right about now. How long did he have before the leader switched back to the old frequency to warn the returning soldiers? Ten seconds? Twenty? This entire plan was already tenuous enough, but it was going to go straight to hell as soon as someone from the house realized what was happening.

But for some reason, no one had responded by the time the boat slowed down as it neared Carrie, who had lowered her hands to her sides and was watching the vessel approach. The two men on the seat had stood up and were clutching their rifles as they scanned the area, looking wary of an ambush.

You have no idea, boys.

He was impressed with Carrie. She had to have nerves of steel to just stand there as the boat came straight toward her. It was either insane courage, or she was too terrified to do anything else. He couldn't see her face from his position, but he guessed it was probably a mixture of both.

The boat slowed down as it sidled up to the dock. One of the men had moved toward the bow, one hand on the gunwale to keep from toppling over. The soldier behind the tall, clear plastic windshield at the helm fixed Carrie with a hard look, hands carefully manipulating the vessel with surprising deftness.

"Don't move!" the man behind the steering wheel shouted. "Stay right where you are!"

Carrie didn't move or say anything back.

The third soldier had started to let his guard down. Maybe it was the sight of Carrie in her jeans and sweat-stained T-shirt, with no signs of a weapon anywhere on her. It was hard to look at the woman and think she was dangerous, especially the way she hardly moved.

Nerves of steel. Or suffocating, mortal terror.

Either/or works for me.

Keo was lying in the grass at the end of the dock, almost completely hidden among the two-foot-tall yard that grew around the house and up and down the shoreline. He watched the boat sidling alongside Carrie's still form and the man at the bow leaping out, landing on the wooden planks in front of her.

The third man slung his rifle and threw a line to the first one, who wrapped it around a wooden post. When Keo saw the man finish wrapping the rope and pull it tight, then straightened up, he pulled the trigger and shot the man in the back.

Even before the soldier went down, Keo was already scrambling up from the warm ground.

It took the two in the boat a few seconds to realize what had happened. Keo didn't blame them. They hadn't heard anything—the suppressor on the MP5SD had done its job. The fact was, they had a better chance of seeing the bullet casing ejecting (if they had been looking in his direction) instead of hearing the actual gunshot.

Keo didn't give them a chance to gather themselves.

He was on one knee, using the higher angle to aim and put the second round into the driver's chest. The shot shattered the protective screen at the same time. The soldier stumbled back and into the third one, and the two of them went down in a tangled heap. The boat rocked but was held in place by the line.

Keo was on his feet and racing forward, shouting, "Get down! Get down!"

Carrie dropped and flattened herself against the dock as Keo ran up at full speed. He hadn't taken his eye or the submachine gun's red dot sight off the boat the entire time and was waiting patiently for the third man to pop back up.

One second…

…two…

There, finally.

Keo shot him once in the chest, then put a second bullet into his forehead as he was falling back down.

He reached Carrie a second later, stepped over her prone form, and checked on the first man. Dead. He swept the boat, making sure the other two weren't going to get back up anytime soon, either.

"Lorelei!" he shouted.

The teenager burst out of the house before he even finished screaming her name. She was carrying their supply bag, which probably weighed almost as much as her. She didn't seem to feel the extra weight, though, and he guessed that was thanks to a combination of fear and adrenaline.

Carrie scrambled back up and Keo helped her into the boat. "What about the bodies?" she asked.

"We'll toss them later," he said.

She looked as if she was about to throw up again but thankfully managed to keep it in this time.

The boat moved under them and Carrie had to grab at the rail for support, almost stepping on one of the dead soldiers. He waited for Lorelei, then helped her onto the boat, too. She wasn't quite as lucky and actually stepped on the driver's open palm.

"Oh God," she whispered, her face pale.

"Later," he said.

He turned, grabbed the rope, and was untying it when the first volley of gunfire sliced through the air and pelted the dock around him, the already-rotting wood disintegrating inch by inch against the barrage.

"Keo!" Carrie shouted.

He looked across the lake and at another dock seventy meters away as uniformed men fired in his direction. Bullets *zip-zip-zipped* past his head and sliced into the water, and more than a few drilled holes into the boat's fiberglass side.

More men were running along the shoreline toward them, assault rifles and legs pumping wildly as they sprinted with everything they had.

Keo tossed the line back into the boat and jumped in after it, landing between Lorelei and Carrie, both crouched behind the gunwale amongst the two dead soldiers. Keo moved behind the steering wheel and grabbed the throttle and pushed it up, doing his best to ignore the fact he was standing on a dead man's arm. It couldn't be helped. There was only so much space inside a twenty-foot boat, especially around the cramped space around the steering console.

The boat roared to life, drowning out the sound of gunfire. Even so, he could hear the *buzzing* noise of bullets *zipping* past his head.

"Stay down!" Keo shouted.

Not that he had to. Both women looked permanently stuck against the bottom, Lorelei with her hands thrown over her head and Carrie doing her best not to look at the face of a dead man staring back at her with lifeless eyes.

The boat shot forward, fighting against his control. He got it turned around and pointed it down the lake even as bullets continued to *zip-zip-zip* around him, punching into different parts of the boat and vanishing into the brown water. He pushed the throttle up as far as it would go and the boat rocked, the bow lifting dangerously into the air as the motor poured on the power and the stern dipped, threatening to go under the lake's surface.

Keo finally allowed himself to duck down into a crouch, still tightly gripping the steering wheel above him with one hand. Thank God the lake was wide enough that he didn't have to worry about driving them right into the shoreline.

He threw a quick look back at the soldiers as they finally reached the dock he had just abandoned. A couple of the men were still firing, but the boat was already a good sixty, seventy meters away and putting more space between them with every passing second. Keo couldn't even hear the sound of gunshots over the motor anymore, even when a bullet snapped off one of the windshield fragments in front of him and disappeared into the dashboard.

Close, but no cigar.

Soon the soldiers faded into the background, and Keo finally stood back up to take full control of the steering wheel. Carrie was rising next to him, looking back at the house. Lorelei was still on the floor, apparently having decided not to risk it, even if she was lying across a dead man's legs.

"You okay?" he shouted at Carrie.

She nodded back. "You?"

"One piece."

"Do we have enough gas to get to Song Island?"

He looked down at the gas gauge. It was almost at "E."

Carrie frowned. "We'll never make it!"

Keo nodded at the skinny trolling motor latched to the bow. "We'll get there. It just might not be as fast as we want." He looked up at the darkening skies and could feel Carrie tightening up next to him. "We'll make it."

She gave him a pursed smile. "If you say so."

"I promise," he shouted. "And I always keep my promises, even if it might take a while."

CHAPTER 17

WILL

"KATE."

"Hello, Will."

"What are you doing here?"

She smiled at him. "I could ask you the same thing."

The Kate he remembered smiled rarely. Which was how he knew all of this was a lie, even if it did feel, sound, and even *smell* real.

"You're not really here," he said.

"I'm not," she said. "I know it's hard to believe, Will, but I have things on my mind at the moment other than you."

"Mabry's keeping you busy."

"I'm always busy."

"Are you still in the state?"

"Maybe. But then, when has distance ever stopped the two of us? Whether you want to admit it or not, there is something that ties us together, you and I. A bond beyond the physical that you'll never have with Lara."

Lara...

Stop it. She can read your mind.

"Oh, Will. You still think you can keep things from me. Haven't you learned by now? When I'm with you, I know everything. I know things you don't even realize you know."

"How are you in my head right now, Kate?"

"There are ways. So many ways that you can't even imagine.

What's that saying you love so much, Will? *'Know thy enemy'?* You'll never know us. Never really know us. Which is why you'll never win."

They were still in Dunbar. He knew that much. Night was falling around him, but for some reason he wasn't anxious at all, which didn't make any sense. Every inch of him should have been tingling at the moment, itching to get indoors. Darkness was not his friend. It hadn't been for almost a year now.

But of course, it was just a dream. Or a figment of his imagination. Or whatever the hell Kate did when she invaded his head.

Trying to make sense of it—any of it—was pointless.

She was wearing a long white dress. It was silk or gossamer. One of those. Almost see-through, though it played tricks with his mind, the hem billowing as if it had a life of its own. She looked radiant, long black hair glimmering under the falling dusk. He couldn't have looked away even if he wanted to, and he didn't want to.

"You always were a charmer, Will," she smiled.

She's in your head.

He forced himself to look away from her, to take in his environment instead. Occupy his mind with other thoughts that weren't so dangerous.

Hide his secrets…

The street looked familiar, and it took him a moment to recognize the strip mall where the soldiers and the U-Haul had taken up residence earlier in the day. Except most of the men in uniform were dead, their bodies spread around the white and orange trailer in an almost semicircle. The gunfight he had listened to with Danny was over.

This is yesterday. Why am I seeing a day that's already happened?

A man with red hair, wearing a military vest, stood over one of Josh's soldiers. The injured man was lying on the parking lot looking up, one bloodied hand raised in some kind of meek defense. Neither one of them seemed to noticed that Will was watching them.

So this is what it feels like to be a ghost.

The man with red hair shot the soldier in the head with a 9mm handgun. Then he calmly ejected the magazine and put in a new one before looking over at the U-Haul nearby. "Open it," the man said.

Big mistake, Will thought, though he didn't know why.

He heard giggling behind him and looked back at Kate. She

stood a short distance away, hands clasped in front of her, a wicked, knowing grin spreading across blood-red lips.

"What's in the trailer?" he asked her.

"You'll find out," she said.

"Kate, *what's in the trailer?*"

"It's a surprise. You still like surprises, don't you, Will? You're going to get a kick out of this one. It was my idea, you know. This town, this little city in the middle of nowhere, was becoming a nuisance." The smile faded, replaced by something dark and danger- ous. "Like a certain little island that should have stayed quiet. This is what happens when you stick your head out and get my attention, Will. I grab a hammer."

The island. She's talking about Song Island.

"Now pay attention," Kate said. "This is where it gets really fun."

He looked back at the man with red hair. There were others gathered around him now. Two dozen or so, mostly men, but a couple of women among them, all well-armed and loaded for bear. They had moved in a rough, jagged circle around the U-Haul, having emerged from the alleys and streets and buildings while he wasn't looking. They stepped over the dead bodies, some going out of their way to move around the pooling blood. A few looked squeamish.

Only a couple of them seemed to notice the fading sunlight. The others, like the man with red hair *(the leader)*, was too busy focusing on the trailer at the center of the death and destruction. There were bullet holes in the sides of the orange and white vehicle. Stray bullets, he guessed, during the gun battle.

The man with red hair pointed at the U-Haul. "I said open it."

Look up, you idiot. Look up!

But the man didn't look up. Instead, he took another tentative step toward the parked vehicle, clenching and unclenching his handgun, one of those fancy Smith & Wesson semi-automatics.

Look up!

Two men with assault rifles moved toward the trailer and one of them grabbed the lever at the bottom, twisted it open, then pulled at the door—but it didn't budge. He paused and exchanged a nervous look with his comrade before slinging his rifle and grabbing hold of the lever with both hands and this time really yanked.

Nothing. The door refused to move.

"It's exciting, isn't it?" Kate said gleefully behind him. "It was such an easy sell, too. Give them something mysterious, something intriguing. They couldn't leave it alone even if they wanted to. Look at them, Will. Most of them are so caught up with it they don't even notice the sun is disappearing, little by little, by little...."

She was standing right next to him now. He didn't know how she had done that.

This is her dream. She can do anything she wants.

They were standing in the middle of the group, people with rifles fidgeting around them, more than a few looking nervously at the darkening streets, some even glancing at the blackening sky. So some of them *had* noticed the setting sun. But not nearly enough, he saw.

"Harrison," one of them said. A woman. Will recognized her from the basement last night. *(Today? This morning?)* "We have to go, it's almost dark!"

Harrison looked conflicted. He glanced back at the U-Haul, then at the others.

He's target fixated. He's so focused on what's in front of him, he doesn't see the danger coming up behind him. Or...above him.

"Yes," Kate said. "That's the idea. Not bad for a civilian, huh?"

"Harrison!" the woman shouted. "We have to go now!"

The others were backing up, their precarious situation finally dawning on them. Half of them looked ready to turn and run, but something was holding them back. They kept shooting quick questioning looks at Harrison.

He's the leader and they're scared of him. Even with night coming, death waiting in the wings, they won't run. Not without his permission.

Idiots!

"Harrison!" the woman shouted again. When Harrison still didn't respond, the woman whirled on the others. "Everyone head to the designated safe buildings! Go! Now now now, goddammit!"

They finally moved. Some of them, anyway, but a few still hesitated, waiting for Harrison's orders, though they too looked on the verge of fleeing.

Then even Harrison turned and ran.

"Hurry, hurry, hurry," Kate said in a singsong voice, and he swore she might have cackled. Or maybe he just misheard?

The two men who had been trying to open the U-Haul had also turned to go when the door flew open behind them and the trailer actually *quaked* against the truck connected to it as something—some*things*—exploded with movement from inside.

There were two of them—no, *four*—coming out of the trailer.

Blue-eyed ghouls.

He recognized one of them instantly. It was the same one he had shot outside Ennis's bar, who took the silver round and flinched but didn't go down.

It didn't go down.

The man who had been trying to open the trailer heard the vehicle squeaking and turned around. It was a mistake. He let out a piercing scream just before one of the blue-eyed creatures landed on top of him, pummeling his much larger frame down to the concrete floor. The ghoul bent and flesh tore and the man kept screaming as blood flowed.

The second man had made it almost out of the parking lot when he heard his friend's howls. He spun around and let loose with his rifle on full-auto, shredding one of the blue-eyed monsters as it was almost on top of him. Blood and flesh were ripped from the creature's skeletal frame, but it kept coming and seemed to smash into the man and drive him down behind a parked blue Chevy, where they both disappeared out of Will's sight.

A woman stumbled and fell. She turned around on her back and was reaching for her sidearm when another of the blue-eyed things fell on top of her. She didn't even get a chance to scream.

Then the ghoul was back up and running, its jaw slicked with fresh blood that was visible even in the darkness swallowing up whole sections of the streets. Gunfire exploded across the city, a continuous cacophony of gunshots and screams.

Then they came. The others. The black-eyed ones.

Harrison's people were scattered—in buildings, alleyways, some poor souls trying to escape in the streets—and their cries filled the air along with the endless *pop-pop-pop* of automatic weapon fire.

"You wanted to know," Kate said.

"You were here last night," he said.

"No. But I have a strong link with the others."

"'Others'?"

"The other blue-eyed ones. Our bonds are stronger, and I can communicate with them over greater distances. Of course, even if I knew you were here, I couldn't have come anyway. Like you said,

Will, Mabry has me very busy these days."

He heard *slurping* and looked behind him at a blue-eyed ghoul perched over one of Harrison's locals. The man's eyes were open and he stared up at the dark sky, mouth quivering as the ghoul suckled rabidly at his neck. The creature looked in a state of frenzy, like a man about to orgasm.

"You did this," Will said. "You planned this…massacre."

"Most of it. But I admit, I didn't expect them to attack so fast and so ferociously. What's that saying you soldiers have? No plan survives contact with the enemy?" She smiled. "Are you impressed, Will?"

"Yes…"

"There's a reason Mabry chose me. He knew my potential."

"The same reason you chose Josh? Because of potential?"

"The young ones are always the most malleable. But yes, he's a lot smarter than many of these…" she looked around at the dead soldiers, the ones he had come to call Josh's men, "…cannon fodder. This is what they're good for. Josh and the other young ones will keep going. What's that saying, Will? The children are the future. So true. So true…"

Will stared at the bodies spread around the parking lot. So many. Soldiers and locals. Spent bullet casings by the thousands. Pools of blood everywhere. And still, the shooting went on and on, along with the screams.

The screams…

"What now?" he said, turning back to face her.

But she wasn't there anymore, and he was no longer standing in the streets of Dunbar.

Instead, he was in Ennis's bar, the same one he and Danny had used as their last stand before escaping through the basement door. He was sitting on one of the stools at the counter, which wasn't covered in dust and time like it had been earlier.

This is her domain. She can do anything, because none of this is real.

She's not really here.

Right?

That didn't explain how she was sitting on the stool next to him, wearing some kind of formal evening gown. It was bright outside the windows, and the sun glinted off her exquisitely long neck as she saluted him with a small glass of brandy. "To your health, Will," she said, and took a sip.

"I didn't know you cared."

"You don't think I worry about you? Running around out here? Trying to stop the inevitable? It's like watching a child standing on the tracks trying to hold back a runaway train. You don't hate the child, Will, you feel sorry for him, because you know the train is going to run him over. All you can really do is try to reason with him, get him off the tracks before then."

"Is that what I'm doing, Kate? Standing on a train track?"

"What do you think, Will?" A bottle of brandy, the liquid inside brilliant orange against the glow of the sun, had appeared on the counter between them. Kate picked it up and poured him a glass. He wasn't sure where the glass had come from, either. "Drink up, Will. We should talk."

"What about?"

She poured with precision, another skill he didn't know she possessed. Or was that the dream? Kate could do things in dreams that were impossible in the real world. But was this his dream or hers?

Or…theirs?

"What about? You, me, this world," she said.

He stared at the glass. Was that real cognac inside? It smelled like it.

"I almost had you in Harvest," she said, pinching her fingers together. "Missed you by that much."

"You tried to kill me."

"Don't be silly. Death doesn't mean what it used to anymore. You of all people should know that by now."

Will picked up the glass and took a sip. The taste was sweet, followed by the familiar warm aftermath.

"The towns, the pregnancies," she continued. "They're all just the beginning. In ten, twenty years, you won't recognize any of this. In a couple of generations, man will have forgotten they were ever in control of the planet."

"Is that the long-term goal?"

"You say that as if there is a short-term one, Will. There isn't. We've shed the mortal coil. Time is no longer the enemy. Days, months, years, even centuries. They mean nothing anymore. You have no idea how long they've been preparing for this."

"So there are more than just Mabry."

She smiled mischievously. "I meant him."

"You said 'they.'"

"Did I?"

"Yes."

She shrugged. "Maybe you misheard. This is just a dream, after all."

She said 'they'...

"You sound very confident," Will said. "Is that why you haven't attacked the island?"

"Ah, the island," she said almost wistfully. "Lara shouldn't have sent out that broadcast. Why did she do that, Will?"

"I don't know..."

"I was content to leave you alone. As long as you left me alone. Because of what we've been through, because of my feelings for you. But then your little pre-med doctor had to send that broadcast, blabbing about the silver to the whole wide world." She sighed. "That complicated things, you know. It's too bad."

She nursed her glass of brandy while watching their reflections in the big mirror behind the bar. That mirror had been broken when he and Danny came through before—when was that? Last night? A day ago?

He was losing track of time...

Kate smiled again. That strange emotion that was at once so human and at the same time so...*wrong*.

"What are you going to do, Kate?" He felt anxious for the first time in a long time, and he tightened his grip on the glass without realizing it. "What are you planning?"

"You shouldn't have left the island, Will. That broadcast was a mistake. You should have stopped Lara from putting it out there."

"You're going to attack the island because of the broadcast?"

She shrugged and said nothing.

"It's too late," Will said. "Even if you burned the island down tomorrow, you won't be able to put the genie back into the bottle."

"Maybe I don't care about putting the genie back into the bottle," Kate said. "Maybe I'm just a spiteful bitch. Or maybe I'm just feeling a little jealous toward that little girl of yours."

"Jealousy and vindictiveness are human traits, Kate."

She laughed. It was almost lyrical. Almost...*human*. "Yes, they are, aren't they? I guess I'm still more of the old Kate than we both thought."

"What would Mabry say if he knew?"

"You're assuming he doesn't already know. Mabry knows every-thing, Will. Everything *we* know. It all comes from him, and it all goes to him. Haven't you figured that out by now?"

She stood up from the stool.

"Kate…"

She didn't seem to hear him and instead turned and walked away, the hem of her dress *swishing* around her legs. She wore high heels, the *click-click* of stiletto points like firecrackers in the emptiness of the city around them.

What happened to the locals? The soldiers? Where did everyone go?

It's just a dream. It's just her *dream.*

Or mine.

Or ours?

"Kate…"

He tried to get up in order to stop her, but he couldn't move. Something was holding him down on the stool. An invisible force of some kind clinging to his arms and legs. He couldn't even let go of the glass in his hand.

"Kate!"

She finally stopped at the door and looked back at him, and a ghost of a smile flashed across her ethereal face. "You shouldn't have left the island, Will. It might not be there when you get back. *If* you make it back."

She opened the door and stepped through. Daylight flooded inside and Will grimaced at the blinding brightness.

"Kate!" he shouted, but his words were lost in the wind, as if he had never said it in the first place. *"Kate!"*

"DON'T TELL ME, another trip to Deussen Park?" Danny said when Will opened his eyes from the dream.

"Shit," Will said.

"The dream or our present predicament?"

"Both."

"Then I'll join your shit with my own shit. Talk about a double-shit burger."

Three of the people they had met in the basement were asleep, dozing somewhere in the darkness. One of the faces visible in a small pool of LED light placed in the center of the room was the woman who had greeted them when they first entered, and who Will remembered from his dream *(Nightmare?)*.

Her name was Rachel. The kid next to her with the M40A3 sniper rifle cradled against his shoulder like a comfortable blanket was Tommy. A third person, Milch, was somewhere to their right, still awake because Will could hear him moving against the hard concrete floor.

Rachel was clearly the leader of this group, and she stared across the room at him now, her AR-15 in her lap. Dirty black hair hung over her shoulders and she gave him the kind of look that was devoid of warmth. She wasn't entirely unattractive. Late thirties, a face lined with hard living and surviving. Her people had taken his and Danny's weapons and equipment when they surrendered less than—how long ago? A few hours.

At least they hadn't taken his watch, and he looked down at the glow-in-the-dark minute hand, which ticked to five after midnight. He heard the *ticking* clear as day in the silence. The monsters had stopped banging on the door hours ago.

Dead, not stupid.

"Who's Kate?" Rachel asked.

Did I say her name out loud?

"Someone I used to know," Will said.

"Ex-girlfriend? Must not have left things in a very good place, the way you were moving around in your sleep, saying her name."

"I shot her."

She gave him a wry look, as if she was trying to decide whether to believe him or not. "Now that's what I call a breakup."

"The funny thing is? She didn't die."

"Just clipped her, huh?"

"No. I shot her in the chest."

Rachel narrowed her eyes. "And she didn't die?"

"Nope."

"Whatever. Keep your little secret."

Danny chuckled next to him. "She doesn't believe you."

"I guess not," Will said.

Rachel looked annoyed. "You never told me what you two were doing in Dunbar."

"We're just passing through," Will said.

"Bullshit. No one passes through Dunbar. It's barely a blip on any map and we're miles from the closest interstate. The only people who come to Dunbar are people who were *coming* to Dunbar."

"That includes you?"

"I was born here. So were most of these guys. It's our city. We're not leaving."

"Doesn't sound like you have much of a choice anymore after last night."

"Wrong."

"Am I?"

"Tomorrow's another day. We'll start again."

"With just the five of you?"

"There are more of us out there."

"You hope."

"I *know*." She said the words with the right inflections, as if she actually believed it. "Harrison made sure we all knew where the safe houses were. There are other basements like this one around the city. We're not the only ones left."

Harrison was the man with the red hair, who Will had watched lead the locals to certain death last night. Probably dead now, like most of his people. There had been a lot of blood and bodies in the dream *(memories?)*.

"You can always leave," Will said.

"And go where?"

"Anywhere but here."

She shook her head. "Dunbar's our home. We're not leaving tomorrow or the day after that."

Will nodded. "You gotta do what you gotta do."

Talk of home made him think of Lara, of the island.

What was that Kate had said?

"You shouldn't have left the island, Will. That broadcast was a mistake. You should have stopped Lara from putting it out there."

The island. He had to get back to the island…

"What now?" he asked Rachel. "What happens to us tomorrow?"

She shrugged. "The only reason you're still alive is because you're not wearing one of those uniforms. I'm willing to believe you're just passing through, but I'm not taking any chances tonight."

Will thought about the locals he'd been forced to kill when he fled Gaine's Meat Market with Danny yesterday.

Right. Just passing through. Totally innocent bystanders here.

"I get where you're coming from," Will said. He looked to his left, where Tommy and the others had taken his and Danny's weapons and packs. The radio was somewhere back there, too. "I need to ask a favor…"

Rachel snorted. "Oh, do you now?"

"I need the radio in our pack."

"What for?"

"I need to transmit a message to a friend about something."

Danny looked over, concern flashing across his face.

"It has nothing to do with you or this city," Will said. "But my friend and I had a scheduled call that I missed last night. I just want to let them know we're okay."

Rachel shook her head. "You can do that tomorrow when you leave the city."

"It's vitally important they get this message. It's a matter of life and death."

"That's your tough fucking luck, isn't it?" she said, her eyes hard.

Will glanced over at Danny and could practically hear his thoughts: *"The island? Something's happening with the island?"*

He looked back at Rachel and the sleeping Tommy next to her. There were three meters between him and Rachel. He didn't know exactly where Milch was, just that he was (probably) still awake. That might be a problem. Tommy, on the other hand, would be easy to handle. He was obviously tired and struggling to keep his eyes open.

The real problem was Rachel…

Doable.

"Go ahead," Rachel said, staring back at him. She placed her hand on the AR-15 for effect. "This rifle's been converted to full-auto. All I need to do is pull the trigger once. You think you can make it across the room before that happens?"

Or not.

Will clenched his lips into a smile. "You're right. It can wait till morning. Besides, my friend is probably asleep by now anyway."

"Definitely asleep," Danny said. "Probably snoring like a horse, too."

"I wouldn't go that far."

"Bear?"

"Shut up," Rachel said. "You'll get your weapons and radio back tomorrow morning and get the hell out of my city. Do anything before then and I won't hesitate to shoot you both."

Will and Danny exchanged a look.

"Go ahead," Rachel said, narrowing her eyes at the both of them. "Try me. I'm having one hell of a shitty day, so shooting the two of you might just turn it all around."

"It can wait till morning," Will said, gritting his teeth.

She's coming, Lara.

Kate's coming…

CHAPTER 18

LARA

"YOU HEAR THAT?" Maddie said. "Listen carefully."

Lara did listen carefully, but after about five seconds of silence, she shook her head. "I don't hear anything."

"I swear it was there. And this isn't the first time, either. I've heard it before. Earlier this morning; and before that, yesterday."

"It could just be the quiet," Lara said. "It plays tricks with your mind. Besides, it's been more than three months. Don't you think they would have attacked by now if they wanted the island back?"

"I guess," Maddie said. "I'd feel better if Will and Danny were around, though."

You and me both, sister, she thought, but said, "What time is it?"

Maddie glanced at her watch. "Five fifteen. When is Will due to radio back in?"

"Before nightfall. We don't have a set time, but he promised to check in with me twice a day, once in the morning and once in the afternoon or evening, depending on his situation."

"You think they found Gaby yet?"

"I hope so."

"I guess they're good at that, huh? Tracking and stuff? They teach that at Ranger School, don't they?"

"I'll ask him when I talk to him again."

Maddie went back to staring outside the east window at the long shoreline in the distance. The horizon was blanketed in a shade of orange and red, like a painting come to life. You wouldn't know how dangerous it all was just to look at it.

Lara tried to remember the last time she had allowed herself to watch the night come with absolute serenity, but couldn't. It had been a while.

Since Will left the island...

"What did it sound like?" Lara asked. "The noise you heard?"

"Like an outboard boat motor."

"How many did you hear?"

"Just one, I think."

"And you're sure it was a motor?"

"I thought it was, but..." She shrugged. "I'm not so sure now. I didn't see anything, so maybe you're right; I might have just been imagining things. It can get pretty quiet when you're all alone up here."

"You should bring one of the kids to keep you company next time."

"That's a good idea, I'll do that."

"Until then, stay alert until Blaine relieves you."

"Will do, doc."

"You should probably stop calling me that."

"Why?"

"Because we have a real doc on the island now. I don't want her to get confused."

"You'll always be our doc, doc."

Lara smiled. "I'll take that as a compliment."

She left Maddie on the third floor of the Tower and headed down the spiral staircase. She had done a good job hiding her disappointment in front of Maddie, but now that she was alone with her thoughts, she gave in to the overwhelming anxiety. It was almost nightfall, and Will hadn't radioed in yet. That wasn't supposed to happen.

Twice a day, Will. That's all I asked. So where's my second radio call?

You better not be messing around out there.

She stepped outside the Tower and into a slight chill. It always got cool around the island near sunset, something that made her look forward to the coming months. November and December wouldn't exactly be Christmas in Louisiana, but anything was better than the daytime heat of October.

Lara did the buttons on her long-sleeve shirt as she walked

across the empty hotel grounds back to the hotel. She spotted figures racing down the front patio and up the pathway toward the beach. Bonnie's girls, trying to get in a final hour along the white sands before dark.

Even with the safety of the island, they had a curfew—everyone needed to be at the hotel by six except for the guards. Benny would be on the boat shack right now. Even limping on one good leg, the young man had proven a worthwhile addition to the group. Not that she really needed him to do much. He and the others posted out there throughout the day were really just an early warning system in case of an attack.

Plan Z, right, Will? God, I hope we never have to use it.

She slipped into the hotel through a side door and walked up Hallway A, then the short distance to an office near the lobby. It was a big room, worthy of whoever was supposed to run the Kilbrew Hotel and Resorts. The plaque on the door was originally marked "Administrator," but someone had put duct tape over it and written in large permanent marker, "Lara's Lair." She suspected Carly, but her best friend refused to own up to it.

Lara's Lair had stainless steel filing cabinets, shelves, and comfortable chairs along one wall. Most of the offices in the hotel were empty, the island's chosen administrators having never had the time to settle in before The Purge. Which made sense since the building itself was never completed. Far from it, with the entire second floor still missing and whole chunks of the first floor unfinished.

She slumped down on the large executive chair behind the equally large desk, which never failed to make her feel like a fraud. It might have had something to do with the vinyl upholstery or the way-too-elegant looking mahogany wood finish. The hand-applied brass nails certainly didn't add to her comfort level. After settling in, she picked up the pen and wrote in the ledger, recording the day's conversation with survivors through the radio.

Japan...upstate New York...Alaska...Beecher in Colorado...and now, just recently, a man claiming to lead a few hundred survivors in London.

All this time, we thought we were the only ones still out there running against the night. I wonder if they all thought the same thing?

There were so many people still left, all of them just waiting for someone to tell them what was happening. Her broadcast had been responsible for that, and they had used her as their in-between to communicate, exchanging ideas about weapons, defenses, and even survival techniques to live off the land.

She couldn't help but feel pride swelling whenever she thought about it. She had done that. A third-year medical student. How the heck did she even get here?

Lara looked up at the sound of Carly's voice. "You decent?"

"No, but that's never stopped you before."

Carly came inside and slumped down into a large loveseat, the furniture's mahogany finish and oxblood vinyl swallowing up her bright red hair. She rubbed her stomach as she looked contently at Lara. "Heard from the boys yet?"

"Not yet." Lara kept writing. "You look happy."

"I had a good meal."

"That's it?"

"I'm a simple girl, Lara. A good meal, good company, my little sister laughing." She beamed. "What more could a girl want?"

"I'm thinking about making a work rotation for the kids. I know they've been spending a lot of time on the beach and exploring the island, but sooner or later they're going to get bored. This should keep them busy."

Carly smiled at her.

"What?" Lara said.

"You're good at this."

"'This'?"

"Running the island. You're really good at it."

"It's only temporary. Once Will comes back—"

"He'll insist you stay in this room, doing what you're doing now."

"You think so?"

"I know how your boyfriend operates. My guess is that's why he brought Zoe—so she can take over the infirmary. He has big plans for you, kiddo."

Lara laughed. "You really think Will thinks that far ahead?"

"It's Will. *Hope for the best, prepare for the worst,*' remember?"

"Maybe." She put down the pen and leaned back in the chair. "He sort of said the same thing when we talked earlier today."

"See?"

"Don't gloat just yet. Zoe can barely stand, much less run the infirmary."

"For now. But she'll get better. Then you'll be stuck in here behind that big desk. Heck, we should get you a permanent plaque as befitting your new position."

"Are you finally admitting you're responsible for Lara's Lair?"

Carly grinned. "I'm admitting nothing of the sort."

"WHAT TIME IS it?" Maddie asked.

"Seven thirty," Lara said.

"He should have called by now, right?"

"Yes."

"I'm sure he's fine. He's got Danny with him. What could possibly go wrong?"

She gave Maddie a pursed smile. "I'm not worried. Why, do I look worried?"

"Just a little bit." Then, as if it should explain everything, "Lara, it's Will."

She smiled again. This time it came out more convincing. Or at least, she hoped so. "I know."

"If they didn't call in today, I'm sure they had a good reason."

"I'm sure you're right." *God, I hope you're right.* "Did you eat yet?"

"Sarah's saved me something in the kitchen. I'll grab a bite when Blaine relieves me in a few." Maddie turned back to the night sky outside the east window and peered out with the night-vision binoculars. "Sounds like they're still going at it."

"Sounds like it," Lara said.

She glanced back at one of the radios on the table behind her. It was permanently tuned in to the FEMA frequency, and although the volume was lowered almost the entire way, she could still make out the endless chatter. Beecher had signed off a few hours ago and it was now mostly foreigners. The clamor of a dozen different languages, accents, and broken English was next to impossible to decipher.

"I can't understand half of the things they're saying," Maddie said. "I can barely understand the guys from New York."

Lara smiled, then glanced at her watch again: 7:34 P.M.

Two times a day, Will. That was all I asked. You can't even do that for me. If I didn't love you so much, I'd hate your guts right now.

She stared at the designated emergency radio on the other side of the table, willing it to come alive, for Will's voice to blurt through the speakers.

Instead, she heard the loud roar of an outboard motor rising in the distance. No, not in the distance. *Closer.*

Lara ran to the south window and looked toward the beach.

"Is that one of ours?" Maddie said behind her.

"I don't know." Lara unclipped her radio and keyed it. "Who's at the beach right now?"

"I am, Lara!" Benny said through the radio. He was on the verge of screaming, trying to be heard over the loud noise of the outboard motor in the background. "I was about to call in!"

She could see it—a small white light moving away from the pier. It was a spotlight on one of the boats. It was moving fast, so she guessed it was one of the bass fishing vessels.

"That's one of ours, all right," Maddie said. She was peering through the M4 with the ACOG mounted scope. "Blaine was using it earlier to recon the area for those sounds I thought I heard."

"What's going on down there, Benny?" Lara said into the radio. "Who's on the boat?"

"It's Roy and Gwen," Benny said. "We saw something on the lake. A white boat. It looked adrift, so they're going to intercept it."

"Goddammit, who told them to do that?"

"I'm sorry, Lara. I tried to stop them. What should I do?"

"Stay right where you are."

She took a breath and tempered down the anger and frustration. What the hell were those two thinking, running off like that?

She gathered herself, then keyed the radio again. "Roy, Gwen…come in. Roy, Gwen, answer me."

She waited, but there was no response.

"They might not be able to hear over the motor," Maddie said. "It can get pretty loud standing right next to it."

"Yeah, probably." Either that, or they were ignoring her. She wasn't sure which answer was more aggravating. "I need you up here—"

"Got it," Maddie said before she could finish. "Go."

Lara nodded gratefully back at her. At least she could count on

Maddie, Blaine, and the others. Carly, and even the kids. They had been together since Texas. Roy and Gwen and the others had shown up on the island recently and were still wildcards, trying to get used to how they did things over here. Or maybe it was her leadership. Maybe they didn't fully respect her enough to do what she told them *not* to do…like running off on a boat to catch something floating in the lake like a bunch of amateurs.

Will would never have this issue.

She raced through the door in the floor and sprinted down the spiral staircase. She keyed her radio as she leaped onto the second floor below and found the second set of stairs. "Blaine, did you hear all of that?"

"I heard," Blaine said through the radio. "What the hell are they thinking?"

"I don't know. Grab your rifle and meet me at the beach."

"On my way."

"What about me?" Bonnie asked through the radio. "Carly's out here with me."

Like all the adults on the island, Bonnie had her own issued radio tuned into the same channel and it was powered on at all times, so whenever someone broadcasted, they all heard it. It was another one of Will's protocols, and its singular purpose was to keep everyone in the loop. It was also why she was fuming that Roy and Gwen were ignoring her. *If* they could hear her radio call, that is.

Yeah, let's go with that. The other answer is too aggravating.

"I need you guys on the patio," Lara said. "Everyone else, stay put inside the hotel, and anyone who isn't already in the hotel, get there *now*."

"Got it," Carly said through the radio.

"Carly…"

"Yeah."

"I need a rifle."

"Gotcha, boss."

Lara burst out of the Tower and jogged across the grounds, making a beeline for the beach. Bonnie was already back outside the hotel's front patio, cradling a Remington shotgun. The ex-model waved at her and Lara waved back.

Carly jogged down the patio steps as she reached them and handed Lara an M4 rifle. "Blaine's waiting for you at the beach."

"What were Roy and Gwen thinking?" Lara said to Bonnie.

Bonnie shook her head helplessly. "I don't even know what they were doing down there at this time of the night. They know better than that. The curfew…"

"They're, uh, involved," Carly said. The other two women looked over at her. "What, you guys didn't know? They've been sneaking into each other's rooms for the last few days. I guess they were down there doing, you know."

"Spare me the details," Lara said, finding herself even more annoyed than before. "I need you guys here. There are other ways on the island besides the beach." She met Carly's eyes. "Remember?"

Carly nodded back. She remembered that night, too. "We got this. Go."

Lara slung the carbine and jogged along the cobblestone pathway toward the beach. "Blaine," she said into the radio.

"I'm on the beach with Benny," Blaine answered.

"What do you see?"

"I think they stopped the other boat."

Lara noticed how quiet it had gotten suddenly. *They shut off the motor,* she thought, and keyed the radio. "Roy, Gwen…can you hear me?"

"I can hear you," Gwen said through the radio.

It took all of Lara's self-control not to tear into the twenty-something right then and there. "Are you and Roy all right?"

"We're fine," Gwen said. "We have them, Lara."

"The other boat?"

"Yes. There are two women onboard. They're both unarmed."

She was halfway to the beach, the wooded area that separated the hotel grounds from the water to both sides of her. Birds took flight as her footsteps warned them of incoming humans.

"Two women?" she said into the radio. "On a boat in the middle of a lake at night?" Alarm bells went off inside her head. "You and Roy need to be careful. It could be a trap."

"What should we do with them?" Gwen asked.

Oh, so now you want orders? she wanted to ask, but instead said, "Bring them in."

"Will do."

The soothing breeze brushed up against her as soon as she reached the soft, mushy sands and heard the slowly lapping waves. It was always colder on this part of the island and was the main reason everyone loved to sneak in an hour or two near the evenings. There was no better place to forget about the state of the world than running barefoot across the white sands.

Which, she guessed, explained what Roy and Gwen were down here at night. She tried very hard not to picture them hiding in the woods somewhere doing…something.

She spotted Benny standing on top of the boat shack, peering through binoculars out at the water. It was impossible to see much of anything too far out beyond the lights along the piers—except for the bright spotlight of the boat that Roy and Gwen were on at the moment. Next to them, she guessed, was the other boat.…with the two unarmed women.

Blaine was moving up one of the piers and Lara jogged past the shack, exchanging a quick nod with Benny. She headed up the middle pier, one of three that stuck out of the beach like the teeth of a fork. The wooden planks clapped loudly under her boots.

Blaine glanced back. "Doc."

"You heard?"

"Two unarmed women in the middle of the lake, at night? Doesn't make a damn bit of sense."

"No, it doesn't."

The loud outboard motor had started up again and the bright light floating on the surface of the lake started moving, this time coming back toward them.

"How did they catch up to the other boat?" she asked.

"Benny said he heard a low whining sound, so they were probably using a trolling motor," Blaine said. "It would explain how they managed to creep so close to the island without being seen. Well, until they were spotted, anyway."

"How did that happen?"

"Benny saw it first with his binoculars. I guess they were drifting and got too close. He said Roy and Gwen were walking back to the hotel when he called them over. It didn't occur to him those two idiots would jump into one of the boats and take off to intercept."

Lara ground her teeth together. She had a lot of things to say, most of them vulgar. But this wasn't the time. Not now. Roy and Gwen had come to the island at the same time as Bonnie and her sister Jo. They were in the same group, and it made perfect sense the two of them would be drawn to each other. It was almost inevitable, in a way.

It didn't take long for the boats to reach them. The bass fishing boat was towing along a white vessel by a rope, and the two women they had caught were sitting on the floor at the front, while Gwen, all five-two of her, stood next to them (too close for Lara's liking) with her Glock in her hand. Roy steered the boat over to the pier and cut off the engine.

Lara stared at Roy, who quickly looked away. She wasn't sure if that was embarrassment or realization that he had done something she didn't approve of. She ignored him *(for now)* and turned her attention to the two women while Gwen tossed a second line over to Blaine. The women were a brunette in her twenties and a blonde teenager peering back at her through long, stringy hair that seemed to shine under the pier lamps.

The older woman met Lara's eyes. There wasn't fear there, just a lot of reluctance. "We didn't mean to start any trouble."

"What are you doing here on a boat in the middle of the night?" Lara asked.

"Looking for a place to stay. We heard a message on the radio. It said to get to an island…"

Lara exchanged a glance with Blaine.

The radio broadcast. *Her* radio broadcast. A lot of things were happening because of what she had sent out into the world. A lot of it was good, but a part of her, deep down, wondered if the bad was around the corner…

"What's your name?" she asked them.

"I'm Carrie and this is Lorelei," the brunette said. "We were just looking for a safe place—"

The *crack!* of a gunshot exploded across the island from behind her.

She spun around and traced the shot back to Benny, standing on the roof of the boat shack. He was looking down his rifle at something further up the beach.

Benny fired again.

Lara looked where he was shooting and glimpsed a figure moving out of the water and darting up the white sands. It was a man, and he was moving *fast*. Sand erupted behind him as Benny fired a third time and missed badly.

"Blaine!" Lara shouted.

Blaine was already pointing his rifle at the two women in the boat. They stood frozen and terrified because both Roy and Gwen had also drawn their weapons.

"I got 'em, go," the big man said.

Lara ran back up the pier, looking right, trying to track the figure's progress as it slashed across the beach, making a straight line for the trees. He was moving too fast for her to see any details, except that he was running in wet clothes and was still somehow managing to outpace Benny's shots. That was one hell of a feat. Could even Will move that fast?

She heard voices through the radio in her hand.

Bonnie, from the hotel patio: "I hear shooting. Guys?"

Maddie, in the Tower with the ACOG: "I can't get a shot!"

Carly, also at the hotel: "What's happening? Is everyone okay?"

Lara leaped off the pier and landed in the soft sand. She almost lost her balance, but managed to regain it quickly enough to run up the beach. She unslung her rifle as she ran and took aim—

—when the man disappeared into the woods.

Shit.

Lara lowered her rifle and pulled up. Her heart was pounding and the adrenaline was pouring through her.

You wanted to be a leader? Well, here's your chance. Make it count.

She keyed her radio. "Someone's in the woods. I repeat: we have an intruder in the woods. Consider him armed and dangerous. If you get a shot, *take it.*"

CHAPTER 19

WILL

TOMMY WOKE UP around one in the morning along with another man, Bratt, to take their turn on guard duty over Will and Danny in place of Rachel and Milch. Rachel had gotten up and disappeared into the shadows while Bratt replaced her in the light, sitting down next to Tommy.

It was dead silent outside the basement, and the only sound was the breathing of the people inside. Will watched Tommy continuing to struggle to keep his eyes open while Bratt looked as if he had gotten his full eight hours, even though Will knew for a fact he had only slept about four since they fled to the basement after the massacre.

And that was exactly what it had been. Rachel and the others didn't want to admit it, but everyone they knew in the city was likely dead except them. Kate's ghouls—especially the blue-eyed ones—had made sure of that. That was bad for Rachel, but it was also bad for him and Danny. They had come to Dunbar expecting to find Gaby. Unless she had made it out of the city before everything went to hell, chances were she was just as dead (or worse) as Rachel's people.

What were the chances she had actually gone around the city? There was a small—very, very small—possibility of that. But unlikely. Dunbar was too big. It would have taken too long to go around. Easier to just go through it. Plus, Gaby would have wanted to look for supplies on the way to Song Island. She was traveling south—and there was only one thing down there.

Home.

The more he turned over all the possibilities in his head, the more Will reluctantly concluded that the chances of finding Gaby now had lessened dramatically. Hell, he wasn't even sure he and Danny were going to survive tonight. Despite Rachel's assurances about letting them go in the morning, Will wasn't too confident there was going to be a morning.

Not with Kate's ghouls out there. Her blue-eyed ghouls.

Four of them. Jesus. There were *four* of them out there right now. One was bad enough, but four that didn't go down even after you shot them with silver bullets?

Then there was what Kate had said about the island, about Lara's broadcast:

"Like a certain little island that should have stayed quiet. This is what happens when you stick your head out and get my attention, Will. I grab a hammer."

He needed to get his hands on the radio. Even if Lara was asleep, someone would be monitoring the emergency frequency twenty-four hours a day in the island's Tower. It was protocol. He should know; he was the one who put it together.

But to get to the radio, he needed to get through Tommy and Bratt. Maybe if he could talk to the kid, get him to understand. It was always easier to convince someone to do something when he didn't look at you as an enemy.

Then there was Bratt. The man was cleaning a silver-chromed Smith & Wesson automatic with a small toothbrush. He was quiet and invisible for a big man—240 pounds easy—with a full graying beard and dark eyes. Bratt hadn't said a word since he sat down.

Will only really needed to convince one of them, so it had to be Tommy. It was a no-brainer.

"Where did you get that?" Will asked the teenager.

Tommy was clutching the M40A3 sniper rifle, the same one he had been shooting during the gun battle yesterday afternoon. "It's my dad's. He taught me how to shoot with it."

"It's a hell of a rifle. Was he a Marine?"

"How'd you know?"

"I've only seen Marines using the M40 when I was in Afghanistan."

"You were in Afghanistan?"

"Danny and me. You good with it?"

"Not bad. I've been shooting with it since I was eleven."

"So, five years ago?"

Tommy grinned. "Eight going on nine, wise guy."

Will smiled back at him, feeling like a pervert on a playground trying to lure a kid into his ice cream truck.

"I always thought I'd enlist when I was old enough," Tommy was saying. "Never got the chance, with everything that happened. What branch were you in?"

"I was Army."

"That's unfortunate."

Will chuckled. "Yeah, well, we all have our crosses to bear."

Tommy glanced briefly at Danny, sleeping with his back against the wall next to Will. "Is he really asleep?"

Will looked over at Danny, then shrugged. "I think so."

"He doesn't look asleep." Tommy narrowed his eyes. "He's faking it, isn't he?"

"He's tired. We've been moving on water and beef jerky for the last couple of days, trying to get home."

"I'm sorry," Tommy said. "If it was up to me, I'd have let you guys go."

There it is. There's the opening.

"I need the radio, Tommy," Will said. "I really need to give my friend a message. It's a matter of life and death."

Tommy didn't answer right away. But he also didn't say no right away, either.

"Tommy," Will said, keeping his voice calm, conversational, "it's just a radio. What's it going to hurt?"

"I can't," Tommy said finally, shaking his head. "Rachel's orders. I'm sorry."

"She doesn't have to know."

"She'll know." The kid shrugged. "Anyways, it's not going to work. Look around you. Concrete walls and floor. It'd be a miracle if you could get a signal out of this room."

"I have to try. You have to let me try. A lot of lives are at stake."

This time Tommy shook his head faster without even taking a moment to think about it. It was a bad sign.

"I can't," the teenager said. "I'm sorry. You'll get it back tomorrow. It's only, what, six hours away?"

Six hours too long…

This wasn't going to work. So he tried another tact.

"You saw them?" Will asked.

"Saw what?"

"The blue-eyed ones."

Tommy looked hesitant, uncertain, maybe replaying what he may or may not have seen in his head. Will knew for a fact Tommy was there at the parking lot along with Rachel. They had seen the four blue-eyed ghouls emerging out of the U-Haul trailer like demons from hell. You didn't forget a sight like that. Will certainly wasn't going to anytime soon.

"I don't know what I saw," Tommy said. "Everything happened so fast…"

"You saw them," Will said. "I saw them, too. Blue eyes."

The kid nodded reluctantly.

"How many of them were there?" Will asked.

"I saw four," Tommy said. "They had blue eyes like you said, and they were fast. I mean, the others—the black-eyed ones—they're fast, too, but these ones were… They were way faster."

"Shock troops," Bratt said suddenly, surprising both Will and Tommy. Bratt's voice was deep and sounded as if he were swallowing gravel with every word.

Dammit. Not now. Can't you see I'm working on the kid here?

"What?" Tommy said, looking over at Bratt sitting next to him.

"Shock troops," Bratt repeated. He hadn't stopped working on his gun and didn't look up. If Will didn't know any better, he would swear the man was talking to himself. "In wars, they're the point of the spear, lightning-quick and mobile. They're sent to break through the enemy lines to lead the way for the rest of the army. That's what they were doing here last night. They were sent into Dunbar for us."

"Us?" Tommy said. "What are you talking about, Bratt?"

"We've been causing trouble. It's Harrison's fault." The *click-click* of meaty fingers slid gun parts into place. "Attacking their convoys around the area, killing their soldiers, all that stupid-ass stuff. I told Harrison he was asking for trouble, but he wouldn't listen." Bratt chuckled—or was that a cackle? "I guess it's kind of an honor. I bet they don't send those blue-eyed freaks out for just anyone, right?"

You're not wrong, Will thought, remembering again what Kate had said:

"This is what happens when you stick your head out and get my attention, Will. I grab a hammer."

"Shock troops," Tommy said to Will. "Crazy, huh?"

Will almost laughed.

Crazy? If you've only seen the things I've laid eyes on in the last eleven months, you'll realize this is the least crazy thing, kid.

He said instead, "Yeah."

"I mean, what makes us so special?" Tommy shook his head. "Nothing. Nothing that I can think of."

You're not. You're just an annoyance to her. That's all we are to Kate, to Mabry. Cockroaches running around, dirtying up their new house. And cockroaches get stepped on if they stray into the light—

He felt it. It was a very soft vibration at first, and there was almost no sound.

Slowly, as he listened more carefully, it grew in volume…

Danny opened his eyes next to him. "You felt that?"

"Yeah," Will said.

Tommy said across from them, "That wasn't just me, right? You guys felt that, too?"

Will nodded and stood up, Danny and Tommy mirroring him.

Bratt followed suit, holstering his sidearm and unslinging his AR-15. "They're coming," he said matter-of-factly.

"I think you better wake the others up," Will said to Tommy.

The teenager nodded and vanished into the darkness. Will heard urgent whispering, then Rachel's groggy voice.

The sound had picked up noticeably and it was definitely coming from above them—the basement door. Will and Danny wandered over to the landing and looked up the flight of stairs. Even in the semidarkness, the steel door seemed to gleam at the other end.

"What are the chances they'll give us back our weapons?" Will said.

"Maybe if you ask nice like," Danny said.

"I did. Again and again."

"Questionable noises weren't coming from the other side of the door then."

Will looked over as Rachel and Tommy emerged from the blackness. Milch and two others, Eaton and George, were moving slowly after them, rubbing the sleep out of their eyes.

"What the hell's happening?" Rachel said.

"Listen," Will said.

Rachel did. So did the others.

Slowly, their eyes wandered over to the top of the stairs. They could all hear it now. The slight vibrations, the dull *thump-thump-thump* of something tapping against the thick metal door from the other side.

"I thought they gave up?" Tommy said, whispering for some reason.

"They did," Will said. "Now they're back."

"They've never done anything like this before," Milch said. He unslung his M4 rifle and held it in front of him at the ready. "Right?" Milch added, looking over at the others. "They've never stopped and start over again, right?"

It's the blue-eyed ghouls, Will wanted to tell them. The black-eyed ones behaved differently when they were around. They became more unpredictable, more creative.

And this time there are four of them out there.

A little overkill, don't you think, Kate?

Will exchanged a brief knowing look with Danny before he sought out Rachel in the semidarkness. "If they get in…"

"They won't," she said.

He didn't buy it for a second. "We need our weapons."

"No."

"I thought we already came to an understanding. We're not a threat to one another."

She didn't answer right away, and Will saw conflict playing across her face.

"Rachel," Will said, "we're not your enemy. If they get through that door—"

"Give them back their stuff," she said to Milch and Eaton before he could finish.

"Thank you," Will said.

"You're definitely going on my Christmas list now," Danny added.

Rachel grunted before turning her full attention back to the door up the stairs. "Don't make me regret this."

Milch and Eaton vanished into the darkness before coming back with Will's and Danny's M4A1s and gun belts. Will took them eagerly, as did Danny. He felt instantly whole again with the extra weight of the pouches, spare magazines, and the cross-knife in its sheath around his left thigh.

"What about our packs?" Will said to Eaton. "The radio's in one of them."

Eaton glanced back into the shadows. "They're back there somewhere."

"We need them."

"Not my problem," Milch said before turning back to the door.

Will exchanged a look with Danny.

"The service in this place sucks," Danny said. "I'm definitely complaining on the comment card."

Will started to move toward the back of the basement when above them the noise had increased and the soft, barely audible *thump-thump-thump* became noticeably faster and seemed to be growing in volume. That stopped him in his tracks and he gripped the rifle, turning to face the door.

What the hell are they doing out there?

He knew for a fact the creatures weren't banging on the metal slab without a reason. Not with the blue-eyed ones guiding them. So what was it, then? How did they plan to get inside?

"What about the side door?" Will asked.

"What about it?" Rachel said.

"There's one, right? That's how you got in here before us."

"Yeah."

"We might have to use it."

"You don't think there are more of them waiting out there?"

"Probably, but it's a better option than facing what's going to be coming through this door."

"Assuming they get through."

"Listen to them," Will said. "They're going to get through. They're just getting warmed up." He glanced at his watch: 2:16 A.M. "And they have hours on their side."

"You're a warm bowl of optimism, aren't you, buddy?" Danny said.

"If we have to, we'll use the side door," Rachel said.

BOOM!

They all took an involuntarily step back from the stair landing. It wasn't the same noise they had been hearing for the last few minutes.

No. This was a single blow. Heavier, stronger, and more damaging. Will had become used to the rhythmic pattern of the ghouls slamming their useless flesh against a door, and this wasn't it.

This was something else. Something more intense.

"Sounds metal," Danny said.

"Yeah," Will nodded.

"That all you got?"

"Yup."

"You're useless."

"I try."

"Shut up," Rachel said, annoyed.

Danny mouthed at Will, *"I blame this all on you."*

"We're going to die tonight," Will mouthed back.

"Captain fucking Optimism. I'm telling Lara."

Will grinned.

"Tommy, go see if you can hear anything happening at the side door," Rachel said.

Tommy rushed off into the darkness. The fact that people could disappear and reappear without warning was a bit disconcerting to Will, especially since he had zero visibility outside the small pool of light provided by the single LED lamp.

BOOM!

"Definitely metal," Danny said.

"Let's find out for sure," Will said.

He jogged up the stairs, where he could still see the doorframe trembling in the aftermath of the last blow just seconds ago. Whatever they were using out there was definitely heavy and doing tremendous damage. He hadn't been counting the seconds between the impacts, but it sounded like every ten seconds.

Which was just about—

BOOM!

Every inch of the door shook, and the brick wall surrounding it threatened to come unglued at any second. And there—a noticeable indentation had appeared at the side of the door, just over where the lever and locking mechanism were.

Footsteps behind him before Rachel's and Danny's breaths hit him in the back of the neck.

"Holy shit," Danny said, staring at the indentation.

"What the hell is that?" Rachel asked, out of breath.

"They're using some kind of battering ram," Will said. "It's the blue-eyed ghouls. They're running the show out there."

"Blue-eyed—" Rachel started to say.

BOOM!

All three of them took a step back as another indentation materialized in the door, very close to the first one. It sounded as if the creatures were literally driving whatever was on the other side into the door with great force, raining one concentrated, massive blow at a time every ten seconds.

"They're going to cave the lock in," Will said. "The door won't hold for long after that."

They hurried back down the stairs just as Tommy reappeared in the light.

"Nothing," Tommy said. "I didn't hear anything on the other side."

"Are you sure?" Rachel asked.

"I'm telling you, there's nothing out there—"

BOOM!

Will swore the entire basement vibrated for a good five seconds afterward that time.

"We gotta split," Bratt said, his gravel voice cutting through the momentary silence. "The shock troops are coming. That's them out there. We gotta go *now*."

Will exchanged a quick look with Danny, who nodded back.

"Rachel," Will said. "He's right. We gotta go."

"The side door?" she said, looking uncertainly at him.

"Yeah."

"We'll never survive out there."

"We'll have a better shot out there than down here when they start coming through that door."

"Not much better…"

BOOM!

"Better than down *here*," Will said, "trapped in this one big room with nowhere to go."

"The door will hold," she said, looking back up the stairs.

Will could tell he wasn't going to get through. Maybe it was fear, or determination, or just simple human stubbornness (he knew a little bit about that last one), but he wasn't going to budge her. She had decided, made her choice, and she was going to live *(die)* with it.

"It'll hold," she said again.

Another *BOOM!* blasted through the entire basement.

They spun around back to the stairs almost as one just as the metal door flew wide open and a burst of cold, rancid air flooded inside.

The first ghoul raced in, its bones *clacking* loudly.

Rachel, Eaton, and Milch opened fire and the creature's forward momentum was stopped by a hail of bullets tearing into it, ripping away flesh and revealing bleach-white bones underneath. Then they lost sight of the ghoul because the black ocean pouring in through the open door swallowed the lone creature up and flooded down the stairs in a quivering obsidian tide.

"Go go go!" Will shouted.

Danny was already running, Tommy right behind him, when Will opened fire on the stairs.

Silver bullets punched through weak flesh and ricocheted off bones. Ghouls fell, flopping down the stairs, while others threw the dead ones over the banisters to make way for more to get down faster.

"Rachel!" Will shouted.

It didn't do any good. He didn't even think she heard him over the roar of blazing gunfire in the tight confines of the basement. Bullet casings sprayed around her and Bratt and Milch and Eaton, the *clink-clink-clink* of empty brass almost as loud as the unrelenting boom of assault rifles firing on full-auto.

Will turned and fled.

He darted into the darkness, guessing *(praying)* at the direction of the side door, using where he had last seen Tommy going and coming out of as a marker. Then he saw moonlight spilling through a rectangular hole in the wall and ran toward it.

Screams erupted behind him. Men's voices, then a woman's.

He kept going, because looking back would only slow him down. A second. Half a second. It didn't matter. Slow was slow, and slow was death.

The floor under him trembled as the creatures landed everywhere. The slapping of flesh against concrete was loud because the gunfire had all but stopped. For a split-second there was no noise at all, until Rachel's screams filled the room and bounced off the walls, then someone began firing with a semi-automatic handgun—

Will saw Danny in the doorway, holding the door open for him. There were no signs of Tommy. "Come on!" Danny shouted. "Can you run any slower, old man?"

Will put on a burst of speed and lunged through the opening and crashed into a brick wall chest-first on the other side. Behind him came the loud *bang!* of the door slamming shut and almost instantly the sound and fury of dozens of ghouls crashing into it from the other side.

Thoom thoom thoom!

Ennis's basement side entrance was one floor below ground, with steps leading up into an alleyway beside the bar. Danny was already halfway up, shouting, "Can't lock the door on this side! Run run run!"

Will pushed himself off the wall and followed as a gust of wind rushed against him about the same time the door banged open and the sound of hundreds *(thousands?)* of crashing bare feet flooded his senses.

Tommy was waiting for them in the alley above, absurdly still armed with his sniper rifle, and was pointing it at the mouth of the alley.

"Go go go!" Danny shouted.

Tommy turned and ran toward the back of the alley. Will wanted to shout at him, find out if he knew where he was going, but he didn't get the chance. Creatures were coming up fast behind him, and he skidded and nearly fell against the dirty floor. He managed to catch himself at the last second, made a quick U-turn, and pursued Danny and Tommy into the darkened alley.

There were no lights, just the weak spill of moonlight from above. Thankfully that was enough to see with, and Will caught sight of Tommy's lanky form moving with surprising speed. The kid was running so fast, so determined to get to the end, that Will wondered if he even still realized they were behind him.

Danny slowed down in front of him, then spun around like a ballerina doing a pirouette. Will kept going, the loud *clattering* of Danny's rifle firing on full-auto behind him even louder in the narrow passageway.

Then he began to slow down, and as soon as Danny fired his last shot, Will stopped, spun, and lifted his rifle.

Danny darted past him a split-second later. "Changing!"

THE FIRES OF ATLANTIS   249

Will opened up on the horde. It was a wall of living darkness, liquid black eyes against the enveloping night. He fired into the center, then swung the rifle left to right, then right to left again. The magazine emptied at an impossible rate, the carbine getting lighter and lighter with every half-second—

"Go go go!" Danny shouted behind him.

Will turned and ran, Danny commencing firing as soon as he was past him.

Up ahead, Tommy was waving them over while holding open a steel door, moonlight glinting off its shiny surface. It was beaten and old, but it was intact, and that was all that mattered.

He ejected the magazine and let it drop to the floor and shoved in a new one while shouting, "Danny! You coming or what?"

Danny was already running back toward him, a big grin on his face. "Aw, I didn't think you cared!"

"Don't tell anyone!" Will shouted back, then pulled the trigger again.

Ghouls stumbled and fell, creating a dangerous pile that the others slipped and stumbled against as they tried to get over to get to him. Will was backing up as he fired, watching with morbid fascination as the black-eyed undead things toppled like dominos, bullets piercing non-existent muscle and dropping more of their kind behind them. They were so crammed into the tight confines of the alley and there were so many of them he was pretty sure he was killing a half dozen *(more?)* with every silver bullet.

He wished he could have said it did any good, but it didn't. It didn't make a damn bit of difference at all because for every single ghoul he killed, a dozen were already scrambling over its lifeless carcass and they were constantly moving forward at an obscene rate.

"Move your ass, Kemosabe!" Danny shouted behind him, his voice shockingly close.

Will hadn't realized he was almost on top of Danny until he spun to his left and saw the open door in front of him. He threw himself inside while Danny unleashed another full magazine into the surging tide of writhing flesh, the harsh sound of bullets snapping and glancing off bones like some kind of strange melody that could only be orchestrated by a mad composer.

Will was turning around when Danny stepped through and Tommy, who had been waiting beside him this entire time, slammed the door shut with all his might. There was the loud (and very satisfying) *clack-clack!* of a large deadbolt sliding into place. Almost instantly, the door shook as the ghouls flung themselves into it from the other side—

Thoom thoom thoom!

—and Tommy stumbled back, disoriented by the brute force on display.

But the door held. *It held.*

"Where the hell are we?" Will said as he took in his surroundings.

He couldn't see anything, but he could hear the sound of his and Danny's instinctive reloading. Not that he needed light to change magazines. He mastered that little trick years ago and hadn't looked back since.

Thoom thoom thoom!

Danny was standing next to him, the two of them in competition to see who was breathing harder and faster and more desperately. It was, he thought, a tie. The fact that they were standing in some kind of darkened hallway with no source of light whatsoever did nothing to make him feel any calmer. Danny apparently shared his apprehension.

Thoom thoom thoom!

Click! A beam of light speared a long hallway with white walls, carpeted flooring, and dust flitting wildly in front of them. "Someone's been shirking their dusting," Danny said behind the flashlight.

Will grabbed his own flashlight from one of his pouches and flicked it on. "Tommy, where the hell are we?"

Tommy stepped in front of them, still sucking in air. He looked back every time the creatures smashed into the door.

Thoom thoom thoom!

Will and Danny had forgotten about the sound. God help them, but they had become so used to it that it didn't even faze them now.

Thoom thoom thoom!

"It's a museum," Tommy said.

"A museum?" Danny said. "In Dunbar? What's the museum for? The crawdads of Louisiana?"

"History of the town. Dunbar is, uh, kind of proud of itself."

"I'm proud of my boxers, too, but you don't see me starting a museum for them."

Thoom thoom thoom!

"Are we safe in here?" Will asked.

"I, uh, hope so," Tommy said, looking back at the door again.

Then—*silence.*

The pounding had ceased without any warning.

All three of them looked back at the door, Will and Danny running their flashlights over it to make sure it was still closed. It was, and the deadbolt remained firmly in place. The frame looked slightly cracked by the vicious assault, but the door itself was still in one piece.

It was quiet around them. Not just inside, but outside as well. There were no screams, no gunshots, not even the soft but familiar *tap-tap* of bare feet. It was as if the ghouls had ceased all activity within the city limits.

"What the hell is this?" Danny whispered.

"Hell if I know," Will whispered back.

It's the blue-eyed ghouls.

Four of them.

Out there, somewhere.

They know we're in here.

They have to know.

So what the hell are they up to now?

CHAPTER 20

KEO

DAMN, THAT PLAN went down the crapper fast.

The guy missed with his first two bullets, but all it took was one stray round to turn this into a very bad night. Fortunately for Keo, he had surfaced on the other side of the beach, with a good one hundred meters separating him and the man standing watch on the boat shack. He would have chastised the guy for being a lousy shot, except Keo didn't think he could have done any better himself.

Looks like we both could use a little more time on the firing range, pal.

He pushed his way into the tree line and kept running. Bullets punched through branches behind and to the left of him as Mister Boat Shack continued to try to take him out. The guy had no chance out in the open when he could see Keo, and he had even less now.

Of course, all it took was one lucky shot…

This wasn't how he had expected it to go down. Then again, he hadn't anticipated finding an island lit up like a Christmas tree, with what looked like bright halogen lamps strategically placed from side to side and front to back, either. Towering solar collector trays ringed the place like a shiny necklace, which meant solar power. In a world without electricity, that alone made Song Island worth its weight in gold.

It also went a long way to confirm Allie's story about a mysterious radio signal she had intercepted months ago that had lured seven of her people here. Those same survivors hadn't kept in touch, which wasn't supposed to happen. That was why Zachary and Shorty had come down here with him (well, mostly Zachary), to check up on their missing friends. It was that knowledge of those potentially missing *(dead?)* people that convinced Keo to take this particular approach.

Carrie hadn't been enthusiastic about his idea when he told her. "You're crazy," she had said. "You're going to get yourself killed. Why can't we just go over there and tell them we're looking for shelter and you're looking for people who had come here before?"

His natural instinct was to respond with a cavalier, *"Because this is the real world, not Fantasyland,"* but instead he had said, "Can't take the chance they turn out to be soldiers. This way, we'll know who they are before they even see us."

The three of them sat in the boat, adrift in the darkness with the island in the background. The string of lamps along the three piers looked like glowing fingers, and he could make out a silhouetted form moving on top of a shack on one side of the long stretch of beach. He couldn't tell if the man (or woman) was armed from this distance, but that was probably a safe bet. The Song Island he was looking at now was worth killing for.

So where did that leave Allie's people?

You owe me big for this, Zachary.

With the trolling motor turned off, the boat moved slightly back and forth on its own accord over the calm lake water. He was certain the guard would eventually spot the white paint on the boat, but so far, so good.

The lone guard didn't concern him too much. It was the tall structure at the back of the island, with the floodlights over its windows. Some kind of lighthouse with an antenna sticking out of it. You could probably see the entire island from up there.

Now that's one hell of an overwatch.

He expected to hear an argument between the girls, but there wasn't one. In fact, neither woman said a word. He gave them their privacy anyway and didn't hurry them along with a decision. It wasn't as if he was going to run out of night anytime soon. Out here, far from land, he felt a certain freedom knowing the creatures couldn't—*wouldn't*—reach him. No wonder Allie and her people refused to budge from their little island—

"Okay," Carrie said behind him. "We'll wait here until you come back."

He looked over. "Are you sure?"

"No, but we'll do it anyway because we owe you."

"You don't owe me anything." He looked at Lorelei. "You don't."

"Yes, we do," Lorelei said, with what sounded like absolute certainty. "We'd be back at L11 right now if it wasn't for you."

"Besides," Carrie said, "you're just sneaking onto the island and finding out what you can and swimming back before daylight, right? If it's not safe, we'll go back to shore. If it is, we'll show ourselves like we just arrived."

"That's the plan."

Carrie nodded. He wasn't sure if that was for his benefit, or hers and Lorelei's. "Okay. We'll wait out here in the dark for you. What could possibly go wrong?" She had said that last part while gritting her teeth.

Famous last words.

"Use the trolling motor if you have to," Keo said. "It got us this close without being spotted, and it should be fine to turn on again if we need it." He paused, then, "Remember, if things go bad—and if you hear shooting, that means things have gone bad—wait an hour, and if I'm not back by then, or you see boats leaving the island and coming your way, take off."

"Take off," Carrie repeated. "Right."

They both looked scared. Lorelei had all but shrunk into the back of the boat, once again trying to hide behind her curtain of blonde hair.

"Just stick to the plan," Keo said. "As long as you keep your distance, they shouldn't spot the boat, and I'll be back before sunrise. We'll be fine. No muss, no fuss."

HE LEFT HIS pack in the boat, strapping just the MP5SD tightly around his body before dropping off the side and into the water. It was cold at first, but his body adapted after a few minutes. He measured the distance to the beach. Not too far. Four hundred meters, give or take. He could do that in his sleep. Thank God for all those summers on Mission Beach back in San Diego.

Keo did calm breaststrokes for the first one hundred meters. He wasn't in any hurry. The night wasn't going anywhere, and he had plenty of time to search the island and do a little exploring. Push came to shove, there was a lot of water he could jump into from just about any part of the island and plenty of woods he could get lost in. He had a lot of experience outrunning pursuers in wooded areas these days.

At the 150 meter mark, he slipped under and didn't come up for another fifty.

As soon as he poked his head back through the surface, he heard the roar of an outboard motor and saw the boat leaving one of the piers, bright spotlight flashing across the lake in the direction of—

Carrie and Lorelei.

On cue, he heard the boat they had commandeered this afternoon fire up its trolling motor behind him. The slow, gradual whine was almost instantly lost in the blare of the loud outboard motor pushing a bass fishing boat across the lake. Waves surged against him, jostling Keo around as the faster vessel shot across the water.

Dammit.

He treaded in place and looked after the boat as it streaked toward Carrie and Lorelei. Fast. Too fast. He couldn't have stopped it even if he was close enough to use the submachine gun. Which he wasn't. Instead, he helplessly watched it catch up to the white boat.

He waited to hear gunfire, hoping that he wouldn't. Carrie still had her Glock, but if she was smart, she would get rid of it before the boat caught up to them. There was no way they were going to fight off a boat that was probably better armed, and he hoped she figured out that before it was too late.

Throw the gun away, Carrie. Throw the gun away…

Thirty seconds later, the boats were now drifting in the lake close to one another, and there still wasn't any gunfire. That was a good sign. Carrie and Lorelei had surrendered and no one had shot anyone. They were still alive. Which meant he could still save them…later, on the island.

Keo turned and went back under the surface and continued toward the beach.

When he came back up again, he was just fifty meters from the impossibly white sands, and the craft with the loud motor was on its way back, towing Carrie and Lorelei's boat behind it. He could just make out four figures in the first boat now. Two were seated and two were standing. He squinted, but he couldn't tell if the two standing were wearing uniforms.

Maybe, maybe not…

He ducked back under and pushed on toward the island, fighting against the jostling waves from the boat's wake a second time.

He was ten meters from the beach when his boots touched something mushy but just solid enough and he began walking up at an angle. He went into a crouch, half-submerged in the water. A quick check to the side found the island boat sidling up to one of the piers, where a man and a woman had appeared and were waiting for them.

Carrie and Lorelei were standing up on the boat now, so they were okay. At this point, both women alive was more than he could have hoped for, especially given the precarious nature of the night.

Of course, their capture changed everything. Without the boat waiting for him out there, he had no place to retreat to—

Crack! A bullet splashed into the lake behind him.

He bolted up from his kneeling position and took off up the beach. Not an easy feat. He was drenched from head to toe and he was carrying extra pounds thanks to the water absorbed by his clothes. Parts of Beaufont Lake were in the pockets of his cargo pants and T-shirt, and a whole lot of it was in his boots. He picked up speed (or thought he did, anyway) with every ounce of water that literally poured out of him. He would probably look like a bloated corpse on the beach if he were to die now.

Swim fast, leave a bloated corpse. Wasn't that the old saying?

Close enough.

IT WAS GOING to take a while before he dried up completely. Maybe half a day, since it was still night and he didn't have the sun to make it go faster. He was shivering, because being out of the water and moving in wet clothes was a lot colder than when he was submerged in the lake.

The MP5SD in hand, Keo picked his way through the woods, skipping round underbrush and trees, making as little noise and leaving as few tracks as possible. The moon provided little light for him to navigate with, but he took comfort in the knowledge that if he couldn't see where he was going, then likely his pursuers wouldn't be able to, either.

Right. Keep telling yourself that, pal.

He was far enough from the lampposts to avoid their halos, and the only creatures that noticed his passing were birds in the trees and random land creatures that were annoyed by his presence, who scampered off. A few squirrels sat and watched him curiously. He grinned back at them. The furry little buggers had become his new lucky charms these days.

I should catch one of them, skin it, and hang its fur around my neck for good luck.

He could certainly use a little luck now. Hell, why settle for a little? He could use a *lot* more than that. It was going to be tricky if he had to fight an entire island full of soldiers, though he was starting to think that wasn't the case. They just didn't act like the men in uniform he had encountered the last two days. Something about them was…different. The vibe was all off.

Groovy, man. We living and dying by vibes now?

Keo took a moment to take inventory of his supplies. Besides the Ka-Bar, the submachine gun was it. Heckler & Koch made excellent weapons, and even wet, the MP5SD would still work like a charm. He fired off a couple of rounds just to be sure, putting two bullets into the ground, the suppressor keeping both shots at minimum decibels.

Satisfied he still had a working weapon, Keo moved on.

He was sure they would chase him into the woods or attempt to locate him from the surrounding fields (with the beach behind him) almost immediately. He was wrong. They were either taking their time, or they were too smart to follow him into the darkness. He would have preferred to keep doing this under the cover of night, but daylight had its advantages too, including drying him out, which would help with the shivering.

He thought he was prepared for what he would find as he reached the end of the woods, but the sight of the hotel startled Keo and left him breathless for a moment.

Daebak. I've died and gone to heaven.

The building was huge, with floodlights spaced out along the walls. And it wasn't even finished yet. He knew that because there were scaffolding and construction equipment visible on the flat rooftop. The lights coming from the rooms, particularly the front patio and lobby, told him that the quiet hum he had been hearing since stepping foot on the island was the product of a power station probably somewhere on the other side of the island where the hotel guests wouldn't notice. That was where all the solar collector trays were sending their juices.

A solar-powered island. God bless the peaceniks.

And there was the lighthouse, about half a football field from the back of the hotel, with a sprawling lawn between the two structures. Or it looked like a lighthouse. Three floors, with a cone-shaped top. Four windows each on the top two floors, light pouring out from the openings. A figure moved back and forth between the windows on the third floor with binoculars. Possibly a woman from the curves.

Keo would have liked to move around the island while sticking to the woods, but once he reached the eastern cliff, he was stuck. The woods only went so far, leaving him with open ground filled with two large empty swimming pools and bird-poop-covered fish ornaments between him and the hotel. From here, his only choice was to retreat back to the beach.

It wasn't an optimal fighting position. Not by a long shot.

A voice, booming across the wide-open space in front of him, snapped his attention back to the hotel. "Keo!"

A woman. Probably the same one from the beach. The fact that she knew his name was expected. Carrie and Lorelei would have given up information on him by now. He hadn't expected them to hold out under interrogation, much less torture, if indeed that was what had happened to them in the last two hours.

"Keo!" the woman shouted again. "We talked to Carrie and Lorelei!"

No kidding, lady.

"We're not soldiers! Or collaborators!"

Keo tracked the voice to the patio, maybe 200 meters from his current position. He fished out his lightweight binoculars from one of his cargo pants pockets and looked through them.

A blonde. About five-five. A taller woman and the large man stood behind her. All three were clearly illuminated by the harsh

THE FIRES OF ATLANTIS 259

glare of lights above them, which also allowed him to see their clothes—civilian pants and shirts, but no uniform. Of course, it could just be one big trap to lure him out. After what he had done to them, first at the marina and then later at the shoreline, he wouldn't be surprised if one of the fake soldiers finally grew a brain.

"I know you can hear me, Keo!" the woman shouted.

She seemed to be looking in his direction, so he guessed she figured out that he didn't have a whole lot of real estate to hide in after escaping the beach. It made sense. This was their island. They would know every inch of it by now. So why hadn't they attacked him yet? Either they were risk-averse, or they didn't want to make this encounter bloody. Of course, he could just be overthinking the whole thing, too.

"This is your chance to keep this from getting out of hand!" she shouted. "Step outside with your hands up!" She paused, probably for effect. "You make us chase you in there, and it's not going to end well, and neither one of us wants that!"

Speak for yourself. I happen to have a lot of recent experience eluding people with assault rifles in the woods.

Keo turned and hurried back toward the beach. He skirted over familiar terrain that he had memorized before arriving at his destination.

He went into a crouch and listened for signs of armed men trying to outflank him.

Behind him, the woman was still shouting, her voice fading a bit with the distance. But the night was so silent he would have to be deaf not to hear her. "Look, we get it! You had no choice! You couldn't be sure who we were! I understand that! I would have done the same thing in your shoes!"

Satisfied no one was moving in on him from the beach, Keo got up and jogged through the darkness and back to the other side of the woods. The woman and her companions hadn't moved from the patio.

He looked to the lighthouse and saw two figures inside now, moving from window to window with binoculars. Searching for him, no doubt. He wondered if they had special binoculars. Night-vision, maybe. That made him take a couple of extra steps backward until he was behind a thick underbrush just in case.

"Keo!" the woman shouted. "Let's talk this out!"

When he didn't respond, the woman turned to the others and said something. When she was done, she went back into the hotel with the tall woman, and a few seconds later a second man came out and took up position outside the patio alongside the big guy.

Keo waited again for the attack he knew was coming.

And waited, and waited…but nothing happened.

He sat down on the ground in his still-wet clothes instead.

Who were these people? If they weren't soldiers, then who were they? Maybe they were even Allie's survivors. But that didn't make sense, either. That lighthouse made a hell of a good broadcasting station, especially with the antenna at the top. Wouldn't they have contacted Allie with it by now? Or broadcasted a "safe and sound" message? They had to know Zachary and the others were waiting to hear back from them. The only reason they hadn't done that yet in the months since they arrived was because they were *(dead)* in trouble. So was that it—

"Keo!"

It was Carrie's voice, coming from the hotel patio.

"Keo!" Carrie shouted again. "It's okay! They haven't hurt us, and they're not going to hurt you!"

He moved back toward the tree line and looked out with the binoculars again. Carrie was on the patio with the boss lady and the two men. The sight of her, standing among the islanders, caught him by surprise. He certainly hadn't expected *this* little development.

"Keo!" Carrie shouted. "They're not going to hurt you! I've been talking to them! That's all we've been doing. Just talking! They know what happened to those seven people you came here looking for! Keo, can you hear me?"

Carrie waited for him to answer, and when he didn't, she turned back to the woman. They exchanged some brief words, the back and forth almost casual. Then the women went into the hotel, once again leaving the two men outside.

What the hell was that about?

Keo remained where he was, watching them and listening for sounds around him. Any noise at all other than the birds in the trees, the scurrying along branches from his furry buddies. Hints that the attack he knew was coming would finally arrive. They certainly knew where he was—or at least, the general vicinity—so what was keeping them?

He got up and moved back toward the eastern part of the woods. There, he leaned out between two trees and peered at the rocky formations below. There was nothing down there except large rocks. No handholds, either, so climbing without equipment was definitely out of the question.

There was only one path out of the woods that he could see. That was straight across the open grounds, past those two empty swimming pools, the unfinished gazebo, and hope and pray he didn't get too close to one of the hundreds or so lampposts that snaked around the place like someone's gaudy idea of showing off to the neighbors during the holidays.

Hey. No one told you you had to come here. Remember?

Yeah, yeah...

THERE WAS A new figure on the boat shack; he could tell the difference by the height and the man's outline. There was also someone new in the lighthouse—just one, this time, going from window to window and peering through binoculars and occasionally talking into a radio. The big man was alone at the hotel patio again.

Presenting one lone guard at each position was tempting. Was that the point? Were they trying to lure him out into the open? To make the first move? Was there really just one person at the beach? Or more inside the shack? Another one hiding in the lighthouse? Or waiting behind the front doors into the hotel lobby?

These people clearly weren't stupid, so anything was possible.

Of course, it could just be his paranoia talking. Or maybe, just maybe, he was giving them too much credit again.

There wasn't really much of a choice when he got right down to it. Run or fight. Or surrender. That last option wasn't really an option. Keo had never been good at surrendering. It wasn't in his DNA. At least he shared that much with his father. Of course, if he had been a better planner, a better tactician, he wouldn't have found himself in these situations so often. Norris could have told him that. The old-timer was always criticizing his (lack of) ability to strategize.

Woulda, coulda, shoulda...

After watching the figure in the lighthouse and the one on the patio for an hour and getting their patterns, Keo waited for his opportunity. When he saw the woman in the lighthouse move away from the south window and the one on the patio turn his back briefly to check the other side of the island, Keo jogged out of the woods. He kept low, bent over at the waist, while still managing to sprint.

He made it to one of the swimming pools less than ten seconds later. He slid along the tall grass and fell off the smooth concrete edge and into the empty and slightly curved hole in the ground. It took him a moment to realize the thing was shaped into a pear and that he had landed somewhere in the shallow section. Which was lucky. If he had chosen the wrong spot, he would have had a pretty long plummet into the deep end.

He moved toward the other side of the pool and didn't have to stand up to scan the lighthouse on one side and the patio on the other. It was two in the morning and he could tell both guards were tired. It was in their sluggish back and forth, the way they held their weapons.

Keo waited for the double turn again, and when it came, he climbed up and darted across the grounds, sticking to the patches of darkness and skirting around the haloed LED lampposts. The damn things were ridiculously bright up close and he had to blink away temporary blindness a couple of times. There were a couple of damaged lights here and there that allowed him to go in a straight line every now and then.

He finally slipped behind a large palm tree *(Where the hell did they even get palm trees in Louisiana?)* and glimpsed the lighthouse to his right, the patio to his left, and the side of the hotel—wicked bright floodlights and all—directly in front.

And there, one of the side doors stared invitingly back at him.

Keo waited again.

One minute. Two…then three…

The double turn.

He dashed through the lights and made the side door fourteen seconds later. He reached for the lever and cranked it and slipped inside, his MP5SD moving up into firing position—

Keo froze.

There was a police Remington pump-action shotgun pointed at his face from one meter away.

"You took your sweet time," the redhead standing behind the shotgun said. "We thought you might have decided to swim back to the shore or something."

Keo's mind raced.

The redhead noticed and grinned. "Yeah, go for it. Three feet? I'm sure there's a chance I could miss. Probably."

"WHAT HAPPENED TO your face?" the pretty blonde asked.

"Birthmark," Keo said. "It was a very painful birth."

"I'm sorry for her."

"So am I."

"Is that why your mom named you Keo? As punishment?"

"She wanted to call me Harry, but it was already taken."

"Really."

"True story."

"I'm sure it is." She paused for a moment, watching him intently. "The plan didn't quite work out, huh?"

He shrugged. "I've always been more of a doer than a planner."

"It would appear so."

The blonde was the clear leader. If he had any doubts before, he didn't anymore. She looked convincing in cargo pants with a Glock in a hip holster. Late twenties (though it was hard to tell these days), watching him with crystal-blue eyes. The redhead, leaning against the wall behind her, looked even younger. She might have been twenty, maybe twenty-one.

They were both staring at him. Really, *really* staring at him.

After the incident at the side door, they had led him to a small room at the back of the building. Some kind of supply closet, with concrete walls and floor. He sat on an uncomfortable metal chair now, hands zip tied behind his back and ankles similarly restrained. The three of them were inside the room, but he could hear a fourth person—a man by the heavy back-and-forth footsteps—in the hallway.

How exactly had he ended up being held prisoner on an island run by two kids?

This is fucking embarrassing.

"We talked to Carrie," the blonde was saying. "You're looking for seven of your friends."

Friends of friends, actually, he thought, but said instead, "What happened to them?"

"They were responding to a message on the radio?"

"Yes."

"When was this?"

He recalled his conversation with Allie. "A while back."

The blonde nodded. "They're dead."

"You know this for a fact?"

"Yes."

"Did you kill them?"

"No."

"Then who did?"

"The people who had this island before us."

"And what happened to them?"

The blonde didn't answer, and neither did the redhead. Their silence was all the answer he needed.

"Ah," Keo said. "This is one dangerous island."

"It can be," the blonde said.

"So what happens now?"

The blonde gave him a long look before glancing back at the redhead. "Do you see it?"

The redhead shook her head. "Nah."

"You sure?"

"Looks okay to me."

"Maybe I can help you ladies out if you'll tell me what you're looking for," Keo said.

"We wanted to make sure you didn't have squirrelly eyes," the blonde said.

"I have no idea what that means," Keo said, looking from the blonde to the redhead and back again.

"No, I don't suppose you do."

"He looks like one of those K-pop guys," the redhead said. "Except for the scar. That's butt ugly."

"Now that's just mean," Keo said.

"K-what?" the blonde said.

"Those Korean boy bands I told you about."

The blonde shook her head. "You do know that I only pay attention to you half the time, and almost never when it involves pop culture?"

The redhead smirked. "Now you tell me." She looked over at him. "Your English is pretty good, K-pop."

"I was born on an American base in San Diego," Keo said.

"Well, that explains it."

The blonde stood up and walked to the door. "Get some sleep and we'll talk again tomorrow morning," she said to him.

"Sleep?" Keo said. "It's going to be hard getting any sleep like this."

"He's right," the redhead said. "The poor guy."

She walked over, stopped beside him, then lifted her foot and kicked the chair over. Keo landed on the hard concrete floor on his side with an *oomph*.

"There," the redhead said. "That's for making us stay up past midnight chasing after your dumb ass. Do you have any idea how much beauty sleep I need per day?"

"Not much, I'm sure," Keo said.

"Flattery will get you pancakes in the morning."

"You have pancakes?"

"Oh yeah, we have a lot of things. There's a big ol' freezer with all kinds of goodies. Be a good boy and don't try anything funny, and we might share some of it with you tomorrow."

"Deal."

The blonde was waiting at the door. "Sit tight."

"Some way to welcome a guest," Keo said.

"You're lucky we didn't shoot you on sight after the month we've been having."

The two women left, slamming the metal door shut after them. Keo heard a lock turning, then saw the big man from earlier look in at him through the security glass, before he, too, vanished. He didn't go very far, though, because Keo could still see his shadow just under the door.

At least they hadn't tied him to the chair, which Keo scooted away from now and laid on his side, his hands still bound behind him. He stared up at the ceiling, at the bright squiggly lightbulb above. It was impossibly bright, though the fact that he hadn't been this close to an artificial light source in a while might have a little something to do with that.

"Hey!" Keo shouted. "Can you at least turn off the light so I can get some sleep?"

He waited for a response. The guy outside didn't seem to have heard him. Or if he did, he didn't care.

"Come on. Do a guy a solid, huh? Geneva Convention and all that? I know you can hear me. Come on, man."

The shadow didn't move.

Keo sighed and closed his eyes.

At least he was still alive, so there was that.

One promise down, one to go...

CHAPTER 21

WILL

"SILVER BULLETS?" TOMMY said. "You mean they actually work?"

"You've heard about them?" Will asked.

"There was a radio broadcast some of the kids picked up a few days ago. Something about silver, ultraviolet lights, and islands." The teenager shook his head. "Harrison dismissed it and we never really tried to put it to use. I mean, the idea of silver... That sounded crazy."

"Because all of this is so clearly *not* crazy," Danny said.

Tommy looked slightly embarrassed. "Harrison made the decision."

"You guys do everything he says?"

"He's the one who put this city together. He organized the resistance in the beginning. I don't think we'd be here without him. For all his faults, he really did save us in the early days. After that, I guess it just became a habit to follow him."

Even in the semidarkness of the Dunbar museum, Tommy looked young and innocent, and Will could easily picture the kid falling in line like the others, including Rachel. She had seemed strong-willed to him, even stubborn, but she too had hitched her wagon to Harrison.

It's hard to say no to a savior.

"This radio broadcast," Danny was saying. "Was it a woman?"

"Yeah," Tommy said. "You heard it, too?"

"I might have caught a snippet or three."

Tommy was talking about Lara's broadcast. The same message that had incurred Kate's wrath. Kate, who at this moment was plotting the island's destruction as retaliation.

Goddamn you, Kate. You're going to haunt me for the rest of my life, aren't you?

They were crouched behind a half-circle entranceway that separated the lobby of the museum with the back of the building, where the administrative offices and back rooms were linked by a long, curving hallway on each side. The spacious front lobby made up nearly sixty percent of the place, with still-intact double glass doors looking out into the moonlit sidewalk beyond. There were half a dozen small windows, but they were too high up to make any difference. Why bother with those when there were the doors?

The museum was made up of old photos, commissioned paintings of the city's founders, and different angles of Dunbar over the decades from cattle town to what it was now. Not much, if you were to ask Will, but then its residents probably saw it differently. There were old maps, clothing, and even six-shot revolvers in dust-covered glass cases. Evidence that mankind once built something here. How long would they last once Dunbar's citizens were scattered into the wind after tonight?

"The towns, the pregnancies," Kate had said. *"They're all just the beginning. In ten, twenty years, you won't recognize any of this. In a couple of generations, man will have forgotten they were ever in control of the planet."*

A couple of generations, Kate? It's hard to remember now, a year on...

He pushed those defeating thoughts of Kate away (nothing good ever came of thinking about Kate) and concentrated on the doors in front of him.

Those damn doors. Those were going to be a problem if the ghouls attacked. Will didn't have any doubts that the creatures knew they were inside. Not after pursuing them through the alleyway.

Dead, not stupid.

So why hadn't they attacked? The twin doors wouldn't last under a prolonged assault. An hour, if he was being optimistic. Less, if he was being practical. Barricading them hadn't been an option. The only furniture in the lobby were a few chairs, a water cooler, and some stanchions that had been knocked over months ago, along with the velvet ropes attached to them. Bringing the heavy oak desks and metal filing cabinets from the offices in the back was too much work. Besides, they had already come up with a plan of retreat for when the creatures finally gained entry into the museum. It wasn't a matter of if, but when.

So where the hell are they?

He could easily make out the abandoned streets on the other side of the doors about twenty-five meters across the lobby. The entire city of Dunbar looked and felt as if it had become stuck in time, like a museum outside of a museum.

Tommy moved nervously next to him from time to time. Danny was on the other side of the half-circle, sitting Indian-style with his M4A1 in front of him as he ate a granola bar Tommy had produced from one of his pockets. The teenager had put away his M40A3 sniper rifle and was clutching a Glock from his hip holster. Will had given him one of his silver-loaded magazines, something they had precious little left of at the moment.

"How're you for ammo?" he asked Danny.

"Three mags for the rifle, all five left for the nine mil," Danny said while chewing and spitting out pieces of granola at the same time. "You?"

"Two for the M4, three for the sidearm."

"I guess we should start conserving. Of course, we could always use Tommy here as a baseball bat. You take the right leg, and I'll take the left."

"Hey," Tommy said.

Will grinned. "Deal."

"Whatever," Tommy said. "Anyway, where should I shoot them with this?"

"Doesn't matter," Danny said. "As long as you put silver into their bloodstream, that's all she wrote."

"Like some kind of chain reaction? Are they allergic to silver or something?"

"Ask him," Danny said, nodding at Will. "He's supposedly the mastermind. I just work here."

Will shook his head. "We don't know. Just that it works better than anything except the sun."

"Hard to holster the sun," Danny said. "I've tried. Burned a hole right through my boxers. Had to go commando for weeks until I could find another pair."

Tommy stared at Danny uncertainly.

"He's joking," Will said.

"Oh," Tommy said.

"Carly wasn't amused, though," Danny went on.

"Who's Carly?" Tommy asked.

"The hottest redhead you'll ever see, kid. I'll introduce you to her when we get to Song Island."

Tommy nodded anxiously.

They sat in silence and stared out the twin doors for the next few minutes, which became the next thirty minutes. Will glanced at his watch every now and then. Between the running and shooting and waiting, it was easy to lose track of time.

Three in the morning. Four hours, give or take, before sunup.

Doable.

Maybe…

"Where are they?" Tommy finally whispered. "They know we're in here, so where the hell are they?"

"Why, you getting anxious?" Danny asked.

"I wish they'd just attack already, that's all. Get it over with." He passed the Glock to his left hand, then back to his right.

"Now you're just trying to jinx us, kid—"

Danny hadn't finished saying the word "kid" yet when the sound of exploding glass cut him off. Their eyes darted back across the lobby to the two front doors. Something had obliterated the long pane of glass that made up nearly eighty percent of the left door, leaving behind just the frame and a big gaping hole. Will traced the trail of destruction to the source—a long metal wrench lying on its side on the floor.

"Now you've done it, kid," Danny said. "I blame this on you, I hope you know that."

Tommy wanted to respond, but either couldn't figure out how, or couldn't make anything come out of his mouth when he opened it.

"You ready?" Will said.

"I was born ready," Danny said.

"Then you changed your name to Danny?"

"What, I told you this story before?"

"Only a few thousand times."

"Hunh," Danny said.

Crash! The second glass door shattered into a thousand pieces, this time against the black metal of a tire iron that *clattered* to the floor. Glass sprinkled the lobby, chunks of it reaching halfway to the three of them crouched on the other side of the room. It was already cool in the building after nightfall, but now that the lobby was suddenly ventilated, the temperature dropped even further.

"Hey, kid," Danny whispered.

"Yeah?" Tommy whispered back, his voice shivering slightly.

"What's the difference between a wife and a hooker?"

Tommy stared at him for a moment. Finally, he said, "I don't know. What?"

"The hooker's cheaper to keep around."

There was a brief pause as Tommy processed the joke.

"Don't think about it too hard, kid; you'll bust a blood vessel," Danny said. He glanced over at Will. "I call dibs on the sniper rifle when he keels over."

"Hey," Tommy said.

Tommy might have continued his protest, except whatever sound was going to come out of his mouth turned into an involuntary gasp when they heard the *tap-tap-tap* of bare feet against concrete, and the streets outside the broken front doors blackened. It wasn't because the moonlight had disappeared, though Will thought that might have been the preferable explanation. Instead, it was because a swarm of ghouls had come out of nowhere and converged on the sidewalk and began squeezing their way through the openings.

The sight of them slashing their skins against the glass shards hanging off the doorframes—thick clumps of black blood wetting the tiled floor—while desperately forcing their way in was hypnotic. There were so many of them it was hard for Will to know where one began and ended and the rest continued. It looked like one continuous squirming flesh, accompanied by the *plop-plop-plop* of blood on the floor and the patter of footsteps growing in intensity with every passing second as more arrived.

"It's about damn time," Danny said. He had dispensed with the whispering. "My legs were starting to cramp anyway."

Will flicked his rifle to semi-auto, leaned out, and shot the first ghoul that was almost through in the chest. The bullet easily punched through the creature's skin and muscle and hit another one—then another—behind it. As the undead thing fell lifelessly *(again)* forward, it was pulled unceremoniously back through the door and the next one flopped inside.

And just like that, the dam broke.

They moved with the same speed and agility, and with the absolute and complete lack of self-preservation that always managed to both fascinate and terrify Will. While he stared, Danny stood up and fired on full-auto, dropping a dozen ghouls on the first volley as they raced across the room. Silver bullets punched through soft, yielding flesh and slammed into bones and muscle.

"Go!" Will shouted back at Tommy.

The teenager gave him a horrified look before stumbling to his feet and running up the hallway to their right. He was moving so fast he was literally tripping over his own legs.

"Changing!" Danny shouted.

Will flicked the M4A1 to full-auto and pulled the trigger.

Ghouls fell, others slipped and slid, and multiple streams of arcing black liquid sprayed the lobby. Not that it did anything to slow them down. Not even close. The surging black wave of amassing flesh began to spread out, at once providing easy targets and *too many* to concentrate on.

"You coming or what!" Danny shouted behind him.

Will stopped firing and turned and ran.

He followed Danny up the hallway, reloading as he went, dropping the magazine and snapping in his next-to-last one. "Stick to the plan!"

"As long as it's not Plan Z!"

"You love Plan Z!"

"You misheard! I said I love zucchini lasagna!"

They ran past offices and closets and didn't bother to stop at any of them. They had checked earlier: the doors were cheap wood and wouldn't last against a prolonged attack, even with a barricade using desks and filing cabinets. Maybe against just the black-eyed ghouls they might have stood a small chance, but that wasn't all they were dealing with tonight. Not by a long shot.

They get creative when the blue-eyed ones are around.

The metal basement door under Ennis was proof of that.

But there was one, a bathroom at the end, that could work. Or, at least, it had the most potential to get them to sunrise. It had a stainless steel door with a large deadbolt on the other side and no windows. It was easily their best choice by a good margin, and the plan was always to retreat to it once the attack began.

Now all they had to do was get to it...

Then something happened. It was so unexpected that Will couldn't have explained how he knew, except that he just *sensed* it.

He slid to a stop. "Danny."

Danny stopped a few meters up the hallway and looked back, then opened his mouth to ask—Will held up his hand and Danny didn't follow through with it.

Except for their labored breathing, they couldn't hear anything.

The building, as it had been just a few minutes ago, was *dead silent* again.

"The fuck?" Danny mouthed at him.

"No clue," Will mouthed back.

They both looked down the hallway—at the empty nothingness staring back. There was no wave of ghouls, no black eyes seeking them out, or moving death nipping at their heels like rabid dogs. Even the telltale patter of bare feet against tiled floor was gone, along with the all-too-familiar *clacking* of bones underneath sagging flesh.

There was just...silence.

Five seconds...

...then ten...

Until a scream pierced the hallway *from behind them.*

Tommy!

They looked back up the hallway and Danny started moving, and Will was right behind him when—

—he heard it, the noise he had been waiting for—anticipating with dread—coming from behind him: the *tap-tap* of bare feet coming, *inhumanly fast.*

He spun back around, lifting his rifle and expecting to see a flood of ghouls making their way up the narrow passageway.

But there was just one.

A tall, silhouetted figure with piercing, almost pulsating blue eyes. It wasn't quite as thin as the ghouls he was used to seeing; it actually looked almost healthy, like the one that was standing outside of Ennis last night.

Ennis...last night...blue-eyed ghoul...

Silver...

It didn't go down.

Will squeezed the trigger.

It was fast and somehow—and Will didn't understand how—the creature was actually *dodging* his bullets! But as impossibly fleet of foot as it was (and God help him, it was *fast*), Will still managed to put two bullets into its chest.

But it didn't go down.

Instead it kept coming, moving with a swiftness that defied logic *(so what else is new?)*, disintegrating the distance between them even before Will felt the last silver round leave the carbine and smash into the curving wall, taking a big chunk of the creature's shoulder with it.

Then it was there, in front of him, batting the rifle out of his hands.

Up close, Will saw black blood oozing out of the holes in its chest. He had put those there with two silver bullets.

Silver bullets!

Will opened his mouth to scream Danny's name, but before he could get anything out, smooth black flesh wrapped around his throat and he was flailing from one side of the narrow hallway to the other. His breath exploded from his half-open mouth and his lungs burned in a sea of fire as it slammed him into the wall.

Where the hell's Danny?

Will's eyes darted left, up the hallway—and saw Danny firing *at another blue-eyed ghoul* running toward him from the other side. The damned thing was dodging Danny's bullets, too. It also had something on its face that almost looked like a grin. But that was impossible. These things didn't grin...*right?*

The creature grabbed Danny by the face and slammed his head into the wall, and a second later Danny's body went slack and crumpled to the floor. The blue-eyed ghoul stood over Danny and there was fresh blood covering its mouth, the bright red liquid glistening in what little moonlight managed to penetrate this far into the hallway.

Tommy's blood...

It looked up at him. No, not at him, but at the first creature, the one holding Will in place with a single hand, as if Will were fifty pounds of nothing. Its fingers dug into his throat, threatening to crush his windpipe with just a little bit of pressure.

And then the creatures did something Will had never seen them do before, that he didn't think they could even still do.

They spoke.

"I told you it'd be easy," the second one said. Its voice came out as a sharp hiss, almost like hot steam venting. It didn't sound the least bit human. It was more than that. More than human. *Beyond* human.

"So you did," the first one said. It manipulated Will's eyes back to its face by turning his head, like a grown man would an infant that was completely and utterly at its mercy.

Forced to stare at it, Will couldn't help but marvel at the smoothness of the creature's skin and its domed, hairless head. Its face was encased in impossibly tight flesh, showing none of the pruned bumps that covered the black-eyed ones. The smooth contour of its skin from the neck up looked almost pristine, like something fresh and newly born. The holes in its chest, where he had shot it, had cauterized in the last few seconds, even if the monster probably didn't consider them wounds in the first place. It sure as hell hadn't acted like getting shot *(with silver bullets!)* had hurt at all.

The eyes were closer to a shade of sky blue, and the unnatural thing's long and bony *(and cold)* fingers were wrapped so tightly around his throat that Will had trouble breathing. He guessed that was the point.

"Will," it said, its voice coming out in the same unnatural hiss. "Kate says you're a hard man to kill. But I told her you couldn't be. After all, you're only human."

"Kate exaggerates," the other ghoul said, and it made a noise Will didn't understand at first, until he realized it was laughter. Soft laughter, as if it didn't quite remember how to do it properly but thought that this was just close enough.

"Would you like to play a game, Will?" the one in front of him asked.

"Kate wants him," the other creature said.

"We'll tell her he resisted. Oops." Lines where lips should be morphed into a smile. "What she doesn't know won't hurt her."

"Mabry will know."

"Mabry thinks she's too obsessed with him. He'll approve of this."

"You've talked me into it." And it, too, smiled. "Go on, then.

Tell him the rules."

"The rules are simple," the first one said to Will. "We'll have a blast—" It stopped talking and stiffened, and its fingers tightened further *(Is that even possible?)* around his throat as the creature hissed, "A knife? Really, Will?"

Cross-knife, Will thought.

He didn't know when he had even reached for it, much less pulled it out of its sheath. But there it was, in his hand, gleaming in the moonlight as it moved in a wide arc from his thigh toward the ghoul's head. He wasn't sure if he was even aiming, but the knife seemed to know where it was going, as if it had a mind of its own.

The ghoul glared at him and there was a glint of something that could have been pity just a split-second before the knife punctured the side of its head. The blade kept going, penetrating the skull—it was surprisingly tough—and Will kept pushing with everything he had—which wasn't much at the moment, but there was just enough—until the hilt of the weapon rammed up against slightly cold flesh and the knife couldn't go any further.

He thought the creature would let out a scream, a cry of pain, maybe even panic, but it did none of those things. Instead, the sparkling blue in its eyes lost their luster and it collapsed in front of him. The fingers let go and Will could breathe again, and he slid down the wall, sucking in air, following the falling motion of the creature with his own. The *clack-clack* of bones as the ghoul hit the tiled floor first, then *thump* as Will landed on his ass.

There was a sharp hissing sound and Will looked up at the second ghoul. It stared at the creature lying motionless in front of him, the cross-knife still embedded in its skull. Then its eyes shifted over to Will and it moved—

The Glock, like the knife, had somehow magically appeared in Will's hand without him ever knowing how it had gotten there. He stopped thinking about it, stopped trying to understand what was happening, and just pulled the trigger.

He fired once—twice—*three times*—hitting the creature in the chest with all three rounds.

It didn't stop it. Of course it didn't stop it. He knew it wouldn't, but he was trained to hit center mass and that's what he did.

The monster shook off the three silver bullets and kept coming.

Will tilted the gun up slightly and fired, creasing the ghoul's right cheek. It flinched that time and actually paused for a second.

For a moment—just a brief, optimistic moment *(Captain fucking Optimism, yeah right)*—Will thought he had forced it to change its mind, that it would now turn and run away.

But of course it didn't.

It lunged at him again, and Will fired instinctively and from point blank range, hitting it square in the center of the forehead. Something that might have been brains—or whatever still passed for brains inside them—exploded out the back of the ghoul's head. The creature's body—emaciated, yes, but somehow stronger and tougher and fuller looking than the black-eyed ones—twisted at the last moment and flopped to the floor, bones *clacking* and blood oozing out of what was left of its skull. The entire back part of its head was gone, leaving just the front.

Will gasped for breath, every successful attempt sending a jolt of pain through his body. He wondered if his old wounds had opened up. It would be ironic if he survived these blue-eyed bastards only to die from a gunshot wound inflicted by a human traitor.

Ironic, or was that tragic?

Who gives a shit.

But he wasn't dead yet, and Will grabbed the cross-knife and jerked it out of the dead ghoul's head. It came out easily, with no resistance whatsoever, just a soft *slurp*. He picked up his rifle and slung it, then crawled on his hands and knees over the two dead bony things to get to Danny.

He reached for the neck first and felt a strong pulse.

When he turned Danny over onto his back, he thought he might have felt a pulse that wasn't there, because the face he was staring down at was covered in a thick layer of blood. Will felt his neck again just to be sure and got the same response. The bleeding must have looked way worse than the actual wound. He hoped, anyway.

He snatched up Danny's carbine, then got a good grip on the back of his friend's shirt collar and began dragging him up the hallway. He kept his eyes glued in front of him, at the half-circle arch into the lobby, and his ears open for any noises coming from behind him. He wasn't entirely sure if he was seeing very much or hearing anything at all over the roaring pain in his chest and throat and ears.

Jesus, was there a part of him that wasn't hurting at the moment?

Stupid question. Of course there wasn't. He didn't even know how he was still moving. It had to be adrenaline. It would hurt later, but for now, he could still make his legs move and keep his grip on Danny, and that was all that mattered.

He moved on automatic pilot, trying not to think about every aching bone and pulsating muscle in his body. It didn't help that Danny was heavier than he remembered. Or maybe he was just getting weaker.

Will glanced back and saw the bathroom door coming up. It was open, unable to close because of the shadow-covered body lying half-in and half-out of it. Tommy. How the hell had the ghoul gotten behind them? They had searched the entire building and found no other way into the museum except through the front doors. The offices didn't even have windows, for God's sake. So how had the blue-eyed bastards sneaked inside?

When he finally reached the bathroom, his suspicions were confirmed. It was Tommy. Or most of him, anyway. It was actually just everything from the neck down, because his head was missing. Teeth marks covered the stump where the head had been attached.

He pulled Tommy's lanky frame out into the hallway to clear the door, then dragged Danny inside. He closed the heavy stainless steel door, then turned the lock and heard the satisfying *click-clank* of the metal bolt sliding into place.

With Danny inside, Will unslung his rifle and scanned the bathroom just to be sure. There were no windows in here, so the other blue-eyed creature had to have gotten in from somewhere else. Maybe another window they had missed. It was dark and they were moving by flashlight, so just about anything was possible.

He fished out the flashlight and clicked it on. He slung the rifle and drew the Glock, then went through the three stalls inside the bathroom again, just to be sure. He found nothing, which made him relax a little bit, though not by much since even just breathing hurt.

He walked back over to Danny and sat down next to him.

Even under the mask of blood, Danny had something on his face that looked suspiciously like a smile. Maybe he was dreaming he was back on the island with Carly. Danny had the right idea. What Will wouldn't give to be back on Song Island right now, walking on the beach with Lara...

He thought about last night's dream. Of Kate again. He hadn't been able to stop thinking about it. The way she had proudly admitted to orchestrating everything that had happened in Dunbar yesterday. The trap with the U-Haul, with the blue-eyed ghouls inside. Four of them.

Four of them…

He glanced at the door. There were two out there. He couldn't tell if they were the same ones from the dream, the same group that had ambushed Harrison's people. But they had blue eyes, and there had been *four* of them when Kate showed him the…what the hell was it? A memory? A dream? More like a nightmare…

So where were the other two now? Did they always work in fours? Or did the other two leave after they had decimated Harrison's people? No, that didn't make any damn sense at all.

Because, obviously, all of this makes perfect sense.

Yeah, that's the ticket.

He stuck his hand into his cargo pants pocket and pulled out the small bottle. Thank God Rachel hadn't taken it from him last night along with his pack and weapons. He couldn't read the label in the dark, not that it mattered. He twisted off the cap and shook out a couple of pills and swallowed them, then realized that wasn't going to work and tossed down two more.

He put the bottle away and pulled his shirt up to make sure his wounds hadn't reopened during the fight. No wetness along his waist, which was good. That was the one stitching he was worried most about opening up again. But Zoe had done a hell of a job, and the stitches were still in place. He'd have to thank her again when he got back to the island.

Now who's being Captain Optimism?

He tucked his shirt into his pants, then picked up the M4A1 and made sure it was still in one piece. He laid it across his lap and leaned back against the wall, trying to see if he could hear them through the door. It was so dead silent he could hear just about everything, including the thrumming in his chest, the creak of his bones, and the throbbing from all the bruises up and down his body.

He wasn't too worried about the black-eyed ghouls, though. They were weak and they didn't have the creativity to break down a metal door. But the others, the blue-eyed ones, were dangerous. Ennis's metal basement door hadn't stood a chance, so if those other two bastards were out there somewhere…

He drew the Glock and laid it on the floor next to him.

Blue eyes or not, faster and stronger or not, they still went down if you got them in the right spot: the head. Or was it the brain?

Either/or.

Just to be sure, he'd just shoot them in the head until there wasn't a head anymore.

Yeah, that's the ticket.

CHAPTER 22

GABY

THE CEMETERY DIDN'T look any less inhospitable in the daylight, but that could just have been the plentiful weeds and scattered debris that had overtaken the place since it had last seen a caretaker. Nothing ever looked the same these days; the cities were always too hollow and unwelcoming, the houses too dark and depressing, and the streets too wide and empty. There was no reason a place where the dead resided would be any different.

Gaby kept to the winding path, staying out of the grass with the girls following closely behind. Donna kept pace behind her, followed by Milly, and Claire brought up the rear with her Winchester clutched tightly in her small hands. Though Donna was older and taller, Gaby had no doubt that when things went sideways—and they usually did, these days—she wanted Claire to be the one standing beside her, shooting.

She didn't remember the front gate of the cemetery being as far as it was or the place being so big. She couldn't see Route 13 from here, but the sunlight danced off a pair of large buildings to her right. Not far, maybe half a mile.

"What's over there?" she asked, pointing.

"Dunbar Airport," Donna said.

"Big airport?"

"Not really. Just a couple of hangars and a waiting room in one of the buildings. Not much to look at, and most of the planes that land there are those small ones. Why?"

"It's always a good idea to reload on supplies whenever you can."

"I remember a couple of vending machines. Drinks and stuff."

Gaby shook her head. "Not worth walking all that way for just drinks and stuff. We'll make do with the supplies we took from the VFW hall."

"You think that'll be enough?"

If it's not, that means we didn't make it to Song Island, Gaby thought, but she decided the girls didn't need to hear that. She said instead, "It should be."

She looked back at Milly. The girl had been quiet since they woke up in the crypt this morning. Not the best morning she'd faced before or since the end of the world, and it had to be worse for Milly, who had just lost Peter. The two of them weren't related, but they shared a stronger connection, one created from survival. She knew what that was like. Her link with Will, Danny, and Lara—those were the kind of bonds she could never have created with her friends or even family before The Purge. It was the kind cemented in fire and combat.

"Hey, are you hungry?" she asked Milly.

The girl looked up, big eyes peering through long, dirty hair. She shook her head silently.

"If you are, tell me, and we can stop and eat again," Gaby said.

Milly nodded. She looked as if she were moving in a stupor, not connected to the world the way Gaby and the sisters were. Gaby would have to keep an eye on her. She owed Peter that at least.

"Claire said you guys had been wanting to leave Dunbar even before I arrived," she said to Donna. "Why?"

"It's Claire's idea," Donna said. "Ever since she heard that radio broadcast, she's been obsessed with it. She plays the tape recorder once every hour, and to anyone who'll listen. It's kind of annoying."

"That's the only reason?"

Donna shrugged. "Harrison... I never liked him. My dad used to teach us about what kind of man to stay away from. You know, when we got older. Harrison fit his description perfectly."

"So why did you stay with them for so long?"

"Dunbar's the only place we know. And besides, the others were pretty cool. Rachel, for one."

"Was she back at the VFW hall?"

"No. She was outside with Harrison. She's like his second-in-command."

"She's really your friend?" Claire asked from behind them. "The woman on the radio?"

"She is," Gaby said.

"She sounds cool."

"She is pretty cool."

"And the island is safe?" Donna said doubtfully. "The creatures—these ghoul things—can't get to it?"

"I was there for three months and they never crossed the water," Gaby said.

"What about the hotel? Tell me about the hotel. You said it had power, which means hot showers, right?"

Gaby nodded. "All the hot showers you want."

"Oh my God," Donna smiled widely. "It's been so long since I've had an honest to goodness real shower."

"You smell it, too," Claire said.

Donna rolled her eyes. "It's not like you smell any better."

"Better than you."

"Oh, shut up."

Claire snorted, but didn't have any comeback for that one. The thirteen-year-old continued to keep watch behind them, eyes roaming the cemetery for potential threats or surprises.

"Can she really use that rifle?" Gaby asked Donna.

"She was good with it before all of this," Donna said. "Now, she goes to sleep with that thing in her arms. It's creepy."

"I heard that," Claire said.

"You were supposed to."

"Whatever."

Gaby smiled. It had been a while since she heard sisterly bickering. In some strange way, she liked it. It reminded her that, whatever happened, sisters would still be sisters even at the end of the world.

"Come on," Gaby said, glancing up at the sun. "The faster we get up Route 13, the faster we'll hit Interstate 10."

"And Song Island after that," Donna said.

"And Song Island after that. Meanwhile, keep an eye out for any vehicles. It'd be nice not to have to walk the entire way there."

"Can you drive?"

"A little."

"Good, because I never got my driver's license."

"I doubt anyone's going to ticket you, Donna."

"No, but she might drive into a ditch and kill us all," Claire said.

Donna groaned. "God, you're stupid, Claire."

"Whatever."

They finally reached the front gates of the cemetery and stepped through it. They turned left, heading back toward the highway in the distance.

THEY HADN'T GONE very far toward the highway when Gaby saw sunlight glinting off the metal dome of a vehicle parked at the intersection between Route 13 and the country road that had led them to the cemetery. The car hadn't been there last night.

She grabbed Donna's arm and pulled her left, toward the ditch and off the road, snapping, "Car."

Behind them, Milly and Claire smartly followed without a word. Gaby slipped to one knee and unslung the M4, flicking off the safety.

Donna was on both knees in the grass, peering forward. "Is that a truck?"

Gaby nodded. It was a big silver truck, about 200 yards further up the road and parked along the shoulder. She couldn't tell what kind of vehicle from this distance, not that she had ever been particularly good at distinguishing one car from another. The end of the world hadn't done a whole lot to fill in that particular knowledge gap.

A man was climbing out of the front passenger seat of the truck now and did something she couldn't quite make out from this distance. Too bad she hadn't grabbed a pair of binoculars. She remembered seeing a few of them on the shelf in the basement under the VFW hall. Will and Danny would have picked one up just in case.

"Hope for the best, prepare for the worst," they would say.

"What should we do?" Donna whispered. She didn't really have to, given how far they were from the highway. Then again, sound did travel these days, so maybe the girl was wiser than Gaby gave her credit for.

She glanced back at Claire and Milly. They were crouched behind them, Claire with her rifle in front of her, looking ready for action. Milly was a quivering mess, and Gaby expected her to jump up and run off at any second.

She looked back at the truck just in time to catch a second figure approaching from the other side of the road. Both men. She could tell by the way they moved. After a while, she began to make out the multiple colors of their camo uniforms.

Josh's soldiers.

Were they looking for her? Had Josh sent them? He would have been informed by now of her escape. There was one thing about Josh—the old and the new—that she knew with absolute certainty: he didn't give up when he set his mind on achieving a goal. Unfortunately, that was her at the moment.

Whatever he had become, whatever he had deluded himself into believing, he was still, at heart, the kid who fell in love with her the day she moved in across the street from him. She knew that because he had told her.

Kid? Did I just call him a kid?

He's not a kid anymore. He's nineteen. Old enough to know better. Old enough to stop lying to himself.

"Gaby?" Donna whispered. "What should we do?"

They were watching her curiously. Donna next to her and the two girls behind them.

Good question.

Options. What were her available options?

She could look at this as a stroke of bad luck, but that was probably not what Will or Danny would have done. No, they would see the soldiers and the truck (but especially the truck) as an opportunity.

Besides, she didn't feel like walking the rest of the way to Beaufont Lake, anyway.

"Stay here," Gaby said, looking first at Donna, then at the thirteen-year-olds. "Don't move from this position, and stay as low as you can until I give you the word."

"I can help," Claire said eagerly.

"Yes, you can—by keeping everyone here safe with that rifle."

She fixed the girl with a hard look and Claire, understanding— which didn't mean she liked it one bit by the way she gritted her teeth—nodded reluctantly.

"Remember, keep low," Gaby said. "Don't make a sound. If anything happens and I don't come back, wait until they leave, then keep going south until you reach Beaufont Lake. Understand?"

Donna nodded without any enthusiasm. Like her sister, she apparently didn't see any point in arguing. Milly just looked mortified by the whole thing.

"Okay," Gaby said. "I'll be back."

She gave them her best smile, then shrugged off her pack and handed it to Milly since Donna was already carrying the supply bag. She got up and began jogging up the country road, back toward the highway. With just the rifle, her holstered sidearm, and spare magazines around her waist, she felt lighter on her feet, though of course that could just be the adrenaline trying to convince her she could, possibly, survive this.

Captain Optimism, right, Danny?

They needed the truck. It was going to make returning to Beaufont Lake easier, faster, and safer. There was no way around it. That truck had a working battery and likely a full tank of gas to be out here by itself. She needed that damn truck in the worst way.

Gaby was fortunate the country road had ditches on both sides, each about four feet deep. That allowed her to slide all the way down to the bottom of one of them and, hunched slightly over, move up the road without being seen.

Or, at least, she hoped she couldn't be seen.

The morning heat had picked up noticeably and Gaby was already sweating after twenty yards of bent-over running. She kept the M4 in front of her the entire time, ready to use at a moment's notice. Her legs carried her forward on automatic pilot, and she kept her eyes focused straight-ahead at all times. She prayed something didn't pop up in front of her—like a tree root—and trip her up. It wouldn't have taken much, given how little attention she was paying to what was on the ground at the moment.

Thirty yards…

…forty…

She watched the soldiers the entire time. There were definitely just the two of them, which was the good news.

The bad news was, there were still two of them, and just one of her.

She gripped the carbine tighter, wishing she had her own weapon. The rifle she had now had proven decent back at the VFW hall, but she understood why Will and Danny were so adamant about holding onto their M4A1s all the way from Afghanistan. Soldiers weren't supposed to bring weapons back home with them, but the two had managed it anyway. *"We knew someone who knew someone,"* was all Will would say when she asked how he had managed that.

She missed her old M4. The feel of this one wasn't quite right, though she imagined it was all in her mind. Probably.

Sixty yards...

She concentrated on the two soldiers to take her mind off the things she didn't have but wished that she did. She still couldn't make out a whole lot of details, but they were definitely both men. Gaby had only killed men so far, but she didn't think she would have trouble pulling the trigger on a woman. A collaborator was a collaborator. And uniform or not, these were still members of the human race that had sold out their kind. She couldn't summon any sympathy for them even if she tried.

Eighty...

They hadn't spotted her yet and seemed to be too busy talking to really pay any attention to their surroundings.

After moving steadily up the ditch for a while, she stopped and went into a crouch. She took the opportunity to glance back at the girls. They were lying on their stomachs and watching her back. Or she assumed they were looking in her direction. She could only really see three lumps in the grass, and that was only because she knew where to look.

She faced forward again and caught her breath: one of the soldiers was turning in her direction when he stopped and seemed to stare right at her from across the distance.

She gripped the M4 tighter and mentally prepped herself to launch into battle—

False alarm.

The man hadn't seen her. He was looking down while trying to open some kind of bag. Then he was turning away, stuffing something into his mouth as he did so.

She forced her fingers to loosen around the rifle.

Jumpy. She was way too jumpy.

When the man had turned his back to her again, she got up and continued along the ditch at a half-trot while slightly bent over at the waist to lower her profile.

Ninety yards...

She was at one hundred when she stopped a second time to get her bearings. The man on her side of the silver vehicle was leaning against the front grill and staring off down the road at nothing in particular. Their lack of attention to the land around them was incredible.

You need better "soldiers," Josh.

She got up again and kept going.

110 yards...

The second one was walking back around the truck and handed the first one a bottle of water. They drank while looking down the highway, back toward Dunbar. They were clearly waiting for someone and weren't going anywhere soon.

130 yards...

She took a second to make sure the fire selector on the M4 was set to semi-auto.

150 yards...

She was close enough now that she could hear them talking. They sounded young, and she could make out blond hair on one soldier, while the other one had a long black ponytail.

160 yards...

She wasn't sure what happened. Maybe she wasn't being nearly as quiet as she thought she was. Or maybe one of them, by some fluke, saw something that alerted him to her presence, the way she had seen the reflection of their truck under the sun earlier.

Either way, one of them saw her, said something, and both men began unslinging their rifles.

Gaby immediately stopped, took aim through the red dot scope, and fired—and *missed.*

Her bullet *pinged!* harmlessly off the hood of the truck. It was a bad shot, but it still made one of them dart for cover, so at least it had some impact. The one that didn't move opened fire on her, the *pop-pop-pop* of his three-round burst filling the air even before her own shot's echo had faded.

Gaby forced herself to stand perfectly still and reacquire her target even as the ground to her right, at shoulder level, exploded and she was showered with loosened dirt and grass. The man was firing too fast, too wildly, probably trying to fight against the same adrenaline that was pumping through every inch of her at the moment.

Whoever these men were, they didn't have the advantage of being trained by a pair of Army Rangers. Will and Danny hadn't held back—not once in the three months they broke her down and built her back up on the island.

She summoned that experience now and forced one of her senses to ignore the sound of bullets *buzzing* past her head.

She corrected her aim, swiveling slightly to the right, and fired again.

This time she hit the man in the waist, and he dropped his rifle and grabbed at the spot where he had been shot. When the man tried to run around the truck for cover, Gaby calmly took aim again and shot him in the back.

The man stumbled and slammed into the hood of the truck and slid down the smooth surface, but by then Gaby was already rushing up the ditch again. This time she dispensed with the slow jog and was in a full sprint mode, peering through her weapon's sight the entire time and searching for another target.

Where's the other one? Where's the other one?

Running forward was the only path open to her. She couldn't retreat, not with one of the (fake) soldiers still alive. He had the truck and she needed it. She knew exactly where the resolve came from: the very real desire to get back home to Song Island at all costs.

That's my truck, asshole!

The second man was moving along the length of the truck, smartly keeping behind cover. Unfortunately for him, thanks to her lowered vantage point inside the ditch, she easily spotted his boots moving underneath the vehicle. The man was clearly trying to reach the back of the truck (a Chevy, as it turned out), probably in hopes of catching her by surprise. Either he didn't know she could see his feet or he was counting on her not picking it up.

When he poked his head out the back, she snapped off a shot. Her bullet shattered one of the taillights and the man jerked his head back instinctively.

Gaby picked up the pace. She was twenty yards away now and she could still see the man's boots, this time holding their position at the middle of the truck. Gaby laid the M4 on top of the ditch, took careful aim, and shot the man in the right ankle. There was a loud scream and the figure crumpled to the ground on the other side of the Chevy.

Gotcha.

She climbed up the ditch and scrambled up the road. The first man she had shot was dead, lying facedown on the hot asphalt in a pool of his own blood. Gaby scanned all the sides of the highway, looking for any potential threats. She hadn't seen any before, but that didn't mean someone hadn't heard the shots and was responding. It was a big road and seemed to go on endlessly in both directions. She hadn't properly realized what a huge task it would have been to travel it on foot until now.

I definitely need that truck.

She skirted around the hood of the Chevy, the rifle ready to shoot the second man on sight. He must have had plenty of time to prepare for her by now. It had taken her how long to climb up the ditch and then jog over? Twenty seconds? Maybe thirty?

More than enough time. Maybe he was going to make a final bloody stand, hoping to take her with him. She wasn't going to give him that chance if she could help it. She was tired of giving people the benefit of the doubt. They always ended up disappointing her, like Josh…

But the man wasn't a threat. Not anymore.

He sat on the highway, back against the driver side door, trying desperately to tie a handkerchief around his bleeding ankle. His face was locked in a tight grimace, sweat pouring down his temple and chin, and he didn't seemed to notice her at all. He was young, too. He couldn't have been more than twenty, and "Darren" was stenciled over his nametag.

Gaby tightened her finger on the M4's trigger.

Darren finally realized she was there and looked up. He didn't make a move for his weapons and only clenched his teeth in pain. "Please, please don't shoot."

Gaby stared at him. He had soft blue eyes and a burgeoning stubble. He didn't look dangerous, but then, none of them did. It wasn't what they did that made them her enemy; it was what they were committed to.

"Please," Darren said again. "God, please, don't kill me."

She wanted to shoot him. It was the smart thing to do. He was the enemy and she was, without a doubt, stuck behind enemy lines. If she let him go, he would alert the others to her presence. If Josh had sent him, he would go back and tell him where she was. Josh would immediately know where she was heading, and what roads she would take.

Letting this man *(boy)* go would be the dumbest thing she could do at this very moment. Will would shoot him. He wouldn't even hesitate.

So why was she?

Gaby breathed for the first time in what seemed like hours and took her finger off the trigger. Darren, seeing her response, sighed with great relief.

"Don't move," Gaby said.

He nodded.

She scooted over and picked up his assault rifle. She pulled his sidearm out of its holster and shoved it into her waistband, then took a step back. "I need your magazines."

Darren began removing them from his pouches and placing them on the road without hesitation. Gaby stepped back a little bit more and gave Darren a quick look, then glanced down the road and waved with both hands at the girls. She hoped they would understand and was grateful to see all three rising and running up the road as fast as they could. From this distance, they looked like stick figures twinkling against the sun.

She looked back at Darren as he took out the last magazine. "Is there gas in the truck?"

He nodded. "We filled it up this morning."

"From where?"

"In town."

"Dunbar?"

"Yes."

"You were there last night?"

"No, I arrived this morning."

"What are you doing out here? Are you looking for someone?"

He looked reluctant to answer.

"Are you really going to make me ask twice?" she said, trying to inject as much menace as she could into her voice. Will wouldn't have had a problem with it, but then, she wasn't an ex-Army Ranger.

"There were people still left in the city," Darren said. "We were supposed to make sure no one tried to leave."

"Did Josh send you?"

"Who?"

She stared at his face. Was he lying to her? The way he had answered the question—quickly, without even taking a second to think about it—made him either the world's best liar or he was telling the truth. Josh hadn't sent him. He didn't even seem to know who Josh was.

If Josh didn't send you, then who did?

"Never mind," she said.

Gaby glanced over again. She could make out Claire in the lead, with Milly behind her, and Donna lagging in the back because of the heavy supply bag she was carrying.

"Where's the key?" she asked Darren.

"Inside," he said. Then, blinking in the sun at her, "Are you going to kill me?"

"I haven't decided yet."

His face turned ghostly white. "Please…"

"Stop begging," she said, fighting the growing irritation.

"Be a man," she wanted to say. *"Accept the consequences of your decisions and your actions. You and Josh and the rest of them."*

Instead, she motioned for him to get away from the truck. He struggled to his feet, then dragged one leg behind him as he hobbled away, leaving a bloody trail in his wake. His eyes shifted down the road for a brief moment.

"Expecting reinforcements?" she asked.

He shook his head quickly. "No, I was just…" He didn't finish and instead looked down at nothing.

She slung her rifle and drew the Glock, then opened the driver side door. The key was in the ignition. She pulled it out and pocketed it, then opened the back door and looked in. There were two cases of refilled water bottles in the back, unopened bags of MREs, and spare magazines thrown haphazardly across the seats.

"How many others are out here?" she asked.

He seemed to think about it. "This far out? Just us."

She fixed him with a hard look.

He swallowed. "I swear."

She didn't know whether to believe him or not. She had never been particularly good at reading faces anyway, but Darren looked too scared to lie.

"I'm going to take your truck," she said.

"Take it," he said quickly.

The girls had reached them by now, Claire clutching her rifle at the sight of Darren. Donna was out of breath and leaned against the hood for support. Milly looked winded but was too busy being queasy at the sight of the dead soldier.

Claire returned Gaby's pack, but her eyes were fixed on Darren. "What are we going to do with him?"

"I don't know yet," Gaby said. "What do you think?"

The girl was eyeballing Darren like a predator. Although he was five-ten and probably had one hundred pounds on the thirteen-year-old, Darren still shrunk back from her intense stare. He glanced from Claire to Gaby, then back again.

Gaby couldn't tell if he was more afraid of her or the kid.

Definitely the kid, she thought with a smile.

CHAPTER 23

WILL

"AM I DEAD?"

"Almost," Will said.

"Thank God," Danny groaned. "Because if I'm dead and your ugly mug's the first thing I see, it's a pretty good bet I didn't go, you know, up there." He hiked a thumb upward, then looked down at his shirt, which was covered in a thick film of dry blood from last night. "All this red stuff mine?"

"Yup. There's more on your face."

"Shit."

"Yup."

"So that explains the sore joints, aching bones, and this wicked pounding inside my skull."

Danny winced as he sat up, pushing back against the wall for support. In the glow of morning that filled up the bathroom, his face was covered in dried blood, and to look at him, it was unfathomable that he was still alive. His nose was crooked and broken at the bridge. Will had stuffed two wads of year-old toilet paper into each nostril.

"Morning?" Danny said.

"Morning."

"We made it."

"Yeah."

"Let's not do last night again."

"Deal."

Danny pulled the tissue paper out and flicked them away. "I hate nosebleeds."

"I wouldn't call what you had last night nosebleeds. More like a blood-gushing torrent."

"That bad, huh?"

"I was pretty sure you were dead. I had a speech prepared for Carly and everything."

"I kinda wish I was." He glanced over at Will, sitting to his right. "You look like how I feel."

"That bad?"

"Worse."

Will didn't feel like moving from where he had been sitting for the last few hours. In-between chewing on a pair of granola bars from one of his pockets, he had downed two more painkillers. His side throbbed and his neck hurt, but he was alive, even if every inch of him claimed otherwise.

"Water?" Danny said.

"Back in Ennis's basement."

He looked over at one of the stalls. "I can't believe I'm asking this, but...toilet water?"

"Went dry a long time ago."

"So what's the good news?"

"We're still alive."

"That'll work. So, you got anymore of the good stuff?"

Will pulled out the light bottle of painkillers and tossed it over. "Finish it off."

"This everything?"

"More in the packs..."

"...back at Ennis's," Danny finished. He shook out two, then decided four was the better number and popped them into his mouth and chewed on them as if they were rock candy. He tossed the empty bottle away and watched it skid across the room. "It wasn't my imagination, right? There was one of those blue-eyed buggers in the hallway."

"Yup."

"I shot it."

"You did."

"With silver bullets."

"Uh huh."

"I mean, I shot the crap out of it. A dozen rounds. At least six."

"Give or take."

"So how the mother truckin' hell did it keep coming?"

"I was going to tell you," Will said. "I saw one of them outside the bar last night. I shot it with a silver bullet and it didn't go down."

Danny smirked. "And you were saving this for…when?"

Will shrugged. "Eventually. We were sort of preoccupied with other things last night. Like trying to keep Rachel from killing us. Then I fell asleep. And you know what happened after that."

"Excuses, excuses." Danny paused, then, "So why are we still alive?"

"Shooting them doesn't work, not even with silver bullets. But taking out the brain seems to work just fine."

"You still need silver for that, or will any ol' bullet do?"

"I have no idea. Let's just use silver to be sure."

"Sounds good to me. That's what they used to call me back in college, you know. Sure Thing Danny." He paused again to catch his breath. "Damn, I could use some water."

"Yup."

They sat in silence for a moment, staring at nothing in particular. Talking was easier than moving, but it seemed to have tired Danny out almost as much as it had Will.

Danny touched the gash along his left temple, fingers sticky from the ointment and disinfectant Will had used to cover it up when there was enough light to work with. He had wiped as much blood off Danny's face as he could, but even so, Danny looked like the result of a plastic surgery gone awry.

Danny flinched. "Goddamn, that hurts."

"So don't touch it."

"Yeah, good idea. You're full of good ideas this morning." Danny nodded at the long trail of dried blood that led to the door. "Is that mine or Tommy's?"

"Both."

"What happened?"

"I don't know. I think one of them found another way in. Waited for Tommy, then…you know." He added, almost as if in afterthought, "It took his head."

"It took his head?"

"Yeah. It took his head."

"The fuck?"

"What I said."

"Did you...find it?"

"No. I don't want to, either."

The bathroom smelled of something rotten, and it wasn't just from their sweat and blood. Will had been breathing mostly through his mouth ever since he struggled to drag Danny inside about four hours ago. Even though there were no windows, visibility had greatly improved and he could feel the warmth of the sun against his skin and face coming into the room from...somewhere.

"So," Danny said after a while.

"So..."

"Blue-eyes."

"Yeah."

"Two?"

"Four."

"Four?"

He told Danny about his dream, the one Kate had shown him. About how they had ambushed Harrison's people.

"Smart buggers," Danny said.

"Bratt had it right."

"What's that?"

"He called them shock troops. The tip of the spear, sent behind enemy lines to break the resistance. That's what they did. Harrison and his people have been causing problems for the ghouls, attacking their convoys, that sort of thing. So Kate sent the four blue-eyed ones to take Dunbar."

"And it was all your ghoulfriend's idea?"

Will sighed. He hated that word. "She claims it was. She was a former ad executive, you know. It's what she used to do for a living. Getting people to do what she wants."

"That how she got you into bed?"

"All she had to do was take her clothes off to accomplish that."

Danny snorted. "Tits and ass is all it takes with you, huh?"

"Pretty much."

"You're such a dude, dude."

"Dude, right?"

Danny chuckled for a moment, then smacked his dry, cracked lips together. "So, four?"

"I saw four."

"In the dream."

"Uh huh."

"And we're sure the dream was real?"

"It didn't feel so much like a dream as they were…memories."

"Whose?"

"She said one of the ghouls'."

"She can do that now?"

"I guess so."

"Man."

"Yeah," Will said.

A few more seconds of silence passed between them before Danny said, "But there were only two last night."

"Two minus four is indeed two."

"So Mrs. Miller was right. Math really does come in handy in real life. So where are the other two?"

"I have no idea."

"Does that worry you?"

"Every second of last night."

Danny's stomach growled. "Excuse me."

"Hungry?" Will smiled.

"Just a tad."

"Well, we know where our packs are…"

"Ennis's."

"Yup."

Danny sighed and reached over and picked up his rifle. "What are we just sitting around here twiddling our thumbs for, then? Let's get this show on the road."

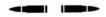

TOMMY'S HEADLESS BODY wasn't in the hallway when Will and Danny emerged from the bathroom, weapons at the ready. There wasn't a whole lot of light back here, and patches of shadows jumped out at them from both sides of the passageway.

They swung left, then right, then stood with their backs together, rifles pointing into the darkness on both sides of them, waiting for something to happen. There should have been an attack from a nest of waiting ghouls, only there wasn't.

"Shoot for the head?" Danny asked.

"Shoot for the head," Will nodded.

"Should have told me that last night."

"I didn't know last night."

"Yeah, well, this broken face is still your fault."

"Relax. You still look pretty."

"That goes without saying…"

Even among the shadows, multiple streaks of blood ran up and down the hallway, including a long jagged trail from when Will dragged Danny to the bathroom. And another big swath of blood, where Tommy's body used to be.

"They take the bodies, right?" Danny said.

"As far as I know."

"Why?"

"I have no idea."

"We should really sit down one of these days and talk about everything we know about them. I'll dictate and you type."

"What makes you think I can type?"

"I dunno, but you look like the typing kind."

"What kind is that?"

"You know, with dainty fingers and such."

They moved toward the lobby, passing the spot where he had last seen the blue-eyed ghouls. He wasn't surprised to find them gone, leaving behind only smeared, clumpy black blood in their wake, too far from the sunlight to have evaporated. There was still a wet quality about the liquid, which shouldn't have been possible given how many hours since they had bled out.

"That them?" Danny asked.

"Yup."

"Blood's still wet."

"Yup."

"How's that possible?"

"Hell if I know."

"Do you know anything?"

Will pointed at the patch of dried red blood on the wall. "I know that's you."

"Damn. Are you sure I'm still alive? Maybe this is just one big freaky *Jacob's Ladder* type of scenario?"

"Are you saying you're Tim Robbins?"

"Hell no. I'm much handsomer."

"Keep telling yourself that, buddy."

"I do every day. Someone's gotta."

They stepped over the blood—a difficult feat, since there was so much spread around the narrow passageway—and continued down toward the lobby, drawn forward by the warmth of the morning heat. There was just enough sunlight as they neared the half-circle arched entrance that they began to relax.

"Right in the head?" Danny said.

"How many times are you going to ask me?"

"So it's the brain."

"I think so, yeah."

"Why do you think that is?"

"I'll let you know when I figure it out."

"When will that be, you think?"

"Five years, two months, one week, and three days from now."

"I'm gonna hold you to that. Anything else you wanna share, now that we're both in a sharing mood?"

"I think Kate's going to attack the island."

Danny sighed. "How many times have I told you? Stop dating the psycho bitches. But do you ever listen to me? Noooooo."

"In my defense, we barely dated."

"You know what I always say about those one-night stands, man. They're killer."

The lobby looked like a war zone, with shards of glass covering most of the tiled floor, scattered among dozens of bleached-white bones. The acrid smell of evaporated flesh and tainted blood hung in the air.

Will started breathing through his mouth again. It seemed like he was doing a lot of that lately.

They maneuvered around the chaos and death and stepped out-side onto the sidewalk and into the hot sun. The street looked even more empty this morning, and the city of Dunbar was eerily quiet, with hardly any wind at all. Debris and spent shell casings littered the streets.

Except for the two of them, there were no sounds or signs of any other survivors.

Danny looked over at Ennis's next door. "You think any of

them made it?"

"Doubt it."

"Maybe Rachel got out."

"You think?"

Danny thought about it, then shook his head. "Nah, I can't even muster up enough optimism for that one."

"Some Captain Optimism."

"I know, I'm really not living up to the title these days. You wanna give it a try for a while?"

"No thanks."

Danny glanced around him for a moment, then said, "So, what else did your ghoulfriend say about attacking the island?"

◄▬ ▬►

ENNIS'S BASEMENT WAS covered in swaths of dried red blood. Or, at least, the part of it that they could see using the light pouring in from the side door. There were still large sections of the room covered in darkness, and Will and Danny scanned the place with their flashlights first and were surprised to find it empty.

They headed straight into the back, where Rachel's people had taken their packs last night. They found what they needed in a corner, some of the contents spilled around the area. Everything was still there, including the radio.

They hurried out and climbed back up to the alley next door, then stepped through another graveyard of bones, this one thicker and deeper and longer than the one in the Dunbar museum. It was impossible to take a step without crunching a femur or snapping a finger or pulverizing ribcages. The lingering acrid smell of dead ghouls was overwhelming, and they had to put handkerchiefs over their mouths and nose to get through the alley on their way in and out.

Will took a moment to gather himself back out on the sidewalk, pulling out a warm bottle of water from one of the packs and quenching his thirst. He spent the rest of it washing as much of the blood and grime off his face and hands as possible. Danny had already wasted two bottles cleaning the dry blood off his face, grimacing and hissing each time he touched his broken nose.

The city hadn't gotten any livelier since they stepped outside the museum thirty minutes ago, though it seemed to have gotten hotter, the streets on both sides of him flickering like mirages.

He found a beat-up red truck on the curb and sat the portable ham radio down on the hood and powered it on. He pressed the pre-set button to bring up the island's designated emergency frequency and adjusted the attached antenna as high as it would go.

"How's this going to work?" Danny asked, drinking the rest of his second bottle. Mostly free of his bloody mask, he actually looked even more bruised and battered in the sunlight, if that was possible.

"What do you mean?"

"So, you're just going to tell Lara that your psycho ex is going to launch an attack on the island, and that she told you herself in a dream?"

"Yeah, I guess."

"And this doesn't strike you as the least bit odd?"

He thought about it. Then, "Lara and I have talked about it before."

"And she believes you?"

"Of course she does."

"Why?"

"Because—" Will stopped.

It was a good question. But whenever he thought about it, he always came back to the same answer: because Lara had seen Kate that night in Harold Campbell's facility back in Starch, Texas. Once you've seen the blue-eyed creatures and had their existence confirmed with your own eyes, it was easier to accept that they were capable of things that weren't always entirely explainable. Danny, for all his involvement in their survival, had never actually seen Kate. Last night was, in fact, the first time he even saw one of the blue-eyed ones.

"Because she's seen them," Will said finally. "Just like you did last night. Did you really believe me before then?"

"Of course," Danny said without hesitation.

"Really?"

"Well…" Danny grinned. "Okay, I had my doubts."

"And after last night?"

Danny sighed and nodded at the radio. "Call the island. Then we have to get the hell back there as soon as we can."

"ARE YOU SURE?" Lara asked.

"Yes," Will said.

"Will, *are you sure?*"

"Lara, she's coming. I don't know how, or when, but she made it pretty clear that she's been ignoring the island all this time because we haven't been worth her attention."

"And now, because of the broadcast, she's paying attention again. So all of this is my fault."

According to Kate, yes, he thought, but said, "Don't blame yourself. It was bound to happen sooner or later. We couldn't hope to stay under the radar forever. We're a loose end. She said as much."

"Kate…"

"Yes."

"Goddammit, Will." He could hear the exasperation in her voice. And maybe a little bit of anger. Or a lot of anger. It was sometimes hard to get all the nuances of someone's tone over the radio.

"Look, anything she says can't be taken at face value," Will said. "Maybe she'll attack, and maybe she won't. Maybe it's because of the radio broadcast, or maybe she's just using it as an excuse. I don't know. But we shouldn't take any chances."

Lara didn't say anything for a while.

"Lara…"

"I'm still here," she said. "What about Gaby?"

Now it was his turn to take a long pause.

"Will, what about Gaby?"

"The island is vital, Lara."

"It's just an island."

"But you're on it. And Carly. And the kids…"

"You have to find Gaby. We don't leave our own behind, re-member?"

He wanted to find Gaby, but he couldn't deny what had hap-pened last night. Kate had all but ended Dunbar and its occupants. It had been so easy, too. That was the most disturbing part. Everyone who was here before last night was dead *(or worse)*, and that included Gaby. Will was still certain she had come into the city. What were the chances she had made it out after last night?

"We'll keep looking for her on our way back," he said finally.

He must not have been convincing enough, because she said, "Will, you can't leave her out there alone. Not again. You can't give up now."

"The island is important, Lara. We can't lose it." He added, "Gaby would understand."

There was another long silence, this time from both of them.

"Do you know where she is now?" Lara finally asked.

"That's the problem. Danny and I tracked her to Dunbar yesterday. If she was still here after nightfall... I don't know. I just don't know. I'll keep looking. But the island, Lara, the island..."

"I know," she said softly, her voice barely audible over the connection. "I know."

He didn't know what else to say and was grateful for the sound of a car engine coming from up the street. He glanced back as Danny turned the corner in a white Ford Bronco.

"Danny found a vehicle," Will said into the mic. "I have to go."

"Find her, Will. Do everything you can to find her."

"Lara..."

"Promise me."

"The island..."

"Don't worry about the island. I'll take care of us here. You just take care of yourself and Danny, and find Gaby. *Find her, Will.*"

If she's even still alive, he thought, but said, "We'll keep looking for her on our way back. But we can't stay out here forever. Not with the island in danger."

"There's something..." she started to say.

"What is it?"

She didn't answer right away.

"What is it, Lara?"

"Nothing," she said. "Nothing that I can't handle. Just find her and come home. In the meantime, I'll look after things here. You trust me, don't you?"

"You know I do."

"Good. I love you, Will."

He smiled. "I'll see you soon."

He put the microphone down and turned off the radio as Danny parked the Bronco in the middle of the street behind him, then hopped down from the raised driver side door.

"How'd it go?" Danny asked.

"It went."

"You told her about Gaby?"

"Uh huh."

"And she was fine with us coming back without the kid?"

"What do you think?"

"Well, I hope you don't mind, but I'm going to tell Carly it was all your idea."

Will grunted. "Sounds fair to me." He nodded at the truck. "Where'd you find that beast?"

"Auto body garage next to a VFW hall on the other side of town. Harrison might have been an idiot, but he wasn't a total idiot. There were a half dozen working vehicles inside, including a fuel truck. Working batteries, too. From the looks of it, they kept all the cars running just in case."

"Any survivors?"

"There was a hell of a lot of blood in the VFW. They had the windows and doors barricaded, but apparently it didn't work. There was a basement in the back, but I heard scurrying from down there and decided I'd rather not investigate further."

"Smart."

"It's been known to happen." Danny watched Will pack up the radio. "Song Island or bust?"

"No choice," Will said. The words came out like gravel. "Can't take the chance that Kate will attack without us there."

Danny nodded. Will knew he didn't like the idea of giving up their search for Gaby any better than he did. But like him, Danny had come to the same conclusion.

The island. They had to protect the island. It wasn't just the beach and the hotel and the solar power, though those were important, too. It was the people on the island.

Lara, Carly, Vera, and Elise....

We can't lose the island. Not now. Not after we've fought so hard to keep it.

"Well, let's get truckin', then," Danny said. "I'm driving."

"You're a terrible driver."

"I'm a great driver. Better than great. I'm a spectacular driver. Back in college, they used to call me Danny the Driver. True story."

THE BACK OF the Bronco was piled high with supplies Danny had raided from the VFW hall, though to hear him tell it, there were probably more goodies in the basement. He had stockpiled a generous amount of MREs, granola bars, and unopened cases of bottled water. He had also picked up weapons and ammo, along with a Mossberg pump-action and a FNH self-loading tactical shotgun.

Will grabbed the FNH from the back and turned it over. Eighteen inches, black matte finishing, and it didn't look as if it had ever been used. It had a metal shell carrier along the left side with six shells already preloaded. The shotgun was semi-automatic, which meant you didn't need to pump it after each shot. Harris County SWAT had been thinking about switching from the Remingtons to the FNHs but had never gotten around to it.

"Nice, right?" Danny said. "For the lazy shotgunner."

"I can dig it," Will said.

"There's a box of ammo in the back if you can find it."

Will had to rummage around the water and lumps of shiny MRE bags before he found the box of shells on the floor. He tossed it into his pack. "This was all in the VFW hall?"

"Most of it."

"Last stand?"

"Looked like it. A hell of a mess. I think they had kids in there, too."

"How could you tell?"

"I just could," Danny said, but didn't elaborate.

"So there were definitely more goodies in the basement," Will said. "An armory, maybe, where they kept more of these."

"Probably."

"It might have been worth it to go down there."

"Not in this lifetime."

"When did you get so queasy around these things?"

"Since shooting them only got me these little keepsakes," Danny said, touching his broken nose, then rubbing—and grimacing—the red gash along his temple. "Now I know how you feel walking around with that face all day."

"Keep your eyes on the road, pretty boy."

"What the hell for? There's nothing out here. Even less than nothing. If there was a name for this place, they'd call it Nothing-land. Nothingapolis. Loadacrapola."

He wasn't wrong. Route 13 out of Dunbar was uneventful. Will was ready for an ambush or at least some kind of activity on their way out, but there was none. The streets remained deserted, and the main highway connecting Dunbar to Interstate 10 was a flat two-lane road with empty scenery on both sides of them. He expected to start seeing farmland and houses soon, but apparently they hadn't ventured far out enough.

'Loadacrapola' is right.

Then Danny said, "Whoa," and slowly stepped on the brake.

Will looked out the front windshield and immediately saw a body lying across the highway where Route 13 intersected with a country road on its right side.

"Body?" Will said.

"Body," Danny nodded.

"Stay sharp."

"I'm so sharp I give myself pinpricks."

Will put down the FNH and unslung the M4A1. The window was already rolled down, so all he had to do was focus in order to listen in on his surroundings. Not that he could hear very much over the churning of the Ford's engines. He did glimpse something to his right in the distance, along the country road. It looked like a ceme-tery.

Now that's not an ominous sign at all.

Danny stopped in front of the body. It was wearing a camo uni-form and lying on its stomach. "Ambush?"

"Doubt it."

"You go out and make sure while I wait in here."

"Don't leave without me."

"Whatever you say, boss."

Will opened the passenger side door and hopped down. He scanned the area—the land to his right, then up and down the highway. He stepped on bullet casings as he moved toward the body.

The figure was definitely dead, fresh blood pooling underneath him. The man's hip holster was empty and there was no sign of a weapon nearby. Will turned the man over onto his back with the toe of his boot. Male, twenties, with a ponytail. "Lumis" was written over his right breast pocket. He hadn't been dead for very long. There were no vultures or crows circling above, so the smell hadn't reached the carrions yet. He had been shot once in the hip, then again in the back.

His right ear *clicked*, and Danny's voice came through the earbud in his ear, part of the comm system they had recovered from Ennis's basement earlier. "Dead?"

"Looks dead to me."

"Give it mouth to mouth just in case."

"I think I'll skip that part."

"Why, cause he's a guy? You're such a homophobe."

Will straightened up and looked around at the flat country land-scape again. There was nothing out here, which made stumbling across a body odd. Someone had to have killed this man. Maybe someone had actually survived Dunbar last night. Maybe that person might have even been Gaby…

Captain Optimism.

"I'm heading back," he said into his throat mic.

He was halfway to the Bronco when he heard rustling and spun back around toward the ditch that ran alongside the country road. He didn't hesitate and ran toward the source of the sound with his rifle at the ready.

"Don't shoot!" a voice shouted as he neared.

Another man in his early twenties, also wearing camo, was crouched in the ditch with his hands raised high. The man was unarmed, sporting an empty hip holster and a makeshift tourniquet around his right ankle. His face was pale and he was covered in sweat, and the name "Darren" was stenciled across his nametag.

"Don't shoot!" Darren shouted again.

"Get up here," Will said.

Darren hesitated, then stood up and climbed out of the ditch with some difficulty. The handkerchief he had tied around his ankle was covered in blood and he winced each time he put pressure on the leg.

Danny had come out of the Bronco and was standing behind Will now, scanning their surroundings for possible signs of a threat. "Looks like we missed the party."

"Looks like," Will said. Then to Darren, "What happened here?"

"We were parked on the road when someone attacked us," Darren said.

"You were in a car?"

"Yes."

"Where is it?"

"They took it."

"Who is 'they'?"

"I don't know," Darren said. He wiped at the beads of sweat dripping down his face. "There were four of them."

"What did they look like?"

"They were girls."

"Girls?"

"Yeah."

"You mean kids?"

Darren seemed to think about the question before answering. "Teenagers, I guess."

Will exchanged a quick look with Danny, who grinned back at him. "Ya think?"

Maybe...

"Was one of those teenagers blonde, tall, about five-seven?" Will asked Darren. "Pretty, despite the bruises on her face?"

"You know, the kind you'd give that right leg to take to the prom?" Danny added.

Darren grimaced at him for a few seconds. Will wasn't sure if it was because of the sun, the pain, the memory of what had happened to him, or maybe all three.

The kid finally nodded. "You guys know her or something?"

Will smiled. "Yeah, we've met. Where'd she go, and how long ago?"

CHAPTER 24

LARA

CARRIE AND LUCY had good things to say about Keo, but more important was what they told her about the "soldiers" and Keo's reaction to them. He wasn't their friend. Far from it.

The enemy of my enemy is friend. Isn't that the old saying, Will?

Then Will called on the radio and told her about Kate. A part of her was still annoyed his ex-girlfriend was visiting him in his dreams. *In his dreams.* But that was the kid in her talking. The pre-med student who had survived The Purge on pure luck. The new her, the one who had been running Song Island for the last few weeks, was concerned about other things.

Like survival. Hers. And Carly's. Elise's and Vera's, too. The new people who had joined them, hoping for a fresh start. Or, at least, a less terrifying existence. All these people who had come here and now depended on her, and she didn't know when it would all fall apart.

That was what concerned her the most. The not knowing. Today, tonight, or tomorrow. Or the week after. She knew one thing: they were sitting ducks. The enemy knew where they were at all times. The island that was such a godsend also made them an easy target. There was nowhere to run or hide, just fight.

Just fight…

Those thoughts swirled around her head as she walked to the back of the hotel.

Survival. Their chances would increase when Will and Danny

THE FIRES OF ATLANTIS   311

returned. But that wasn't for a while. A day at least. Maybe two. Gaby was still out there, too. The thought of losing her because Will had to rush back home tormented Lara.

Roy was sitting on a chair outside the makeshift jail cell, an old inventory room with a steel door, when she turned the corner. He glanced up when he heard her footsteps.

"Did you eat yet?" she asked.

"Not yet. Blaine's supposed to show up in thirty minutes." He looked nervous this morning, and she guessed he had been waiting for this—the two of them talking—since last night. "Lara, about what happened ..."

"We're not talking about that right now, Roy."

"I just wanted to say I'm sorry. Going out there was stupid—"

"Later," she said, cutting him off. "For now, go get something to eat."

He looked confused. "Are you sure?"

"Yes." She peered through the security glass.

"Lara, about last night, with Gwen..."

She gave him a reassuring smile. "Roy, we're all adults here, aren't we?"

"Yes."

"It's fine. You found someone. I'm happy for you. For Gwen, too. And about what you did... Well, it worked out for the best. I'm not saying it was the right thing to do—and yes, I'm still pissed off you did it—but no one died. That's all that matters for now."

He nodded, looking not pleased exactly, but relieved. "Just be careful with him. I've seen guys like this before."

"What kind of guys is that?"

"The dangerous kind," Roy said.

She nodded. He was talking about West and Brody, two men Roy had traveled with since The Purge. He was right. Those two were dangerous men. Every now and then, she wondered whatever became of West...

"Go grab some breakfast, Roy."

"Just be careful with him," Roy said again before heading down the hallway.

"Roy," she said after him. When he stopped and looked back, "Don't ever do that again without asking for my permission first. Do you understand?"

He nodded and pursed his lips. "I understand."

"Go eat some breakfast."

She waited until he turned the corner before reaching for the key that hung from a hook. She unlocked the makeshift cell door and pulled it open.

Keo looked up from the floor where he was sitting with his back against the far wall. A white plastic plate with thick dripping syrup rested between his bent legs while he shoved the last piece of fluffy pancakes into his mouth using a flimsy plastic spork. Crumbs from biscuits were sprinkled liberally on his clothes and around him.

"Frozen pancakes," he said.

"Frozen pancakes," she nodded.

"Tastes just like the real thing."

"They are the real thing. Just thawed out. How'd you like the biscuits?"

"What's not to like? The only thing missing are eggs and sausages."

"We were thinking about bringing a hog or two onto the island and letting them run wild in the woods."

"I always wanted to try my hand at being a pig farmer."

She picked up Roy's chair and set it down in front of the open door, then sat down on it. She leaned forward and smiled at him. "You don't strike me as the farming type, Keo."

"What do I strike you as?"

"Dangerous. That's what everyone says."

He shrugged. "I've been called worse."

He hadn't moved from the floor and his eyes watched her curiously, first dropping to the Glock in her hip holster, then to the open door behind her. Ten feet of space separated them. It wasn't very much and she wished it were more.

He was tall for an Asian-American. Six-one, easily, and was obviously in good shape. Muscled; more toned than huge like Blaine. Fast, too, she thought, remembering last night. If she had any doubt that he was, as Roy said, dangerous, one look at that long scar along one side of his face took it away. This was a man used to violence, even before the world came to an unceremonious end.

So what were the chances she wasn't about to make the biggest mistake of her life right now?

You wanted to be the leader, so lead. This is what it means to lead.

The hard choices. The tough calls. This is it.
So lead.

She replayed everything Carrie had told her about this man in her head for the fifth time in as many minutes. The soldiers at the marina in Dulcet Lake. The ones on the shoreline of Beaufont the next day. The man was dangerous. A professional, she had thought when she heard about what he had done. She had come so close to telling Will about him during their radio call this morning.

So why hadn't she?

Because Keo is dangerous. Too dangerous.

And after West and Brody, Will would never agree to let me do this. And maybe he's right, and I'm dead wrong, because that's exactly what I'll be if I misjudge this man.

But she had other information Will didn't. She had seen Keo up close and in person. She knew what he had done, why he was even on the island. The fact that he had saved Carrie and Lorelei and never asked for anything in return and in fact had shouldered the responsibility of bringing them down here with him...

"I'm Lara, by the way," she said. "We didn't get a chance at introductions last night."

He stuck a finger into the leftover syrup and licked it clean. "You know what I miss most about the end of the world, Lara?"

"What's that?"

"IHOP. Best damned pancakes in the history of the world. Their French toasts with fruit topping and sweet cream? To die for."

"I don't think we have any of that in our kitchen."

"Heaven without the fluffy clouds?" he smiled.

She smiled back. "Carrie told me you were headed somewhere else, that you only came here to find out whatever became of your friends."

"I'm keeping a dead man's promise. It was the only reason he came down here with me in the first place. I figured, what the hell. It's already on my way."

"The seven people."

"Yeah."

"So you don't know if they actually made it to the island."

"Nope."

"But I didn't lie to you last night. If they did make it here, then they're probably dead. My group only survived because we got lucky.

Does that answer your question?"

"Yes, if you're telling the truth."

"What reason would I have to lie? Look at where you are now."

He chuckled. "Point taken."

This time, it was her turn to watch him closely. She thought he looked almost relieved by what she had told him. Then again, she didn't know this man at all, and she could be misreading him completely.

God, please don't let me get everyone here killed.

"So what's next for you?" she asked.

"I move on."

"Santa Marie Island."

"That was the original plan."

"Who is she?"

"What makes you think there's a 'she'?"

"There's always a she, Keo."

He grinned. "I met her when all of this first happened. We got close, and like a fool, I told her I'd meet up with her later. It's been four—five?—months since, and I'm still trying to make good on it. Hell, I don't even know if she's still alive."

"So all of this could be for nothing?"

"A big fat nothing, yup."

"Must be true love."

"Sure, that's one way to look at it." He nodded at the Glock at her hip. "Can you use that thing?"

"Yes," she said without hesitation.

"I believe you." He picked up the spork and sucked at the syrup clinging to it. "So what happens now? You going to lock me in here for the rest of my life? Even after how Carrie and Lorelei told you what a swell guy I am?"

She leaned back in the chair. "I have a proposition for you, Keo."

"I thought you already have a boyfriend."

"You wanna hear it or not?"

He gave her a noncommittal shrug. "Not like I have a choice."

"I'm expecting an impending attack. It might be today, or tonight, or tomorrow. But it's coming."

He gave her a knowing look. "The soldiers I ran into yesterday."

She nodded. "You told Carrie you thought it was a staging area.

She also told me about the boat that was going up and down the lake. It was watching us."

He nodded. "They were reconning you."

"Here's my offer, Keo. Lend us a hand, and I'll give you everything you need to reach Santa Marie Island. It beats swimming over there."

"I don't know, I can swim pretty far, as you saw last night."

She continued as if he hadn't said anything. "I'll give you a sailboat with an outboard motor and plenty of fuel and supplies to last for weeks out in the Gulf of Mexico. The way I hear it, boats are in pretty short supply these days."

"I'm sure there's one lying around somewhere…"

"Not according to what Carrie told me."

"Carrie talks too much."

"She wants to stay here. Lorelei, too."

"Are they?"

"You mean, am I going to let them?"

"Yes."

"I am," she nodded. "There's no reason not to."

"That's big of you."

"It's common decency."

"I've heard of that. Never had much use for it."

She smiled at him. "That's not what the girls told me."

"Like I said, they talk too much." He sucked on the spork again. "I could always just walk to Texas."

"Yes, you could. It's a long way, but hey, maybe one day you'll actually make it. Hide in basements at night, walk in the day. Of course, you might run into those soldier buddies of yours again, or some nutcase with a sniper rifle who decides he wants your stuff." She shrugged. "Who knows, you might even find a working vehicle."

"You've thought this through."

"I've been out there, Keo."

"All right. I'll play along. What exactly do I have to do to win this great prize of yours, Barbie Barker?"

"I don't need you to fight our battles for us. I just need you to help me delay the attack."

"Delay it?"

"Yes."

He seemed to think about it, then gave her that noncommittal shrug again. "For how long?"

"A day. Two. Whatever you can give me. I'm going to get reinforcements from two Army Rangers either later today or the day after. But I'm not waiting around to find out when the attack is coming."

"You want to attack them first."

"Yes."

"Ballsy."

"No," she said, shaking her head. "Just desperate."

He actually looked impressed. For a moment, anyway. Then he was back to pretending he didn't give a damn about her or the others on the island. "Sounds like you have it all figured out, Lara."

Except for the part where I mess up and trust the wrong man and get everyone killed as a result.

"The question is," Keo said, "are you really willing to put your life, and the lives of everyone on this island, into the hands of a stranger with a gun? Because that's what you're about to do. Are you *certain* you're not going to regret that decision?"

"IS THIS SMART?" Carly asked.

"I don't know," Lara said.

"Can we trust him?"

"I don't think we have a choice."

"What did Will say?"

"I didn't tell him about Keo or last night."

"Oh."

"Should I have?"

"I don't know," Carly said. "I guess that's why you get paid the big bucks. To make decisions like this."

"Yeah," Lara said. "The big bucks."

If I'm wrong, we're all dead.

Then again, if I don't do this, we're probably all dead, anyway.

"If all else fails, there's always Plan Z," Carly said.

"God, that's such a stupid name."

Carly chuckled. "Isn't it, though?"

They both smiled. Mostly because they didn't know what else to do. Carly, more than anyone, knew what was at stake here. Not just her own life, but her sister Vera's, too. The fact that she was making a decision that could take away both lives hung over Lara like the Sword of Damocles.

"We're probably all going to die," Lara said.

Carly laughed. "Yeah. Probably." Then, after she had settled down, "I have to tell you, the image of Kate out there pulling the strings makes for a pretty icky visual." She shivered a bit. "I liked her, you know. We were friends."

"I know."

"But I don't think we were ever as close as you and me right now. The age difference and everything. She was always kind of..."

"What?"

"I don't know. I guess out of my league."

"I didn't know the two of you dated."

Carly snorted. "She wishes."

They leaned against the railing on the hotel's front patio and watched Keo and Roy across the open grounds in silence for a moment.

The two men were observing Kendra and some of the kids as they worked on a patch of land that Kendra told them had the best soil for growing vegetables. They had found everything they needed to loosen the earth from the supply shacks in the back, including rakes, shovels, and more variety of hoes than Lara knew existed. Kendra had been disappointed they didn't have a tiller machine, which would have made everything easier. In one of Will and Danny's forays on land for supplies, they had picked up a crate full of seeds from one of the home improvement warehouses. It wouldn't be long now before they could begin planting along the rows being carved out.

If they were still alive in a week from now, anyway. A lot of things could happen in a few days. All she had to do was look at the last couple of weeks for evidence of that.

"I know what you're doing," Carly said.

"What's that?"

"Giving him a tour of the hotel, then showing him everyone eating breakfast together in the dining room. And now showing him the garden, with Kendra and the kids. Danny told me about this. The Army calls it psy ops. Psychological warfare. Hearts and minds, right? You're trying to convince him without actually saying a word that the island is worth saving by showing him the people on it. I mean, the kids, Lara. Who could resist Elise and Vera covered in dirt? You'd need a heart of stone, and I don't think Keo has one. At least, not the Keo that Carrie and Lorelei told us about."

"You give me way too much credit, Carly," Lara said before she smiled to herself, hoping that Carly hadn't caught it.

"Slick," Carly said, grinning at her. "Real slick, boss. I always knew you had it in you."

SHE STOOD WITH Keo on the beach. He had taken off his boots and was enjoying the sensation of bare feet soaked in the cool and clear Beaufont Lake water. Elise, Vera, and Jenny, fresh from helping Kendra with loosening dirt for the garden, were fighting against the waves in front of them, cleaning off the dirt and grime of their hard work. The girls hadn't bothered to change into bathing suits given how everything on them was dirty. She guessed this way they were hoping to kill two birds with one stone—clean up themselves, and their clothes, too.

Blaine's silhouetted form on top of the boat shack watched them carefully; he was there just in case Keo decided he wanted the boat and supplies minus the whole risking his life part. That was why she only wore her Glock in a hip holster. Worst-case scenario, Keo would be armed with a handgun while Blaine had the M4. Maddie was also watching them from the Tower with the ACOG-equipped rifle while Roy and Carly were on alert back at the hotel.

She hadn't counted on the girls showing up suddenly on the beach, though. If things did go bad and he grabbed one of them…

Please, God, don't let me be wrong about Keo.

"If you were me, how would you do it?" she asked. "Delay the attack."

"You seemed to be awfully sure there's going to *be* an attack."

"You saw it yourself. The staging area with the soldiers."

"But that's not all. You have inside information."

That's one way to put it, she thought, and said, "I know it's coming, yes."

"Okay." He seemed to think about her question for a moment. Then, "It's been a whole day, so by now they would have gotten reinforcements. Men to replace the ones I took out yesterday. You're looking at a dozen assaulters at least. Two, maybe three dozen, if you're really SOL."

"What else?"

"The fact that they're willing to commit to assaulting the island at all, given how isolated you people are, tells me you've pissed either them or their ghoul masters off. I'm guessing that radio broadcast of yours had a little something to do with it."

She smiled. After Carrie and Lorelei mentioned he knew of her broadcast, she had been waiting for him to put two and two together. "Finally figured it out, huh?"

He chuckled. "I know I look it, but I'm not that dense. But yeah, it took a while."

"What finally gave me away?"

"Your voice sounds more echoey on the radio."

"I recorded it in the Tower. It's an enclosed space."

"How'd you find out about the silver?"

"Trial and error."

She sneaked a look at him. He was watching the girls frolicking against the waves. She couldn't quite read his reaction. Maybe he was marveling at the sight…or was it complete indifference?

I can't read this man. I'm about to put the lives of everyone on this island into the hands of a stranger whose face I can't read with any certainty.

"Will you help us, Keo?"

He looked over at the boats docked along the pier. One of them was a sailboat—small enough to be handled by one person, with a powerful outboard motor that would have had no problems taking him south and to the coast of Texas. The boat Carrie and Lorelei had come in sat among them, looking almost quaint next to the more travel-ready vessels.

This is it. This is where he proves me right or wrong.

She didn't realize it, but her hand had moved closer toward her sidearm. She shifted her eyes slightly to the right and saw Blaine watching them closely, his rifle gripped in front of him at the ready.

"And you'll give me one of those boats, plus fuel and supplies?" he asked. "Everything I need to make it to the Texas coast?"

"Yes," she said, and hoped her voice wasn't nearly as anxious as it had sounded to her own ears.

She waited for his answer, but he surprised her by chuckling softly to himself.

"What's so funny?" she asked.

"A year ago, you wouldn't have liked me." He was watching Elise and Vera building castles in the sand while Jenny, Sarah's daughter, did backstrokes nearby. "In fact, you would have hated me, and justifiably so. I've done things you couldn't imagine."

"I'm sure you had good reasons."

"No," he said, and laughed, though it was devoid of humor. "Not really."

"You've changed. We all have. Adapt or perish."

"I've gone soft is really what's happened." He sighed. "The organization would have put me out of my misery months ago."

"'Organization'?"

"The people I used to work for."

"They don't sound like very nice people."

"Nope. They were most definitely not." He looked over at her. "I'm not promising anything, you understand? I'll do what I can, but it might still not be enough. But maybe it'll buy your boyfriend time to get back here and put up a proper defense."

"I'm willing to take that chance."

"First things first," he said. "I'll need guns, ammo, explosives, and at least one person to lend a hand. So, I asked you the question before, and I'll ask it again: Are you really willing to put your life, and the lives of everyone on this island, into the hands of a stranger with a gun?"

◄━━▮ ▮━━►

OVER THE MONTHS, Danny had organized the subterranean space under the Tower into a makeshift armory. Lara had been surprised when she first saw it, but Danny had single-handedly done a magnificent job. He had halved the basement, with emergency supplies like rations, crates of MREs, cases of small bottled water and five-gallon coolers—half of them unopened, the other half refilled with tap water—and equipment up front. The back contained the weapons, ammo, and silver that hadn't been melted down yet. There were green ammo cans filled with silver rounds stacked high in one corner and even more housed in regular moving boxes. The rest of the non-essentials, like clothes and personal items, had been transferred over to the hotel and put in a "lost and found room" in the back where anyone could take what they needed.

As a result, the basement looked bigger than when she was last down here two months ago. The room was longer than it was wide, extending away from the northeast cliff. Lara had never measured the space, but she guessed it was ten yards at its widest and at least twenty at its longest. LED lights, powered by the solar cells around the island, lined the ceiling, with battery backups hanging from wall hooks.

"When do you expect your boyfriend back?" Keo asked. He was standing in front of the racks of rifles. She couldn't tell if he was impressed or indifferent by the selection Will and Danny had collected over the months.

"Best-case scenario is later tonight," Lara said. "Worst-case scenario is…God knows."

"So I'm a stopgap, is that it?"

"You said it, not me."

His laugh echoed slightly in the contained room. "At least you're honest about it." He pulled an M16 from the rack. "You got rounds for the M203?"

The M203 was the grenade launcher attached under the barrel of the rifle. It was the same type of weapon that had almost ended her life when Kate's people last assaulted the island.

She gestured at the crates around them. "Be my guest."

"I'll also need my guns back."

"They're in the hotel."

He nodded. "So. Where are my volunteers?"

BLAINE AND BONNIE had joined her and Keo on the third floor of the Tower. She expected to see Blaine there. He had volunteered almost as soon as she brought it up earlier, but Bonnie's presence was a surprise.

"How's this going to work?" Blaine asked.

Keo leaned against one of the windows, looking over his submachine gun. He looked overly well-armed with the addition of the M16. "I just need you to do the driving."

"What about me?" Bonnie asked.

He shrugged. "I guess you'll be there in case he gets shot."

Bonnie and Blaine exchanged a worried look.

"Just you against that army out there?" Blaine said.

"Don't be so dramatic," Keo said. "Even with reinforcements, it's still a makeshift group of assholes in homemade uniforms. And besides, numbers isn't going to play a part in this."

That didn't seem to really reassure either Blaine or Bonnie, and Keo didn't look like he cared too much about their reactions.

"You guys don't have to go," Lara said. "I can ask for other volunteers."

"I'm good," Blaine said without hesitation.

"Me too," Bonnie said, though not nearly as quickly. She scrutinized Keo across the room. "Tell me one thing: You're not going there just to get yourself killed, right? You *want* to come back here?"

"That's a dumb question," Keo said, looking almost offended by the mere suggestion. "I don't have a death wish. I wouldn't be doing this if I didn't think I could walk away from it. I just wanted to make sure you know what you're getting into, that's all. People are going to die. Maybe the two of you will be among them. You need to understand the risks. But trust me when I tell you, I'm not going there to get killed. I got places to go and people to see."

That seemed to reassure them somewhat.

"Last chance," Lara said. "Speak up now—"

"I'm good," Blaine said again.

"Yeah, me too," Bonnie nodded, and this time she said it quicker and with more conviction.

Lara wanted to tell them something reassuring, make a speech that would ease their minds. She tried to come up with words that Will would say to rally the troops as they prepared to go into battle.

Instead, the only thing she could think of to do was glance down at her watch. "Let's get something to eat before you guys go."

"Maddie's relieving me in a few hours," Blaine said.

"Okay, I'll send her over earlier."

If having someone in the Tower twenty-four hours a day was important before, it was imperative now. So she, Keo, and Bonnie walked down using the spiraling cast-iron staircase while Blaine stayed behind.

Keo wandered ahead, and Lara used the moment to walk beside Bonnie.

"I'm volunteering because I want to, Lara," Bonnie said before Lara could ask the question that had been on her mind since she saw Bonnie waiting for them on the third floor.

"Can I ask why?"

"You don't know?"

"Should I?"

"Because someone had to, or else you would have volunteered. And we couldn't allow that."

"'We'?"

"Carly, me, Benny, Roy… Everyone."

The 'we' strikes again.

This wasn't the first time the island had made a decision for her because they believed it was for her own good. It was ironic because she was supposedly running the place in Will's absence. And yet, whenever they felt like it, the others always got together and discussed what was best for her. She should have been angry about it, even pissed off, but she couldn't, really, because they were almost always right.

"One of us had to go with Blaine and Keo," Bonnie continued. "Carly wanted to. So did Maddie. And Benny and Roy, and even Jo and Gwen. But in the end, we decided I was the best choice."

"Why you?"

Bonnie laughed. "You sound so surprised."

"I…" Lara began, but didn't finish because everything she would have said would have come out as an insult to Bonnie.

"I know," Bonnie said with a grin. "The ex-model? I don't blame you. All I can say is, you have to trust me, because compared to the rest, I'm the best choice. I was always athletic as a kid. I played basketball when I was in high school and I've stayed pretty active over the years. It was either stay skinny by sweating your ass off or throw up everything you ate, and I was never good at chucking food."

Lara smiled.

"So yeah, between everyone, I'm the obvious choice," Bonnie said.

"All of this, so I wouldn't volunteer myself?"

"Yes." Bonnie gave her an earnest look. "You're important to the island, Lara. More than the rest of us."

"I don't know what to say, Bonnie."

And she didn't. She had no idea whatsoever. Because Bonnie was right. She would have gone with Keo and Blaine if no one else had stepped forward. Keo had made it clear—he could have done with one, but he preferred two. Three people gave them the best chance at success, and right now, they needed success in the worse way until Will and Danny could come home.

"Thank you," Lara said. It was the only thing she could think of to say, and it felt too simple and unworthy of Bonnie's sacrifice.

She wondered if Bonnie had even heard her, though, because the other woman looked preoccupied with Keo, who was walking ahead of them. "You really think he's as good as he thinks he is?" she asked.

"From what Carrie and Lorelei told me, he's pretty damn good," Lara said.

"And you think this could work?"

"I hope this works."

"What happens after that? I know you just want to delay them for a few days until Will and Danny can get here. But what happens *after* that?"

"I don't know," Lara said quietly. "I'm just trying to get us to tomorrow first…"

CHAPTER 25

GABY

SHE SHOULD HAVE killed the kid. Darren. Well, he wasn't really a kid. He was older than her by a few years, but to Gaby, anyone with a rifle who couldn't put up a fight was a kid. Of course, killing Darren went out the window as soon as he started crying. Even Claire had looked almost sickened by the sight of that.

So they had left the collaborator on the side of the road and taken his truck. It was a Chevy Silverado, though one truck was the same as another to Gaby. It had a high perch, which allowed her to see a lot of the road up ahead, something that she liked. It was also powerful, and she finally understood why boys loved their trucks so much. It was hard not to feel as if you could run over just about anything behind the wheel of one of these monsters because, in all likelihood, you probably could. All she needed from it at the moment was to get her to Song Island.

Donna and Milly were stuffing themselves with food and refilled bottles of water in the back. Claire, who sat shotgun in the front passenger seat, leaned over every now and then to grab some for herself. Each time she did, Gaby resisted the instinct to tell her to put on her seat belt. She had to keep reminding herself that she wasn't the girl's mom, though she felt a strange connection to her, even more so than to Milly, whom she had known longer.

It was still morning, and the sun baked the empty vastness to both sides of them. The hot asphalt road shimmered and looked like water in front of her, and the nothingness made her feel like she was daydreaming. It should have made her comfortable and lulled her into something resembling serenity, but instead it only made her more alert and sit up straighter in the leather seat.

It was Josh. She couldn't stop thinking about him. About what he had become, what he was doing. She kept looking at her side mirror, expecting to see him coming up behind her at any moment, declaring his love for her, that he was doing all of this for her, while bringing along a small army of lackeys.

Keep lying to yourself, Josh. Maybe one day you'll actually believe it.

"Is it far from here?" Claire asked after a while. She talked through a mouthful of bread and pieces of sausage.

"Where'd you get that?" Gaby asked.

"Back here," Donna said, holding up a blue plastic Tupperware with more sausages inside. "It's pork."

"How's the bread?"

"It's about a day old. Still pretty good, though."

Donna pulled off a chunk and leaned forward. Gaby gobbled it up and chewed for a moment, keeping one hand on the steering wheel and her eyes outside the windshield the entire time. The last thing she needed was to run them into a ditch while trying to eat. All those "Don't Text and Drive" commercials flashed through her mind all of a sudden. That and those "Click it or Ticket" billboards.

The good old days…

Donna was right. The bread was still pretty good. Then again, it had been a while since she had last eaten some. They had frozen dough on the island, but these actually tasted fresh. Or, at least, one-day fresh. Donna handed her one of the pork sausages and Gaby devoured that, too. It was even better when she stuffed the remaining parts into the bread and ate it like a hot dog.

"They must have a pig farm or something," Donna said. "And fresh flour."

Gaby nodded. She wondered how much Donna knew about what was happening out there, with the collaborators and the towns, while she was stuck in Dunbar all this time with her sister under Harrison's protection. But she decided not to ask. The sisters knew enough to be scared of the soldiers and what was out there at night, and those were the only two things she needed them to know at the moment.

"You know how to cook?" she asked Donna.

Donna shrugged. "A little."

"She thinks she's good, but she's terrible at it," Claire said.

"At least I can cook," Donna said.

"Barely."

"Ugh, you're never eating anything I cook again."

"Promise?"

"You say that now—"

"Look!" Milly shouted, leaning between the front seats and pointing not up the road, but to the right of the highway.

Gaby took her foot off the gas slightly and the Chevy slowed down, going from forty to thirty, then twenty, as she saw what Milly was pointing at: a white two-story house being ravaged by a raging fire. The building was part of a farm, flanked by a red barn and some kind of storage shack. After leaving the cemetery behind, farmland and the houses of the people that tilled them had begun popping up.

"Whoa," Claire said, leaning against her door. She had rolled down the window and the girl stuck her head out a bit. "It's really burning that sucker up."

They were almost past the house, and Gaby swore she could feel the flames all the way over here, adding to the already terrible morning heat. Donna and Milly moved toward the back right window to get a better look at the flames.

"Should we stop?" Donna asked.

"No," Gaby said without hesitation.

"What if someone needs help?" Milly said.

"It's too dangerous. After what happened with the soldiers, I don't want to take any chances."

Gaby gave the house one last look, scanning the grounds around it. She couldn't detect any signs of movements or vehicles in motion in the front yard or along the manmade dirt road that connected it to the highway.

She added pressure to the accelerator and the Chevy began to pick up speed again.

Donna and Milly continued gazing out at the burning house, eventually moving from the side window to the rear windshield as they passed it by. Gaby looked briefly over at Claire, and the girl, bread stuffed into her mouth, gave her an approving nod.

Gaby smiled back.

"HOW MUCH FURTHER to Beaufont Lake?" Donna asked.

"I'm not sure," Gaby said. "After we reach I-10, it's about half a day, I think. The good news is that the road out here is pretty empty, so we should make good time. But depending on how long it takes us to reach Salvani, we might have to find a place to spend the night."

"I was hoping we'd get there today."

"Me too," Milly said.

"But you know where to go?" Claire asked. "Even without a map?"

Gaby nodded. "Once we hit I-10, we turn right, then left on Salvani. After that, it's a straight drive down south."

She glanced at Claire, then at Donna and Milly in the backseat, and hoped she had been convincing enough. They looked satisfied, so she probably had been.

The truth was, without a map, she was just guessing. She had traveled from Texas to Louisiana with Will and Lara, but she had never taken the wheel during any part of the drive. She even spent most of that trip asleep in the backseat *(with Josh)*. Even during the helicopter ride with Jen, she was just a passenger, and she slept through most of that, too.

But it seemed like a pretty straightforward trip. Hopefully.

"I can't wait for a hot shower," Donna said wistfully. She took a sip from a bottle of water and made a face. "And cold water. With ice. That would probably be the best thing ever."

"It's not bad," Gaby said. "The soft bed and your own room is a close number three and four."

"I've never stayed in a hotel before," Claire said. "Is it a nice hotel?"

"The parts that are finished are."

"How unfinished is it?" Donna asked.

"You'll hardly notice."

"She'll notice," Claire said. "She complains about everything."

"I only complain about *you*," Donna said.

Claire smirked. "See?"

They went back and forth for a few more minutes, but by then

Gaby had automatically tuned them out. She found it easy to do after the tenth time they started in on each other. Not that she ever thought about telling them to stop. She just assumed this was their way of coping, the same reason Danny joked his way through a firefight. It was their natural response, their sanctuary.

She couldn't help but share Donna's enthusiasm. How long had it been since she tasted cold water? Or stood under a hot shower? Had it really been weeks since she laid down on her own soft bed? God, she missed that the most.

Thinking about all the comforts waiting for her back on the island only made her long to see signs of the I-10 highway in the distance. Any sign at all. It would be hard to miss: a tall concrete structure rising up from the flat landscape she had been traveling for the last—how long had it been?

Gaby glanced at her watch. 9:15 A.M.

Had they only been on the road for less than forty minutes? Of course, she had only been driving at forty miles per hour. The slow speed was a combination of not being entirely confident in her driving skills and a wariness of what lay ahead. She had very little experience driving, but even more so when it came to these big trucks—

Sunlight reflected off something metallic in the road, and her left leg went down on the brake before she realized what it was: a barricade, consisting of two vehicles parked across the lanes and spilling onto the shoulders on both sides. It wasn't an accident; she could tell that much even from a distance. The cars had been parked on purpose to block the road.

Claire saw it, too, and immediately stopped her back and forth with Donna.

"What?" Donna said. Then she, too, saw it. "Oh no, that can't be good."

Gaby slowly eased her foot off the gas pedal until the truck was moving at a snail's pace. Claire had already picked up her rifle and put it in her lap.

"Power up your window," Gaby said. Claire did, and Gaby did hers at the same time. "Girls," Gaby said, looking up at the rearview mirror, "move behind the seats. Milly, get on the floor. Stay hidden."

Donna moved behind Gaby while Milly did as she was told. She was small enough that she was able to sink all the way down to the floor on her bent knees until she was hidden completely behind Claire.

Gaby checked to make sure her rifle was still leaning against her seat, the stock resting on Claire's side so it wouldn't accidentally fall and become tangled with her feet while she was busy with the gas and brake.

Outside, the vehicles took the shape of a white four-door sedan and a beat-up red truck. Both cars looked like they had seen plenty of use; the sedan's paint was peeling and its windows were rolled down. The truck's windows were down too, and both looked empty.

Looked empty, anyway.

Gaby knew better. Cars didn't stop in the middle of nowhere and park themselves nose to bumper. Certainly not out here, with only the spread-out land and farmhouses (including one that was burning somewhere behind them) resembling civilization. She guessed they were either halfway to the I-10 by now, or pretty close.

God, she hoped they were almost there.

The Chevy was thirty yards from the obstruction when Gaby came to a complete stop. She kept both hands on the steering wheel because if she had to jam down on the gas pedal, the truck was going to shoot forward like a rocket. When that happened, it was going to fight her with everything it had, which was a hell of a lot.

She did what Will taught her and turned the options in front of her over in her head.

There were a few that she could think of right away. The sedan and truck were no match for the larger Chevy, and she could probably power her way right through them without suffering too much damage. But there would be some damage, and she wasn't sure if she wanted to risk that. At least, not yet. Not as long as she had other options.

Which were…?

The ditches, she knew from earlier, were too deep to drive across. That seemed to be the entire point of positioning the two cars across the road in the first place. Even if they couldn't completely overlap the shoulders, enough of them did that it left little space for her to maneuver the wide truck around without ramming the bumper on one car or the front hood on the other. So she would have to go down the ditch and come up on the other side if she wanted to avoid impacting the vehicles entirely. Was the Silverado powerful enough to pull that off? She had no idea.

She could retreat. That was the third option. She didn't particularly like it, but it was there. Going backward meant heading in the wrong direction, though. Home was up ahead, not behind her. So that was out of the question.

"Gaby?" Donna said. She was pressed so tightly against the seat that Gaby heard her even though she was whispering. "What are we going to do?"

"We can ram them," Claire said.

"Ram them?" Donna said. "You're crazy."

"Why not? I bet we could."

It had been less than thirty seconds since she had stepped on the brake. In that time, the highway remained empty except for their vehicle and the two in front of them. She expected a head, followed by a weapon, to appear behind one of the cars at any second, signaling that this was an ambush as she *(knew)* feared. The Silverado's raised seat gave her a good view of her surroundings, but at the moment she couldn't see anything to indicate this wasn't just some freak accident.

Yeah, right. And I'm on a Sunday drive in the park with some kids.

She waited, but nothing happened.

There were no heads, no weapons, and no signs that someone was hiding behind the vehicles. Or around them. There were just two dead cars that shouldn't be there but were and an empty field to the right and left of her.

Up ahead was I-10…

Maybe she was overthinking this. Or maybe someone *had* set up an ambush here a while ago but gave up when they didn't find any takers. That was possible, too. You could only wait so long until you got tired and moved on. Maybe those vehicles were actually dead.

Maybe. So many maybes.

It was starting to get hot inside the truck with the windows rolled up, and Gaby glanced down at the AC controller when she caught a flicker of movement in the rearview mirror.

A man, cradling a rifle, was sneaking up on them from behind—

"Get down!" Gaby shouted, at the same time shoving the gear into reverse and slamming her foot down on the gas pedal. The truck lurched backward with such awkward force that Gaby was thrown forward into the steering wheel and had to hold on with everything she had.

The Silverado's tires screamed as it reversed. Or was that more of a shrill? She swore she could also smell rubber burning, but that could have just been something her frenzied mind was making up on the spot.

She felt rather than heard the *THUMP!* as the truck rammed into the figure behind them and she glimpsed something flying through the air, flashing across her side mirror. It was big and dark and seemed to be failing wildly, and it was there one split-second and gone the next.

Keep going! Don't stop! Don't stop!

She didn't stop and she kept going, pushing back against the seat while gripping the steering wheel with all her might. A dark black lump flashed by to her left, lying on the road *(I guess he landed)*, just as a flurry of movement tore her eyes away to a *second man* emerging out of the ditch to her left. She didn't get a good look at his face—the truck was moving too fast—but he was definitely wearing slacks and a T-shirt, so he wasn't one of Josh's people. Not that it mattered at the moment. The shotgun clutched in his hands was what was important.

Then Claire screamed her name.

Gaby snapped a look in the girl's direction and saw a *third* figure climbing—lumbering, really, because the man was huge and moved with great difficulty—out of the ditch to their right. The AR-15 looked like a toy in his hands. The man stopped and took aim and opened fire.

"Stay down!" Gaby screamed.

She kept her hands tight around the steering wheel even as the truck continued to reverse, the sound of peeling tires now lost in the string of shotgun blasts pounding the air, joining the AR-15 as it pelted the truck. She hoped and prayed she was going in a straight line back down Route 13 even as the front windshield shattered and glass shards *zip-zip-zipped* around her head. In another second, the entire windshield seemed to disintegrate until there was nothing left.

"Gaby!" Claire shouted. "Watch out—"

Before the girl could finish, the ground gave out under them and they were going down. Then her view out of the rectangular hole that used to be the windshield changed positions and she found herself staring up at the cloudless sky, bright sun hitting her full in the face. Without the glass to protect her, the full force of the heat was overwhelming and she had to blink even as the sound of the truck's rear tires spinning fruitlessly against the ground forced its way into her senses. She still had her foot pressed down on the gas pedal, though she wasn't sure why because they didn't seem to be moving at all.

They were upended, with the truck's bumper resting on the bottom of the ditch and the tires fighting for purchase against the dirt wall. She looked to her right and saw Claire clinging to her seat, hands over her head, dazed and confused.

Gaby pulled her foot off the gas pedal and reached for the M4 lying across her and Claire's seats just as the driver side door was yanked open with a loud squeal of metal grinding against metal. The man had to be immensely strong because opening a door *upward* took a hell of a lot of strength, and yet he had done it almost effortlessly.

She gave up on the rifle and went for her Glock instead.

The large man with the AR-15 was trying to pull her out with one hand even while he kept the door pried open with one bulging shoulder. Trying? No. He was succeeding. Meaty fingers dug into her flesh, and she couldn't have fought him even if she wanted to. He was so much stronger that she didn't think he was even exerting any force whatsoever as he yanked her toward the open door.

She twisted in her seat and saw his eyes go wide at the sight of the gun in her right fist. He opened his mouth to say something—maybe to ask her not to shoot—but before he could get a word out she shot him in the chest, the discharge deafening in the tight confines of the vehicle.

Behind her, either Donna or Milly began screaming. By the shrill noise, she guessed it was probably Milly. Gaby had been wondering when the girl would finally let it all out. She guessed this was as good a time as any.

The big man—who was probably shorter than her, though he made up for it with width and at least one hundred pounds—let go of her arm before stumbling back, looking more stunned than hurt. The door slammed back down, but Gaby could still see him through the cracked driver side window. The man's rifle was slung over his shoulder and he was clawing for it. He looked confused, as if he couldn't quite figure out where the rifle was, or remember how to breathe.

She shot him a second time in the chest, shattering the driver side window in the process.

"Aim for center mass," Will always said. *"The biggest part of the body is your best target. Only delusional idiots aim for the head in a gunfight."*

The man crumpled to the bottom of the ditch on his stomach.

She was about to leap out of her seat *(Get out of the car! It's a death trap! Get out of it now!),* when she heard glass shattering behind her, from across the front seat, and Claire screaming. Gaby twisted back in that direction. She hadn't gotten completely around when she saw a familiar face, the same shade of red hair, leaning in Claire's suddenly open passenger side window with a shotgun in his hands.

But she was still halfway around when the man ruthlessly shoved the barrel of his weapon against Claire's cheek, then glared at her from behind the girl's head. "Go ahead, see if I don't blow this little girl's head open like a melon before you get that gun all the way around."

Gaby froze.

Harrison.

She stared at him, then at Claire, fastened to her seat as if she was glued to it, too afraid to even move. There was a big bump in the girl's forehead where she had slammed into the dashboard because she wasn't wearing her seatbelt. For the first time since she had met her, Gaby saw very real fear in the thirteen-year-old's eyes.

"It's okay, Claire," Gaby said. "Everything will be okay."

"Don't lie to the girl," Harrison said. "It's unbecoming."

Gaby gripped the Glock. It was still pointed in the wrong direction—at her steering wheel—but it wouldn't have taken much to swing it sixty more degrees, lift it slightly, and shoot Harrison on the other side of Claire. Of course, that would require better aim than she had proven herself capable of with a handgun. And he was standing *right behind Claire*, using her small head as a shield.

The crying continued in the backseat. Gaby couldn't be sure if it was still just Milly or if Donna had joined in.

Options. What were her options?

Will said there were always options. She just had to see them.

So what were her options now?

She couldn't see them. God help her, she couldn't see any of them.

"Don't make me say it again," Harrison said. "Put down the gun or I'm going to splash this little girl's brains all over you. You know I'll do it."

"Yeah," Gaby said. "I know you'll do it."

"So what are you waiting for?"

She threw the Glock out her window. "Don't hurt her."

Harrison kept the shotgun pressed into Claire's cheek with one hand and reached down with the other. He brought the hand back up and tossed something to her.

Gaby looked down at a pair of steel handcuffs in her lap.

"Put one around your right wrist and the other around the steering wheel," Harrison said.

"Why?"

"Because I said so."

Options? What are my options?

None. I don't see any.

God help me, I don't see any...

She picked up the handcuffs and did as he instructed. The metal bit into her wrist and she instantly regretted it. "Now what?"

"You're going to sit tight," Harrison said.

He snatched up Claire's rifle and tossed it into the ditch. Then he grabbed her M4, which had slid into Claire's side of the truck, and stepped backward before disappearing completely from her field of vision. She heard him moving around the ditch, climbing up and then scrambling over to the other side, though she couldn't see him because the truck was pointing up at the sky at the moment.

She looked into the backseat, at the weapons that Darren and his friend had brought with them. There, an AR-15, lying between Donna and Milly—"Donna, the rifle, hurry."

Donna stared back at her as if she couldn't understand what she was saying.

"The rifle!" Gaby said, just loud enough to get through to her.

She could hear Harrison moving around the truck, reaching the other side...

"Give me the rifle!" Gaby said again, louder this time.

Donna finally understood and reached for the rifle. She picked it up by the barrel and was holding it out to Gaby when the back passenger window exploded and showered the teenager and Milly with glass shards. Both girls screamed and the rifle fell. The girls threw their arms over their heads while Milly sank even lower into the floor behind Claire's seat. Gaby couldn't tell if they were hurt or just terrified, but she saw fresh blood on the upholstery in the backseat.

The loud, unmistakable sound of a shotgun being racked filled the air, then Harrison was standing next to her on the other side of her shattered window. "Nice try," he said, then hit her in the face with the stock of his weapon.

Gaby actually heard her nose breaking, then tasted blood in her mouth as her head laid back against the comfortable headrest. She tried to shut off her senses. She wanted to go to sleep, but the sun was still beating down on her and she was able to open her eyes just in time to see Harrison pulling open the door with some effort.

He reached in and unlocked the handcuff around the steering wheel. He grabbed her by the arm and pulled her out of the truck roughly, throwing her down into the ditch. She landed on top of the short but large man she had shot earlier and scrambled to get away.

She was straightening up when Harrison hit her in the gut with a balled fist. She doubled over from the pain before falling back down to her knees in the grass. Thick blood dripped down around her in clumpy streams.

Are those mine? Yes. I think so.

Harrison towered over her, his bigger frame blotting out the sun. "You should have stayed out of my city. Everything was going fine until you showed up. Everything that's happened, it's all your fault."

She looked up at him and shook her head. "No," she said, but before she could continue defending herself, he punched her in the face—right in her broken nose. All the pain in the world seemed to come down on her at that very moment.

Someone screamed, then someone else joined in.

She heard her name just before the loud roar of another shotgun blast silenced it.

BOOK THREE

RUN AND GUN

CHAPTER 26

KEO

"THAT'S ONE NASTY scar," the woman, Bonnie, said.

"You should have seen the other guy," Keo said.

"Worse than that?"

"He's dead, and I'm not."

"Hunh."

"That's what he said."

The redhead *(Auburn hair? Close enough)* with the supermodel good looks was crouched on one knee at the bow of the eighteen-footer, as if she expected someone to start shooting at them from the shoreline at any moment. She had a Remington tactical shotgun slung over her shoulder and wore a gun belt with a sidearm, though the combination of the deadly items on someone that gorgeous struck him as somehow unnatural.

The boat they were traveling in was used primarily for bass fishing, with two seats in the middle, one behind the steering wheel, and two pedestal seats—one in the back next to the loud outboard motor and the other up front where Bonnie was crouched next to at the moment. It was also the same boat they had used to intercept Carrie and Lorelei last night. No wonder it hadn't been much of a chase. The damn thing was fast.

The big guy, Blaine, was maneuvering them toward the shoreline. His target was a spot about half a kilometer up the road from a burnt out marina and what looked like the blackened foundations of a fire-gutted house.

"Coming up," Blaine announced.

Keo freed his MP5SD and moved from his seat and toward the bow, then crouched next to Bonnie. He still had the M16 with the M203 grenade launcher. It was a heavier weapon—about nine pounds loaded—than the submachine gun and felt like a baseball bat thumping against his back.

Bonnie glanced nervously at him. "You've done this before, right?"

"What's that?"

"This, what you're about to do."

He shrugged. "First time for everything."

She gave him a horrified look. "Are you kidding me right now? Tell me you're just kidding me."

He looked back at Blaine instead. "Bring her in easy. Fifty meters."

Blaine nodded, then pulled back on the throttle. The boat slowed noticeably before continuing forward on a glide. A tall ridge and muddy banks greeted them, but no signs of another living soul anywhere. There was a long field on the other side crowded with overgrown and sun-bleached grass. That would come in handy if there was a sniper out there waiting to pick him off. If he was lucky, Blaine's bigger form would make a more tempting target and give him the early warning he needed to retreat.

I'd shoot him first, too.

It was hot and Keo was already sweating under his T-shirt. Both Bonnie and Blaine looked similarly drenched and uncomfortable under the unrelenting heat.

"Shore's coming up," Blaine announced.

Keo stood up and put his submachine gun away. He waited until the boat slipped onto the muddy bank before leaping out. He grabbed a line Bonnie tossed to him and tied it around a boulder nearby. After the islanders climbed out after him, he tightened the rope and made sure it wasn't going anywhere. The last thing he wanted was to swim back to the island. Once was enough, and he was closer last night.

He glanced at his watch: 11:13 A.M. "There and back again by five should give us a ninety-minute cushion."

"It's your operation," Blaine said.

"As long as we're on the water by the time the sun goes down,"

Bonnie said. She might have involuntarily shivered when she added, "I don't like the idea of being caught out here at night."

Keo took point. He climbed up the ridge and went into a crouch before scanning the area. Despite the oppressive weather and lack of shade, the grass had grown three feet high from the ridgeline all the way to the road on the other side. Route 27, according to a map Lara had shown him. Blaine and Bonnie climbed up behind him.

"I don't see it," Keo said. "You sure this is the right spot?"

Blaine nodded. "Should be."

"'Should be'?"

"It's here," Blaine said, with just a little more conviction that time. He stood up to survey the area before crouching back down. "I see it. It's where it should be."

"Take the lead, then."

Blaine picked up a car battery he had brought with him, got up, and jogged through the grass. Keo followed, Bonnie right behind him with two red plastic cans of gas in each hand. She was surprisingly strong for such a skinny beanpole.

The big man was leading them toward an old tree about thirty meters from the flat highway. As they neared it, Keo began making out a large object. Square-shaped, covered in some kind of brown tarp and repurposed grass that blended it, if not perfectly, then just enough into the surrounding field to make it mostly invisible to passing eyeballs unless you knew what you were looking for and where.

They slowed down as they reached the vehicle sitting underneath the makeshift camouflage. Blaine grabbed one side of the tarp and pulled it, revealing a black Dodge Ram that looked to be in reasonably good condition.

Blaine tossed Keo a key. "Pop the hood."

Keo got a whiff of stale air when he opened the door. Apparently they hadn't needed to use the Ram in a while. He leaned in and pulled the lever. "How many of these things do you guys have stashed around the lake?"

"About a half dozen," Blaine said. He stuffed the battery back into its slot and reconnected the wires. "Most of them still have some gas left in the tanks, but we bring enough extra just to be sure."

Behind him, Bonnie had finished pouring the two cans of gasoline into the tank. She closed it back up now and tossed the empty cans into the back, then wiped her hands on her shirt and made a face at the smell.

When Lara had told him that Blaine knew where to get a vehicle and they would need a battery for it, Keo hadn't been convinced. But the more he got to know these people, the more he realized he was dealing with seasoned survivors and not civilians fumbling their way through the end of the world.

Most of that, he thought, was the result of good leadership. Lara, and this Will guy whom Keo hadn't met yet. He wasn't entirely sure he wanted to, either. Keo had never gotten along especially well with Army guys. His father had been proof of that, and subsequent encounters with grunts during his career with the organization had never turned out especially well. As much as he didn't have any use for career soldiers, Keo suspected they thought the same about him and his ilk.

Blaine slammed the hood down and walked back over. "How far up the road?"

Keo did the calculations in his head, replaying snapshots of the map and where he had encountered the weekend warriors. Or collaborators, as Lara called them. "Twenty kilometers north, but since we're on the wrong side of the lake and we'll need to loop around the south end, add in an extra ten. Thirty kilometers, give or take."

"How much is that in miles?" Bonnie asked.

"Just a shade over eighteen," Keo said.

"Eighteen miles," Blaine nodded. "As long as we don't get held up by anything, we shouldn't have any problems making it back down here by five, and we'll be on the island thirty minutes later."

"Sounds like a plan. Let them know we're off."

Blaine unclipped his radio and keyed it. "Song Island. Can you read me. Over."

"Loud and clear, Blaine," a voice answered. It was one of the women, Maddie. Song Island, Keo discovered, had a lot of very capable women. Gillian and Jordan would definitely have fit in like gangbusters.

"We're heading off now, Maddie," Blaine said. "Wish us luck."

"Good luck and see you when you get back," Maddie said.

Keo climbed into the front passenger seat while Blaine slipped in behind the wheel. Bonnie settled into the back and leaned in between the two front seats. She gave Keo a long, curious look.

"What?" he said.

"Are you sure this is going to work?" she asked.

"No, but it'll be fun to find out."

Bonnie sat back with a heavy sigh. "Oh God, you're going to get me killed, aren't you?"

"That's the spirit," Keo said.

YOU REALLY THOUGHT *it was going to be that easy, huh? Think again, pal.*

They were exactly where he last saw them yesterday, gathered around the red two-story house near the shoreline. Except this time there were more vehicles and more men guarding the roads and standing along the docks. He counted almost two dozen uniforms, likely more scattered elsewhere that he couldn't see.

The radio clipped to his hip squawked, and Blaine's voice came through at half volume because he had lowered the volume halfway. "How's it look up close?"

He told Blaine about what he could see and what he couldn't.

"Damn," Blaine said.

"Yeah."

"What's the plan now?"

If I'm smart, I'll go back and shoot you and the girl and take the truck and not look back until I'm halfway to Texas.

"Sit tight," he said instead.

Blaine and Bonnie were waiting for him about three kilometers up Route 410. They had stopped even further back than that before pushing the vehicle with the gear on neutral for almost two extra kilometers so they wouldn't give away their approach. Well, he and Blaine had pushed anyway, while Bonnie steered. Keo had hiked the rest of the way. It was a pain in the ass, but necessary since sound traveled these days, especially car engines. Even with all those precautions, he kept expecting gunfire coming his direction at any moment.

He was probably 200 meters from the red house, just further back than when he was last here with Carrie and Lorelei, and well hidden behind a brown building that was once a house before a fire gutted it years ago, leaving behind three walls and not much else. Keo was crouched along one of those still-standing sides, peering through his binoculars up the road at men transferring supplies from the house and parked trucks over to the docks. One of the men was looking through a box and pulled out night-vision goggles and tried it on.

Looks like they're getting ready for a night assault.

The sentries at the two-story structure, including the one on the rooftop, looked alert. Two men paced the road almost exactly halfway between him and the shoreline. One of them was carrying an M249 Squad Automatic Weapon, an ammo belt wrapped around his shoulder and waist like he was a bandito out of a Western. That was the first time Keo had seen a machine gun in the last year, and he wondered where they found that little beauty.

"Are we still good?" Blaine said through the radio. "Keo?"

Keo didn't answer right away. Then, "Nothing's changed. Just more targets."

"Maybe we should come up with another plan," Bonnie said.

"I'm listening…"

"I didn't say I had any ideas. I just think we should go back to the island and talk it over with Lara. Or wait for Will and Danny to come back tomorrow."

"They're going to attack tonight," Keo said.

"How do you know that?" Blaine said.

"They brought night-vision goggles."

"Oh, shit."

"Yeah," Keo said.

He put the MP5SD away and reached for the M16. Besides the extra two pounds, he also disliked the length of the rifle, but the M203 grenade launcher more than made up for that. Keo opened the ammo pouch along his right hip and took out a 40mm grenade round—the size of a deodorant dispenser, except cylindrical and with a bulbous head—and fed it into the tube under the barrel.

The M203 had an effective range of 400 meters, which was more than enough to take out the house and maybe a few of the trucks. They were still moving supplies back and forth, so if he could knock out the vehicles and what they were carrying, all the better. Maybe they had ammo in there, or if he was really lucky, things that went *boom*. Some secondary fireworks might even result in collateral damage.

The house, though, was the main objective. Besides being the biggest and easiest target, he counted at least a dozen soldiers inside (and the one on top of it). If he could take it out, that would probably cut the invasion force in half, or close enough. Hell, if he was really lucky, he'd take out their command and control, too. That would really cripple them. Even weekend warriors needed someone to give the orders.

It wasn't a bad plan. Best of all, it was a *safe* plan, with minimal risk to his scalp. He felt even a little bit like a coward shooting from a distance hidden behind the gutted house, but what the hell, these soldiers were about to invade an island full of women and children. Keo had done a lot of bad things in his life, but he wasn't going to sit by and let that happen.

I'm an asshole, but I'm not a fucking *asshole.*

The M16 came with a second sight for the grenade launcher toward the front of the barrel, and Keo flicked it into position now. He remained crouched but scooted a bit further out from behind the building, then moved left toward the road until he could see (and shoot) around the wall. He spent a few seconds adjusting for wind and elevation.

It was going to be a hell of a shot, but firing a grenade launcher wasn't quite the same as shooting a rifle. It was mostly about angles and adjustments and letting the round do all the work. Unlike shooting a rifle from long-distance, an explosion was easier to "miss" with and still be effective. He was also comforted by the fact that he had extra ammo in his pouch if the first shot went astray.

See, adjust, and fire again. So simple even a baby could do it.

Of course, he would have loved to get closer. Maybe another fifty meters. Oh, who was he kidding. A nice, round hundred meters would have been ideal.

He aimed for the roof, hoping to land a round somewhere in that vicinity so the resulting impact would take out the second floor and collapse it down onto the first. If not, a second shot into one of the walls would just about do it. The one thing Keo knew for sure was that if one grenade didn't accomplish its goal, two—or hell, three—usually got the job done. Usually—

Clink!

The sharp sound of metal grinding against metal made Keo

stand up and spin around, his finger sliding away from the grenade launcher to the main trigger. He was prepared to fire, to spray and pray (Thank God he had kept the fire selector on three-round burst), but instead Keo lost a second processing what he was seeing.

It was a kid.

A goddamn kid.

He was sitting on a shiny new bicycle in the middle of the road, wearing one of those plastic shell helmets that was supposed to protect him from cracking his head if he fell. He had on wrist and knee pads and brand new Nike sneakers. The kid couldn't have been older than ten, sporting a white T-shirt that was stained in equal measure with sweat and what looked like chocolate.

He stared at Keo, as if he couldn't believe what he was seeing.

Join the party, pal.

Then the brat reached down and unclipped a rectangle black object housed inside a holder along the bike's down tube, where a water bottle was supposed to go. The kid pulled out a walkie talkie, and Keo remembered what Carrie had told him after the marina shootout back at Lake Dulcet. It was how the soldiers knew there was a boat at the marina in the first place.

"They're spies. Lookouts. Their job is to go around the city looking for survivors. The guys in uniform come later. That's how they found us. One of those stupid kids spotted us and the trucks swooped in."

"No," Keo said, taking his finger off the M16's trigger, hoping that would have some kind of effect. "Don't do that, kid. You don't want to do that."

The little bastard didn't hear a word he said. Or if he did, it never registered, because he lifted the walkie talkie to his lips, pressed the transmit lever, and shouted into it, "There's someone here! There's someone down the road! And he's got a machine gun!"

Aw, hell.

Keo turned back around and saw the two soldiers in the road looking in his direction. Because he was standing now, they saw him immediately and started pointing.

When Keo glanced back at the kid, the little tyke was bicycling away at full speed, the *clink-clink-clink* of his chains against heavy metal frame.

"Yeah, you better run, you little bastard!" Keo shouted after him, but he hadn't gotten "bastard" completely out when gunfire split the air and bullets *buzzed* past his head.

He ducked instinctively and moved back behind the wall, which started coming apart piece by piece in front of his face. He slipped down to one knee and tried to wait out the *pop-pop-pop* of a carbine shooting, which meant the guy with the M249 hadn't opened up yet. Of course, it was only a matter of time. Chances were the guy was waiting to get closer. Either that, or he wasn't comfortable firing that heavy weapon standing up—

The wall behind him disintegrated before he could finish the thought, ripped apart by a barrage of *brap-brap-brap* gunfire that seemed to go on and on and on.

The M249 light machine gun had just joined the party.

"Keo!" Blaine shouted through the radio. "What's going on? Keo!"

Keo could barely hear Blaine's voice over the roar of the machine gun fire. He didn't know how far the two soldiers were at the moment, but he guessed they would keep together, which meant slowly moving up the road toward him. At the moment, staying down and keeping his head from being detached from his shoulders by one of the SAW's 5.56mm rounds seemed the more prudent move.

He swapped the M16 for the MP5SD then glanced to his left, wondering if there were more pieces of the house still standing back there when the machine gun suddenly stopped firing.

Keo sucked in a breath, thought, *The hell with it, you only live once,* and stood up behind what was left of the wall. There wasn't much remaining, just about four feet of brick and mortar reaching up from the ground.

The two soldiers were still on the road. One of them was slightly crouched over and moving cautiously forward, but he was a good fifty meters away still. His partner was farther back and struggling to feed the ammo belt into the M249. That was the problem with belt-fed weapons. You never know when the next round was going to jam and ruin your day.

The one with the M4 saw Keo stand up and snapped off a shot. Too quick and the round missed by a wide margin, not even hitting what was left of the house wall. Of course, in the guy's defense, there really wasn't *much* left to hit.

As the man adjusted his aim, Keo returned fire. The man staggered down to one knee, so Keo guessed he had hit something. He kept pulling the trigger because fifty meters was a hell of a distance for the MP5SD, and Keo wasn't taking any chances. He only stopped shooting when the soldier collapsed to the road on his stomach and didn't move.

The one with the light machine gun saw his partner go down in front of him and tossed his jammed weapon and took off running back down the road. Keo was taking aim at his fleeing form when he saw something else—two of the trucks parked in front of the red house had fired their engines and were starting to move, their tires peeling and tossing dirt into the air around them.

"Keo!" Blaine was still shouting through the radio. "What's going on? Are you alive?"

He didn't waste time responding. Instead, he slung the MP5SD and brought out the M16 again, then calmly stepped out from behind what was left of the house wall and carefully took aim with the rifle.

One hundred meters for a grenade launcher designed to blow the crap out of something from four times that distance was almost child's play. It was such an easy shot even a baby could have pulled it off. And he was definitely more skilled than a baby.

Nice, you almost believed it that time!

The trucks were burning rubber up the road, men in uniforms hanging on for dear life in the back, swarms of dust scattering in their wake. The soldier who had ditched the SAW had to dive out of the path of the oncoming vehicles when they were almost on top of him. He rolled comically sideways and landed somewhere in the ditch.

"Keo!" Blaine shouted through the radio. "Answer me, dammit!"

Blaine might have said something else, but his words were lost against the sound of the grenade launcher belching out a dull but incredibly satisfying *ploompt!*

The 40mm round landed near the closest truck as it was halfway to him. The driver, predictably, reacted badly to the sight of an explosion ripping a hole in the road directly in front of him and showering his windshield with chunks of asphalt. The man jerked on the wheel and the truck looked as if it had hit an invisible wall, turning sharply to the left and then rolling over onto its side before spinning forward once, twice, three times. It finally settled back down on its roof, sending showers of glass everywhere.

The second truck, seeing the first one spinning out of control in front of it—peppering the road with metal and plastic and aluminum, along with the two sad bastards who were in the back—came to a screeching stop, the smell of burning rubber filling the air.

Keo pulled back his right hand and found the main trigger on the M16 and fired, stitching the second vehicle's front windshield with a series of three-round bursts. They were close enough now— less than fifty meters, he guessed—that it wasn't too hard of a target. Of course, he was firing again and again just to be sure. God knew he had realized his shortcomings with long-range shooting recently.

Two men inside the front cab ducked as their windshield caved in on them. Men in the back dropped out of sight and one jumped down from the truck, lost his footing, and started crawling toward the back bumper for cover.

Keo backpedaled as he fired again and again, glimpsing more figures racing up the road behind the vehicles, weapons swinging wildly in front of them. There were simply too many of them. Way too many. So what else was new?

His eyes darted briefly to the two-story red house in the background. He thought about sending a 40mm grenade toward it, but that choice went out the window when he saw sunlight flashing off additional trucks blasting up the road.

Then he heard something—coming *from behind him.*

He glanced back, wondering how the hell they had outflanked him, and was shocked to see the Dodge Ram coming up on him fast. Blaine was behind the wheel, Bonnie in the front passenger's seat holding onto the dashboard for dear life.

I guess they're more useful than I thought.

Keo grinned at them—saw their terrified faces staring back— before he turned around and looked up the road. He grabbed a second 40mm grenade out of his pouch and reloaded the launcher. He did his best to ignore the sound of the Ram's brakes squealing behind him as it came to a stop inches away. He was guessing it was inches away, because he actually felt the wind pushing against the back of his neck as Blaine nearly ran him over with the Dodge.

See, adjust, and fire again. So simple even a baby could do it.

The men from the house were about to reach the first two dead-in-the-road trucks while the driver and his passenger took the opportunity as Keo reloaded to scramble outside and run for cover behind the back bumper.

Wrong hiding spot, Keo thought, and fired and listened to the equally satisfying second *ploompt!* as the second round sailed.

This time the grenade hit its intended target, vanishing through the windshield of the second truck. The resulting explosion ripped across the vehicle and shredded the two men hiding behind it and tossed two more into the road, their clothes and hair and skin on fire. They might have been screaming, but it was hard to hear over the roar of flames and tires.

"Keo!" Bonnie, shouting behind him. "Come on!"

He tossed the M16 onto the ground and turned and nearly ran into the scorching hot hood of the truck. It was *inches* behind him. Jesus Christ. Blaine really did almost run him over seconds ago. He stared across the hood at Blaine, who stared back at him wide-eyed.

"Keo!" Bonnie shouted again.

Keo snapped out of it and ran around the Ram.

Bonnie saw him coming and threw the passenger side door open and he jumped inside, landing in her lap. She grabbed him with one hand, her other arm reaching across him and slamming the door shut, shouting, "Go, Blaine, go!"

Blaine didn't need any encouragement. He shoved his foot down on the gas pedal and the Ram began reversing up the road, the big man's hands gripping the steering wheel with such intensity Keo wondered what it would take to pry them loose if he needed to.

Bonnie struggled out from under him and scooted over to the middle of the front seats. "Jesus, we thought you were dead."

He was about to answer when bullets punched through the front windshield and *zipped* past his head and tore into the truck upholstery around them.

"Christ!" Blaine shouted.

The big man spun the steering wheel even as rounds slammed into the vehicle's side and front hood, the constant ring of *ping! ping! ping!* filling the air. Then a second later they were facing the right direction—back down the road—and the truck was picking up speed again with every breath Keo took.

Bonnie screamed when the back windshield exploded under a hail of bullets and they were showered with glass. She threw her hands over her head and kept it down, unwilling to come up even after the last piece of glass fell away.

"We're good, we're good," Keo said, looking back up. Then to Blaine, "Nice driving."

"Thanks," Blaine said, though he hadn't looked away from the road or even relinquished an ounce of pressure on the steering wheel.

Keo glanced out the blown back window. He didn't see any pursuing vehicles, just the two wasted ones blocking the road. The first was still resting on its roof, while the second one was engulfed in flames. Two trucks were trying to get around them, but one had run into a ditch and men were trying to push it out to no avail. The fourth truck didn't even make the attempt.

"Are they following us?" Bonnie asked.

"No," Keo said. He glanced at his watch. "Get to the island by six, right?"

"Yeah," Blaine said, almost breathless.

Keo reached into the back and pulled his pack over. He unzipped it and took out a bottle of water. It was freezing cold a few hours ago and was just cold enough now. Hell, that was more than he'd had in almost a year.

He sat back in his seat and took a sip, flicking broken glass off his clothes and picking them from his hair. He hoped he hadn't been cut by flying shards. God knew he already looked like a mess with the scar and a broken nose that hadn't entirely healed properly yet. The last thing he needed was a piece of glass sticking out of the other cheek.

After a while, he realized Bonnie was staring at him. "What?" he said.

"Did that go as you planned it?" She wasn't being sarcastic, either; he could see it in her eyes. She was hoping he would say yes, because that would mean it was mission accomplished. Or close enough.

"The idea was to stall them until the Army Rangers get back and you can put up a proper defense for the island, right?"

"Yes…"

He looked at the truck's side mirror, back at the flaming wreckage behind them. "Then maybe. I guess we'll find out tonight one way or another…"

CHAPTER 27

WILL

TWO DOWN, TWO to go.

So where were the other two blue-eyed ghouls?

The question nagged at him from the time they climbed into the Bronco to when they were halfway up Route 13, with I-10 still hidden somewhere in the distance.

According to the map, thirty minutes would take them to the interstate, and from there another hour on the highway before hopping off for the small roads at the town of Salvani. Song Island lay further south. Another hour, give or take, thanks to the nonexistent traffic. If they could locate Gaby somewhere along the way, there was no reason why they couldn't be home by nightfall. He was looking forward to that. More than anything, he wanted to see Lara again. Imagining her in his mind's eye had become harder with each passing day.

And yet...

Two down, two to go.

Where did the other two go? Why weren't they in Dunbar last night? The only explanation he could think of was that they had split up. Which had benefited Danny and him. He wasn't sure he could have fended off four at once, even knowing a bullet to the head *(Silver bullets? Or would any ol' bullet do?)* could finish them off, whereas they simply shrugged off everything else.

That was good and bad news. The good news was that you could kill them with a bullet to the head. The bad news was that you had to shoot them *in the head* and destroy the brain. The average human melon had a circumference of fifty-six centimeters (give or take), with the brain residing in the top portion. So take fifty percent away from the initial size, leaving the shooter with, at best, a target circumference of twenty-eight centimeters.

Not a difficult shot in and of itself, but when the target was moving—and there was no way in hell those blue-eyed bastards were going to stand still and let him zero in on them—it was another matter entirely. He had gotten lucky with the two from last night. The first one by way of the cross-knife when it was standing still, gloating over its victory, and he had caught the second one at almost point-blank range with the creature coming right at him. Even an amateur could have made that shot.

Shoot them in the head. Right. Easy peasy.

"At the risk of sounding like Carly," Danny said, "what are you thinking?"

"Where did the other two blue-eyed ghouls go?"

"And you definitely saw four in that, uh, walkabout of yours."

"Definitely. I mastered counting in elementary school."

"I wouldn't know. I was too busy making out with Suzy by the jungle gym."

Danny had both hands on the steering wheel. His broken nose and bruised face looked even more noticeable against the burning sun and dry wind blowing through the open windows. Both of their clothes, weighed down by the gear they were carrying, were damp against their seats. Will would have preferred to drive with the air conditioner blasting, but knowing Gaby was out there somewhere made that impossible. They were also driving much slower than before—barely forty miles per hour now—just so they wouldn't miss seeing or hearing anything that could point them to Gaby's whereabouts. The idea of driving past her now, after all but giving her up for dead thirty minutes ago, was an unsettling thought.

"Given their whole hive mind thing," Danny said, "it doesn't make sense they didn't launch a second attack after you took out the first two."

"That's what concerns me."

"So maybe they weren't in Dunbar. Maybe they were out here in Nowheresville doing…something else."

"Or tracking someone else."

"Gaby?"

"Best-case scenario."

Danny chuckled. "Our best scenario is that two blue-eyed ghouls are hot on Gaby's trail. Didn't think I'd be saying that anytime soon."

"Desperate times call for desperate best-case scenarios."

"So we know she left L15 with two locals, then left Dunbar with three. Where do you think she picked up the third stray?"

"In Dunbar, maybe. Or—" Will stopped when he saw the smoke rising in the distance. "Slow down, Danny. Two o'clock."

Danny eased the Bronco down to thirty-five, then twenty, miles per hour. They leaned forward at the sight of smoke hovering over the remains of a house. Recently, from the looks of it.

"Someone must have left the oven on," Danny said.

"I see a road," Will said, pointing.

Danny pulled the truck off the highway and onto a manmade dirt road, past an open gate, and drove them toward a farm. The remnants of the house were flanked by a red barn to one side and what looked like an unattached garage or possibly a supply shack on the other. There were a couple of vehicles parked in the wide, expansive yard.

Will picked up his M4A1 from the floor and scanned the property. Like most of the land they had passed since leaving Dunbar behind, the ground was flat and baked brown. There were no animals grazing, no signs of horses or cows, or whatever it was the owners had been raising before The Purge. Then again, he hadn't seen a large land animal running free for almost a year now, so the complete lack of livestock didn't add to the potential (if any) threat around the area.

The road was rough, but the Bronco's tires traversed it without trouble. They reached a front yard covered in dead grass, and Danny parked behind a white pickup that was so old Will couldn't place its make or model. A black minivan that looked out of place sat on the other side of the property. It had Mississippi license plates.

"Someone's far from home," Danny said. "Hell of a time to take a vacation."

"It might be worse where they're from."

"I somehow doubt that, Kemosabe."

"Yeah, you're probably right."

They climbed out of the Bronco, weapons at the ready, and spent another few minutes giving the property a cautious look-over. There was a slight breeze, but not enough to chase away the sweltering heat or keep the ruins of the house from smoldering in the aftermath of what looked like a ravaging fire. There were no bodies that he could see or signs of a battle.

So what started the fire?

"No Silverado," Will said.

Darren, the twenty-something soldier who Gaby had shot in the ankle earlier in the day, told them Gaby had continued up Route 13 in his and his dead partner's Chevy Silverado truck. They were hoping to run across it sooner or later.

"Fire must have been raging something purty when she came through here earlier," Danny said. "You think she kept going?"

Will thought about it. "She's a smart girl. And taking into account she's dragging along three people..." He nodded certainly. "I don't think she'd stop. We taught her better than that."

"We would totally rock as parents. Separately, I mean. With, you know, girls. Not that there's anything wrong with the other thing."

"How about we make sure no one's in the minivan first before we start making marital plans, Mrs. Doubtfire."

"Certainly," Danny said, mimicking a high-pitched female voice.

They approached the van from separate angles. Will peered into the open front passenger window while Danny did the same on the driver's side. A pink watermelon-flavored Little Tree Air Freshener, long past its smell-by date, hung from the rearview mirror. Will used that same mirror to look into the back of the van before opening the side hatch to make sure it was really empty.

Old soda cans and water bottles littered the floor. A pair of men's shirts, shorts, and sandals. He picked up old footsteps in the ground from the side hatch outward, but they were barely noticeable.

"It's been a while since they used the van," Will said. "It would make sense if they came all the way from Mississippi. Maybe they exited the interstate to see what was out here, found the house, and decided it was as good a place as any to settle down."

"Here?" Danny said. "There's nothing here, buddy."

"Maybe that's the point. This far from civilization, if they hunkered down, they could go unnoticed for a while."

Danny circled the van. "Dunbar's nearby."

"They might not know that."

"So where are they now?"

Will looked back at what was left of the house. The charred frames that were still standing told him it used to be a two-story building. They moved toward it, trying to glimpse anything that might give an impression of who had been in there or what had caused the fire. The flames had mostly burned themselves out, leaving behind embers to give off more than enough heat to make getting too close uncomfortable. They stopped about ten meters away from what used to be a front wooden deck. There wasn't much left except for the concrete steps that led up to the front door.

"Guess no one's home," Danny said.

"But something—or someone—had to have started the fire."

"Spontaneous combustion?"

"That's one theory."

"What's another one?"

"No idea."

"Hunh. So what now?"

Will glanced back toward the road. "Come on, we're burning daylight. Gaby was smart not to stop, and we should have done the same thing."

"Too late for that."

"Just don't tell her when we finally catch up."

"Mum's the word."

They started walking back to the Bronco when a flicker of movement—*from the barn*—caught the corner of Will's eye and he stopped on a dime and spun. Danny did the same, and they stared across forty meters at the large twin doors that had swung open.

"I guess someone's home after all," Will said.

"Awesome," Danny said. "Let's go see if we can borrow some milk and sugar."

They changed direction and moved toward the barn, approaching it from two different angles the way they had the minivan earlier. Will kept his eyes on the open alley doors in front and the closed loft door directly above those. If there was a sniper inside, he would use the higher perch to shoot from, but Will couldn't make out any holes or makeshift gun ports.

The barn doors remained open, but no one had shown themselves yet.

They took the first twenty meters without fanfare, taking their time but moving steadily forward. Will scooted slightly right to eyeball the bottom of and along the slanted roof. Danny did the same on his side.

"Anything?" Will asked.

"Squadoosh," Danny said. "Unless they have an invisible sniper. If they do, that would really suck."

Finally, one of the barn doors opened even wider and a pair of tanned arms appeared in the sunlight. "Don't shoot!" someone shouted. Young and male. "We're not armed!"

"Step outside!" Will shouted back.

The owner of the outstretched hands stepped out of the barn. Tall, jeans and a white T-shirt stained with something red. *Blood.* The man squinted in the sunlight and his hair was a mess. Will couldn't see a gun belt or a weapon, but that didn't mean there wasn't something behind his waist.

The man had moved a foot outside the building when Will said, "Stop."

He did.

"Turn around," Will said.

The guy gave him a confused look.

"Like Cinderella," Danny said.

Another confused look.

"Just to make sure you're not armed," Will said.

He understood that and turned around a full 360 before facing Will again. He had wisely not lowered his arms the entire time.

"You said 'we,'" Will said. "Who else is inside?"

"My girlfriend," the man said.

"Her name wouldn't happen to be Gaby, would it?" Danny asked.

The guy shook his head. "Um, no. It's Annie."

"Oh well, worth a shot," Danny said.

———

LANCE AND ANNIE hadn't arrived from Mississippi by themselves. There had been six of them four months ago. That number was trimmed to two after last night.

"They had blue eyes," Lance said, trembling noticeably as he talked. "They played with them. I mean, they *played* with them. I'd never seen anything like it."

"There were two," Annie said.

Will and Danny exchanged a knowing look.

They stood around the Bronco with the weary couple. Both Lance and Annie still looked shell-shocked from last night's harrowing encounter with the ghouls.

"What do you mean by 'they played with them'?" Will asked.

"They let Toby out of the house," Lance said. "Then they made him run into the fields. At first I thought the black-eyed ones would be all over him, but they weren't. They just stood around and watched. Then the new ones—the ones with blue eyes—ran after him. Then...there was a lot of screaming. Toby. I would know his voice anywhere."

"They gave him a head start?" Danny said.

"Yeah," Lance said, as if he could barely believe his own story. "Those things... they didn't act like the others. I think they were controlling them. I know that sounds crazy...right?"

"It's not that crazy," Danny said.

"You've seen them too, haven't you?" Annie said, staring at them.

"Yeah," Will nodded. "What happened to the rest of your people?"

"They killed them," Lance said. "One after another. They started with Toby, then Danielle, then Sally..."

"...then Howard," Annie finished.

"We hid in a room under the floorboards inside the main bedroom when they first attacked the house. I guess the homeowners were using it to store valuables. We saw bundles of money in there."

"There was jewelry, too."

"We stumbled across it by accident when we first moved in. We didn't really have any uses for it until last night when they came. Usually they don't bother with the house. We make sure the place is completely dark at night and we seal ourselves into the rooms. We had barricaded the windows and doors, too."

"Every night?" Will said.

Lance nodded. "It's a lot of work, but it's worth it. Until last night."

"What happened last night?"

"Usually the black-eyed ones might sniff around. Sometimes they'll even bang on the doors or windows. But then they always leave when we don't show ourselves. But last night, they didn't stop. They just kept at it. I don't know how, but they managed to break down one of the windows."

It's the blue-eyed ghouls. The others become unpredictable when they're around...

"We barely got into the hidden room in time," Annie said. "Then the screaming started..."

"They played games with them," Lance said, and his eyes drifted over into the fields that surrounded the property. "It's so quiet at night, you can hear a long way even through walls."

Annie reached over and squeezed Lance's hand.

"What about the house?" Will asked. "What happened to it?"

"We burned it down," Lance said. "After last night, there wasn't any point in staying. And they were in there..."

"They?"

"The creatures. They were hiding in the basement. When we came out of the secret room, we could hear them moving around under the house."

"Lance thought we might be able to kill a few of them," Annie said. She was staring back at the house now. The smoke had all but vanished, leaving behind just a twisted, blackened carcass. "I don't know if it worked, or if the basement is still down there under all that. Should we...find out?"

Will exchanged another look with Danny.

"There could be a couple of Mister Blue Eyes down there," Danny said. "Might be worth it to find out."

"Through that?" Will said. "It'd take the whole day to sift through the wreckage. We don't have that kind of time with Gaby still out there."

"You mentioned her before," Lance said. "Who's Gaby?"

"A friend of ours. We've been looking for her since Dunbar."

"We saw a lot of vehicles coming from Dunbar all morning."

"Was one of them a Silverado truck?" Danny asked.

"I don't know, I didn't see one. Annie?"

She shook her head. "I don't know what a Silverado looks like. And I only got glimpses of them from the barn."

"But there was something else," Lance said. "We heard shooting from farther up the road."

"How long ago?" Danny asked.

"I don't know, I think thirty or forty minutes?"

"The timing's about right," Will said. He looked back at Lance and Annie. "You guys can come—"

"Yes," Annie said before Will could even finish.

Lance grinned sheepishly. "What she said."

THE CHEVY SILVERADO was inside a ditch, resting on its back bumper with the front grill facing the cloudless sky. Harsh sun beat down on its chrome and hood, streams of sunlight piercing bullet holes that stitched the front windshield. There was a dead man outside the driver side door with two bullet holes in his chest. All the car windows were broken, with glass sprinkled liberally over the seats and spread out among the splashes of blood.

Will climbed up the ditch and back onto the highway, where the Bronco idled in the road. Lance and Annie were standing outside in the sun glancing around.

"Bad news?" Lance said, looking over.

"Not good news," Will said.

He blinked up the road at Danny, walking back from a lone red pickup parked across one of the two-lane roads. He was dropping spent bullet casings from one hand.

"Anything?" Will called.

"There was a second car," Danny shouted back. "Some kind of half-assed roadside ambush."

"To stop the Silverado."

"Looks like it. And these," he said, flicking one of the bullet casings in Will's direction.

Will crouched and picked up a 5.56x45mm brass casing. Assault rifles. Probably M4 or AR-15. God knew there were plenty of those just lying around these days.

God bless the Second Amendment.

"There's a dead body up there," Danny said. "Poor bastard decided to go up against the Silverado and—surprise—lost. Any signs of Gaby?"

"No, and that's a good thing."

"Pray tell."

"No body means she's still alive."

Danny peered up the road. "They must have taken off in the third car. That thing's leaking motor oil. I get the feeling they intended to dump it, grab the first vehicle that came across their little slapdash barricade, but—" he looked over at the undercarriage of the Silverado "—I'm thinking that didn't quite work out as planned. That car can't be moving very fast at all. If we haul ass…"

"So let's get to hauling," Will said.

DANNY WAS ABLE to track the motor oil stain on the highway from the Bronco's driver seat. This way, they would know if the vehicle unexpectedly left the road. It hadn't so far. Will just hoped they could catch up to it before it reached the interstate up ahead. It was going to be difficult, leaking motor oil or not, after that.

He hung out the window listening for sounds that didn't belong and scanned the horizon just in case the trail they were following proved deceptive. Lance and Annie pitched in, the couple leaning out their windows while armed with Will's and Danny's binoculars.

They were ten minutes into the pursuit when Will said, "How's it looking?"

"It's looking," Danny said. "Whatever they're driving, it's leaking good. No wonder they were so hot to switch vehicles. I'm guessing the red pickup must have been in worse condition or else they would have taken it instead."

"We're pushing up on time here, Danny. If we don't find her and hit the interstate soon, we're not reaching Song Island by tonight."

"I know, I know."

They drove on for another few minutes, the only sound coming from the wind rushing through the vehicle and the engine churning under them.

Behind them, Lance asked, "Anything?"

"Nothing," Annie said. "Just a lot of empty land. God, there is so much emptiness out here. We were so lucky to find the house."

"Yeah, lucky."

"I mean before last night," Annie said softly.

"I know what you meant, babe. I didn't mean anything by it."

Will imagined them smiling at each other back there, trying to comfort one another as best they could. The same way he would do with Lara…

"Aw, shit," Danny said beside him.

Will looked out the windshield and saw it.

A lump in the road: *a body.*

Danny slowed down as Will picked up his M4A1 and looked into the back at Lance and Annie. "Stay inside."

They nodded silently back.

Danny stopped the Bronco, and Will opened the car door and hopped out. He heard Danny's door opening behind him, but he was already moving quickly toward the body, scanning the ditch to his right and the landmass beyond. He didn't bother with his left side because he didn't have to—Danny was covering it. Traces of leaked motor oil zig-zagged in front of him, already drying in the heat.

The body was thirty meters away and Will reached it first. He felt a tightness in his gut at the sight of blonde hair blowing against a slight wind. The lump lay on its stomach, arms awkwardly folded under it, as if the woman had attempted to stop her fall as she fell.

She was wearing shorts, a long-sleeve shirt, and sneakers. Blood gathered under her, glimmering against the harsh sun. He crouched next to the body and slowly, almost hesitantly, turned the woman over onto her back.

A girl. Young. Maybe seventeen.

But not Gaby.

"Is it her?" Danny said behind him.

"It's not her," Will said.

The girl's face was partially covered in blood, and there were deep cuts along her cheeks and temple, likely from glass. From far away, she might have been mistaken for Gaby, but Will knew Gaby's face well enough to see through the scars and blood.

"They dumped her," Will said. "She was probably still alive at the time."

"One of the girls with Gaby?"

"Maybe."

Will thought about searching the girl for clues but quickly dismissed it. She looked at peace, and considering what she had gone through, she didn't need him digging around her pockets.

"What's the word?" Danny said.

"Let's go." He got up and they jogged back to the Bronco. Will could feel the urgency in every one of his bones. "She's still fresh. Five minutes. Maybe less. We're catching up to them."

"Shitty car," Danny said. "They're probably moving slow, too. Good for us and good for Gaby. We get her and head home. No muss, no fuss."

"Yeah," Will said, glancing down at his watch.

12:40 P.M.

Too close. We're cutting it too close...

CHAPTER 28

GABY

SHE WAS STILL dazed from the pain, trying desperately to make sense of what was happening to them, when Harrison stopped the car and threw Donna's body outside. Then he climbed back in and drove off, leaving Claire's sister to die in the middle of the highway. She was vaguely aware of Milly sniffling next to her, just barely able to stop herself from outright bawling, while Claire pressed the rag down against Gaby's mouth, trying to stop the bleeding from her broken nose.

Gaby's entire body was on fire, and the scorching sun that turned the backseat of the old Dodge Neon into an oven didn't help. She couldn't tell how Claire was handling the situation because she could barely make out the girl's face through the haze that blanketed her vision. Claire wasn't crying—she could tell that much because the girl was so close to her—but Milly was doing enough of that for both of them.

Harrison had taken their weapons and tossed them into the trunk before putting all three of them into the vehicle. The handcuffs dug into Gaby's wrists, but she found herself grateful for them because the biting metal sensation took away some of the pain coursing endlessly through the rest of her body. Every inch of her face hurt, and her nose was clearly broken. If only her high school friends could see her now, they might not even recognize her.

She struggled to sit up and was only able to do so with Claire's help. The thirteen-year-old took the blood-soaked rag away because she wasn't bleeding anymore. She couldn't tell if the sun was overly bright this afternoon or if something was wrong with her eyes. Maybe a loosened socket or two. She wouldn't be surprised if she was bleeding internally, too. It felt like it.

"Donna…" she said.

Claire, sitting to Gaby's left, shook her head silently. The girl looked resolute in her determination not to let any emotion show on her face, though when she glanced forward at Harrison, sitting directly in front of her, the hate shone through. Milly had turned herself into a ball to Gaby's right, arms folded across bent legs and her head placed between her knees, like a tortoise hoping to escape from all this.

Harrison drove in silence. What was that he had said when he pulled her out of the Silverado?

"Everything was going fine until you showed up. Everything that's happened, it's all your fault."

Screw you, Harrison.

There were a lot of things wrong with that statement, but she was sure Harrison wasn't in the mood to debate them. Not that she was, either, as her eyes drifted from his face, reflected in the rearview mirror, to the Remington shotgun lying across the front passenger seat, the stock facing him. As luck would have it, she had sat up in the middle of the backseat and there was nothing at all between her and the weapon. All she had to do was lean forward and reach for it—

Harrison's eyes shifted, picking her up in the rearview mirror. "You're up."

Sonofabitch.

"What happened to Donna?" she asked.

"The same thing that'll happen to you and the kids if you make trouble."

"Donna wasn't making trouble."

"She was going to die anyway." He shrugged. "I saved us both the hassle. You should thank me."

I'll kill you instead.

Claire tensed up next to her. It never occurred to Gaby just how small Claire really was until now. The driver's seat completely covered her up, which meant Harrison couldn't see her.

As the fog began to clear from her head, Gaby's mind went to work. She turned over everything that had happened, that was happening, and that would likely happen if they were still here, in this car with Harrison, when night fell.

Options. What were her options?

She couldn't think of one at the moment. The shotgun was her best bet, but with Harrison already alerted to her conscious presence, her chances of reaching it before he struck was, at best, fifty-fifty. At worse, he was baiting her so he could hurt her some more. She wouldn't put it past him to play games. He seemed sadistic enough to get his jollies out of something like that. And there were the handcuffs. Grabbing the shotgun and using it was going to be problematic with her limited mobility.

Her other option involved Claire. The girl was able and willing to act, but how? Maybe, if Claire could distract Harrison long enough for her to reach the shotgun...

"Where are we going?" she asked.

Harrison didn't answer right away. Maybe he didn't know. She guessed that Interstate 10 was somewhere in front of them, at the end of Route 13. At the moment, the road looked never ending, just another mile of flat highway and sunburned farmland to the sides. There were so few houses and nonexistent businesses that they might as well be traveling across another planet. Mars, maybe. Was Mars this hot?

"The kids said you were taking them to an island," Harrison said. "The radio broadcast. You believe it. About the bloodsuckers not being able to cross bodies of water."

"Yes," she said.

Stall for time. That's what Will would do. He would stall for time while he came up with other options. Because there are always options.

I just have to see it...

"It's true," Gaby continued. "Silver bullets. Bodies of water. They're all true."

"And ultraviolet?"

"I don't know about that one."

She couldn't tell if he believed her. His face, in the rearview mirror, was placid. But then it always looked that way. Even back in the VFW basement when he admitted to beating Peter to within an inch of his life because he *"had to be sure"* Peter was telling the truth. There was a casualness about Harrison that bothered her. That, and a clear mean streak, a desire to inflict pain because he could. It was as simple as that. Some people, she had come to learn, were just born mean.

I'm going to kill you, Harrison. It's just a matter of time.

She must have been staring at him without realizing it, because Harrison looked up at the rearview mirror and snickered at her reflection. "You want the shotgun? Go for it. It's right there. All you have to do is grab it. What are you waiting for?"

She didn't move. She didn't reply and didn't grab for the weapon.

What are my other options?

She was watching Harrison's face when she picked up something in the distance. A slab of gray concrete rising out of the ground like some mirage. At first she wasn't sure if it was her imagination, but the longer she stared, the more certain she was that it was the real thing.

Interstate 10! Finally!

Harrison saw it too, and he eased the Dodge down to a slower rate of speed. It wasn't just the interstate in front of them that got his attention, but also the outlines of businesses on both sides of the road. Gas stations, maybe even strip malls. They were still too far away—a mile? two?—to really make out any details, but after so much nothingness, the sudden appearance (silhouettes?) of civilization was unmistakable.

Then Harrison stopped the car completely and leaned forward against the steering wheel, peering out the dirty windshield. It took her a few seconds to see what he was looking at: men on horseback, loitering on the road near the buildings, still so far away that they looked more like slivers of shadows than actual figures.

The posse. L15...

She knew immediately who they were and wondered if Harrison did, too. By the way he was staring—part confused, part intrigued— she wasn't so sure.

"They're soldiers," she said.

He didn't respond. Had he even heard her?

"They'll kill you," Gaby said, thinking, *And us, too. Or worse, they'll take us back to the towns. Back to Josh. Back to the blood farms. Back to breeding for future generations of ghouls to feed on.*

Harrison leaned back against his seat, his eyes still focused on the figures dancing across the highway toward them now. She could practically see through the back of his head to his mind as the gears turned, as he tried to come up with a new plan of action. The only path for him at the moment was to go backward. He couldn't go around the soldiers, even if he could survive the ditches and attempt to go around them by using the open land. The Silverado hadn't managed that feat, and it was a hell of a lot more powerful and sturdier than the car they were riding in at the moment.

Gaby looked over at Claire, saw the girl staring back at her. Waiting *(begging?)* for her to do something.

Options. What are my options?

The idea of staying another day with Harrison was too much. What would he do to her? To the girls? She couldn't even understand why he kept her alive. Did he plan on using her for other purposes? She shivered at the thought.

The hell with that.

Gaby caught Claire's eyes again and nodded her head slightly forward.

Claire gave her a questioning look: *"What?"*

She rocked forward slightly—*just enough*—to let Claire know what she wanted her to do. The girl stared back for a moment, then a light went off behind her eyes. She nodded back and grinned.

That's my girl.

Gaby steeled herself, turning forward again. Harrison was still concentrating out the windshield, both hands on the steering wheel, a foot no doubt poised over the gas pedal just in case. He hadn't put the car in neutral, which was smart of him. But he hadn't put it in reverse yet, either.

She took a big breath and snapped a quick glance at the shotgun resting on the front passenger seat. She looked just with her eyes while keeping her head facing forward.

How far? About four feet of space between her and the weapon.

Just four feet.

She could do it.

It was just four feet...

"Now!" Gaby shouted.

Claire rammed her entire body (all eighty or so pounds of it) into the front seat. She was so small and slight that she didn't get nearly as much force into it as Gaby would have liked, but it was enough to rock Harrison forward, knocking him momentarily off-balance. He must have also stepped on the accelerator involuntarily, because the Neon lurched forward a good three feet before he was able to jam down on the brake again.

Gaby threw herself between the two front seats. She reached forward with both handcuffed hands, lunging for the shotgun. When Harrison stepped on the gas pedal, the weapon actually swiveled toward her, decreasing the distance between her and it. But as soon as her fingers brushed against the stock, Harrison stepped on the brake and the shotgun *slid forward* and off the seat and onto the floor!

With no choice and her body already stuck between the two front seats, Gaby changed course and swung left at Harrison. She balled her handcuffed hands into fists a split-second before she slammed them into the side of his face. She wasn't sure if that little stunt hurt him or her more, because both her arms and entire body were vibrating from the impact.

Keep moving! Keep moving, or you're going to die!

Gaby shoved the rest of her body through the front seats, and with her knees braced against the armrest—one knee actually dipped inside a cup holder—she rained blows down on Harrison, summoning as much force as she could muster with each strike. Her entire body screamed and her broken nose felt as if it would break free from the rest of her face at any second.

Harrison was caught off-guard and seemed to be struggling with keeping the car from going forward and warding off her attack at the same time. If her blows were having any impact, he didn't show it, especially when he swung his right *(sharp)* elbow and caught her in the chest. Stabbing pain flooded her, as if she had been impaled by a sword.

Well, at least he didn't go for my nose again, she thought even as she fought through the bursting sensations and continued hitting him with her balled fists over and over again. Except now Gaby had begun using the steel handcuffs, angling the metal just right, in order to cut into Harrison's temple and face with every successful contact.

Blood sprayed the air between them.

She must have done a hell of a better job than she thought, because Harrison took his foot of the brake and somehow stepped on the gas and the Dodge started moving forward again. His face was bloody, his eyes lolling in their sockets, and his body went slack against the seat.

Gaby stopped hitting him long enough to lean over his body, grab the door lever, and jerk on it. The door swung open and she leaned back, put both feet against Harrison's shoulder, and pushed with everything she had. He didn't fight her—he didn't look as if he were capable of fighting her. Thank God he wasn't wearing his seat belt, because his body toppled toward the open door and disappeared into the air, landing with a solid *thump!* against the highway moments later.

"Gaby!" Claire shouted behind her.

Gaby looked back at the girl, saw her pointing, and turned toward the front windshield.

The horsemen were coming right at them at a fast gallop. There had to be at least a half dozen of them, and there was no confusing the camo uniform they were wearing.

Josh's soldiers. I hate it when I'm right.

She climbed into the driver's seat, jammed a foot down on the brake, and pulled the gear into reverse. She grabbed the steering wheel and switched her foot over to the gas pedal, pushing down as far as it would go until she felt it touch the floor.

"Hold on!" she shouted.

Here we go again, she thought as the Dodge began to reverse up the highway.

She struggled to keep it straight, using both the rearview and side mirrors, jerking the steering wheel left and right the entire time, trying to compensate for the drift. It was amazingly harder to drive backward than she had expected, but then, she knew that all too well. The last time she had tried this, she ended up in one of the ditches…

And the horsemen were coming. She had no idea horses could move that quickly.

She kept backing up, praying she was going straight enough. The last thing she needed was to go into the ditch *again.*

"Left, left!" Claire shouted behind her.

Gaby jerked the steering wheel left, knowing full well she was overcompensating but unable to relay that information to her hands.

"No, no, your right, your right!" Claire shouted.

Gaby righted the steering wheel and saw the ditch flashing by in her rearview mirror.

"Straight, straight!" Claire shouted.

Gaby grinned. Her own personal highway traffic controller. Now if only she could find Claire a pair of bright orange sticks—

Pek-pek-pek!

The front windshield cracked and Gaby heard a *whistling* sound as a bullet sliced past her right ear—an inch from taking it off completely? Two?—and tore off a piece of her seat's upholstery. More rounds slammed into the hood, the *ping-ping!* of metallic ricochets echoing in the air.

"Get down, get down!" Gaby shouted.

She didn't look back to make sure both Claire and Milly had obeyed orders because Gaby was too busy looking forward at the horsemen galloping up on them. Jesus, were horses supposed to be able to move that fast?

They were close enough now that she could make out six of them, like camo-wearing cowboys, a couple sporting baseball caps to keep out the sun. The country sky was thick with gunfire, bullets screaming around the car, digging chunks out of the road outside her window. The only reason she was still alive, she imagined, was because the soldiers were riding and shooting at the same time. It looked easier in the movies, but was apparently not so in real life.

But they weren't completely terrible shots, either. Enough bullets were hitting the Dodge that smoke began venting out of the hood, and Gaby kept hearing glass breaking. The headlights, the windshield... Where else did the car have glass? And how long before every single one of them was shattered?

We're going to die. We're going to die on this miserable piece of sun-drenched highway. I'll never get to drink ice cold water or sleep in my own bed again, or take a hot shower. I should have never gotten on that damn helicopter...

Then she heard an explosion and braced herself for the car to be engulfed in flames. But that didn't happen. The hood was still in one piece and though smoke continued to rush out from underneath it, the sound hadn't come from in front of her. It had come from under the car, which meant—

The Neon began fighting her and she knew one of front tires had been punctured. Oh great. She had barely managed to get this far on four good tires, now she was swerving dangerously left, then right, then left again on just three.

What else can go wrong?

"Gaby!" Claire shouted.

"I know, I know!" Gaby shouted back.

She struggled with the steering wheel and searched out the shotgun and found it on the floor of the front passenger seat. There was no choice now. If she kept backing up, she would end up in the ditch again and that would be it. If the Silverado hadn't been able to survive that kind of drop, there was no way the sedan, in its current sad state, would even come close.

"Stay down!" Gaby shouted just before she slammed down on the brake.

The car swerved, coming to a stop with the front bumper pointing at the left side shoulder and the front passenger side facing up the highway. Gaby put the car in park and lunged for the shotgun. In order to reach the weapon, she had to lay across both front seats, and when she scrambled up on her knees, the first thing she saw was one of the horsemen *right outside the window*.

Gaby pulled the trigger, prayed that Harrison had a shell already racked, and was rewarded with a loud blast that, in the closed confines of the car, was ear-splitting. The buckshot tore off pieces of the open window, but enough of them made it through and hit their intended target. Red splotches spread across the rider's shirt as he fell out of the saddle.

The other soldiers, seeing one of their own go down, reined up twenty, maybe thirty yards away. Gaby threw herself back down to the seats as gunfire filled the air once again.

The *ping-ping-ping!* of bullets punching through the Dodge's side, the warbling shrill of Milly screaming at the top of her lungs and her own labored breathing filling her ears all in one loud rush. Then there was another *boom!* as one more tire exploded and the car dipped slightly behind her.

Gaby gripped the shotgun and kept her head down. Glass pelted her from every direction, the noise of bullets *whistling* above her head like missiles. It was impossible to rack the shotgun and load a new shell while still handcuffed, so she had to grab the forend with both hands and pulled it back before returning her finger to the trigger.

She bided her time, keeping her eyes on the open front passenger door window above her, waiting for a head to appear on the other side like last time. But they had apparently learned their lesson and no one came close enough for her to shoot. They didn't have to, either, because they could destroy the car from a distance just fine, which seemed to be what they were trying to do. The seats around her were perforated, the dashboard to her left literally coming apart by the second, and glass continued to rain down on her, cutting her arms. She might have been bleeding from her face *(again)*, but she couldn't be sure.

She didn't know how long she lay there across the two front seats holding the shotgun, small and large shards of glass falling off her body with every slight movement she made or breath she took. It could have been a minute. Or a few seconds. Hell, it could have been an hour for all she knew.

We're going to die. We're all going to die.

There was a silver lining, though. If she died out here, she wouldn't have to face Josh again. So there was that—

Silence.

She looked up, shocked by what she was hearing—or *not* hearing.

The shooting had stopped.

A trick? Were they moving toward her now? Maybe they wanted her alive after all. Or maybe they thought she was already dead. All she had to do was look around her at what was left of the Dodge's interior and realize it was a miracle she wasn't already bleeding to death from a dozen bullet holes—

Pop-pop-pop as a new round of gunfire erupted, but this time the walls of the car were unaffected. They were shooting *over* her.

What the hell?

She was still trying to figure out what was happening when another volley joined in, except these new ones were coming *from behind her.*

At first she thought some of the horsemen had somehow managed to outflank her. Those horses could probably maneuver over the deep ditches better than a car, but if that was the case, why didn't they just run up and shoot her through the driver side window?

She was about to flip over onto her back and face her attacker when she felt a rush of wind and the door creaked open first. Gaby had no choice and scrambled up to her knees, turning the shotgun around.

A familiar voice said, "Whoa there, G.I. Jane."

A hand grabbed her by the shirt collar and jerked her off the seats and through the open door like she weighed less than Milly.

She was unceremoniously deposited onto the hot asphalt road, where she gasped for breath and looked up, then grinned at the figure crouched next to her, firing with an M4A1 rifle across the Neon's hood.

"You're a sight for sore eyes," she said.

Danny didn't take his eyes off his scope as he continued shooting, calmly pulling the trigger again and again. "We'll talk about your terrible choice of fighting positions later, missy. Right now, grab the kids and head back to Big Willie."

She looked over at Will, positioned behind the open door of a parked truck behind them, also firing calmly over her and at the horsemen farther up the highway.

Gaby scrambled up and opened the Dodge's back door. Claire, her small body practically merged with the floor, looked up at her with wide eyes. "Come on," Gaby said, and held out her hand. Claire took it and Gaby pulled her out. "Run to the truck!"

Claire glanced past her at Will.

"They're my friends," Gaby smiled.

Claire nodded and ran off, smartly keeping herself as low as possible.

Gaby looked back into the car and found Milly on the floor behind the front passenger seat. "Milly, come on."

The girl hesitantly held out her hand and Gaby took it, pulling her toward the door. Milly leaped into her arms and Gaby, holding her tight, began backpedaling.

"Danny," Gaby said.

"Right behind you," Danny said. He fired two more shots before ejecting his magazine, making sure to catch it and put it away before slamming in a fresh one. "Go go go."

Gaby turned around and ran, Milly clutching her so tightly she could barely breathe. She kept as low as possible while still running, which was amazingly hard with Milly's weight pulling her down to the road.

Will said, "Hey, kid," as she ran past him.

"Hey, Will," Gaby said. "You look like shit."

"Don't tell Lara."

"I won't if you don't tell her about my face."

"Deal." Will switched his rifle to full-auto, said, "Danny," before firing off a single, continuous burst.

Danny ran toward them, using Will's fire as cover. When Danny was back at the truck with her, Will switched back to semi-auto and continued firing off one round at a time again.

Gaby put Milly down behind the back bumper of the truck next to Claire. She took a moment to compose herself, her chest pounding so loudly she had difficulty hearing Milly's sniffling. Gaby had to put one hand against the truck to steady herself before leaning back out to look up the highway.

There were four riderless horses out there now, two moving along the right side shoulder while the other two had escaped into the ditches and were grazing on sunburned grass. Their riders lay still on the road. The remaining two soldiers were fleeing up Route 13 at a fast gallop as Will fired casually after them, but by now they were already too far away to be picked off.

"What happened to your face?" Danny said to her.

"What happened to yours?" she said.

"Touché."

Will fired a final shot, then walked back to them, reloading his rifle as he did so. "Anyone missing an arm or a leg or have holes where there shouldn't be extra holes?"

Gaby shook her head and wiped at trickles of blood along her arms where falling glass had cut her. None of them were too deep, thankfully. "Just a couple of scratches. I'm good."

"Yeah?" Will said, watching her carefully.

She gave him her best smile. "Good enough for now. Thanks for the rescue."

"It's a good thing we didn't stop at that sushi place down the road," Danny said. "You know how much I love roadside sushi."

She looked at Will, then at Danny, this time more closely. They were still the same guys she knew, but in the week or so since she had last seen them, they looked beaten up, bruised, and battered. Danny, in particular, had a broken nose and cuts along his face, as far removed from the California blond surfer she was so used to. Will still looked like Will, which was to say, tired and weary, but somehow still moving around. But then, Will always did hide his wounds well.

"Man, you guys look like total crap," she said.

"You should see the other guy," Danny said.

"Bad?"

"Worse."

"What could be worse than the sight of you two?"

"Dead."

"Yeah, that's definitely worse."

Will had turned back up the highway. She walked over and stood next to him and looked over the roof of the Dodge. She hadn't realized just what bad shape the vehicle was in until she got enough distance from it. All four tires were punctured and every window was broken. There had to be dozens of holes across the length of the car that she could see and probably more that she couldn't on the other side.

My God. How did we survive that?

Will fished out a pair of binoculars from his pack and peered through them.

"The interstate," Gaby said. "They're guarding it, aren't they?"

"Looks like it."

"How many are up there?"

"A dozen," Will said, lowering the binoculars. "Horses aren't the only thing they're riding around on. Looks like they have technicals, too."

"Technicals?"

"Improvised fighting vehicles," Danny said, walking over. "Basically, they put a machine gun on top of a truck."

"Oh."

"How many?" Danny asked.

"Two that I can see," Will said.

She saw a vehicle—maybe a truck—moving up the road toward them. She could just barely register the silhouette of a man standing in the back. Then a second truck appeared and joined the first, the two of them riding side by side.

"Here they come," Gaby said.

"Come on," Will said. "We're not going to survive a stand-up firefight against those."

Danny circled the vehicle over to the driver side while Will slipped into the front passenger seat. Gaby opened the back door and was surprised to find two people already inside. A man and a woman, both in their twenties.

"Oh yeah," Danny said. "It's a little crowded back there. But that's what laps are for, right?"

Gaby held open the door for Milly and Claire as they squeezed into the back. "Milly, sit on my lap."

The girl nodded. She had stopped crying and her cheeks were covered in dried tears, but she looked ready to start all over again at a moment's notice.

Gaby closed the door as Danny started up the truck and reversed. Then he somehow swung the vehicle around until he had it turned a full 180 degrees. He stepped on the gas and they were flying down the highway, away from Josh's approaching soldiers.

It was a tight fit in the back. Even though the other two people were doing their best to make themselves small, they had to fight for space with weapons and boxes of supplies piled on the floor. Claire ended up sitting on one of the boxes while Gaby had to place her legs over another one, with the edge of crates poking into her ribcage.

Danny looked up at them in the rearview mirror. "Just think of it as a studio apartment and ignore the smell. Annie and Lance, that's Gaby. I have no idea who those kids are, so don't ask."

"We're sorry about your friend," the woman, Annie, said.

"Friend"? Gaby thought, then, *Oh, she's talking about Donna.*

"Thanks," Gaby said, and wondered if Claire had deduced the same thing.

Gaby looked over her shoulder and out the back window.

Two trucks—the "technicals"—were coming up the road after them, but they weren't going to catch Danny anytime soon. At least, she hoped not. After surviving Harrison and reuniting with Will and Danny, the idea of having all of that ripped away now was too difficult to stomach.

Will looked into the backseat and observed her for a moment.

"What?" she said.

"How's the face?" he asked.

"It hurts. What do you think?"

He smiled, then took something out of one of his cargo pants pocket and tossed it to her. "Something for the pain."

She caught the bottle. It didn't have any labels, and there were only a few pills left when she opened it. She didn't ask him what the pills were because she trusted Will. Gaby swallowed two of them.

"Where are we going?" she asked.

"There has to be a back road, another way to the interstate and around what's waiting up there."

"And if there isn't?"

"Then we'll do what we always do," Will said. "Hope for the best and prepare for the worst."

CHAPTER 29

LARA

"EVERYONE'S IN ONE piece," Bonnie said through the radio. "I don't know how, to be honest with you. I think one of them had a machine gun. We could hear it shooting from miles away."

A machine gun. Jesus.

"Where are you now?" Lara asked.

"Almost home. Thank God. I can see the sun starting to set, or maybe that's just my imagination."

"I'll see you when you get back."

"Okay. Over."

Lara put down the radio. "They're on their way back."

Carly moved over to the north window and peered out with her binoculars. "I see them coming down the road now. Sarah will be relieved to have them back."

"Blaine?"

"No, Lara, she's been nervous about Bonnie. Of course Blaine."

Lara smiled. "I wasn't sure."

"Everyone's getting some nookie these days except us."

"Danny will be back soon and you can make up for lost time."

"Done, and done," Carly said. "Has Will radioed in yet?"

"Not yet."

She looked down at her watch: 5:29 P.M. It would be dark in less than an hour, and Will hadn't called yet. If he was on his way, he would have told her so. But he hadn't, which meant he was nowhere close to home and was busy doing something else *(like surviving)*. For some reason, she wasn't surprised by that. She just hoped he had spent all that time out there looking for Gaby.

No one gets left behind, Will. Find Gaby. Find her and come home to me.

"Looks like all that time you put into convincing Keo paid off," Carly said. "How did you know he'd go for it? Or come through with flying colors?"

"I didn't. Hope for the best, prepare for the worst, remember?"

"Well, you did good, kid."

"Only if they don't attack us tonight."

"You think they might anyway? Even after what Keo did with that grenade launcher?"

Lara shook her head. "I don't know. That's the problem. I don't know anything for sure." She picked up the radio again. "Roy, come in."

"What's up?" Roy answered.

"Blaine and the others are headed back now. I need you to get one of the fast boats ready just in case they need a hand. Grab a battery out of the supply building and get Maddie to help you gas it up."

"Will do."

"I heard some Russians on the radio today," Carly said behind her.

"Russians?" Lara said.

"Yeah. They were talking to some Italians."

"What were they saying?"

"I have no idea. The Russians were talking in Russian to the Italians, who were talking Italian back at them. It was, uh, kind of confusing for everyone, not to mention super surreal."

Lara smiled at the thought. She'd done that. Got people around the world communicating with one another. Even if they couldn't understand a single word the other was saying, her broadcast had connected them by letting them know there were other survivors out there. That, she found, was what they needed to hear most—that they weren't alone.

We started something. Now all we have to do is survive it.

Yeah, no pressure.

BLAINE AND THE others didn't shove off from shore on their way back to the island until five minutes after six. They were cutting it close, and Lara only allowed herself to breathe easier when they were halfway home and she could see their boat in the distance, with the sight of the sun dipping in the horizon behind them. She still didn't feel comfortable sending people out there, and she didn't think she ever would be.

It was beginning to darken, and still no word from Will. That meant there was no chance he was coming back today. A part of her always knew they'd have to survive another day without him. Maybe that was why she took such a big gamble with Keo.

"How many?" she asked Keo later while he was eating in the dining room.

Keo tore apart a white bass and gobbled up the meat. "Over twenty, easy. They were definitely preparing for an assault."

"One hundred percent sure?"

He nodded. "They were loading supplies onto boats when I showed up. And they had night-vision gear."

"Even after you killed some of them, they were still coming…"

"Like I said: they really have a bug up their ass for you people."

Will was right. Kate's coming, and nothing's going to stop her.

Keo grabbed a glass of water and gulped it down and didn't stop until he had drained the entire thing. Even Blaine and Bonnie, eating across the table from him, looked impressed. Lara exchanged a brief grin with them.

"Ice cold water," Keo said, putting the glass down. "Worth its weight in gold these days, especially in the summer."

Lara had already eaten with the others two hours ago, so she was the only one at the table not pulling apart fish at the moment. Blaine and Bonnie still looked a bit shell-shocked by their experience, and to hear them tell it, they hadn't really done much except dropped Keo off, then picked him back up when the shooting started. Keo, who had been in the middle of the firefight, didn't look the least bit fazed. At first she thought it was an act, a tough guy façade. She only had to watch him eating for a few minutes to realize that wasn't the case.

"What happened exactly?" Lara asked Keo. "It sounded like you had to improvise."

"There was a kid," Keo said. "He ruined the plan."

"We didn't see him," Bonnie said. "But then we had to stop the truck pretty far away so they couldn't hear us coming."

"Carrie told me about them," Keo said. "The soldiers are using them as lookouts. They send the brats across the cities to look for survivors, then radio in if they find any." Keo wiped fish oil from his lips. "I should have shot the little bastard."

Lara and Bonnie stared at him.

"I said *should* have," Keo said. "I didn't, for the record."

"So, in your expert opinion," Lara said, "do you think you stopped them?"

"Stopped them? Not even close." He shook an ice cube out of his glass and popped it into his mouth, crunching it loudly. "Delayed them, maybe."

"Maybe?"

He shrugged. "I don't know these ghouls as well as you do, so I can't predict what they're going to do next. I would have liked to take out more. That house, for instance. But situations being what they were…"

"The kid," Lara said.

"Yeah. The kid."

"They're using children," Bonnie said, shaking her head. "It's hard to believe they'll stoop that low."

"It's actually pretty smart," Lara said. "Kids are impressionable. Adaptable, too." She thought about Elise and Vera and how the two young girls had carried on despite everything they had been through. "You give them a job and they'll glom to it. Especially if you make them think it's the most important thing in the world. And by extension, they're important for doing it."

"Yeah, well," Keo said, "I still think I should have at least stolen the little tyke's bicycle. That was a pretty sweet-looking ride."

***

"THERE ARE PLENTY of rooms left to choose from if you don't like the one I picked out for you," Lara said when she was walking with Keo up Hallway A after dinner. "This is assuming you're at least staying the night."

"It's a little too dark out there to be sailing, don't you think?"

Keo said.

"I didn't want to presume. You've already done more than enough to earn everything I promised you. We're grateful. I'm grateful."

"Are you propositioning me?"

"What?"

He laughed. "I'm just messing with you, Lara."

"Oh." Then, because she thought she had been blushing just a bit, "You're anxious to get going."

"I made a promise, and I'm way overdue."

"She doesn't know you're trying to make your way over?"

"No. We didn't exactly plan to separate. It just came up at the last minute, so we didn't put any kind of communications system into place, the way you have with your boyfriend. You guys are a lot smarter than us."

"We have our moments."

"But it's not going to last, you know."

"What do you mean?"

"Regardless of how many times you push them back, delay them, or repel a full-on frontal assault. You can't do it forever. Sooner or later, if they want this island bad enough, they'll get it. And when that happens, a lot of people will die."

She didn't answer him because she knew he was right. She had spent countless days and hours thinking about it, trying to find a way out, a way that would keep them all alive. And each time she failed to see the answer. Always.

They walked in silence for a moment, the only sounds coming from their footsteps against the hallway and the slight hum of the lightbulbs.

"What would you do if you were in my position?" she finally asked.

"The odds are against you," he said with that matter-of-fact tone that annoyed her, but at the same time she found herself grateful for because it was the *truth*—or at least, as he saw it. "Even with the Army Rangers, you won't be able to keep the island indefinitely. I understand why you don't want to leave. The hotel, the power supply, the beach… Hell, I'd risk it just to have ice water every day, but that's me. I've survived past my sell-by date even before the world went kaput. Bottom line? There's no reason why you and the others can't start again someplace else."

"Where would we go?"

"I can't tell you that." He paused, then added, almost reluctantly, "This island is a paradise, Lara, but it's not worth dying for. What's that old saying? 'Home is where the heart is'? These days, it might be enough just to have a home that isn't constantly under attack."

⬤

IT WAS ALMOST dark outside when she stepped out onto the hotel patio with Keo's words echoing inside her head.

"The odds are against you... This island is a paradise, Lara, but it's not worth dying for."

Wasn't it, though? If Song Island wasn't worth spilling blood for (and God knew, they already had, too much), then what was these days?

She just wished Will were here with her. Right now, she would be satisfied with just hearing his voice.

She looked toward the Tower, where Carly was still posted with Jo, Bonnie's little sister. The two of them were moving from window to window with night-vision binoculars. Lara had doubled up on the watch to improve their chances of catching an attack if Kate decided to send her collaborators anyway. It was dead quiet out there, so if they were coming by boat (which they would be—was there any other way?), even using those trolling motors, they would give away their approach.

"This island is a paradise, Lara, but it's not worth dying for."

Maybe. Maybe not.

Lara unclipped her radio and said into it, "Everyone in position?"

"Lake looks quiet from up here," Carly said. "Jo and I are good to go."

"Keo's coming up to relieve you later tonight, Carly."

"He's staying?" she asked, sounding surprised.

"For tonight." Then, "Roy?"

"Beach is clear," Roy said.

"Piers, too," Blaine said.

Blaine and Roy had the beach tonight, with Bonnie scheduled to relieve Roy in an hour, and Gwen for Blaine an hour after that. Not that she expected two people on the beach to repel a full-scale attack. But if they could see an assault coming, it would give them time to set up the real defense at the hotel and, if necessary, start putting Will's Plan Z into motion.

God, that's such an awful name for a plan that's supposed to save our lives, Will. We need to come up with a better, more optimistic-sounding one.

"Benny?" Lara said.

"Looks good from up here," Benny said.

Lara glanced up at the roof of the hotel behind her but couldn't see Benny up there. He wasn't alone; Stan the electrician and Kendra's son Dwayne were also up there somewhere. Lara had been hesitant to make use of twelve-year-old Dwayne until she saw him shoot with his bolt-action rifle. Even Benny and Blaine were impressed. The kid was, easily, the best shot on the island. She hadn't asked the boy if he had ever shot anyone before, because she didn't really want to know.

She listened to the others calling out through the radio. Gwen and the fourteen-year-old Derek were with Sarah, along with Carrie and Lorelei, in the hotel lobby. They had looked nervous when she walked through the room a few minutes ago. She didn't blame them and she wondered if they were thinking the same thing:

"We're prepared…but are we really?"

She didn't know the answer to that, and she wouldn't know until the real thing. Lara prayed none of them had to find out tonight.

One more day. Until Will and Danny come back.

And then what? We do it all over again, because Kate isn't going to stop. She's going to keep coming, and coming, because what's one or a dozen more human sellouts to her?

"This island is a paradise, Lara, but it's not worth dying for," Keo had said.

Maybe he was right. Maybe…

Her radio squawked and Carly's excited voice came through. "Lara. It's your boyfriend on the radio. Should I tell him you're busy?"

Lara smiled and ran down the patio, then across the grounds toward the Tower. She felt ten years old again and didn't care.

If she was going to die tonight, at least she'd get to hear Will's voice first…

CHAPTER 30

WILL

ONCE THEY REALIZED they weren't going to catch up to the Bronco, the technicals slowed down, then stopped completely. An hour after that, they resumed traveling cautiously up Route 13, showing surprising patience. Then again, he guessed they could afford to take it slow and easy—the night was their ally.

Will checked his watch for the third time in the last hour: 3:16 P.M.

Three and a half hours before nightfall, give or take.

Josh's soldiers were a kilometer out before he could actually see their vehicles as more than just flickering mirages under the sun. One was a bright cherry red mid-size Toyota Tacoma. The other was a gray full-size Nissan Titan. Both trucks moved on large tires and each had a soldier in the back positioned over an M240 machine gun *(Where the hell did they find those, and where can I get one, too?)* mounted on the roof by bipods. There was a driver and a passenger in each vehicle, making the total number six, unless there was additional personnel in the truck beds that he couldn't see from his position. That was unlikely. It was way too hot to be lying down back there.

Not that he could see everything from the side of the ditch where he had been positioned for the last hour, bathing in his own sweat. Wearing the assault vest didn't help, but Will was used to discomfort, especially with the smell of upcoming combat lingering over the horizon.

He lowered the binoculars and keyed his radio. "They're on approach. One klick."

Danny's voice came through Will's right ear. "Two little piggies went to market, while the other little piggies stayed home. Two little piggies in trucks, with more little piggies in the back with machine guns. Two little piggies are about to get shot, and they'll be crying *wee wee wee* all the way home."

Will opened one of his pouches, pulled out a granola bar, and took a bite.

"What are the chances we're making it to the island today?" Gaby asked through his earbud.

"Not while they're out here," Will said.

The problem was the flat terrain around them. It didn't matter where they drove, on or off the highway, because the soldiers would be able to spot them from a safe distance. That would lead to a car chase and a running gunfight. The Bronco was a decent vehicle, but it wasn't going to stand up against two trucks with mounted machine guns. And those were just the bad guys they could see. There were probably *(likely)* more waiting closer to the interstate. A radio call later and they could easily run into an ambush without realizing it.

No, they weren't going to avoid this. That much was clear now. The soldiers knew exactly where the Bronco had turned off the road, and it was there they were moving toward at the moment. Hopefully, they hadn't also seen him and Danny making their way back up Route 13 on foot using the ditches as cover.

Hopefully.

"Better to shoot our way through, anyway," Danny was saying. "Funner."

"'Funner' isn't a word," Gaby said.

"You're wrong and I'm righter," Danny said.

Will imagined Gaby rolling her eyes back at their temporary base, where she was staying at the moment with the girls and Lance and Annie. The farmhouse was the best they could do in a pinch, since retreating all the way back to Dunbar was a non-starter. Gaby had mentioned a cemetery, but that was too far back, though he was impressed when she told him she had stayed in a crypt the previous night.

The enemy trucks were close enough now that Will could hear the sounds of their engines, even at their current slow, almost painfully deliberate pace. He swallowed the last piece of nearly stale granola down.

He didn't have to use the binoculars to see them this time, with the Tacoma in one lane and the Titan in the other. The men in the back were swiveling the mounted LMGs around, looking for targets. They were scanning the ditches, fully expecting some kind of an ambush. The bipods holding up the weapons looked firmly attached to the roof.

He slipped the binoculars into his pack and scooted backward until the curved angle of the ditch allowed him to slide all the way down to the floor. He unslung the M4A1 and leaned back against the cool earth wall and waited.

"They'll be on top of you in five," Danny said in his right ear. "Try not to screw this up like you always do."

"I'll do my best."

"That reminds me of a joke…"

"Of course it does."

"Two high school best friends are sick and tired of being virgins, so one day they cook up a scheme to both get laid at the same time. One of the boys comes up with the perfect girl to seduce. So they go on the Internet and watch hundreds of videos about what girls like. When they're finally ready, they plot their move. One day, as their target is walking home from school, our virgins jump out of a bush and both shout at the same time, 'Hey, you wanna have hot sex? We guarantee we'll please you!' The girl squeals, 'Ew, gross!' Then she points at virgin number one and says, 'I'm going to tell mom, Rob!' And runs off. Virgin number two is understandably confused. He turns to his buddy and says, 'Dude, we are so screwed! Why didn't you tell me she was your sister?' To which virgin number one replies, 'Well, her room's right next to mine and she's always screwing guys every night, so I figured she'd be pretty easy!'"

"Gross, Danny," Gaby said.

"You gotta be there, I guess." Then, "Speaking of which, one minute until they're on top of you, Kemosabe."

"Roger that," Will said.

Not that he needed Danny to tell him. He could hear the tires crunching against the hard asphalt. He guessed they were moving ten, maybe fifteen, miles an hour. From this distance, the drivers could see the bright red barn and the two-story house where Gaby was currently watching from, along with the Bronco parked in the front yard.

"I counted six," Will whispered into his throat mic.

"Sounds about right," Danny said. "Four inside, two in the rear. Speaking of rears—"

"Be careful, guys," Gaby said, cutting him off. "I don't like the look of those machine guns."

"Neither do I," Danny said. "950 rounds per minute is not my idea of a fun prom date."

"What's the range on that thing?"

"Don't worry; they're not going to be shooting at the house until they're way closer."

"That doesn't make me feel better, Danny." She sighed, then, "Where did they get something like that, anyway?"

"Probably the same place they got the rifles and ammo, and army boots, and MREs…"

Will glanced up just as the first truck—the Tacoma—was directly on the road in front of him. There was a slight squeak as the gunner swiveled the machine gun around on its bipod. The M240 was a heavy weapon at just under twenty-eight pounds, which was why it was more effective when mounted instead of being carried by a single soldier. It utilized an ammo belt, which was the source of the *clink-clink* noise he was hearing now as the dangling bullets tapped against the metal of the car.

"You good?" Danny said in his right ear.

"Go for it," Will whispered back.

"I call shotgun," Danny said just before a loud *crack!* rang out.

Will was moving even before the shot had finished its echo. He stretched up to his full five-eleven height and his vision filled with the cab of the Tacoma that had stopped directly in front of him.

Danny fired again, then again, and again. Calmly, putting every bullet where he intended them.

The driver was fumbling with the gear, trying to reverse, when Will shot him in the left temple, shattering the closed window in the process. The man slumped forward, his head slamming into the horn and causing it to fill up the countryside with a headache-inducing blare.

Then the *brap-brap-brap-brap* of one of the M240s firing, overpowering even the loud car horn. Bullets weren't hitting the ditch around him, so Will assumed the man was trying to hit something else *(Danny)* down the road and still didn't know he existed.

Will couldn't see the Titan from his position, with the Tacoma in the way. He had to climb out of the ditch before he could see the rest of the road.

The Tacoma wasn't going anywhere. He had shot the driver and Danny had taken out the front passenger and the one manning the machine gun in the back. But while the Tacoma was down, the Titan was still alive and kicking, its machine gun firing at Danny's position, the *clink-clink-clink* of bullet casings pelting the bed of the truck like falling rain. A second soldier was adding his own fire, standing behind the open driver side door. Will couldn't tell if the passenger was still alive on the other side of the truck. Not that he wasted too much time thinking about it.

He shot the machine gunner in the back, then put a second bullet into the man's collarbone as he was falling down. The sudden silence of the M240 must have surprised the driver, because he stopped shooting up the highway and looked back, saw Will, and swiveled his rifle around just before a bullet chopped through the door's open window behind him. The soldier stumbled forward, looked surprised, then collapsed to the ground in a heap.

Will maneuvered around the Tacoma, sweeping it for signs of movement, before moving on to the Titan. There was no body outside the front passenger side door, and when Will got closer, he saw the third man slumped over the dashboard with a neat bullet hole drilled through the windshield in front of him.

"We good?" Danny said in his right ear, his voice barely audible over the blaring horn.

Will didn't answer until he had completed a full circle around the two vehicles. He reached into the driver side window of the Tacoma and pulled the dead man off the horn. Blessed silence.

"Right as rain," he said into his mic.

"Anyone hurt?" Gaby asked.

"My butt's a little sore from sitting down for the last hour and change," Danny said.

"So what? You want me to massage it for you or something?"

"Would you, please?" Danny said.

THEY DUMPED THE bodies on the highway and drove the trucks back to the farm where the others were holed up. They had been careful not to damage the vehicles during the firefight (bullet holes in windshields and broken car windows didn't count) and as Will expected, there were more 7.62x51mm ammo for the M240s and supplies in the backseats. The machine guns would come in handy, and Will had no intention of giving them up now. He was already thinking about ways to set them up along the island's perimeters in preparation for one of Kate's assaults…

Gaby and the others came out of the house while they were driving up the dirt road. The farm was surrounded by fields of dry grass, which made it like every other homestead they had passed since starting up Route 13 out of Dunbar. At one point he imagined that horses, cows, and other livestock grazed the vast acres and kept the family fed. They might have even raised enough to sell at the market.

The two-story house wasn't anything special, but it looked sturdy, with a front porch and peeling paint, along with evidence of rotting foundations if you looked closely enough. For their purposes, it would work just fine.

The thirteen-year-old girls, Claire and Milly, stayed close to Gaby the entire time. Milly looked just as shell-shocked now as when Will first saw her, but Claire seemed to be amazingly composed for someone who had just lost a loved one. According to Gaby, the girl he and Danny had found on the road earlier was Claire's sister, Donna. In so many ways, Claire looked like a younger version of Gaby—strong, determined, and way tougher than most people probably had given her credit for in her pre-Purge life.

"Nice rides," Gaby said.

"The machine guns will come in handy on the island," Will said.

"Pump out some silver rounds for those belts and we got ourselves a bona fide ass kicker or two," Danny said.

"We can't use our silver bullets for them now?" Gaby asked.

"Wrong caliber," Will said. "We'll fix that when we get back to the island—"

He was cut off by the distant sound of car engines.

"Or not," Danny said.

Will took out his binoculars and turned back to the highway. Men on horseback, maybe a half dozen, were galloping alongside a light green truck heading in their direction.

"How many?" Gaby asked behind him.

"At least six on horseback and a technical," Will said.

The caravan stopped about half a kilometer away, and men climbed out of the back of the trucks and began taking up positions, the vehicle moving to straddle the two lanes. The riders climbed off their horses and began spreading out, some sliding down the ditches along the shoulders. They were already passing around bottles of water.

"Are those little rascals doing what I think they're doing?" Danny said.

"Yeah," Will said. "Looks like they've come prepared to stay a while."

"Does that mean they're not attacking?" Lance asked. He sounded almost hopeful.

"Maybe their friends have the answer," Danny said.

He was looking down the other side of the highway as another technical appeared and parked across the lanes, while more men in uniforms climbed out of the back. There were no horsemen on this side, but Will counted seven men in all, including one perched behind another machine gun mounted on the roof of the vehicle.

"What are they doing?" Annie asked, sounding already panicked.

"They're boxing us in," Will said.

"Why?" Lance asked.

Will glanced at his watch. 3:59 P.M.

"Does this mean we're not going to the island?" Milly asked, her voice on the verge of cracking.

"I don't know," Gaby said. She walked up beside Will and exchanged a look with him. "What now?"

He glanced back at the house, the barn next to it, and a smaller building they had checked earlier that contained farming equipment. Then he looked at both sides of the highway one more time to make sure the soldiers still weren't moving. They weren't. His first instincts were correct: they were settling in.

Night is their ally. But it's not ours.

"Will?" Gaby said. "What now?"

"We get ready for nightfall," Will said.

◀━━▌ ▌━━▶

"HOW ARE YOU for silver bullets?" he asked Gaby as he handed her a box of ammo from one of the two technicals.

"I'm out," Gaby said. "I used everything up in Lafayette when me and Nate got caught in the pawnshop."

"I'm sorry about that."

Gaby nodded. "He was a nice guy."

"Yeah. He was a good soldier, too. We could have really used him at the island."

"I don't even know what happened to him, Will. Not really, anyway."

Gaby was looking at Claire, standing across the yard from them, watching the road. Will had given her the FNH shotgun and it hung across her back, its thirty-nine inches just a foot shorter than her entire frame. A large pouch bulged against her hip, stuffed with extra shotgun shells. She had learned surprisingly fast when he showed her how to load and fire the weapon less than thirty minutes ago. The girl was a natural, which again reminded him of Gaby.

"Are you sure about that?" Gaby asked.

"Not really," Will said. "Fact is, if we need her to start shooting, we're already in trouble."

"Just don't give Milly one of those, okay?"

"I don't think you have to worry about that."

Gaby followed Will back to the house. He glanced up at Danny, watching the roads from one of the open second-floor windows. He had chosen a spot that gave him a clear view of both sides of Route 13. Lance stood next to him with binoculars, peering left, then right, then back again every few seconds.

"We should have brought Tommy's rifle," Danny said down at them.

"Shoulda woulda coulda," Will said.

Danny made a gun with his fingers and said, "Pew, pew," up at the road.

"Who's Tommy?" Gaby asked.

"A kid we met in Dunbar," Will said. "He had a sniper rifle. He was pretty good with it, too."

"What happened to him?"

Will shook his head, recalling Tommy's decapitated body in the hallway outside the bathroom in the Dunbar Museum. The next morning, it was gone.

They take the dead. Why the hell do they take the dead?

They walked up the rickety steps to the front porch and stood underneath the awning. It was old and cracked and there were holes up and down its length, but it still provided a welcome respite from the heat. They stood in the shade and looked back out at the yard, Claire's tiny figure standing sentry, the sun-drenched road beyond.

"Everyone's dying around us, Will," Gaby said quietly.

"Not us."

"What makes us so special?"

She peered out at him through the broken nose and bruises around her face. Even with all of that—and all the cuts and scratches from the helicopter crash, if he looked closely enough—Gaby was still just the eighteen-year-old girl he and Danny had molded and trained to be a killer on the island. He guessed she would never outgrow that image in his head.

"We're not," Will said. "We're just well-prepared. And we have something to live for. Don't underestimate the importance of that."

"The island," Gaby said.

"No, not the island. The people on it…"

◄▬▬▮ ▮▬▬►

"YOU RADIOED SONG Island yet?" Danny asked.

"Not yet," Will said.

"What's keeping you?"

"I don't know what to say."

"Good news and bad news. Good news, we found Gaby. Bad news, reunion time won't start until tomorrow. Don't tell her we'll probably die tonight, though."

"Good advice, Danny."

"That's what I'm here for." Then, "Sunset at 6:30, give or take."

"Yup."

"They got us by the balls."

"Does it hurt?"

"Kinda, yeah. And itchy, too. Is it supposed to itch?"

"When was the last time you bathed?"

"You're asking me?" Danny sniffed him. "You smell like week-old cabbage. No, I take that back. That's giving week-old cabbage a bad name."

Will smiled. Pouring bottles of water over himself took away some of the stink, but it wasn't nearly enough. "I'll shower when I'm dead."

"So soon, then?"

Will smirked. "Captain fucking Optimism."

Danny chuckled. He was leaning on one side of the open window across from Will. The main bedroom on the second floor gave them a perfect view of Route 13 and the soldiers at both sides of the road. With only one vehicle parked across the lanes, it was less a barricade and more of an invitation. Will knew a fake opening when he saw one, and he was looking at two right now. Danny had come to the same conclusion.

"Maybe we should give it a shot anyway," Danny said, alternating between looking out the window and finishing a can of SPAM with a steel spork. "Give them what they want. You know me; I'm a people person."

"We'd never make it. Even with the M240s on each truck. A machine gunner out there is a sitting duck. We proved that."

"Maybe we can move it inside the cab."

"How?"

"I dunno. I'm just throwing out ideas. That's me. The idea man."

"We'd never make it," Will said again. "Not with the girls and the kids."

"When did you get to be such a Debbie Downer all of a sudden?"

"I'm just being practical. The ones along the ditches are the problem. They'll pick us off because we'll be sitting ducks in the middle of the road. Before we know it, the ones on the other side will flank us, cut off our retreat." He shook his head. "No, there's no way around that. And they know it."

"I hate sitting and waiting. Did I tell you that? They used to call me Action Danny back in college."

"So I hear." He glanced down at his watch again. 5:31 P.M. "It'll be dark soon, and they're still out there."

"'They'?" Danny said.

"Yeah. They."

"Oh. *They.*"

The other two blue-eyed ghouls. They're out there somewhere. Waiting for nightfall.

Always waiting…

"Maybe we got lucky and they're not around here anymore," Danny said. "Maybe they went home. They have homes, don't they? Maybe when you put down the other two, they got scared and ran off."

Will didn't say anything.

"Of course not," Danny said. "When has anything ever been easy with you around?"

"You blaming all of this on me?"

"I thought that was pretty obvious." He shoved another chunk of SPAM into his mouth. "We need a new plan."

"We already have a plan. Sit and wait and see what they do, and react accordingly."

"That's a sucky plan. Come up with a better one."

"You know what they say about plans."

"That yours suck?"

"No plan survives contact with the enemy."

As soon as he said the words, he thought about Kate. She had said the same thing back in Dunbar. In the dream. The nightmare. One of those.

He looked out the window and scanned the flat empty landscape around them.

Are you out there, Kate? Are you pulling the strings right now?

"That's what I'm afraid of," Danny said.

"What's that?"

"Contact with the enemy. The *real* enemy. The last time that happened—" he touched his broken nose "—I got just a little bit uglier. I mean, sure, I'm still male model material compared to you, but a guy can only take so much abuse before he starts losing gigs, ya know?"

◄▬▬▮ ▮▬▬►

GABY, LANCE, AND Annie were downstairs hammering the closet doors they had pulled off the rooms on the first and second floor over the windows as well as the front and back doors. They had found everything they needed from the shack on the property, including buckets of rusted nails. Lance, who didn't look as if he had ever picked up a tool in his life before The Purge, handled a hammer surprisingly well, while the girls, Milly and Claire, pitched in as best they could.

Will had no illusions that the barricades were going to hold, but putting them up gave everyone something to do and took their minds off what was about to happen in less than an hour. It was either this or watch them staring off into empty space, waiting for the inevitable darkness to fall.

Gaby glanced over when he came down the stairs. "We're almost done. What about the upstairs windows?"

"Three windows—main bedroom and two additional rooms in the back," Will said. "We'll save the rest of the doors for them."

"What if we run out?"

"We'll pull the floorboards. There's just dirt under them anyway."

The house was old and the stairs groaned. The wallpaper was peeling, and the floorboards were real wood that could be easily ripped free with the proper tools, like a hammer or a prying bar. Everything moved and creaked as they walked around.

Lance sat down on a couch and drank deeply from a warm bottle of water. His clothes were soaked, his was face flustered, and his tired, hollowed eyes sought out Will. "They're not going to hold. You know that, right? I told you we had them up at the other house, too. They broke in after a couple of hours."

Gaby and Annie didn't say anything. Even the two girls seemed to greet the matter-of-fact comment with subdued acceptance and were paying more attention to the heat. The temperature had been tolerable earlier, but now with the windows covered, it had become insufferable.

"We don't need them to hold," Will said. "They just need to keep them out for a while."

"And then what?" Lance said.

"Then we make our stand on the second floor."

"What about the basement?" Gaby asked. "Those have always worked for us in the past."

"Against the black-eyed ghouls, it's a no-brainer. But not with the blue-eyed ones around." Images of Dunbar and the basement under Ennis's flashed across his mind. "They're too smart. Even if they couldn't get through—and that's a big *if*—there are the soldiers to worry about. If we seal ourselves down there, we're trapped with only one way out."

"Like what we did to the other house," Annie said softly.

"What did you do?" Gaby asked.

"We burned it down because we thought there might be creatures—the things you call ghouls—in the basement."

"Did that kill them?"

"I don't know. We never checked."

"We'll make our stand on the second floor," Will repeated. He glanced at his watch again. "We need to finish up soon, so let's get it done."

Lance got up and held out his hand, and Annie took it and the two of them exchanged a private smile. Will thought they looked almost resigned to their fates as they walked past him and up the stairs. Claire and Milly followed, leaving him on the first floor with Gaby.

The nineteen-year-old stood next to him and looked after the others. "It's going to be close," she said, keeping her voice low enough that the others couldn't hear.

He nodded. "So what else is new?"

"These blue-eyed ghouls... They can be killed?"

"Yeah, but you have to shoot them in the head."

"Regular bullets or silver?"

"I don't know. We'll default to silver just in case. I stabbed one of them in the head with my knife and that seemed to work, too."

She glanced down at the cross-knife at his hip. "I really gotta get me one of those."

"I'll make you a copy when we get back to the island. Deal?"

"Deal."

They walked up the stairs together. Slowly, as if they had all the time in the world.

"So it's the brain," Gaby said. "Which would explain why you say they're smarter than the others. They actually still have brains."

"As good an explanation as any."

Gaby smiled at him through her scars, bruises, and broken nose. "I thought you were dead after we split up in Harvest."

He smiled back. "Someone once told me I'm too stubborn to die."

"They're probably right." Then, she surprised him by hugging him in the middle of the stairs. "I knew you'd find me. I always knew you would."

Will hugged her back and felt her body trembling in his arms. He decided she didn't need to know that he was prepared to leave her behind, thinking she was dead, until he found out differently just a few hours ago.

Instead, he said, "There's someone else who'll be glad to know you're still alive…"

"GABY," LARA SAID through the radio. She sounded breathless and happy. "It's good to hear your voice again."

"That's funny, because I've been hearing your voice a lot these days," Gaby said, smiling across the window at Will.

They were back in the main bedroom on the second floor of the house, with the portable ham radio sitting on the windowsill between them, its antenna sticking outside the open window.

"The broadcast," Lara said.

"How did you know?"

Lara told them about other survivors who had reached out to her through the radio because of the message she had sent out into the world. People from Russia, the United Kingdom, and even some kid living on an island in Japan.

"Wow," Gaby said. "That's amazing. I didn't know there were so many people still out there."

"Neither did they," Lara said. "I guess this is why Kate's so pissed off. We unwittingly brought everyone together. At least, over the airwaves. People are starting to coordinate as a result. Guys in New York are talking to guys in San Francisco. Will, there are two groups in East Texas that we didn't even know about until now."

Gaby passed the microphone to Will. "All of that's great, but I'm more worried about the island right now," Will said. He sneaked a look outside at the darkening skies. "Are there any signs of an attack yet?"

Lara didn't respond right away.

Will and Gaby exchanged a worried look.

"Lara," he said into the mic.

"Do you trust me, Will?" Lara said finally.

"You know I do. Implicitly."

She told him about some guy named Keo and the two women he had been traveling with. What they had seen back on shore, including more men in uniforms roaming Louisiana, and a staging area higher up Beaufont Lake. He listened and didn't interrupt, absorbing everything she said, especially what she had attempted—and succeeded—with this Keo guy.

"I think it might have worked," she said. "I guess we'll know for sure tonight."

"And everything's ready just in case it didn't?" Will asked.

"Plan Z…"

"Yes."

"Everyone knows their roles," Lara said. "I just hope we don't have to use it." She paused for a moment, then, "I knew you weren't going to make it back today, Will. That's why I made the choices I did."

"You did the right thing, Lara."

"Did I? Maybe I just made things worse."

"Things can't get any worse, babe. Besides, the island's still there, isn't it? You're still safe. And the others, too."

"Yes…"

"So you made the right choices."

"I wasn't sure…"

"Don't doubt yourself. You're smarter than me. Always have been."

"You're the one who kept us alive all these months."

"Not by myself."

"You and Danny…"

"Danny's just a dumbass with a gun."

"Hey," Danny said. He was sitting on the big mattress behind them, cleaning his rifle. "Leave me out of this."

Will ignored him and said into the mic, "We'll be back tomorrow. Gaby, Danny, and me. And some other people, too."

"You keep picking up strays," she said. "Looks like we have that in common."

He smiled. "I guess we just can't help ourselves."

He looked outside at the falling night again, at the soldiers milling about on both sides of the highway. The trucks had turned on their headlights. Waiting, just waiting, because they had all the time in the world.

They do, but we don't.

And it seems to get shorter every day…

Will turned back to the radio. "It's getting dark, and we both have a long night ahead of us."

"Be careful," Lara said. "You too, Gaby. I don't want to lose you guys again."

"What am I, chopped liver?" Danny said behind them.

Will held the mic toward Gaby, who said into it, "Get a glass of cold water ready for me, Lara. I also wouldn't mind if someone went into my room and made the bed. I might have left it a little messy."

Lara laughed. "Your highness's wishes are my command."

Gaby nodded at Will, then stood up and walked over to where Danny was, her way of giving Will some privacy with the radio.

"We'll be home tomorrow," he said into the mic. "Wait for me, okay?"

"Someone recently told me that home isn't where I'm staying, but where the person I love is," Lara said. "Come back to me, Will."

"Tomorrow…"

"Tomorrow," she repeated.

CHAPTER 31

KEO

"YOU THINK IT worked?" Blaine asked. "Earlier today?"

"I don't know," Keo said. "Maybe."

"We should have blown up that house. Or taken out one of those docks and the boats. Maybe if we'd stayed longer instead of running so quickly…"

"Then all three of us would be dead right now." Keo shrugged. "We did what we could. If they're smart, they'll accept today's losses and regroup."

"And if they're not that smart?"

"Look around you, Blaine. These people took over the planet. I'm not talking about the human puppets. I'm talking about the ones pulling the strings. The creatures that Lara called ghouls. They're not stupid."

Blaine nodded. "You're right. Anyway, if they want this island, they're going to have to take it over our dead bodies."

That's what I'm afraid of, Keo thought, but said instead, "That seems to be the consensus with everyone here."

"Lara's a smart woman. She'll get us through this."

Keo didn't doubt that the blonde was smart, but sometimes it took more than smarts to survive an unwinnable situation. Sometimes you just have to accept that you can't win and move on. Or run. He had done plenty of both in his life.

And that's what I should have done earlier today, too. Run the hell away from here and these people as fast as I could.

So why the hell am I playing guard duty?

Isn't it obvious? Because you're the dumbest man alive.

Keo sighed to himself.

From up here, he had a view of every inch of the island with the exception of the forested western half. He could see why Lara had someone up here twenty-four seven. It was a hell of an overwatch. Armed with the ACOG-mounted M4, a good shooter could pick off targets on the beach or boaters coming from the shorelines almost at will. Not him, of course. His skills were more close and personal-based.

"I was here when the island came under attack the first time," Blaine was saying. "It was a hell of a night. Bullets everywhere. People dying."

"They attacked the place before?"

"Over three months ago. Will and Danny were here that time."

"You guys made it through okay, apparently."

"Barely." He lowered the binoculars and glanced up at the sky-light above them. "They almost took down the Tower with one of those grenade launchers you used back at the staging area."

Keo peered up at the full moon. It was a cloudless night, which was good for them because it extended their coverage of the surrounding lake.

He looked down at his watch: 8:16 P.M.

"Are you staying?" Blaine asked after a while.

"No," Keo said. "I'll help out as much as I can until I leave to-morrow."

"Thanks for that."

Keo chuckled. "Don't get the wrong idea, Blaine. I'm stuck here for now, so if they attack, my ass is on the line, too."

"Hunh. Good point."

They didn't say much after that, and Keo was glad Blaine wasn't the type who felt the need to fill every second with noise. Shorty had been one of those.

The silence was finally broken by their radios squawking, and they head Lara's voice. "Keo, Blaine."

Blaine answered his radio first. "What's up?"

"Anything?" Lara asked.

"Nothing yet." He glanced over at Keo for confirmation. Keo shook his head. "All quiet up here."

"If you see anything, I want to hear about it. Anything at all."

"Roger that."

Keo moved to the south window and looked off at the stretch of white sands along the beach. There was a figure standing guard on top of the boat shack. Either Bonnie or Roy, though Keo hadn't completely memorized their guard shift yet. A second figure walked in and out of the dozen or so halos along one of the piers. Tall and slender, so that was probably Bonnie. He turned a bit to the right and looked over the roof of the hotel and spotted two more figures, one crouching, the other standing. There were supposed to be three people up there tonight.

"Doesn't she ever sleep?" Keo asked. "Lara."

"A few hours here and there since Will left the island," Blaine said. "I don't know how she does it. She must drink two or three cups of coffee every morning."

"Where do you guys get coffee anyway?"

"We got stacks of the stuff in freeze dried form. Sarah says those things last anywhere from two to twenty years in the pantry, and indefinitely in the freezer. You don't know how much you miss coffee until you've smelled it in the morning."

A flicker of movement against the moonlight caught his attention just before their radios squawked again. This time it was an excited female voice. Not Bonnie, but one of the other women. Maybe the short one?

"I see something on the water! I think it's coming toward us!"

Keo adjusted his binoculars and picked up multiple white lights skirting across the lake at a snail's pace, moving gradually in their direction. The object was too far away and too hidden by darkness to make out any details, but Keo had seen enough of them to know what the lights belonged to.

"I see it," Keo said into his radio. "It's a boat."

"What kind of boat?" Lara said through the radio. Her voice was shaky and she was breathing hard.

Keo turned the binoculars downward and saw a figure racing toward the beach. Damn. How'd she gotten out of the hotel so fast? The woman really didn't sleep.

"It's still too far away to tell," Keo said. "But it's moving slow, which means it's big."

"Or it could be trying to sneak up on us," Carly said through the radio.

"No. It's got its lights on."

"Keo," Lara said, "I need you on the beach with me. Maddie, head to the Tower and take his place."

"I'm on my way," Maddie said.

Keo nodded at Blaine, then slipped through the door in the floor.

He saw Maddie racing in and out of the lampposts that dotted the hotel grounds as he exited the lighthouse/radio tower. They exchanged a brief nod and he jogged off as she darted into the building behind him, slamming the door after her.

Keo glimpsed dark figures moving around on the hotel rooftop as he ran past. Three up there at the moment, including the twelve-year-old, what's-his-name. Civilians were usually queasy about kids and guns, but Lara had put the tall kid up there anyway.

She's ballsy, all right. Gotta give her that.

He made the beach a few minutes later. The short woman with the impressive rack, Gwen, was on top of the supply building to his right, while Bonnie, the tall ex-model, was at the other end of the beach to his left. He wondered if their placements were on purpose, because that was how he had sneaked onto the beach last night. The result of Lara adapting?

He found her at the end of the middle pier, standing underneath one of the bright LED lampposts that lined the walkway.

"What's out there, guys?" Carly asked through the radio. She sounded anxious.

"It's definitely a boat," Lara said. "And it's headed toward us."

"Hard to miss the island. We are lit up like a Christmas tree, re-member?"

"It's a yacht," Keo said. He had been thinking about it during the walk over. "It's the right size. Two, probably three decks from the position of the lights."

Lara glanced back at him. "You've seen yachts at night before?"

"I've boarded one or two in my time."

"At night?" she said doubtfully.

"Hard to board a boat in the day when they can you see you coming."

He stopped beside her and peered through his own binoculars. The boat was really moving slowly, as if it was in trouble. Was it leaking? Damaged? Still, he could just make out a bit more detail now. From the front, it was difficult to tell how many decks the vessel had, but its sleek white paint job was clear enough against the blackness.

"How many people does something like that hold?" Lara asked.

"I'm guessing anywhere from five to ten cabins. So two, maybe three per would be comfortable. But you could squeeze in more if you had to. You'd need at least five crewmen to keep something like that running, with eight to ten being preferable."

"It looks pretty big."

"The beam can be anywhere from five to ten meters."

"What's a beam?"

"The width of the boat."

"Oh."

"Something that wide is probably thirty to fifty meters long."

"Is that big?"

"For a yacht? That's luxury yacht territory. It's a moving bed-and-breakfast, basically. Can you hear its engines?"

"Barely," she said, straining to hear.

"That means it's got a really quiet engine. Whisper quiet, they call it."

"You know your yachts."

"Like I said, I've had to board one once or twice in my old job. Of course, that just means I know my own limitations. You need to take something like that, I'm your man. You need someone to keep it afloat? That's not me."

Lara hadn't said anything in a while, so he glanced over. He could see her mind working, processing the information.

"Oh, shit," he said.

"What?" she said. "I didn't say anything."

"I know that look."

"You don't even know me."

"I don't need to know you to know *that* look."

She smiled almost sheepishly. "I was just thinking…"

"Of course you were…"

"…that it might be nice to have a moving bed-and-breakfast on hand."

Keo had to laugh. "You're seriously thinking about it, aren't you?"

"It wouldn't hurt to have something like that around just in case. Hope for the best, prepare for the worst, as Will would say. Besides, wouldn't you like to ride something like that to the Texas coast?"

"I'll make do with a sailboat."

"Think about it," she said. Then, into her radio, "Tower, I need you to keep an eye on the rest of the lake in case this is some kind of distraction. I don't want someone sneaking up on us again."

"Roger that," Blaine said through the radio. "What about the boat?"

"Let's wait and see what they want. They're not trying to hide their approach, so that's a positive sign." She said to Keo, "Can they turn off those lights manually?"

He nodded. "They're letting us see them on purpose." Then, "We should probably step back."

"Why?"

"In case they have snipers onboard."

"You think…?"

"Can't be too sure, right? You saw the boat and you're already making plans to acquire it. And they've seen what you have on this island. Even from a distance—"

"The power," Lara said. "They know we have power."

"And lots of it," he nodded.

She turned and headed back down the pier, lifting the radio to her lips again. "Gwen, make yourself as small as possible back there. Bonnie, head back toward the tree lines for now."

At the end of the pier, Gwen went into a crouch on top of the boat shack and Bonnie retreated up the beach toward the woods.

"Are we expecting trouble?" Roy asked through the radio.

"No," Lara said. "Just in case."

Just in case, Keo thought. Apparently that was the island's motto.

"What now?" he asked her.

"I don't know." He thought he might have heard the first sign of a strain in her voice. "I wish Will was here. He'd know what to do."

"You're doing pretty well on your own."

"For now," she said. They stopped at the end of the pier and looked back at the approaching lights. "You said a boat that size had to have a big crew."

"At minimum, five people just to keep it running."

"They can't be Kate's soldiers. It's too obvious."

"Who's Kate?"

"This bitch we used to know," Lara said, but she didn't elaborate. Instead, she narrowed her eyes and said, "If they're hostile, it might be too late to do anything about it once they're closer." She paused for a moment, and he could almost see that mind of hers spinning again. "Can you sink something like that? I mean, by shooting it?"

"You can sink anything if you shoot it enough," Keo said.

She continued staring at the approaching lights, her lips twisting, face contorting with indecision. He felt almost sorry for her. It wasn't just her life at stake here. It was the others, too. Blaine, Maddie, the girl with the big rack behind them.

And the kids. He didn't even know their names. One of them was Ellie or something. Janet? Wang?

You don't even know their names. So what's the point?

Because they're kids.

Goddamn it, because they're kids…

"There's a way to find out if they're friendlies," Keo said.

"How?" Lara said, looking at him.

"It's your island, and it's your people. If you tell me to go ahead with this, you could be putting them all in unnecessary danger. Or you might be saving their lives. But ultimately, you're going to have to decide, because once I start, I can't stop. And whatever happens because of it will be on you. You understand?"

She stared at him, clearly confused. But that confusion quickly gave way to understanding, and she nodded. "Thank you, Keo."

He sighed. "Don't thank me yet. This is either going to work out and everyone will live happily ever after, or it's going to blow up in both of our faces and everyone's going to end up dead."

TWO NIGHTS ON this island, and I'm soaked from head to toe…again.

He slipped into the water from the eastern half of the island and swam in the darkness laterally—not toward the approaching yacht, but where he expected it to be at a certain point. His biggest advantage was that he could see the boat just fine to his left along with the island to his right.

Keo swam at a leisurely pace, slowing down and treading water only when he could feel the waves pressing against him more urgently than before. The vessel, bright white against the black canvas, glided in front of him, its half-dozen floodlights on full blast. They definitely weren't trying to hide themselves. Either they actually did come in peace, or they really, *really* wanted the island to think that.

From his angle, he was able to count all three decks on the boat, with the highest one also the smallest. He eyeballed the length of the craft at just over forty meters, so he wasn't too far off when he had guessed from the pier. Keo let it glide smoothly across the water in front of him and read the name written along the side: *Trident*.

He reached the boat's stern just as it was passing him by and grabbed at one of the two ladders half-submerged at the back. He thought he had missed it for a moment but felt smooth metal at the last second and tightened his grip, then let himself be dragged through the water. He reached out with his other hand, got a good grip on the wet ladder, and slowly began climbing. The only sound other than the engine was the tricolor Mexican flag flapping from a long metal staff above him.

Keo crawled onto the lower deck, dripping pools of Lake Beaufont everywhere. A large floodlight created a giant halo with him in the center. This part of the boat was designed for lounging and easy access to the water. Fortunately, there was no one around at the moment to see him. He didn't worry about being overheard, either. The churning engine, "whisper quiet" or not, still overwhelmed most noises around him, especially at night.

He swung the MP5SD forward and flicked off the safety, then darted out of the pool of light.

Keo could feel the vibrations of the boat's engine room under his bare feet, humming as it pushed the *Trident* at a ridiculously slow pace toward the island. The boat was definitely moving at speeds well below its capability. So what was the point of that?

Even from his limited angle in the back of the luxury yacht, he could see the well-lit beach of Song Island spread out like a huge welcome mat. The piers in front, the long stretch of white sands, and the ring of solar-powered collector plates looked like glittering jewelry.

Windows and glass doors in front of him provided a nice view of a dimly lit dining room. No movement, so he ignored it and moved to the side toward one of the ladders leading up to the main deck. Keo climbed as quickly as he could, very aware that he was still dripping water with every rung he took.

He was almost at the top when he heard voices. He flattened his body against the ladder as two men walked past above him. Male voices talking in English, with heavy footsteps. He couldn't quite make out what they were saying, though they sounded excited.

Keo waited until the voices faded before continuing up.

He swung over the rail and landed in a crouch in the back of the main deck, the MP5SD swinging in front of him at the ready. Keo scanned the boat, wondering what he looked like at the moment if someone spotted him. A tall barefoot guy in wet black clothes with a silenced submachine gun. He wouldn't blame them if the first person who spotted him started shooting. He would, in their shoes.

Maybe this wasn't such a good idea after all. He was operating under the assumption that the people on the boat had ulterior motives. Lara thought the same, which was why she had agreed to let him take this approach.

"Don't shoot unless you have to," she had said.

"Trust me," he had replied, "if you hear shooting on the boat, there's a very damn good reason for it."

She had nodded solemnly back at him.

Tough girl, he remembered thinking. *Tough call. Ballsy call.*

He was impressed with her. Keo wasn't a leader; he didn't give orders, but he appreciated people who could. Lara was one. He wondered if she had known she possessed that kind of fortitude before the world crapped out on them. Not everyone knew their full potential until they were faced with a cliff and had to take the leap. Lara had, in his eyes, passed with flying colors.

He was squatting in another lounging area, one that was open to the moonless sky, with a darkened room in front of him. Sofas, chairs, and a bar. Entertainment center. The bridge was above him on the upper deck, and he moved toward another rung of ladders and climbed again. He wasn't dripping quite as much water this time and didn't encounter voices above him, either.

He went into a crouch next to the ladders and took a moment to orient himself with the boat's layout. Then, after about ten seconds, he found an unlocked door and slipped inside.

Another entertainment room, with a big-screen TV on a wall with a wide array of media players and electronics facing comfortable sofas. There was plenty of evidence that the place had been lived in, but the details were hidden in semidarkness. He slipped through the spacious room, reaching a spiral staircase to his right that led back down to the main deck. The bridge was in front of him and around a slight turn in the narrow passageway.

He tiptoed down the hallway, then peered around the corner and into the bridge through an open door. There were two men inside, one standing at the helm, the other one next to him looking through binoculars at the island. They wore gun belts with sidearms in hip holsters, and an AK-47 lay across an empty chair, another one leaning against the console. Their backs were to him, so he couldn't see their faces and only caught glimpses of their reflections in the wide windshield up front. The one with his hands on the steering wheel was wearing a white captain's hat that didn't look like it quite fit him.

They were in the middle of a conversation, so Keo leaned back and listened.

"How many do you see?" the "captain" asked.

"Just three," the other one said.

"What does Rod say?"

The man with the binoculars grabbed a radio off the console and said into it, "Give me a count, Rod."

"I see two," a third muffled voice said through the radio. "But I saw four about thirty minutes ago when we were on approach. One's gone and one's just disappeared. I think one of them went into the woods."

"Where'd the fourth one go?"

He's behind you, Keo thought.

"I have no idea," the man named Rod said.

"Do you have a shot?" the captain asked.

Rod didn't answer right away.

"Rod," the captain pressed, "do you have a shot?"

"One's moving around too much," Rod said. "But the other one's pretty still. He's crouched on top of a building. Looks like a storage shack. Short fucker, too."

"Can you take him?" the second man asked.

"Probably," Rod said.

"'Probably' isn't good enough."

"Yeah, well, that's all you're gonna get," Rod said. "Take it or leave it."

The captain grunted. "We should have put Hank up there instead. He always follows orders."

"Rod's okay," the second man said. "You think they got diesel in that place?"

"Fat chance of that. But you see those things around the island? Those are solar panels. That means they have a constant reliable power source. When was the last time we had that?"

"So we're definitely doing this, then."

"Hell yeah," the captain said. "Tell the boys to stay hidden, but get ready. We'll see what kind of firepower they have first."

"I still think we should have taken the lifeboats inland instead of just showing up with lights flashing."

"It's called a Trojan Horse. And it's worked before. If it ain't broke…"

"…don't fix it," the other man finished.

There was a slight tremor in their voices. It wasn't fear. Keo recognized it from all those times he was deployed into a new arena.

It was excitement.

Clang-clang from behind him, coming from the spiral staircase that connected the main and upper decks.

Keo hurried back down the hallway and slipped behind the staircase just as a bearded man wearing a sweat-drenched T-shirt climbed up the steps. The man had a shotgun slung over his back and a gun belt was riding low around his waist. He was turning, the staircase moving him from left to right as he climbed higher and higher.

Keo slung the MP5SD and slowly, silently, slid the Ka-Bar out of its sheath.

He took a breath, and just as the man put his foot onto the wooden floor of the upper deck, Keo lunged forward and slapped one hand over the man's mouth and stabbed him once, twice, three times in the side before the man could get out his first startled gasp. Keo kept his grip over the man's mouth as he lowered the still-twitching body to the floor. Blood poured out of the gaping wounds and over Keo's fingers, but he ignored the warm sensation.

His eyes remained fixed down the hallway, toward the bridge hidden around the bend. He could still hear them talking.

"You think they have women on the island?" one of them was asking. It sounded like the one with the binoculars.

"What are the chances they don't?" the captain said.

"It'll be nice to get some new ones onboard."

The other man chuckled. "Just keep it in your pants until we have the whole place locked down."

"Remember, we get first dibs."

The bearded man had gone completely still in Keo's arms. He lowered the body all the way to the floor and wiped blood off his hand against the man's dry pants.

"Rod sound a little rebellious to you a while ago?" the "first mate" was asking.

"A little," the captain said. "Probably cabin fever. We've been at sea for way too long."

"Must be."

Keo tugged the shotgun from the lifeless body and stood up. He would have used the MP5SD, but the suppressor wasn't going to make a lot of noise. And right now, he needed to make noise. Enough that Lara could hear all the way from the island.

"Don't shoot unless you have to," she had said.

"Trust me, if you hear shooting on the boat, there's a very damn good reason for it," he had answered.

He headed back down the hallway and turned the corner, and as soon as he stepped inside the bridge, the captain saw his reflection in the glass.

The man looked over his shoulder. "Who the fuck are you?"

"You the captain?" Keo asked.

The "first mate" turned around and went for his sidearm. Keo fired and the man's head disintegrated in a hail of buckshot that continued and spiderwebbed the windshield behind him, splattering chunks of brain and skull against the console.

Keo racked the shotgun and swung it back over to the captain. "I asked you a question."

"I—I guess," the man said.

Keo stepped forward and pulled the man's sidearm out of its holster. It was a fancy silver chrome six-shot revolver. "Nice gun."

"Thanks," the captain said.

Keo shot the man in the right kneecap with his own gun. The captain howled in pain and fell to the floor. Keo grabbed him by the back of his shirt collar and dragged him across the room, then deposited him into a corner.

"Stay," Keo said.

Even through the captain's high-pitched cries, Keo heard footsteps pounding across the boat, originating from outside the bridge. They weren't being the least bit subtle about it. Then again, they probably didn't know what the hell was happening.

He slid the revolver into his waistband and leaned out the door just as a bald man poked his head up the spiral staircase. Keo lowered the shotgun's iron sight over the melon-size target.

Nice and juicy, just the way he liked them.

CHAPTER 32

GABY

SHE SHOULDN'T BE this afraid. If her chances were decent when she was lugging around three girls, then having Will and Danny beside her was a hell of an improvement. But of course all those times didn't involve a small army of Josh's soldiers pinning her inside a farmhouse in the middle of nowhere and the knowledge that the coming night was going to bring out something worse.

Four.

Will said there had been four of them in Dunbar. He had killed two. Four minus two got you two.

Four.

Four!

She wasn't sure she wanted to see them. Just hearing stories about the creatures—from Will, from Lara, from Blaine and Maddie—was creepy enough. She had never actually felt the need to ever come face-to-face with the abominations.

Gaby shivered slightly and was glad no one was around to see it.

She was on the second floor, crouched at the head of the stairs, looking down at total darkness. Ten feet. That was all that separated her from the first floor, where the ghouls would come in first. Unless, of course, they decided to try climbing the two-story house. That was possible, too.

"They can be creative when the blue-eyed ones are around," Will had said.

Gaby shifted her bent legs to keep them from falling asleep. Lance was sitting against the wall next to her, an AR-15 loaded with silver ammo in his lap. His eyes were focused on the peeling wallpaper in front of him, just barely visible in the streams of moonlight filtering through the main bedroom further down the hallway to their left. The door was open and Danny's silhouetted form stood still, peering out the slots they had left in the window after covering it up with slabs of countertop from the second-floor bathroom.

There wasn't enough light to see much of anything, though her eyes had adjusted to the darkness and her mind filled in the missing pieces. She couldn't see Will on the first floor, but she could hear him moving from one barricaded window to another every few minutes. Nightfall had come an hour ago, and they were still waiting for signs of an attack.

Because it was coming. She knew that for a fact. There was no way they were getting through tonight untouched.

Gaby was in the center of the second floor, with two bedrooms to her right and a bathroom at the very end. All three doors had been removed to cover the first-floor windows and reinforce the main bedroom. Closet doors, along with whatever else they could take down, had also been used to block the other windows along the floor. It wasn't impossible to get through the barriers, but it would take a lot of force and there wasn't a lot of leverage to be had while clinging to the outside. Just the same, they had sealed up the other bedroom windows with dresser, beds, and furniture.

Better safe than sorry. Always better safe than sorry.

She felt reasonably safe up here. It was the first floor that they had to worry about. The fortification would hold for a while, but not forever. Sooner or later, the ghouls would batter their way through. And if they couldn't, then their human allies could open the door, literally, for the creatures. Then there would just be the stairs to block their path.

A *click* in her right ear, and Danny's voice. "Anyone huffing and puffing down there yet?"

She heard him loud and clear through the earbud, connected to a Motorola radio clipped to her hip. Danny and Will only had two of their assault vests, but Danny had brought along an additional comm rig when he came looking for them days ago and found Will outside of Lafayette. She reached up and pulled at the plastic band wrapped around her throat. Gaby didn't think she would ever get used to the constricting feel of it against her skin.

"Nothing in the front yards," Will said. "You?"

"I got zilch and nada," Danny said.

"What about the soldiers?"

"Still hanging around. Buggers aren't leaving anytime soon. All dressed up and nowhere to go."

"Ghouls?"

"I see them."

"How many?"

"How do you say 'a shit lot' in Spanish?"

"What are they doing? How are they reacting to the soldiers?"

"They're leaving them alone."

Gaby keyed her radio. "How do they know to leave the soldiers alone? Is it the uniforms?"

"Maybe," Will said.

"Like with the hazmat suits."

"Likely."

"Aw, shit," Danny said.

"What is it?" Will said.

"Buckle up your seat belt, kids, here comes trouble. And the bitch brought friends."

Will didn't respond. Gaby waited impatiently, wanting to ask what they were seeing, but somehow managed to bite her tongue. She felt a pair of eyes on her and glanced over at Lance. He was watching her and had been for a while. Questions flooded his eyes, but like her, he was exercising amazing restraint. Lance was in his late twenties but looked older.

"I don't know," she said, shaking her head at him.

He nodded, grateful for at least that much.

Then Will's voice, finally, in her right ear. "Gaby."

"Yeah," she said.

"Remember: shoot them in the head."

"In the head," she repeated. Then, "How many of them are out there?"

"Four."

"*Four?*" Gaby said, almost shouting the word out.

"You think it's a new group, or did they get reinforcements?" Danny asked.

"I have no idea," Will said. "I can't tell them apart. One blue-eyed fuck looks like the other to me."

"You're such a racist."

"*Four?*" Gaby said again.

"It's probably because of what Willie boy did back in Dunbar," Danny said.

"Or protocol," Will said. "They operate as squads of four. They lose two, they replace two. Or maybe it's an entirely different group. That doesn't seem likely, though."

"Maybe one of them's your ghoulfriend."

"Ex-ghoulfriend."

"What are they doing, Will?" Gaby asked.

"The black-eyed ones are staying back along with the soldiers. It's just the shock troops."

"Shock troops?"

"That's what this guy back in Dunbar called them. It's not a bad theory."

"What was that guy's name, Brick?" Danny said.

"Bratt," Will said.

"Ah, that's right."

"What happened to him?" Gaby asked.

"He didn't make it," Will said.

Of course not. What a stupid question.

Gaby heard a soft tapping noise and looked over at Lance. His fingers were moving nervously against the side of the AR-15 while his eyes had returned to the same patch of dirty wallpaper in front of him.

"Lance," she whispered.

He glanced over. "Hmm?"

"You okay?"

He nodded and tried to smile. "Yeah. You?"

"We'll be fine. Will and Danny are really good at this. Just do what we talked about, okay? *Exactly* what we talked about, and you'll get through this fine."

"Okay," he said, and made another futile attempt at a smile.

She turned back to the stairs and peered down at the pool of darkness below, wondering just where her ability to suddenly bullshit with such conviction came from. She had never been a particularly good liar, but these days, lying came easier. She wanted to think it was because Lance needed the assurance, but maybe it was for her own benefit, too.

A *click* in her right ear, followed by Danny's voice. "Gaby."

"Yeah?" she said.

"You've never seen one of them before, right?"

"No…"

"Come take a look."

Gaby stood up and said "Stay here" to Lance then jogged up the hallway toward the bedroom.

Danny peeked over his shoulder as she approached. "It's time you find out what all the crazy kids are talking about. It's a real gas, man."

Gaby moved across the large bedroom, looking briefly over at Claire, Milly, and Annie huddled on the floor next to the king-size bed. Claire had the FNH gripped tightly in her hands, while Milly was lying across Annie's lap, her eyes closed. Annie stroked the girl's hair, the two of them finding comfort in each other. Claire, though, was all business. She caught Gaby's eyes and nodded. Gaby smiled back at her.

She's going to make a great soldier one of these days.

Gaby reached the window and slid against the wall across from Danny. They had left plenty of slots to see out through, with the biggest being a few inches wide. He pointed at the front yard, lit up by the moonlight. It was amazingly bright out there and she could make out a lone figure standing next to one of the trucks with the mounted machine guns.

The first thing she noticed was the way it stood—tall, like a human male. It also looked noticeably healthier than the other ghouls she was used to seeing, which usually made her think of loose flesh draped over skeletal remains. And its eyes. If she couldn't quite make out the details of its body, she had no trouble seeing its eyes.

Blue eyes. Blue fucking eyes.

She always believed Will and the others when they told her about the existence of the blue-eyed ghouls, but maybe there was a part of her (a very, very small part) that was doubtful. But here, now, staring down the window at one of them—and being watched back by it—she felt a hollowness in the pit of her stomach.

They're real. Jesus, they're real.

In some ways, she thought she knew the world. Even after The Purge when she was confronted with an all-new set of realities, she had become accustomed to it and understood its rules: Stay out of the dark. Silver kills. Bodies of water. Now there was something new, and suddenly everything was upside down again. It was almost enough to make her want to scream and pull out her hair.

"There and there," Danny said.

She followed where he was pointing and saw a second one standing next to the supply shack on the left side of the yard. And there, a third, perched on top of the same building. Three pairs of blue eyes glowed in the darkness.

Radiant blue, like diamonds...

"Three," she said, her voice coming out strangely calm *(Why am I so calm?)*. "You said there were four."

He pointed again. "And heeeeeere's Johnny."

The fourth blue-eyed ghoul emerged out of the sea of black, moving with impossibly fluid steps for something that shouldn't even exist. It was pulling a man behind it by a strap it held almost nonchalantly in its right hand. The other end of the line was wrapped around the man's neck, like some kind of dog leash. The man didn't struggle against his restraints or seemed capable of resistance. All the fight had clearly been beaten out of him.

The ghoul and its "pet" stopped about ten feet from the front door of the farmhouse. It tugged at the leash and the man staggered forward until he was standing beside his "master" before falling (gratefully, tiredly) to his knees. The man had distinctive red hair, the color providing an absurd contrast next to the black-skinned creature with the smooth black skull.

The man lifted his head and looked in her direction. Blood coated his face from forehead to chin, and he peered across the short distance through badly bruised eyes.

Harrison.

She always wondered what had happened to him after she pushed him out of the car. Now she knew.

Gaby keyed her radio. "That's Harrison."

"Yeah," Will said in her ear.

"You've met him before?"

"No."

"How did you know who he was?"

"It's a long story."

"The guy from Dunbar?" Danny asked.

"Uh huh," Will said.

"What's it doing with him?" Gaby said.

She had no love for Harrison. She hated the man's guts. He had killed Peter, all because he *"had to make sure."* That phrase haunted Gaby. They were such simple words, but there was nothing simple about the result.

"They like to play," Will said through her earbud. "They played with Lance and Annie's friends last night. And they were toying with us back in Dunbar, too. They called off the dogs when they had us trapped just so they could have more fun. It's all a game to them. A sick, bloody game."

"I've been telling Willie boy," Danny said, "that if they like games so much, we should introduce them to Parcheesi or Monopoly. All the fun and none of the fatality. Win-win."

The other blue-eyed monstrosities in the yard hadn't moved. The one on the roof of the shack continued to stare in her direction while the other two remained perfectly still, as if waiting for the show to began. There was an effortlessness about the way they just stood that unnerved her, as if they could stay in that pose all night and never have to move for even a second. It was so...*unnatural.*

"Here we go," Danny said softly.

The ghoul tugged on the leash, and Harrison stood up obediently. Gaby braced herself for what she thought she knew was coming when the creature beckoned its captive toward it. Long, delicate fingers reached toward Harrison's throat, and when they pulled away seconds later, the leash was no longer attached. It had freed him.

Why?

When Harrison realized this, he groped at his neck to make sure. He stared at the creature, then around the front yard, before finally up at the second floor. She wondered if he could see her and Danny peeking back at him through the slits. Maybe just her eyes. Was that enough? Did he know she was up here? For some reason, she hoped he didn't. The prospect of her name being shouted out loud in front of those *things* made her shiver.

The blue-eyed ghoul opened its mouth and said something to Harrison. Its voice was too low for her to hear from up here.

Its voice.

It's talking!

"Oh yeah, apparently they can talk, too," Danny, seeing her reaction, said from across the window.

Harrison was backpedaling in the yard now. First slowly, then quicker, while glancing wildly around him. Then he did what she knew he would do—what she feared he would: He ran toward the farmhouse and straight to the front door. He disappeared under the window and a second later she heard loud banging from below.

Then Harrison's voice, pained and panicked. "Open the door! Please, open the door! Let me in! You have to let me in!"

The ghoul tossed away the rope and watched Harrison. There was a look on its face, something she had never seen before on the creatures. It looked *amused.* She turned slightly and saw the same look on the faces of the other three.

They're enjoying every second of it.

The loud banging continued for a while along with Harrison's voice. "Please! For God's sake, open the door! You have to let me in!"

Like hell, Gaby thought, when the banging suddenly stopped.

Harrison reappeared outside her window for a moment before whirling around, expecting an attack at any second. So did she. They were both surprised that none came. Harrison turned and fled up the yard. Then he stopped, seemed to be trying to get his bearings, before taking off again, this time running alongside the house and disappearing.

The creatures hadn't moved. They simply watched him go. Waiting.

For what?

"There he goes," Danny said.

"Are they just going to let him go?" Gaby asked.

He shook his head, and in a voice that was odd for Danny, he said solemnly, "No."

The first ghoul to move was the one perched on the shack. It leaped off the building and darted off in the same direction that Harrison had gone. Then a second one took off, followed quickly by a third, until all four had vanished from the yard.

There was just silence again.

"What are they going to do to him?" she whispered.

Danny shook his head and didn't answer.

A minute passed, and she was only aware of her shallow breathing.

Five minutes...

She looked across at Danny again, hoping to find some answers from his expression. There weren't any. He was waiting and listening like her. Maybe he knew something more, but he didn't say it. She was going to click her PTT and ask Will when a scream pierced the night air.

Harrison.

It was shrill and loud and seemed to go on and on and on.

She had never heard that kind of scream in her life. It wasn't just that he was in pain. There was mortal terror in every second of it.

And my God, did it seem to keep going, and going…

She had difficulty reconciling that voice with the hardened man who had beaten Peter half to death (or if he hadn't done it himself, had ordered it), then later tossed Donna out of the car to die on the highway. She wanted not to feel sorry for him, but she did anyway.

Gaby didn't know how to interpret her feelings. Was it weakness? He was her enemy. She shouldn't care what was happening to him. Or was it strength? Was courage being able to feel empathy even for your enemy? She didn't know. She only knew that no one, not even Harrison, deserved what was happening out there at this moment.

No one…

She looked back at the girls huddled in the corner. Annie had placed her hands over Milly's ears and the girl looked half-asleep in her lap. But it was Claire's eyes that Gaby saw. The thirteen-year-old's face was placid, unmoved by Harrison's cries.

Click. "Gaby," Will said in her ear. "I need you back at the stairs."

"On my way," she said, and walked quickly across the room.

She was glad to leave the window, because the further she moved away from it, the harder it was to hear Harrison's continued screams. Until finally she was back in the hallway, and she couldn't hear the dying man anymore.

Lance looked over at her. "They're doing it again, aren't they? Like last time. Back at our house. They're doing it again…"

She didn't reply. Instead, Gaby sat numbly back down at the head of the stairs, then flicked the fire selector on her M4 from semi-automatic to burst fire. She longed for her own weapon, or at least something with full-auto capability. At least she had silver bullets in her rifle again, so there was that.

THE FIRES OF ATLANTIS 423

"Remember: shoot them in the head," Will had said.

Right. Shoot them in the head.

Easy enough…

THE NEXT TWO hours ticked by in silence, inside and outside the farmhouse. The lack of noise—or any sounds at all—was nerve-wracking.

Blue-eyed ghouls.

She could have lived the rest of her life without seeing them in person.

Not just one, but four.

Four!

She shivered again in the semidarkness and looked quickly to see if Lance had noticed. She shouldn't have bothered. Lance had dozed off, the AR-15 positioned awkwardly across his lap. She thought about taking the rifle away from him. The last thing she wanted was for him to wake up suddenly and start shooting. And the barrel was pointed right at her, too…

The neon hand of her watch ticked to 10:16 P.M.

Not even close to sunrise. When did the sun come out last time? Around seven?

All we have to do is survive nine more hours.

Oh, that's it?

The *clicking* noise in her right ear made her jump slightly. "What's the word, daddy bird?" Danny said through the comm.

"Jack shit," Will said.

"How long does it take to eat Harrison? The guy was kind of thick around the ankles. An hour? Two?"

"Oh, nice."

"What? Too soon?"

"Way too soon."

"Oh, come on. It wasn't like we really knew the guy. You know what they say about gingers."

Tap.

Gaby's eyes darted up to the ceiling.

Tap tap.

She reached down and squeezed the Push-to-Talk switch connected to her radio. "I hear something."

"Sorry, kid, I tried to hold it in," Danny said.

"No, above us."

"What was it?" Will asked.

"Footsteps. I think."

She looked across the hallway and saw Danny, still stationed at the window, craning his head upward toward the ceiling.

Tap tap.

"I hear it," Danny said.

"Ignore it," Will said. "They're just probing the roof, looking for a weak spot."

"What if they find it?" she asked.

"Then we're shit out of luck with a fist full of ham sandwiches," Danny said.

Gaby listened intently to the noise above her when it suddenly stopped.

She breathed a little easier.

They're probing. That's all. They're just probing for weaknesses.

"Gaby," Will said in her ear.

"Yes…"

"Stay where you are. You're in the perfect spot right now. And wake Lance up."

She smiled. "How'd you know?"

"He's not one of us."

Gaby felt a flush of pride. *"One of us."* Her, Danny, and Will. The three of them. In this post-Purge world, it meant the world for him to include her.

She turned to Lance and put her hand on his shoulder, giving it a slight nudge.

He opened his eyes and snapped awake, looking around before locating her through his groggy haze. "What's happening?"

"You were asleep."

"Oh." He rubbed his eyes, then wrapped his hands back around his rifle as if it were his lifeline. The barrel was still pointed at her…

Gaby turned back to the stairs. Or the pitch blackness at the other end. She could really see only the first half dozen or so steps, with the rest hidden in the shadows.

"Heads up," Danny said in her ear.

"I see it," Will said.

Gaby glanced to her left, past Lance and into the open bedroom door at Danny. He had taken a step away from the window and had lifted his M4A1 slightly.

"Danny," Gaby said out loud. "What's happening?"

"They're back," he said through her earbud.

"The blue-eyed ones?"

"Ol' blue eyes. Maybe they want to serenade us. Sing us to death." Then he added, his voice rising noticeably, "Shit."

"What is it?" Will said through the comm.

"I only see two of them."

"Find the other two—"

Something that sounded like an explosion rang out, drowning out Will's voice. Gaby moved on instinct, diving further up the hallway, away from the stairs, just as the first pieces of rubble came tumbling down from above her.

The roof. *It was caving in on them.*

"Lance!" she shouted.

He was struggling to his feet, legs wobbly from sitting too long, and hadn't straightened all the way up before the roof crashed down on top of him. He let out something that sounded like a scream *(A squeal?)* before he was pummeled by falling slate tiles. One of them broke over Lance's head and he stumbled, somehow managing to brace himself against the wall, as more roofing material flooded down on top of him one by one by one.

Then it came down.

It.

One of the creatures. It fell down from the sky like some arch-angel, minus the wings and halo and good intentions, landing in a crouch next to Lance. It straightened up, its body impossibly long, spindly arms and legs extending in what little light was available in the second-floor hallway.

Glowing blue eyes searched her out, and finding her, zeroed in.

It was gripping something long and shiny in one of its hands. Moonlight glinted off the smooth surface of a sledgehammer.

"Gaby!" Will shouted in her ear.

She was too busy scrambling back up to her feet to respond. She didn't think and didn't waste a second. She simply reacted, lifting the M4 and pulling the trigger. The carbine bucked in her hands and the sound of the three-round burst in the close confines of the hallway was like three powerful thunder strikes, one after another.

Her aim was true, and she hit it with all three rounds in the chest.

But it didn't go down.

It didn't go down.

Instead, it looked back at her and grinned before tossing the sledgehammer away. Then it took a step forward. *Pow!* A bullet hit the creature from behind. That same bullet punched through flesh and *zipped* past her head before disappearing into the wall behind her. *Slurping* noises as thick, coagulated black blood burst out of the fresh hole in the thing's neck and splashed with a sickening *plop* against the floor.

"Gaby, get down!" Danny shouted from the other side of the hallway.

Her mind was reeling, the sight of the creature still standing after she had put three silver bullets into its chest making it hard for her to think straight.

"Remember: shoot them in the head," Will had said.

Shoot them in the head!

The creature wasn't looking at her anymore. It was already turning and bounding up the hallway toward Danny, who was firing, having switched to full-auto. Bullets pierced the creature's body and embedded into walls as Danny tried to track its constantly moving and shifting form. It was *dodging* his gunfire. How was that even possible? Were they really that *fast*?

Stupid question, because she could see it with her own eyes.

Danny's silver rounds that did land were penetrating the creature's body and continued on, *zip-zipping* up the narrow space like flies buzzing, slamming into the wall around her. She had to duck to keep from being hit by a stray bullet, and suddenly the prospect of dying by friendly fire was very real.

In a crouch, Gaby lifted her rifle and tried to get a bead on the creature as it fled away from her *("Shoot them in the head!")*. Before she could fire, she lost track of it as it disappeared into the room. It was suddenly on the floor and Danny was under it, fighting for his life, and she couldn't make out where the creature ended and Danny began.

Instead, she reached down and pressed the PTT, and shouted,

"They're inside! Will, they're inside the house!"

Where the hell was Will? Couldn't he hear what was happening up here? What was he doing down there? What—

There was a massive *BOOM!* and the entire house shook from its foundations all the way up to its ceiling, as if a bomb had gone off on the floor under her.

The first floor. Will.

What the hell was happening down there?

She started forward toward the stairs—

—when a second creature fell through the same hole the first one had made with the sledgehammer and landed in an elegant crouch in front of her. It made so little noise, and there was so little effort in its movements, that for a moment the sight of it straightening up, stretching its body like some twisted, deformed ballerina, startled Gaby to the core.

It had its back to her as it rose to its full height—it was at least a foot taller than her, maybe more—and turned around. Gaby became instantly mesmerized by its ethereal blue eyes. Like two impossibly bright orbs washing over the darkened hallway, reaching into her very soul.

It opened its mouth, revealing twisted and cracked brown and yellow teeth stained with oozing black liquid that looked, for some reason, as if they, too, were alive and wiggling.

"Wanna play?" it hissed, eyes glinting with mischief in the moonlight.

CHAPTER 33

WILL

THE DARKNESS DID things to you these days. It lulled you into a
strange state of numbness with its overwhelming silence, the
unnatural sense of calm that seemed to pervade everything, while at
the same time it made you dread all the things out there that you
couldn't see.

Inevitable. Night after night.

Are we just living on borrowed time? Is that all it is?

Tonight. Tomorrow night. The week after. The next month?

*How long can we keep the island? How long can we keep fighting them
before it becomes too much? Before the costs are too great?*

How long...

He had to shake himself to rid his mind of those depressing
thoughts. Being downstairs by himself didn't help. The most he
could do to keep busy was move from window to window, checking
every corner of the front yard. He couldn't really see the soldiers on
the road from here, but he knew they were still out there, somewhere.

When they finally came, he was able to concentrate on the matter at hand. His senses were never more razor sharp as they were
during the preamble to combat. He felt it now, the hyper awareness
of his surroundings. Every sound, every flickering image, and every
glowing blue eyes.

As he watched them toying with Harrison, he realized just how
different these creatures were. They were the same, but not—an

entirely new breed of what he was familiar with. Radically different. More *dangerous*. This was why they had kept the other ghouls back in Dunbar. Because this was their show. Their sport. Harrison was a warm-up and now they were coming for the main event. He and the others inside the house.

So where were they now? What was taking them so long?

Will glanced back at the staircase behind him. It was too dark to make out much of anything on the first floor even with the slivers of moonlight filtering in through the barricades over the windows, one next to him and the other one on the other side of the door. He could just make out the stair landing—

There was a loud crash from above him, and the entire house shuddered.

He reached for his radio. "Gaby!"

He waited for a response, but there wasn't any. Instead, he heard the *pop-pop-pop* of an M4 exploding from the second floor. Three-shot burst. Gaby's rifle, because Danny still had his M4A1 and he would have either used single shots or gone full-auto.

Will abandoned the window as more gunfire erupted from the top of the stairs. In the packed confines of the house, the sounds were thunderous, but they couldn't quite drown out the voice. Danny's, shouting between gunshots. He wasn't using the radio, either. That was a bad sign.

The first floor. Stay on the first floor! Don't abandon—

Then Gaby's voice, blasting through his earbud. "They're inside! Will, they're inside the house!"

He was at the stairs, grabbing for the wooden globe on top of the newel, when shadowed movements flickered across the wall in front of him. Figures, moving outside one of the windows, their shapes casting across the room by moonlight.

He spun back around and saw the indistinguishable shapes moving on the other side of the window he had abandoned just seconds ago. As soon as he saw them, the silhouetted forms raced away again.

What—?

The explosion (or was that *explosions?*) shredded the window, the barrier over it, and a large section of the house around them. Will dived to the floor as chunks of the wall and even the porch buzzed over and around his head, sharp pieces embedding into the floor inches from him. Debris rained down across the room and his ears were buzzing. He was sure he had gone temporarily deaf *(Please let it be temporary)*, though that couldn't possibly be the case because he could still hear continuous gunfire from above him.

Grenades? Did they just use grenades on the wall?

Jesus Christ.

He looked up from the floor, expecting the entire house to come tumbling down on top of him at any second. But it didn't. Somehow, by some miracle, the second floor remained where it was—above him—despite the jagged, gaping hole across the room looking out into the moonlit yard. Absurdly, the door next to it had remained intact, as had the repurposed lumber they nailed over it. Smoke from the explosion poured out of the house, and he became aware of the chilly night air for the first time in the last few hours.

He managed to scramble to his knees, glad he hadn't lost the M4A1 during his swan dive. Pieces of wood and glass fell off his shoulders and back and head, and there may or may not have been a trickle *(or two or a dozen)* of blood flowing down his face. His ears were still ringing, which made the sight of two figures, both in camo uniforms and gas masks, stepping through the hole in the wall and moving against the lingering smoke look like monsters in a bad dream.

He couldn't hear his carbine firing, but he could feel it bucking against his hands.

The first man slumped forward while the second one tried desperately to track him in the smoke. His vision was likely blocked by the limited view of the gas mask.

Sucks to be you.

Will put a bullet into the second man's right eye. He stumbled awkwardly before collapsing into a pile.

Will struggled to his feet. His equilibrium was off and he swayed left, then right, then left again. The coughing fits didn't help him adjust any quicker as he reached out with his free left hand, got a grip on something solid, and finally managed to steady himself.

Or as steady as he could get, anyway. The room had begun to spin and he considered falling back to the floor, where it would be so much easier to regain his senses. The world had looked pretty stable from down there, and he didn't remember coughing nearly as much, either. Up here, though, the smoke was everywhere, and it was hard to just breathe.

The wall he was touching shook, but he had a hard time tracing where the vibrations were coming from. Behind him? Above? Maybe from outside the house. It could have been more steady gunfire from the second floor. Gaby and Danny were still up there. So were Lance and Annie and the two girls.

What's happening up there?

He made to turn back toward the stairs to go find out when he saw the shadows shifting once again out of the corner of his eye. He spun back around just in time to see a pair of blue slits glowing in the swirling smoke.

They were coming—*launching*—at him.

Will reflexively struck out with the rifle, because lifting it and firing would have taken more time—a second, maybe two, that he didn't have. The M4A1 vibrated on contact, both his arms shaking long after he had swung from right to left, his body turning with his momentum.

It didn't fall very far and it was back up on its feet even before Will could right himself. It attacked again, springing like an animal on all fours, barreling into his chest and knocking him back. He groped for the wall but couldn't find it and briefly had a feeling of being weightless as he was thrust through empty air before crashing back down to earth.

He was in the back hallway, past the stairs leading up to the second floor. The door was farther behind him, invisible in the darkness. For a moment, he waited for another blue-eyed ghoul to break its way through that side of the house—

Concentrate! Focus!

The creature climbed up the length of his body and he felt (impossibly) cold dead fingers wrapping around his throat, over the plastic band of the mic. A pair of glorious gems in the blackness bore down at him even as thin, pencil-like lips curled into a smile. It leaned down until its face—the deformed shape of the skull obvious behind smooth black flesh—was inches from his own.

Will stared up at it, fumbling with his fingers for the cross-knife in its sheath along his left hip, cursing himself for losing the rifle. He hadn't even remembered when he had lost it. Hopefully it was still somewhere nearby.

The rifle.

Lara called it superstition, but he called it habit.

She's probably right. I am superstitious about the damn thing. I should tell her that when I get back to the island.

I love you, Lara, please forgive me for dying.

He couldn't breathe. How long had it been since he took his last (smoke-filled) breath? A second ago? Two seconds? Ten? An hour?

The creature's fingers were tightening with every erratic heartbeat he managed, and he momentarily rejoiced at the touch of the cross-knife's smooth handle.

The brain.

Go for the brain.

Will pulled the knife out and swung it upward in a wide arc—

—but the sharp point never reached its destination. The creature's other hand had intercepted his swing well short of its intended target.

Oh, shit.

"We know," it hissed at him. "Didn't Kate tell you?" It was holding his hand up in the air with hardly any effort. "We know what happened with the others. *How* it happened. You didn't think we'd let you get away with it twice, did you?"

He could hear its voice, which meant he hadn't gone deaf after all. Thank God.

"Don't worry," the creature hissed. "It's not going to end that easily for you, Will. Kate made us promise her this time. I think she has big plans for you. Of course, she didn't say anything about punishing you for what happened at Dunbar first."

Its lips curled into a devilish grin.

He somehow found the strength to look away from its face to his own hand, suspended in the air, the cross-knife *(Go for the brain!)* frozen in place. It didn't even look like the ghoul was exerting any effort at all. It was so strong. So fast and so strong. What chance did he have against an army of these things? What chance did Lara and the island have?

Lara. At least I got to talk to her one last time.

Please forgive me for dying.

His vision was faltering and the creature's fingers were still tightening, and Will swore he could feel cold bones cutting into the skin around his throat. Was that even possible? Who the hell knew? He didn't. Right now, all he could do was lie on the floor and wait to die, wait to be taken, wait to be given to Kate…

BOOM!

The hallway trembled, as if it had been hit by an earthquake.

The walls, the ceiling, and even the floor underneath him quaked in the aftermath of the shotgun blast at such close proximity.

Will's eyes snapped open because he could breathe again.

Air!

The creature was still perched on top of him, but it had turned its head and was glaring at something behind it. Chunks of its shoulder and neck were gone, and blood arced out of the ruptured flesh and splattered the wall next to it in a grisly shower of thick, clumpy black blood.

Will looked past the ghoul and saw a small figure standing at the mouth of the hallway, holding a shotgun.

Claire. It was Claire. The little girl with the FNH semi-automatic shotgun.

How'd she get down here?

Claire fired again—the massive *BOOM!* lighting up the hallway a second time.

The blue-eyed ghoul's head jerked backward as buckshot tore into its face, shards of shiny white skull shattering and imploding in the air. Meaty globs of foul-smelling flesh hit Will in the face before he could turn his head in time.

Then his left hand was free and Will wrestled it loose from the ghoul's grip, even as the lifeless *(again)* body on top of him flopped sideways to the floor. The creature's form was so much lighter now that Will found it difficult to understand how this almost feathery thing landing next to him was the same creature that had, just moments ago, smashed into him like a five-ton elephant.

He sucked in air like a drowning man, scrambling up from the floor, trying desperately to command his legs to work properly. Maybe it was the lack of oxygen, or the throbbing pain. Despite what the creature had said about promising Kate *(What the hell did that even mean?)*, it sure didn't seem to care that it was about to crush every bone in his throat.

Claire was standing in front of him, staring at the dead *(headless)* body resting in a thick pool of its own blood. She didn't seemed to notice him as he finally got back on his feet and grabbed the wall to steady himself, the creature's flesh and blood caking his face and clothes like a second layer of rotting skin.

Goddamn, it smells.

The continued loud clatter of gunfire from the second floor told him everything he needed to know—it wasn't over. Far from it.

The gunfire snapped Claire out of it, and the girl rushed over and grabbed his waist with one hand—the other still clutching the shotgun—to keep him upright because, even though he didn't realize it, he needed her help. She was a small, frail thing, but she gave herself up as a crutch so he could stand on wobbly feet.

"My rifle," Will said, his voice coming out as a croak. "My rifle," he said again, louder and clearer this time.

"I don't know," Claire said. Her own voice was strained but somehow still impossibly calm.

She's going to make a great soldier…if we survive this.

"What are you doing down here?" he asked.

"They told me to run," Claire said.

Gaby and Danny…

He clutched the knife in his left hand, thanking God he had held onto it all this time, and searched the darkness for his rifle, doing his best to squint through all the pockets of shadows. There were no traces of the carbine anywhere. Of course, there was so little light that it could have been right next to him, and if he didn't step on it, he might never find—

Claire gasped.

Will looked up at a new pair of blue eyes piercing the darkened living room from the jagged hole in the wall. Its tall, elongated frame looked theatrical against the light of the moon splashing in behind it. Will couldn't figure out if it really was that tall or if the angular shape of its body added to the preternatural deceit.

He reached down and pulled Claire's arm away from him, pushing her back into the hallway. She went willingly.

The creature's eyes shifted from Will to the dead carcass of the other ghoul lying on the floor behind him and Claire. What was it the creature was seeing? Was it the twisted body of its friend? Comrade? Maybe even a lover? Did they even love anymore?

"Kate made us promise her this time. I think she has big plans for you."

What the hell does that mean?

Will reached for the holstered Glock at the same time the creature moved, but he only groped empty air. *The Glock was gone.* He hadn't realized it until now, but he should have sooner. The gun belt felt lighter, but in all the moments of trying to survive, trying to just learn to breathe again, he had missed it.

He switched the knife to his right hand and prepared himself for the inevitable when Claire fired next to him. She was standing so close that he swore this time he really did go deaf from the noise of the shotgun blast. She didn't stop with one shot, either.

The girl fired again and again, the self-loading gun allowing her to shoot without having to manually rack the weapon each time. She was so small she would never have managed it anyway, though Will was awestruck that she somehow held onto the shotgun after every shot. What was she, eighty pounds soaking wet?

The blue-eyed ghoul didn't come straight at them. Oh no, it wasn't going to make it that easy. Instead, it was running sideways— left, then right, then back again—like some kind of goddamn leaping animal. Buckshot from Claire's blasts caught it in the sides, the thighs, and even took a big piece off its temple. The creature was almost on top of them when another blast hit it full in the chest, making a hole so absurdly wide that Will could actually *see through it*.

And yet it kept coming.

Will waited for Claire to fire again, but she didn't. Or she couldn't. The FNH had seven shots. Had she fired all seven?

Fuck it.

He launched himself forward at the oncoming creature. He saw its radiant blue eyes widen, registering shock a split-second before he hit it straight in the chest with his entire body, catching it while it was still in the air. He thought he might have heard a grunt from the undead thing, or maybe that was just air wheezing out of the gaping hole in its chest.

Something wet and thick slathered across Will's face, joining the remains of the first dead ghoul, as he tackled the creature. They both fell to the floor in a heap, but Will had the momentum and he was up first. He shoved his left arm against its neck to pin it to the wooden floorboards, putting every ounce of strength he had into it. Even so, it was already getting back up, its strength unimaginable for something so sickly looking.

It was hissing at him. He couldn't be sure if they were words or just guttural sounds. He didn't give a damn. Its eyes bored into him. It didn't quite look so amused or smug anymore, and for a second— just a split-second—Will allowed himself a momentary surge of triumph.

But it wouldn't stop moving against him. Of course not; what was he thinking?

It had managed to pull its head up from the floor and its hands were reaching for his throat when Will slammed the cross-knife into its temple. He didn't stop pushing down down *down* until the guard smacked into the bone and the end of the knife pierced the floor-board on the other side of the thing's head.

The creature went slack almost instantly under him.

"Will!" Claire shouted.

He looked back at Claire, shoving shells from the pouch into her shotgun, her hands fumbling with the ammo because her eyes were elsewhere. He followed her gaze to the hole in the wall, knowing full well what he was going to find out there.

He wasn't disappointed.

There were hundreds of them crowding around the ragged opening, and those were just the ones he could see. But there was something wrong with the way they moved. Or *didn't* move. They weren't pouring inside the house even though there was nothing to hold them back. Instead, they were peering tentatively at him.

No, he was wrong; they weren't looking at him.

They were looking at *the creature under him*. The dead blue-eyed thing he was crouched over was the center of their universe. It, and only it, as if he didn't exist at all. They weren't running, or charging, and there was none of the rabid intensity he was so used to.

"Will, what should we do?" Claire shouted behind him.

"Don't move," he said.

"But—"

"Don't move."

Will looked down at the creature lying still, dead *(again)*, on the floor. Blue eyes, not quite as bright as before, stared accusingly back up at him. He pulled out the knife, then grabbed as firm a grip as he could on the smooth, oozing black skull and lifted it up.

The mass of quivering figures outside the house seemed to go absolutely still as one. He saw something in them, in their responses, that he hadn't seen in a while. Since that night back in Harold Campbell's facility. And he could smell it, too. It wasn't the two dead creatures' flesh and muscle and blood that drenched him from head to toe.

No, this was coming from the hundreds *(thousands?)* of undead things that gathered outside the house.

Fear.

They were afraid.

Will looked down at the blue-eyed ghoul, then, getting a better grip on the smooth head, began sawing the neck with the cross-knife.

"Oh God," Claire said behind him just before he heard retching, followed by the smell of vomit.

He kept sawing...

CHAPTER 34

GABY

SOMEONE WAS SCREAMING inside the bedroom, but it was impossible to tell if it was Danny, Milly, Claire, or Annie. She guessed it had to be either Milly or Annie, though it was a stretch that Milly could produce that kind of ear-splitting sound. It couldn't be Claire, who was as strong as a rock. And she knew for a fact that it couldn't possibly be Danny, because she had never heard Danny scream in his life. At least, not in fear like this.

Not that she could have done anything to help them anyway, because the blue-eyed ghoul was right in front of her, grinning like a madman. There was something amazingly human about its expression—a twisted, nightmarish version of what a man would look like if he simply gave in to all his base animal urges.

She pulled the trigger on the M4 again and got off another three-round burst. Just a lone silver bullet found its target this time, snapping a piece of flesh off the creature's shoulder blade as its body slid to the right to dodge the other two rounds. Then, without missing a beat, it was moving forward with that same unnatural fluidity that shouldn't be possible.

Impossible. All of this is impossible.

It grabbed the rifle by the barrel and yanked it out of her hands. The move was so effortless that for a moment it took her breath away. She staggered back, unsure if she even had control of her legs anymore. She reached down to her hip for her sidearm and drew the Glock as the creature watched her, head cocked to one side, eyes glowing magnificently in the semidarkness of the narrow hallway.

She aimed for the head—

"Remember: shoot them in the head," Will had said.

—and fired.

It flicked its head to one side, and the bullet sailed harmlessly past it and hit the master bedroom doorframe at the other end of the second floor.

"Remember..."

She fired again.

It moved its head left, and again the bullet disappeared up the hallway, but this time it vanished into the darkened bedroom. She prayed she didn't accidentally hit Danny or one of the girls.

"...shoot them in the head."

She squeezed the trigger again and again and again—

The creature continued coming toward her, its head snapping left, then right, as if it were sashaying, a dancer with absolute control over every inch of its body, every slight twitch. Its head bobbed and weaved like a boxer.

And it kept coming...

It was three feet away when she fired her final shot and watched the bullet graze its cheek, taking away flesh and cutting into bone underneath. There was a thin trickle of black blood before the wound seemed to seal itself up.

It stood so close to her now that she could feel its breath— acidic and strangely warm—against her face. It watched her struggling to reload the Glock, her fingers trembling from the adrenaline and terror and the sight of this undead thing standing so close to her that it could reach out at any moment and lick her face.

She managed to put the magazine in and worked the slide, and as she lifted the weapon there was a blur of black skin and the gun flew from her hand. Her arm stung from the blow and she backpedaled again in shock.

It followed and grabbed her by the shoulders, smashing her into the wall. The entire house shook. Or maybe that was just her imagination. The world that existed from her toes to her head definitely trembled because she couldn't focus on any one thing anymore as pain exploded through every fiber of her being.

She slid to the floor, thankful that the wall was there to prevent her from collapsing like the sad sack of useless meat she felt like at the moment. Her ears might have been bleeding, and she couldn't feel the shape of the earbud in her ear anymore. When had she lost that? And where was the radio? It was gone, too. When had that happened? Maybe it was for the best, since she couldn't hear much of anything anyway, even the gunfire from below her.

Will.

And Danny from the main bedroom. Was he shooting? Was that the *pop-pop-pop* of automatic gunfire? Or something else? Maybe all the noises were being conjured up by her mind, which at the moment might have been on fire.

Was that possible? Could her mind actually be burning?

And pain. There was so much pain...

She couldn't feel her left arm, which had jammed into the wall first. Was it broken? She couldn't move it no matter how hard she tried. So maybe.

And what the hell was that ringing in her ears?

It was crouching in front of her, long bony legs bending at awkward angles. Its smooth skin, pulled taut over a sharp skeletal frame, reminding her of all those anorexic supermodels in lingerie catalogs. *Eat something,* she wanted to say to it, then maybe laugh in its face. Of course, when she opened her mouth to do just that, only a slight gasp came out.

Had she even opened her mouth? Could her mouth even move?

It touched her cheek with one long, slender finger. There was no fingernail, only a fleshy nub. The contact was surprisingly gentle, almost like a lover's caress. She didn't feel very loved, though, but trying to pull away was not working. She only managed to turn her head slightly, but even that took a lot of effort, and the creature simply grabbed her chin with its other hand and forced her to stare back at it again.

"I knew someone," it said, hissing out the words.

Unfathomably bright eyes pierced through her as if they could touch her soul, but she didn't see what she expected to see. There was no glaring evil on the other side, just something that, once upon a time, was human, but wasn't anymore.

"She looked like you," it said.

It turned her head carefully left, then right again, as if to get a good look at every inch of her face, to memorize every line, every bruise and healing scar. The broken nose from this morning and the cuts from the helicopter crash that still hadn't fully healed yet, and might never.

"Not as pretty, but close," it said.

The crashing of gunshots. Danny and Will. Fighting for their lives against how many more of these monsters inside the house? Three? One was definitely inside the room with Danny, so were the other two downstairs with Will? How was Will going to fight off two when she and Danny could barely survive one each?

We're dead. We're all dead.

If we're lucky…

The creature turned its head, looking back toward the bedroom, just as a small figure emerged out of the blackness.

Claire.

The thirteen-year-old was holding the shotgun Will had given her. It still looked ridiculously massive against her slight frame. Claire was running toward them when she slid to a stop in front of the pile of debris—and Lance, still buried under them—as the ghoul feasted its eyes on her.

"Shoot it!" Gaby shouted. "Shoot it in the head!"

The creature was standing up when Claire fired, the shotgun blast so loud in the narrow passageway that Gaby physically flinched at the explosion. The ghoul turned its body slightly right as most of the buckshot glanced off its shoulder, the rounds punching through soft flesh and embedding into the wall.

Then it moved toward the girl.

No, not Claire! Stay away from her!

Gaby's eyes darted down to the floor.

The Glock. Where the hell was the Glock?

There!

Less than three feet away. She lunged for it, throwing her entire body forward with everything she had, unsure if it would even work until her chest slammed into the floor. That was a stupid move. More blinding flashes of pain, but she gritted her teeth through them and she reached for the 9mm handgun, wrapped her numbed fingers around it—

She struggled to sit back up.

The creature was almost on top of Claire, who had backed up and fired again. A large chunk of the ghoul's thigh disintegrated, but the creature kept advancing, undeterred. It could have reached Claire faster, she realized. She had seen it move with blinding speed when it wanted to. But it wasn't at the moment. Why not?

Because this is a game. It's playing with her.

It's all just a game to them...

"Hey!" Gaby shouted.

It turned and looked back at her, and its mouth curved into a grin.

"Run!" Gaby shouted, not at the creature, but at Claire. "Go to Will! Go now!"

Claire climbed over the debris and Lance and darted down the stairs.

The ghoul didn't seem interested in pursuing Claire anymore. It only had eyes for her again. "Still want to play?" it hissed.

"No," she said, and shot it in the right kneecap.

The gun was steady in her hand. She didn't know how that was possible, but it barely moved as she fired.

The creature's leg buckled, and as it went down, she shot it again, this time in the left kneecap, forcing it to involuntarily kneel in front of her.

Then she saw it in its eyes.

Understanding.

It knew what she was doing, and it wasn't smiling anymore.

It started to get up when she shot it again, but this time her hand moved slightly for whatever reason, and she hit it in the cheek. The impact snapped its head upward like a spring. Before it could fully recover, she shot it in the center of the face. Its nose—or what was left of it—exploded into tiny chunks, and something punched its way out of the back of its skull, sticky wet goop splattering across the walls.

The creature flopped sideways and lay still.

It wasn't as dramatic as she thought it would be. One second it was on its knees, as if in worship, and the next it was lying in a pool of its own oozing black blood, blue eyes still incandescent in the semidarkness. It might have even been looking back at her. Or maybe through her. What mattered was that it didn't move again.

She struggled up to her feet. It was difficult. Her left arm wouldn't respond no matter how hard she tried. She stumbled over the twisted carcass—it looked more emaciated in death for some reason, and less powerful—and up the hallway.

She stopped for a moment at the sight of Lance, buried in debris, bright red blood pooling under him with the halo of moonlight falling through the opening in the roof. Gaby looked toward the stairs. She couldn't hear anything from down there. Not a single sound. And she couldn't see anything, either. The other end of the staircase was completely swallowed in darkness.

Crying, coming from the master bedroom. Annie. Or was it Milly?

She climbed over the debris and Lance—she felt like throwing up while doing it—and fumbled her way to the open bedroom door. She lifted the Glock as she neared it. There was just enough moonlight shining through the still-barricaded window that she could make out a figure on the floor, near the center of the room.

Danny. God, don't let it be Danny.

As she stepped closer, the shape on the floor became clearer.

Don't let it be Danny...

It wasn't Danny. It was one of the ghouls, lying on its back. Where she expected to see blue eyes, there were instead two black holes. Except they were much bigger than eye holes were supposed to be. The head lay in a thick puddle of congealed blood, blackened against the moonlight. Danny's cross-knife was buried in the creature's forehead up to the guard.

"Danny!" Gaby called out.

"Over here," a voice said.

There was a *click!* and Danny's face was lit up by a flashlight beam. He grinned back at her through a layer of blood. A mixture of black and red, like some kind of Kabuki mask. It was impossible to tell where he was bleeding, or where he wasn't.

"Can you move?" she asked.

"My right leg's broken," he said. "Too bad, cause that's my dancing leg."

"Annie?"

Danny moved the light away from him and across the room at Annie. She was still huddled in the corner with Milly, the two of them having folded up into a ball, arms encircling each other in mutual defense. Both were crying softly, unwilling to look up even when Danny's flashlight illuminated them.

"The other girl..." Danny said.

Gaby looked back toward the stairs.

"Go," Danny said.

"What about you?"

"I got this situation well in hand. The busted leg's just to make it fairer."

She managed a slight smile at him before stumbling her way back down the hallway toward the stairs, fighting the urge to throw up again as she stepped over Lance and the debris a second time. The fact that Lance's face, turned to the side, was clearly visible in the pouring moonlight made her gag slightly.

She finally reached the stairs and hurried down.

"Will!" she called out. "Claire!"

Her voice echoed, but there was no reply. The only sound was the loud echo of her footsteps. She was halfway down when a silhouetted figure moved in the darkness below her. She stopped and lifted the Glock.

"Don't shoot!" a small voice shouted.

Claire.

Gaby sighed and ran down the rest of the way as Claire stepped back. The thirteen-year-old was still clutching the FNH in both hands, and she didn't look hurt or bleeding. Then again, it was so dark on the first floor that Gaby could barely see where she was stepping. She could tell where Claire was looking, though, and she turned in that direction.

Will.

He stood with his back to her, standing near a large hole in the wall of the house. The loud boom that she had heard earlier, she guessed. Some kind of explosion. Will was holding his M4A1 at his side, not in any threatening manner, and was looking out at the front yard.

"Will," she said, a lot quieter than she had meant to.

Will glanced over his shoulder. "You okay?"

"Alive."

"Danny?"

"Alive, too."

He nodded and looked forward again.

Gaby turned to Claire. "You okay?"

Claire nodded. "Annie and Milly...?"

"They're fine."

"I saw Lance..."

"Yeah." She looked back at Will, but said to the girl, "Stay here."

She walked to Will and almost stepped on a body lying on the floor, hidden in the shadows. She looked down at a twisted black and pruned carcass. Or what was left of it. The head was missing. The monster wasn't the only evidence of a fight down here. There were also two men in uniforms lying unmoving on the floor, both wearing gas masks. She didn't have to ask Will what had happened to them.

"Will," Gaby said. "What happened to the others? The black-eyed ones?"

"They're still out there," Will said. "There's a lot of them."

"How many?"

"I don't know. Maybe thousands."

"Why haven't they…?"

She didn't finish her question, because by then she was standing beside Will and looking out the hole in the wall. There was something else there in the middle of the jagged opening. It was a decapitated head impaled on a long, thin piece of broken wood. The head was hairless and the smooth skin gleamed in the moonlight. When she looked back at the dead creature behind her, she was able to put two and two together.

"Where…?" she whispered.

"Outside," Will said. He wasn't whispering, she realized.

She looked out the house and into the yard again. Will was right. The ghouls hadn't gone anywhere. They were still outside.

All of them.

She could only see the first few hundred through the opening. The rest were hidden in the darkness beyond the power of even the moon to reveal. Not just in the yard, but around the house. The sides, the back, and well into the fields, too.

Her heart pounded at the sight of the creatures amassed outside. Their eyes, always creepy even when there was just one of them, were unfathomably terrifying with so many gathered at one spot. They looked like uncertain children, tentative and afraid. At first she thought they were looking at Will, but she was mistaken. They were staring at the head he had placed in the middle of the hole in the wall, which looked like the crooked mouth of a cave opening.

There was, she knew with great certainty, absolutely nothing to stop the thousands of undead things out there from coming into the house at any moment. Even silver bullets would only kill so many before the rest overwhelmed them in an unstoppable tidal wave of black death. And then what? They could head up the stairs, but against that many, they would never survive the night. She didn't have to look down at her watch to know that they had hours— *hours*—to go before sunrise.

But the creatures weren't attacking. They stayed where they were, swaying slightly against each other, a mass of squirming black flesh, almost indistinguishable against the night. There was something odd about the way they looked at the head, with a mixture of fear and awe and something she hadn't really seen from them before.

It was indecision. They didn't know what to do.

"Will," Gaby whispered. "How did you know it would work?"

"I didn't," Will said. "But the blue-eyed ones control them. I just didn't know to what extent." He paused, then, "There were two more…"

"They're upstairs. Dead."

"Good." Will pulled out his cross-knife and handed it to her, the silver gleaming brilliantly against a stray stream of moonlight. "Bring them down here. Just the heads."

⊲▬▮   ▮▬▷

IT WAS STICKIER than she had expected, and the smell made her want to retch every few seconds. She was no stranger to blood these days, but this wasn't really blood. At least, not anymore. It was like washing her hands in tar, and she wondered if she would ever be able to clean them off—really, *really* clean them off—after tonight.

Cutting the heads hadn't been easy with one hand. Her left was still effectively useless (though she didn't tell Will that), but she found that pressing down on the creatures' chests with one knee and slicing with her right hand was good enough. It took a lot of work, but thank God it hadn't been as difficult to saw through bone as she had anticipated.

The black blood dripped from her fingers as she stood next to Claire and watched Will prop up the two heads on two separate objects sticking up from the floor. With the first makeshift spike, Will had broken a hole in the floorboards with the heel of his boot, then rammed the piece of wood into the dirt ground and set the head on top. He did a similar thing now with the two new heads she had brought down, using a lamp for one, shoving the exposed neck into the spot where the lightbulb was supposed to go, then setting it down on the ground. He used a rifle he had picked up from the floor for the other one.

If she thought the sight of the three decapitated heads side by side was disturbing, she felt better at how uncomfortable, how *frightened* the black-eyed ghouls looked outside where they continued to amass in the hundreds and thousands.

Claire stood next to her, both of them keeping a safe distance behind Will. He hadn't moved, so they hadn't, either. She wasn't sure how long they stood on the first floor, in the darkness, waiting for something to happen.

But the ghouls never came in. They remained outside for the rest of the night and through the early morning hours. As far as she could tell, they barely moved at all and continued to huddle against one another, shoulder to shoulder, chest to back, peering in at the three severed heads, as if transfixed.

Around midnight, Will ordered her and Claire upstairs.

Annie was asleep in the corner, on the floor, with Milly snoring in her lap. Danny had (somehow) stood up and was peering out the window through the slots. He was using his rifle as a crutch and had wrapped pieces of lumber around his broken right leg with duct tape. He drank water and kept in constant contact with Will downstairs through their radios. Like Will and her, he had lost his earbuds during the chaos, but both of them had managed to keep their radios in one piece.

Gaby wanted to pick up Milly and put her on the bed, but she didn't have nearly enough feeling in her left arm to lift her own hand, much less carry the girl. So she sat on the bed with Claire instead and listened to the thirteen-year-old gradually fall asleep, until eventually she was snoring in tune with Milly and Annie. Claire was still clutching the shotgun against her chest as if it were a childhood teddy bear.

She stayed awake throughout the night and morning, watching Danny as he stood, unmoving, by the window. Every now and then, he asked her to take out some food from his pack and they ate. It didn't occur to her until much later that he could hardly move.

"You okay?" she asked as he chewed on some stale jerky.

"Sure," he said, giving her a smile.

Danny had rinsed blood off his face with water, leaving behind a gash along his cheek and another one across his temple that he had treated. Those new wounds, along with his broken nose, ruined the California surfer good looks. But scars, she knew, would heal. It was the ones you couldn't see that lingered.

"You did good, kid," Danny said after a while.

"Thanks."

"Not just tonight. The last few weeks, too, to hear Willie boy tell it."

"I did okay."

"Don't be so modest. We did so good with you, I told the guy downstairs we should open a school. Willie and Danny's School of Asskicking. What do you think? If you refer a friend, you get a free ammo can filled with silver bullets as bounty."

She smiled. "Sign me up."

"I'll do that. Now, go to sleep," Danny said. "I'll wake you in an hour for your turn at the window."

She didn't argue. She simply didn't have the strength.

Gaby lay down on the bed next to Claire's snoring form. She didn't think it would happen, but as soon as she closed her eyes (*Just for a little bit*), she was asleep.

DANNY WAS STILL standing by the window when she opened her eyes and struggled up on the bed.

"Danny," she said. "You were supposed to wake me."

"You feel that?" he asked.

She did. The warmth inside the room. The brightness of the walls. The bloody stains on the floorboards looking more ghastly somehow in the morning light. And the small remnants of blood that Danny had failed to clean off his face during the night.

Morning!

"We made it," she said softly, afraid that if she said it too loud it might jinx it.

Danny nodded. "Told you."

She looked down at Claire, who had crawled over to sleep in her lap sometime during the night. Annie and Milly were both snoring on the floor in the corner, Milly curled up in a fetal position. The girl looked cold despite the sun that highlighted her dirty round face.

"So what now?" she asked.

"We go home," Danny said.

"Can we?"

"I don't see why not."

She carefully untangled herself from Claire, then climbed off the bed and walked across the room to the window. She looked out at the empty front yard. The grass was trampled and there were signs everywhere that hundreds *(thousands)* of ghouls had been down there last night. The trucks, she saw with some relief, were still where she had last seen them, and they looked to be in the same condition.

"Will?" she asked.

"Still giving head downstairs."

She smiled, then peered out across the farm at the highway in the near distance. She expected to see trucks—or technicals, as Will and Danny called them—staring back at her, waiting to finish the job, but they were gone, too.

"The soldiers?" she said.

"They made like bananas and split sometime around sunrise," Danny said. "My guess is, they realized we had a secret weapon—" he glanced at Claire's snoring form on the bed "—and decided not to risk it. What is she, twenty?"

"Thirteen."

"The hell you say."

"Uh huh."

"Damn. That girl saved my life last night."

"How did she manage that?"

"When Frankly Dead Sinatra came through the door, she was the one who distracted it long enough so it didn't rip my heart out when it had the chance. Hit it with that shotgun of hers, like she was swinging a mallet at a county fair. I guess she didn't want to risk shooting it for fear of hitting me. Thank God. Have you ever been shotgunned?"

"No."

"Take my word for it, kid; you're gonna want to avoid it if you can."

"I saw her outside in the hallway. She saved my life, too."

"Technically, you owe me since I'm the one who told her to run." He looked over at Annie and Milly. "I told them, too, but they weren't quite as good at following orders. Anyway, when ol' Blue Eyes was distracted, I managed to judo it and got on top and did my thing with the knife." He mimed it for her. "I feel sorry for it, actually. It never stood a chance."

"I didn't know you knew judo," she said.

"I didn't tell you? Judo and me go way back. She still calls me every time she's in town. She loves to wrestle, oh boy, does she ever."

Gaby couldn't help but laugh. Even her left arm didn't seem to be hurting quite as much as when she had first opened her eyes a few minutes ago. Well, that wasn't quite true, but she figured as long as she told herself that, the pain was manageable.

Mostly, anyway.

EPILOGUE

THEY DIDN'T LIKE seeing him around, and though they did their best to hide it, it was never really good enough. Sometimes he wondered if they were trying at all, or if their hatred for him managed to seep through anyway despite their best efforts. Not that it mattered. Their opinions didn't have any effect on him either way.

He had been *chosen*. It was something they would never understand.

"Something's happening over there," Travis said. "Turner says there's a lot of shooting. He could hear it from half a mile away."

"On the island?" Josh asked.

"Yeah."

"What did he say was happening?"

"He's not close enough to know for sure, but he says it sounds like a gun battle, and it's been going on for the last thirty minutes."

Josh liked being out here, in the open at night. It was such a luxury after so many months of hiding in smelly basements and other people's houses, and he took advantage of it whenever he could.

This is the privilege of the chosen. Freedom.

He leaned against the patio railing on the second floor of the red house overlooking Beaufont Lake. A pair of men in uniforms walked along the docks, and there were more on the other docks up and down the shoreline. Just over thirty men in all. Josh had arrived before nightfall with twenty soldiers to augment the twenty or so already here. Except when he showed up, there were only twelve left. Eight were dead.

"They hit us," Travis had said. *"They had a grenade launcher."*

Josh hadn't bothered to ask for details, because it didn't matter.

Thirty-two men wasn't going to be enough to overwhelm Song Island. He was already hesitant to move on them with forty, but without Will and Danny, he thought it was doable. *Just women and children mostly,* he had thought.

"What should we do?" Travis asked now. He sounded nervous when he added, "What does *she* want us to do?"

Travis was in his thirties and could have passed for Josh's dad. He used to be some kind of supervisor at a construction company and was used to giving orders, which made him ideal to take over this group, now that the guy who was supposed to lead them had gone and gotten himself dead earlier today. Caught in an explosion, according to Travis.

"She hasn't told me yet," Josh said.

"When was the last time you talked to her?"

"Earlier today, before I came here."

"I thought they slept in the day?"

"They do."

"So how…?"

"If she wants you to know, she'll tell you," Josh said, cutting the older man off. "Tell Turner to get as close as he can without being seen and find out what's happening on the island."

Travis nodded. Josh could tell he wanted to say something else, but Travis turned and went back into the house instead. The glass door opened and slid shut behind him. Like everyone these days, even though he was safe in the night, Travis couldn't quite shake the nervousness and preferred to stay indoors when possible.

And for good reason, too. Josh could see them out there, skirting around the spotlights his men had set up around the perimeter. After two attacks in two days, Josh wasn't going to take any chances. He had men all the way up the highway watching everything—

Josh smelled it before it even announced its presence. They gave off a scent that was different from the black-eyed ones. Travis probably couldn't tell the difference, but he had never really been around these new breed of ghouls. Josh had. Too many times to count.

So he didn't have to glance back at the tall, silhouetted figure standing in the shadows behind him, blue eyes glowing softly against the darkness.

"Why haven't you taken the island yet?" the ghoul asked. Its voice, like all the other blue-eyed ones, came out as more of a soft hiss, almost like a lisp. It was male, though sometimes it was hard to tell, even for Josh. "It's become a haven. A beacon of hope. It has to be taken at all costs."

"We don't have enough people," Josh said. His voice was calm and steady. The trick was not to let them know you were afraid. "I've sent for more. They're coming tomorrow, with additional supplies."

"And you can take the island then…"

"Yes."

"Are you certain?"

"Yes," Josh said. Did his voice just quiver a little bit? Of course not. He wasn't afraid of them. He didn't have to be. He was one of the chosen. "Where's Kate? She usually gives me the orders herself."

"She's busy."

"With what?"

"It's none of your concern, meat."

"You don't scare me."

"Don't I?" It sounded amused that time.

Josh fought the urge to whirl around and face the creature. It was testing him, trying to see if it could get under his skin. But he wasn't afraid. Why should he be? He was one of the chosen. He didn't have to fear anymore.

"Tomorrow," the creature said. "No more excuses. You'll take the island tomorrow."

"What about Gaby? Kate told me she's still alive."

"Don't worry; we'll save your precious lover for you."

"Don't hurt her."

The creature might have snickered. "Just do your part, meat. We'll bring your female to you, as promised."

"I'll take the island, don't you worry," Josh said. "What else—"

He stopped. He didn't have to look back to know it was gone. He could feel it in the way the air hung and the sudden loss of the familiar scent.

Josh refocused on the calm water of Beaufont Lake in front of him instead.

Pros and cons: What were they?

Pros: Gaby was alive. Thank God. She had escaped L15 and hadn't perished inside the cave outside of town as reported by his men. *(Those idiots.)* She was stuck outside of Dunbar now. Trapped and surrounded and outmatched. But they wouldn't harm her once they killed the others. Will and Danny, and some kids he didn't know and didn't care about. Gaby was all that mattered. Gaby had always been the only thing that mattered.

Cons: He would storm Song Island tomorrow once the replacements showed up. They had no shortage of manpower these days. All the civilians in the towns were volunteering by the dozens. It had to be the uniforms. Everyone was a sucker for uniforms. It was why he had come up with the military idea in the first place. Even Kate hadn't thought of it. She and Mabry were already replicating his success in the other states and around the world. Soon, he'd join them in the global effort to domesticate the planet. But that was for later. For now, there was Song Island to deal with.

Conclusion: Gaby was alive and soon they would be reunited. He had failed to convince her before, but he couldn't give up now. Gaby was too important. She was *everything*. Even if he had to lock her up for a month or a year. Sooner or later, she would come around. He just needed time. And to get that precious time, he would have to take Song Island and show Mabry he could do more than just think outside the box, that he could act—and do it successfully—too.

He was one of the chosen, after all.

One of these days, humanity would thank him. They would write books about him. Maybe he'd even get his own national holiday. Wouldn't that be something?

Josh smiled into the darkness and looked south, where he imagined Song Island was.

Tomorrow. It would all be over tomorrow.

There would be violence. It was inevitable. Lara wouldn't just let him land on the island. They would have to take it by force. Overwhelming force.

The white beaches were going to run red with blood.

So be it.